Skin of a Sinner by Avina St. Graves

Published by Avina St. Graves

Contact the author at avina.stgraves@gmail.com

Editing and Proofreading by Nice Girl, Naughty Edits

Chapter Art by Zian Schafer

Character Art by Zian Schafer

Cover by Graphic Escapist

Formatting made with Atticus

Paperback ISBN 978-0-473-69304-6

eBook ISBN 978-0-473-69306-0

First Edition

Author's Note

Is the love interest a problematic, obsessive, walking red flag that belongs in prison? Yes.

Would he chase you through the woods, blow your back out and tell you to take it like a good girl? Also yes.

But would he steal your panties? Watch you sleep? Mark your name into his chest? Kill for you, then treat you like a princess? I think you know the answer to that.

And you know what? Us girlies are proud to call his red flags green.

Oh, and on a very serious note, this book is a work of <u>fiction</u>. It does not mean I condone the characters' actions.

Skin of a Sinner is a standalone dark romance book with flashbacks, no cliff-hangers and a guaranteed happy ending.

Happy reading x
A St. Graves

Triggers

Stalking, dubious consent, consent-not-consent, primal kink, somnophilia, light degradation, forced orgasm, blood play, breeding/ unprotected sex, kidnapping, murder, graphic violence, gore, torture, drugging, sexual assault (groping and verbal), depression, anxiety, prescription medication use, mental illness, eating disorder, (male) genital mutilation, drugs, swearing, speech impediment, poverty, child poverty, child abuse (psychological, physical, and sexual)

The opposite of triggers (for some people):
Praise, pet names, masks, some groveling, an absolutely obsessive, possessive, over the top MMC

PLAYLIST

Slow Down - Chase Atlantic

Reflections - The Neighborhood

King for a Day - Pierce the Veil

Bulls in the Bronx - Pierce the Veil

My Medicine - The Pretty Reckless

Make Me Wanna Die - The Pretty Reckless

De Selby (Part 2) - Hozier

Closer - Nine Inch Nails

Kicks - Barns Courtney

Yayo - Lana Del Rey

Prisoner - The Weeknd, Lana Del Rey

Fireworks - First Aid Kit

Teenagers - My Chemical romance

Mr. Brightside - The Killers

My strange addiction - Billie Eilish

Everybody Talks - Neon Trees

AVINA ST. GRAVES

Lonely Boy - The Black Key
Don't Speak - No Doubt
Stolen Dance - Milky Chance
Blood In The Cut - K.Flay
The Less I Know The Better - Tame Impala
Elephant - Tame Impala
Cinnamon Girl - Lana Del Rey
Smells Like Teen Spirit - Nirvana

"I hate and I love. Why do I do this, perhaps you ask.
I know not, but I feel it happening and I am tortured."

- Catullus

.

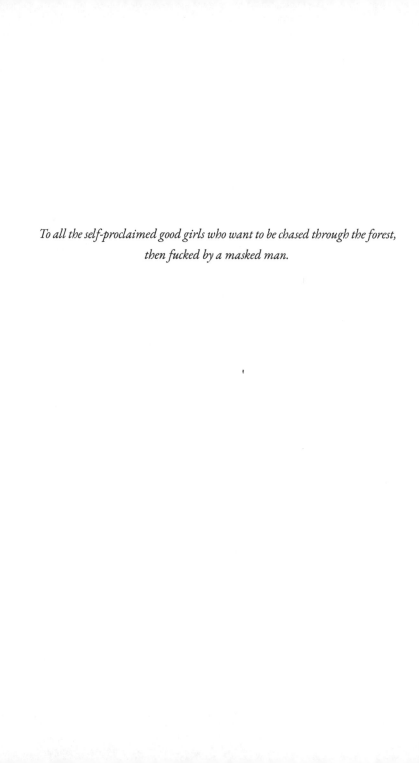

To all the self-proclaimed good girls who want to be chased through the forest, then fucked by a masked man.

CHAPTER 1

ISABELLA

"I'M SORRY, PRINCESS. I didn't mean to wake you."

It's *him*.

He's here.

He's back.

No, no, no, this is wrong. This is all wrong.

He left me, and he didn't say goodbye. He promised me that we would always be together, and *he left*. What is he doing here? Why is he here? Why—

Bile lurches up my throat as I spot the crimson splatter crawling up the wall, pooling on the wooden floor and painting his skin with the poisonous color. I've seen him stained with red, smelling like iron and danger, but never like this. Not with drops freckling around his steel eyes and dripping from his dark hair.

The liquid glistening from his black gloves and matting his shirt is a haunting contrast to the bloody knife in one hand and, in the other, a mask with bright red crosses through the eyes that watch my every move. Stitched lips stuck in a taunting smile dare me to make a sound.

I wish I had never come down from my room and ignored the cries of terror.

A scream catches in my throat, choking me, but I can't look away from the mutilated fingers spread across the dining table. Or the pink concoction trailing down the side of Greg's face, coloring the duct tape over his mouth.

Or the welts marring his body.

Long, angry red lines, two inches wide, crisscross over his arms and legs, some breaking skin. I would recognize those marks anywhere. I know how much each slash would have hurt.

This was done with a belt. *Greg's* favorite belt.

The same belt that's wrapped around his throat, turning his face a deadly shade of purple.

He did this.

Roman did this.

Greg was a piece of shit who deserved whatever was coming for him, but not *this*. The man who housed me for the past four years is—was—a functioning alcoholic who had no issues with tormenting his foster child, and letting his son, Marcus, play along in abusing me.

Slowly—*so slowly*, Roman sheaths the knife to his thigh and places the mask on the table, as if I am a frightened animal that might spook at a sudden movement.

"Go back upstairs. I'll come to get you once I'm done."

The deep timbre of his voice vibrates through every crevice of my being, commanding my attention. I slap a hand over my mouth to suppress a sob as I stagger back.

He's real.

He's actually *real*.

2

This isn't some deranged dream. It takes everything in me not to retch. He was never meant to come back after he tore my heart from my chest and handed me to the wolves to feast on.

After twenty years, I've finally proven to myself that I can live without him. He's shown me that he was nothing more than a tortured soul I grew up with because, in the end, he left.

Three years ago, to the day, he showed me that I was no one. That's what hurts the most, because he wasn't just anyone; he was everything to me. He was every smile that curved my lips, every laugh that rattled my chest, every dream that didn't end in tears.

Everything meant nothing when compared to him.

But to him, *I* was nothing.

Roman sidesteps to block my view, but there's no unseeing the damage he's done to Greg... And Marcus. *Oh God.*

The sight of my naked foster brother, hanging from the ceiling by his wrists, is forever ingrained into my mind. *Roman did that.* Violets and blues blossom in violent splotches across every inch of his pale skin, so dark the red seeping from his cock blends in with the bruised flesh. Or at least, that's where the appendage is *supposed* to be.

I know Marcus had one before tonight. I've felt it pressed against me when I didn't want it to. I've endured it too many times. What does that say about me that I can't bring myself to feel any remorse, only disgust?

I take one step back. Then another.

A sob breaks free from my lips, and then Roman's hands are on me, keeping me there. His fingertips caress my face as he gently wipes away the tears he caused, replacing them with the blood tainting his gloves. I try to push him away, to slap his hands off me, but touching him only makes everything worse.

"No, no, shh. It's okay. Don't cry, alright? I've got you." His voice is so much deeper now; there's no denying the years that have passed.

Even though the sleeve of my shirt separates us, his touch sets me aflame. But I can't look at him—the boy who hurt me more than anyone else. Hot tears burn my cheeks, pooling at the corners of my lips.

I gasp for breath as the scents of lingering bourbon, blood, sandalwood, and cinnamon engulf my senses. Even covered in blood, Roman smells better than his shirt, which I hide beside my bed.

Roman's taller now, more foreboding, with lean muscles lining every inch of his body.

The muscles in his arms ripple when he moves. He pulls me closer, and no matter how hard I try to stop it, he's too strong. He's still everything to me. I hate it.

Warm lips press against my forehead, as a cry rips through my throat. The memory of the last time I felt them is ingrained into my mind, etched so deep that it isn't just a mark; it's who I am.

"Don't touch me," I plead, attempting to push him away. He doesn't move an inch, holding me tighter, like he's worried I'll be the one to disappear.

If he keeps touching me, I'm afraid I'll forget how deep the wounds he left behind are.

"You were always a heavy sleeper." He chuckles to himself as if it's an inside joke.

The gloved hand caresses my cheek as he presses his forehead to mine. The touch is so loving and tender, as if I might actually mean something to him. But I should know better—I *have* to know better. I won't survive if he leaves again.

As I tilt my head up to look at him, his lips stretch into a sinister smirk. Glancing at Marcus and his missing *appendage*, Roman pulls out the knife

4

and nudges the back of my trembling hand, saying, "Would you like the honors, Princess?"

Marcus's cries are muffled by the tape covering his mouth. The sound breaks my trance, and when I pull away from Roman this time, he lets me.

I wish I had the strength to hurt Marcus the way Roman is, not just for vengeance for everything my foster brother put me through, but to prove to myself that I can take care of myself in every possible way.

I wipe away the tears with the back of my hand, spreading the congealing blood he left behind on my cheek. My other foster brother Jeremy is safe at camp, but what about... "Where—where's Millie?" My foster mom stood by and watched, but she doesn't deserve to be tortured for it. She's a victim too.

He shakes his head, a pinch between his brows, looking at me as if he was hoping to hear something else fall from my lips. "She's okay."

"What does 'okay' mean?" I step back when he reaches for me, and the frown deepens.

I turn around. Surveying. Studying. Holding back my meager dinner that's rising up my throat. I've seen him beat someone into a pulp with his bare hands. I've watched bones break beneath his baseball bat. But *this?*

He's done it now. He's gone too far this time.

There's blood *everywhere*. Ripped flesh, torn appendages, and missing limbs. This isn't just murder; this is the definition of a bloodbath.

"What have you done?" My voice quivers as I knock my knee against a shelf.

The room sways, and I can't breathe. He steps in front of me, but that just makes the dizziness worse. I can't look at him. I need to go back to pretending he doesn't exist.

"What have you done, Roman?" I tremble, trying to stop my lungs from burning, but the match has already been lit, and there's nothing to stop it from spreading like wildfire. "What—what is this? What are you—I can't do this. *I can't do this.*"

I fall onto my knees and clamber backward, choking on air before I empty the contents of my stomach onto the floor. He grips my arms and pulls me to my feet, making me dry heave against his chest. "Deep breaths, Bella. Don't look, alright? Just focus on me."

He feels so warm and comforting, like I'm finally back home. But it's all *wrong*. I thrash in his grip, desperate to get away. I can't do this after all the pain he's put me through and everything that happened. He was the only thing standing between me and the demons on the other side.

Demons like Marcus.

Roman left me to fend for myself, and I almost died because of it.

There was a time I was willing to give him every fractured piece of my heart. I thought he loved every broken part of me. He said I was perfect.

But Roman Riviera is a liar.

Every family before this one got rid of me. My mother is gone. I wasn't enough for my father. And, *God*, I thought there was a chance I could be enough for him.

"No." I gasp. "*No!*" *Stop touching me.* Nothing makes his hold on me falter, keeping me prisoner in the arms of the man who is my reminder of every part of me that I lost the day he left. "You're crazy. You're fucking *crazy.*"

"I prefer the term 'artist,'" he quips.

Is he seriously *joking* right now? "What is your fucking problem? Why are you here? You left, so you should stay gone."

I was getting better. Every day, it was getting a little easier. I found hope—feeble as it was—that I would one day turn my back on this town and scrub every stain from me, once and for all.

I found a purpose in looking after Jeremy, my little foster brother. It wasn't much, but I knew even the smallest voices could make the largest impact. Whatever came after was worth making sure Jeremy went to bed unafraid of waking up in the morning.

The muscle in Roman's jaw feathers. "Go back to bed. I was hoping to finish up without disturbing you."

Without disturbing me.

So what? Is he only here so that he can leave me again? Have I always been a tool for his own sick enjoyment?

Back to bed.

Without disturbing me.

The words echo over and over, building and filling until it tips over the brim.

I'm so foolish for thinking he might be back for me. That he might stay. I should have known better. He always had a thing against Marcus. He's just tying up loose ends. Why am I not surprised?

I shove him in the chest. Hard. It's not enough for him to let go, but it catches him off guard long enough for me to slap him. "Fuck you, Roman. I hate you."

The excited sparkle in his eyes disappears, recoiling from my words. He *knows* what it means for me to say his name. "You don't mean that—"

"*Leave,*" I hiss, finally looking at him and his beautifully savage features. Why won't Roman fight me back? Why the hell won't he react to my hits when it's clear he doesn't care about me?

Marcus's muffled screams fuel my fire—every time I was silenced, every time I had to sit there and just take it, *deal* with it—I want to let it all out. I want this place to burn.

Fuck Marcus. I hate him, too. He can die along with his pig of a father, for all I care.

Did Roman think he could show up here after three years, torture and slaughter my foster family while I sleep upstairs, and then just *leave*? All over again. Through the tears, I can only make out the outline of the sharpened edge of his jaw and the dip in his cheeks. Even the shape of him is too much.

"I don't want you here." *Lie.* "You're a monster."

"It's me," he pleads, cupping my tear-stained face to pull me closer. "It's your Mickey."

I kick my legs out, hoping to make an impact with something—anything. "I don't know who you are anymore."

"Bella—Bella, please. It's me. Mickey. I'm *back*. I'm going to get you out of here." His touch is all-consuming. The scent of his cologne seeps into my mind, and I want to give in so badly.

"You abandoned me!" I've said it enough times to myself that I sound like a broken record. Saying it out loud to the culprit feels like finding a trove of rot and dead bones that should have stayed buried.

"I know. And I'm sorry, I—"

"Sorry," I echo. The tears stop, as I see him with complete clarity.

All the words bubbling in my chest want to pour out—all the times I've had to say, *"thank you,"* and smile at men after they hurt me. I'm so fucking sick of it. He doesn't get to say sorry and expect everything to be forgiven.

"Sorry?" My breath comes out in short pants, and he lets go of me, knowing what's about to happen. He always knows. "You're sorry? *Sorry?* You don't get to be sorry!" The more I say the word, the less believable it sounds. "You don't get to come here and act like everything is alright. Do you even know what they did to me? You left me for *dead*, Roman. You're a coward." I shove him, even though he's not holding me anymore. "A fucking coward!"

He doesn't back away as he should. He doesn't give me the space I need, but instead continues staring at me with those steel-grey eyes that darken every time his olive skin touches mine. As he moves only slightly, our bodies are still only a hair's breadth away.

It feels far too good to let out the anger that's been simmering in my veins for years. Only, I'm not sorry Roman is taking the brunt of it.

My voice comes out raw as my chest heaves. "I can't believe I trusted you and gave you all of me." *Shove*. "I regret ever laying eyes on you." *Shove*. "I regret speaking to you." *Shove*. "I regret ever meeting you." This time, when I shove him, he doesn't budge. His arms encircle my waist, and he presses his cheek against my head. "I *hate* you, Roman. I fucking hate you. You're the worst thing to ever happen to me. I hate you. I hate you. I hate you."

I repeat myself.

Over.

And over.

I don't know how long I spend yelling, kicking, and scratching. He takes every bit of it without letting me go, not even for a second, rubbing soothing circles on my back. His tender caress continues even when my body is drained of energy and all my fight evaporates, leaving me limp in his hold as he whispers, "I'm sorry. I didn't want to leave you. I'm back. There's nothing that will separate us now."

I've stopped hearing Marcus's cry in the background. I don't have the energy to care that my foster father is dead in the seat, only a few feet away from us. Or that the man who tormented me for the past three years is bleeding out.

I'm so exhausted from everything.

When will it be enough? When will I be able to truly live?

But only two words are swirling through my head: *He's back*.

I want to believe him.
But Roman Riviera is a liar.

CHAPTER 2

ROMAN

14 Years Ago

Roman: 8 years old – Isabella: 6 years old.

I hate this part of the city as much as I hate the other.

I hate school. Doesn't matter which school, I know I'll hate it. I hate Steve.

I think I hate Steve more than I hate Troy, and I've only known Steve for three weeks. I've learned he yells louder when I speak in a language he doesn't understand. Idiot. Yelling tires him out—I think it's because of the beer he drinks. He leaves me alone the sooner he starts yelling. Then I can run to the room I share with some boy half my size and another guy who's older than us and thinks that makes him better.

He's not better. I'm still teaching him this lesson.

I hate those two boys too, Josh and Perez, but since we all agree that we hate Steve more than we hate each other, we haven't killed each other yet.

I'll give myself another month in this place before I'm sent to another home. After being expelled from all the other schools on the city's eastern side, Margaret said they had no choice but to move me to another area where they can "accommodate" my *different* needs.

I'm not sure what that means, but at least I don't hate Margaret—except when she gives me that look where her eyebrows pinch, and I know she's about to sigh, "Again, Roman?"

She tries to make me talk about my feelings. She also likes to bring me snacks. I know it's a bribe because I'll do anything for a Pop-Tart.

I'm always so freaking hungry.

Even if she feeds me, all adults are stupid. She's as useless as the rest if she can't do anything about Steve. Or maybe she doesn't want to.

But I heard Steve say a couple of words to describe his wife that I think works well for Margaret (sometimes): *Fucking Bitch.* I don't know what it means.

Maybe I'll ask the teacher about it.

I even told Margaret about going into Steve's basement one night without food and not leaving the cold room until the next night.

A whole twenty-eight hours—wait. Are there twenty-eight or twenty-four hours in a day?

Ugh. It doesn't matter because I saw her write *"active imagination"* after I told her last week. That was three weeks after I hit a teacher on the first week of school and ended up here... at another school. In my defense, the teacher called me a menace when I wasn't being one.

So I showed him what a real menace looked like.

Then that stupid teacher called me an *"attention seeker."* Frick him.

Anyway, I have a plan. Perez said there's one other school in the area. If I get kicked out of this school and the other, Margaret said they won't have a choice but to move me to another city or a group home. And then her brows will pinch, then she'll say, "Again, Roman, really? We talked about this."

Not like moving me would make any difference. All the schools will be crap, and all the teachers will be the same.

The vice principal of Woodside Elementary and Ms. *Something* are saying the same thing the last school told me. I'm only listening to snippets of it as we walk to class.

We're here to support you, Roman.

We understand moving to another school in the middle of the year is very scary.

All the other kids are going to love you, Roman.

We want what's best for you, Roman.

It's what they all say. But they don't mean it, because if they did, they wouldn't make me live with someone like Steve.

Or Troy.

The dad at the last house was a fan of throwing things to practice his aim. He liked using us kids as moving targets. The mom of the house did her best to make up for it by making sure there was food on the table every day, even if it was just a slice of bread.

The mom at my current house sucks as much as the dad. The last time either of them remembered to feed the three of us was yesterday morning.

I am *fucking* hungry, to say the least.

But whatever, I'll be gone soon enough, and who knows if the next house will be worse than Troy and Steve combined.

The school here has classrooms spread around to circle the main field. All I'm focused on is the corner, where there's a blind spot between the fence and a building. No one would know someone is there unless they walk that way.

It's perfect.

We enter the locker area between two classrooms, and Ms. Something takes my empty bag from me to put it on a free hook. She doesn't wait for me before going into what I'm guessing is my *temporary* classroom—before I get moved, that is.

I turn my head in time to hear two boys laughing at a little girl rummaging through a bag. Her dark pigtails fall over her face as she turns away from them when one of the boys—the skinny one—says, "Hey, Isa." The uglier one hits the skinny one's shoulder, snickering like he can't wait for the joke. "Say raspberry."

They both burst into a fit of laughter, throwing their heads back as if it was the funniest thing they've ever said.

It's not. How the hell is saying *raspberry* even funny?

The girl looks up at the two boys, bottom lip quivering and eyes glistening as she hugs herself.

Get a grip.

I roll my eyes and follow the vice principal into the classroom. Those types of bullies are boring and weak, always running their mouths, and wouldn't know what a punch is until it hits them. Once it does, they either figure out how to throw one back and make it fun for me, or they cry and beg. Both outcomes seem good to me, especially when they end up doing both.

Other than finding out the classroom I share a building with is two grades below me, nothing eventful happens in class with my overenthusiastic teacher trying to convince everyone learning is fun.

As soon as the lunch bell rings, I grab my bag and beeline to the blind spot tucked away in the corner.

All the other students exit the rooms and head straight onto the field and playground, making this corner of paradise all mine. At this time of the day, the sun sits just right, so the place is only partly covered by shade.

Splinters threaten my skin as I slide down the fence and onto the pavement. The sun sears my face, but I'd rather burn than be cold in the shadows. I'm not interested in feeling the sharp chill again.

Not after Steve put me in the basement.

My stomach sinks angrily when I open my backpack. I shouldn't have gotten used to finding food in my bag rather than a pencil, book, and beer bottle cap. I expect nothing less from useless Steve.

Would Margaret call *this* an active imagination? Frick her, and frick Steve. She'd probably call the house, and Steve would tell her a heroic story about how he slaved away making my lunch, only for me to forget it. Then I'd hear that line I hate hearing everyone say about me.

Attention seeking.

They're wrong. I don't want their attention. There's nothing good that can come from it.

Even the basement wouldn't be all bad if it wasn't so cold and quiet and I wasn't so hungry. No one to yell at me? No one to hit me?

As I said, the less attention, the better.

It's safe in there. But scary. And my lungs do that weird thing where they hurt, and it gets hard to breathe. I hate it.

Attention seeking.

Stupid, stupid, stupid Margaret.

Grabbing the used textbook and blunt pencil, I let my hands do all the talking while my brain continues flashing pictures I can't keep up with. It's so loud I wish it would shut up for two minutes.

Thick, angry strokes of graphite form shapes on the lined page. Circles and triangles, one right after the other, until a boy smiles with his razor-sharp teeth while the people around him scream.

My hand freezes as a chill falls over me—like the feeling of being watched. I snap up at the intruder with a glare, and the girl stiffens in shock.

She looks just like a cartoon with her big brown eyes gawking at me... right before the familiar look I know all too well transforms it.

I've seen it on the cartoon mouse—I think his name is Jerry—when he sees Tom or when I come into class bruised and bloodied. Fear.

Her bottom lip trembles like it did when the two boys teased her in the locker area. She gulps as she looks between the field and me, then back at the field, like she's trying to decide who's the worst monster.

When she drops her head down, I'm about to breathe a sigh of relief, but then she goes ahead and ruins my lunch by walking over to me.

I scowl at her. She's clearly decided I'm less of a threat to her than Skinny and Ugly. Her worn sneakers scuff against the concrete pavement as she shuffles to a spot a few feet away from me. I stare at her, daring her to look me in the eye.

I don't care if this was her spot before, because this is my spot now.

Until I leave, at least.

Minutes pass, and the tension radiates from her as she sits there, staring at the wall, still like a rock. So freaking still. Now, because of *her*, my hand doesn't want to work. Nothing is going onto the page the way it should. The straight lines are curved, and the curved lines are straight.

I'm not feeling it, and it's all her fault.

I've seen kittens less nervous than her. If I listen closely enough, I'm convinced she isn't breathing, and the lack of sound coming from her is pissing me off.

It's so quiet. What the hell is her problem?

"Loosen up," I snap.

I'm not touching her, not even looking at her. She just needs to chill out.

With a squeak, she yanks her bright pink bag to her chest with shaky hands. It's one of those nice backpacks with glitter and stuff on it. I bet

16

she's actually a fancy pants. Her parents probably packed her lunch. With her ridiculously wonky pigtails, I'm sure they put some stupid note in her bag, saying they love her and hope she has a good day.

She's not like those annoying rich kids, though. None of those idiots would be caught dead wearing shoes with holes in them or a shirt that has to be at least three sizes too big.

Still, the kid in front of me doesn't look like she's ever known what it's like to be locked in a basement or what it feels like to have a heated fork brand her skin. I bet she gets tucked into bed every night, like in all those books the teachers read.

Spoiled brat.

The sharp sound of a zipper opening snags my attention. I watch her small hands pause for a second before digging into her bag to grab a worn stuffed toy. It's some character from a show I watched once—when I was at a house that had a TV.

Something about a mouse. Or a rat. Macky Mouse or something?

Whatever the thing is, it looks just like the little earrings she has on. It's like she's obsessed with the pest. Troy set up traps all around the house to kill them.

Her eyes dart up to me, and I look down like she isn't there. Happy—or at least not stiff and staring at a wall—she places the toy next to her with her delicate little hands and arranges its legs to sit upright by itself.

When she pulls out her lunch box (a ripped plastic bag), I can't keep my attention hidden anymore.

What does she have? Is she one of those kids that gets a well-balanced diet with that triangle diagram thingy? Maybe she's one of the lucky ones who gets leftover dinner for lunch. A kid at my other school got to bring takeout for lunch, and the ass would show it off to everyone in the class.

He stopped bringing them in once I started taking them from him.

Pigtails sets the plastic bag on the ground next to the toy. I wait with bated breath as she takes out the contents.

First, she pulls out two crackers—the ones that are drier than sand but do their job filling you up—and gives one to the toy as she nibbles on the other.

What the heck?

The thing isn't real, and she's giving her lunch to a toy? I knew she was spoiled, wasting food like that. If she isn't going to eat it, then I will.

The mouse shrinks back when she catches me watching. But I don't look away, tapping my pencil on the paper, waiting to see what else comes out of her lunch bag and if she's going to waste that too.

I can already tell the next thing isn't just a cracker. It's too big to be. My mouth waters at all the possibilities of everything it could be.

My hunger doesn't stop when she pulls out her pathetic-looking lunch. It's just two thin slices of bread, partly squashed from sitting inside her bag without a container. Even though it doesn't look like there might be anything inside, I'm still salivating.

I'm about to scream at her for being such a spoiled brat when she tears the bruised sandwich in two, squishing the butter through the rip. But my mouth slams shut when Pigtails holds her hand out, buttered bread offered to me as if I'm someone to be pitied.

"You shouldn't share your food," I bite out at the same time my stomach grumbles.

Her big eyes drop away from my face, and her bottom lip quivers again. Does this girl ever stop crying? Life sucks. Get over it. No use crying about it.

"Oh," she says, voice so soft I almost miss it. "I thought—"

"Thought what?"

"I thought you were hungry," she whispers, lowering the food onto the plastic bag directly between us.

She pulls out a reading book from her bag, and I watch her flip page after page while nibbling on her sandwich timidly. When the last bite disappears, she places the cracker next to the remaining bread and pulls the doll into her teeny arms, quietly reading her book.

It doesn't matter how long I stare at her or how long I pretend to look away, my stomach doesn't stop groaning, and she doesn't spare a second glance at the remainder of her lunch—the same lunch sitting closer to me than her.

Tentatively, I inch my fingers toward the food, waiting for her to snatch it away from me as the other kids sometimes do. But she does the opposite. She gives me this sad little smile that kicks me in the gut when I take the first bite.

It's awful. Both her sad look, and the crap I'm eating.

The bread is probably drier than the cracker next on my list of things to eat. The butter isn't even spread properly, as Troy's wife would. She always made sure she got the spread to every corner, and nothing was too clumpy or too thin, and it would *always* go into a container to stop it from becoming mush.

This tastes like a child made it, and the butter is only in the middle of the bread. I stuff the rest into my mouth, not bothering to savor it or enjoy the feeling of something other than water in my stomach, just in case Pigtails changes her mind.

Too caught up in filling my face, I miss the prickle of her stare until she finally asks, "What's your name?"

Her voice is so soft and delicate, like a princess who always has flowers in her hair, a big puffy dress, and a blinding smile.

I run my tongue over my dry lips, trying to get some moisture on them after eating the driest food ever. My eyes drift to the drink bottle that's now next to the plastic bag. It's the super crinkly plastic kind from the grocery store that's thrown away once it's empty.

She shouldn't be so giving. Someone is going to take advantage of it one day and hurt her.

"It doesn't matter." My nose wrinkles as I grab the bottle and inhale a healthy amount of the liquid, leaving her half of it. "I'll be gone soon anyways."

"Oh."

She sounds sad. Why does she sound sad?

The bell rings, and she doesn't waste time packing away her stuff and scurrying off like her tail is on fire.

The next day, I spot the pigtailed girl in the locker room again at the end of recess, standing in the corner while Skinny and Ugly laugh. Something in my stomach churns when I see the tears running down her cheeks, her face burning red like she's been crying for a while. Then she wipes them away with her sleeve and hides behind her hair when the final bell rings.

I didn't see her at the gap in the corner during the break. I thought she found another place where she could hide from the world.

I guess I was wrong.

She runs to her classroom before the two idiots can say another word, and I watch as they cross the foyer and into the room behind me.

There was one other thing I learned yesterday: Skinny and Ugly are in my class. And Skinny and Ugly like to pick on the younger grades.

20

I know their type; the bad kids who think they're invincible just because someone smaller than them can't fight back. Like Pigtails.

When lunch rolls around, I follow them out and wait for them as they grab their bags and disappear to one of the benches near the back of the school. Before Skinny can put his ass on the seat, I sink my grip into the back of his shirt and yank backward. I kick my leg out, so he stumbles over my foot and loses his balance, landing on the ground with a solid thud.

Ugly is as stupid as he looks because he lunges for me, with no form or practice, all rage. He stops screaming when my fist collides with his face, and he rears back, squealing like a little baby.

Skinny tries to scramble to his feet, but my foot lands on the side of his ribs. "What's your problem, dude?" he hisses, clutching his side.

"Talk to the mouse again, and I'll do a lot worse to your stupid face," I sneer and snatch one of the backpacks. I almost hit them again, just because it isn't empty like mine.

"Who?" I'm not sure which one speaks.

"Pigtails."

Without a second glance at them, I shove one of their lunch boxes into my bag and storm away. I can feel them gawking at me, probably nursing their wounds at the same time.

They won't tell the teacher. What are they going to say?

He hit us because we were picking on the girl two grades younger than us.

I don't think so.

She's already there by the time I get to our spot. The rat doll thing is perched next to her, holding half a cracker, while the other is between her teeth, nibbling away like a rabbit as she reads her book.

The same pathetic sandwich is on the same useless, ripped plastic bag. Her pigtails are messier than yesterday, with one sitting near the center of her head and one just above the ear, tied with mismatching hair ties.

Her shoes are holey. A church would be jealous.

Her top is ripped.

The second she sees me, she becomes the same scared mouse from yesterday, hunching her shoulders and staring at the ground as if she's willing me to go away.

I drop beside her, and she flinches, even though I am a safe distance away.

That needs to stop.

I'm not going to hurt her. Other people can try to.

Besides a sideways glance of curiosity, she doesn't acknowledge me as I pull out Ugly's or Skinny's lunch box, clicking the side open and revealing the type of lunch I thought *she* would have.

A banana and a decent slice of bread with chicken, mayo, and greens layered in the middle. I push a finger into the bread, checking that it wouldn't pass as cardboard.

"Eat." I shove the whole container in her direction and grab her untouched sandwich.

Her eyes grow wide as I take a bite of the awful *thing*—I'm not even going to call it food.

I bare my teeth out of reflex when she snatches the bread from my hand.

"What do you think you're doing?"

Her pigtails swing side to side as she shakes her head frantically, trembling as she rips her sandwich in half to push it back into my hand.

Is she serious right now? She's going to hog a sandwich and a half all to her—

She also tears the other sandwich in half, leaving one on the container and bringing the other to her lips.

"We'll each have a side," she says.

I shove the sandwich she made into my mouth and swallow it down. The other one tastes better than anything I've eaten in a long time.

Her gaze is trained on me with keen interest. "I thought you shouldn't share food."

"Shut up. You don't count."

She looks up at me with her little button nose and ridiculous hair, and her eyes sparkle with something I can only call admiration. She's looking at me like I'm her savior. Just because of a piece of bread?

If she doesn't stop acting like this, she will get eaten alive by people far worse than the two boys, who are probably still crying over a bit of pain.

But she doesn't look away; with each bite, the light in her eyes only grows brighter. That look... I've never seen that look before. At least not when I'm involved.

And I don't know if I like it.

It's weird.

I clear my throat to end the silence as I bounce my foot. "Roman."

Her little forehead wrinkles. "Huh?"

"My name."

She blinks. "Oh." Does this girl ever say more than a few words? What is wrong with her? She clears her throat and frowns at the ground between us as she says, "Woah-man."

"What? No. *R*oman."

She sucks her bottom lip and hides part of her face behind a pigtail. "*Woah*-man."

"No, it's—" I snap my mouth shut.

What did Ugly and Skinny tell her to say yesterday? Raspberry...? The angry beast—the same one that Margaret is always telling me I need to learn to control—rears its head.

Those dickwads.

23

"It doesn't matter." I try to save her from feeling bad. "I don't like the name anyway."

She looks back up at me, almond-shaped eyes glossed over, and I want to yell at myself for making them that way.

In her sweet voice, she says, "I do."

"Why?"

I've never liked my name. No one has ever said it with any sort of love or care. It's thrown around like some kind of insult.

The book she was reading flips to the cover page, where there are twelve drawings of different men and women with golden leaves around their heads and what look like white sheets wrapped around their bodies.

A tiny finger points to one of the men whose eyes are narrowed, covered in armor with a spear in one hand and a shield in the other. "He looks like a Woahman, just like you."

"It says his name is Ares."

She nods thoughtfully. "*But* he looks like a Roman." The 'R' still comes out as a 'W.'

"It says he's the God of War."

Brown eyes peer at the writing, and her mouth moves like she's sounding out the word. I don't think she knows what it means.

I shrug. "Still don't like it."

She twists her lips, looking around our nook like she might find a response somewhere. Her attention lands on her toy, and I practically see the lightbulb go off in her head.

"How about Mickey?"

My lips twist into a scowl. "Are you calling me a rat?"

The hold she has on me the second she laughs is immediate. I've never heard anything like it. There's joy in there, but something more. It's like the feeling I have when I finally have a meal or when the sounds in my head stop.

"No, silly. He's a *mouse*. You can be Mickey, and I can be Minnie." She sighs in wonder as she hugs the decrepit thing to her chest. "Mouses are my favorite."

Mice, I think.

It's fitting for her.

"What if I don't want to call you Minnie? What can I call you then?"

The look that flushes her face is worse than getting kicked in the balls. I've disappointed her. I'm not sure why.

She chews her lip. "Isabella. But everyone calls me Isa."

Her name triggers some distant memory. "I'll call you Bella." Because she's the only person I've ever met who deserves to be called pretty. Even with her messed up hair and inside-out ripped t-shirt.

"But—"

I stop her before she tries to protest. "I like Bella."

Her smile is bright enough to stop the sun, and with it, maybe even my plans of escaping this place.

CHAPTER 3

ISABELLA

PRESENT

Roman pulls away once the bleary haze takes root in my bones, numbing me to my thoughts.

"Wait here. I'll be right back."

Where would I go? I wasn't the one who left in the first place. I'm still caught in the web of our making, stuck under a roof where every breath feels like it could be used against me.

I barely register the feel of his lips pressed against my forehead before he leaves. I hardly hear the slap of boots hitting wood, leaving me to stare blankly at the line of scarlet splatter on the flyers stuck to the fridge.

It's hard to think the fridge containing leftover dinner is in the same room as the man slaughtered by my childhood love. It doesn't match the purge mask sitting in a pool of blood on the table, right next to yesterday's newspaper, Millie's cross-stitch supplies, and Greg's severed fingers.

The dishes drying on the rack don't match the body hanging from the beam in the living room. Mundane things surrounded by broken parts, which are all out of place. It's just like my hollow heart.

There was never any hope in this house. No one here saw a future beyond these walls, or the hardware store Greg and Millie own—*owned*.

Marcus was always meant to suffer because of his own sick desires. Greg was always meant to die facing the consequences of his actions, whether drinking or sitting idle. And me? I was always meant to be broken by the boy who put me together.

It's funny how life turns out.

Roman could hurt me a thousand ways, and he wouldn't need to lay a hand on me; a single word, and I would be done for. The sight of his back as he walks away would be enough, and nothing would put me back together.

All the broken shards that made up my being would catch in the wind, and I'd never be complete. Not that I ever was. But he made me feel like I could have been one day.

Frantic movements pull me from the darkness, and it takes more energy than it should to turn my attention to Marcus, who's wriggling and shuddering helplessly. I assume he knows how tonight will end.

The last meal he ate will be the overcooked chicken I prepared. The last person to lay their hands on *him* will be who I thought was my other half. But the last face he sees will be mine.

Little Isa.

Pretty Isabella.

Or his personal favorite: *fucking slut.*

His eyes plead with me as he cries, probably praying I will be the angel sent from above to save him. He's right about one thing: I am an angel. But I wasn't sent, I fell. I descended through the sky with burning wings, landing outside Eden in the land writhing with serpents. Because Roman pushed me out.

I don't realize I've started walking until I'm in front of him, slowly tearing the tape so he feels every bit of it.

The second his thin lips are free, he gasps for air like it's his first time breathing. "Isa, pl—you've gotta help me. You've gotta—he's a fucking lunatic." He blinks fast, swinging his petrified gaze between me, the stairs, and the knife block on the kitchen bench. I keep my eyes on his face, ignoring the blood draining from the hole where his appendage used to be and the liquid clumping in his bloodied chest hair. "There—the knife. Cut—"

"Did I look this pathetic?" I ask, emotionlessly.

Like a child sniffling as the tears mixed with sweat and snot? Was this me? Did I look so deserving of the torment too? Wide, innocent eyes so full of delusion that I thought someone might actually come to save me.

"What are you talking about? Just get the fucking—"

"No."

Mouth agape, he pauses. "What did you just fuck—"

"Shut the fuck up," I spit.

His eyes widen, and his face loses its color.

Good. He's scared. He should be.

"You don't get to speak to me like that anymore." My voice shakes as I say it.

There's something cathartic about seeing him like this, limited by a prison of someone else's making. I've never squirmed away from a little bit of blood—I've seen Roman covered in it enough times. This is fucked up beyond comprehension.

Usually, I'd rather walk away than cause someone's downfall. I wouldn't call it being the bigger person; I'd just say it's because I've had enough.

He hurt me. He made my life hell. He made me scared in my own home. He made me hate every second of my life.

Now, he's at my mercy.

My fists tremble, wanting to be unleashed on something—anything. But the thought of touching Marcus again sickens me to my very core. He's laid his filthy hands on me for years, and I guess life comes full circle; Roman, the man who used to keep Marcus at bay, will be the one who kills him.

I reach for the shelf and grab the first thing I can wrap my fingers around. Then I throw it at him with every bit of force I can muster. One right after the other, I keep throwing everything I can get my hands on. His participation trophies, bolts, tools, photo frames, ornaments, leaving red marks on his skin.

He buckles and screams, but I don't stop throwing item after item, until I keel over and throw up again from the sight of the blood splashing across the room.

"You're going to die tonight, you fucking pig," I spit. "And after everything you did to me, I'm going to enjoy watching." I take a step forward and point at him with a shaky finger. "You're a pathetic piece of shit who preys on women, and you're going to suffer for all the times you've assaulted me."

"Are you seriously mad about that right now?" He swings as he jerks, flapping his feet in a fruitless attempt to reach the ground. "Grow up. Untie me."

"I was a child," I snap, then turn to Greg, shaking my head at the sight of him and the belt around his throat. It's mortifying, yet the perfect form of justice. "I didn't need to grow up." I wanted my dead mother. I wanted my father, who didn't want me. I wanted not just to be loved but to feel it too.

"Isa, get the fu—"

I slap the tape back over his mouth, silencing him. Sometimes when angels fall, the serpents devour them. Other times, they learn to live with them.

"I'd say rest in peace, but I hope you never find it." It feels liberating to let it roll from my tongue.

The back of my neck prickles with awareness right before I hear Roman come down the stairs.

"He better not have said anything he shouldn't have." The rage in Roman's voice is well hidden underneath his sinister veneer.

I don't need to look at him to know he's giving Marcus a smile that's all teeth. Because my foster brother looks at me again, pleading with his eyes for *my* help. How the tables have turned.

Marcus never stopped when I asked him not to push or touch me. This household turned its back when I cried because his hand slipped beneath my shirt. There's a certain peace in knowing that he will die realizing that no one will come to save him. That I will be part of his downfall.

Behind me, something drops to the floor, but I don't want to risk looking at Roman to figure out what it is. I should be grateful that it sounds too heavy to be another body, so maybe it wasn't a lie Millie is alive after all. Or perhaps she's seconds away from joining her husband.

Roman's shoulder brushes mine as he moves past me. I know he wouldn't hurt me physically. But I'd rather have scars on my body than my soul.

He all but saunters to Marcus, twirling the switchblade between his fingers as if he were putting on a show. "You know where you went wrong?"

Marcus sobs, flicking his bloodshot eyes between me and the monster I helped create. I bite the inside of my cheek, feeling like I need to say something, but the words are nowhere to be found.

"You fucked with my girl." Roman chuckles darkly, glancing at me before saying, "And you should *never* fuck with my girl."

The tip of the blade digs into the corner of Marcus's jaw, blooming red as it follows the path to his chin. His thrashing only makes the cut deeper, more vicious, a thorned rose rather than a smooth lily.

I edge back, tripping over my feet as I stumble to a wall for support. I can't look away, but the sight of the gore makes me tip over to gasp for air.

"You're lucky she's here. If not—you and me—we would have been having fun all night long."

A boulder lodges in my throat, scraping along the walls of my neck.

Roman hums a made-up tune as he continues carving all sorts of shapes into Marcus's already deformed skin. Stars, hearts, circles, his own initials—that he promptly slices through—undeterred by Marcus's squeals of pain muffled by tape. Roman watches his handiwork with intent eyes following each motion, his body leaning forward as if in a trance, like a child doodling in class. Each glide of his hand is purposeful, going deeper in certain areas while barely grazing the flesh in others. As if he's trying to stop Marcus from bleeding out.

As if he's tortured someone like this before.

I wipe my trembling hands along my bare thigh and cover my mouth to silence my sobs. Marcus keeps looking at me to help him. Some sick, twisted part of me wishes Greg was still alive to be a bystander in his son's demise.

I don't know what I feel. Guilt? Fear? Disgust? Anticipation? I feel all of it, yet none of it. Each swirl of emotion is so visceral but still so dull, as my mind refuses to comprehend the scene before me.

This is fucked up on every single level.

I know I should call for help. I need to stop Roman before he kills Marcus. I *should have* saved him when I had the chance.

But I can't do anything, paralyzed in my spot, focused on trying not to pass out.

Roman pauses, looking up at Marcus with an eerie innocence that makes my stomach clench. "Do you want me to let you go?"

I stiffen and everything goes silent. He wouldn't... would he? The Roman I knew would burn the entire city down before letting someone who hurt me walk free. But three years will change someone.

My foster brother nods slowly, sending me a questioning look. I swallow. Would Roman really let Marcus go? This is the question in both our heads, but I know for a fact that Marcus won't be asking if Roman will let *me* go. He's selfish. There's no planet where he'd give a shit about what happens to me.

"It doesn't seem like you want to be let go," Roman practically sings, swirling the knife around Marcus's cheek without breaking the skin.

Marcus swings his head from side to side violently, shaking his whole body. He doesn't seem to care about the pain he's causing himself because he doesn't stop.

Worse, I can't seem to care either.

"That's better." Roman smiles in the same way a tiger would before tearing through its dinner's neck. He may like inflicting fear, but what he loves most is making them beg. "Apologize to my girl."

It's on the tip of my tongue to say, *it's fine. He doesn't have to.* But I want to hear him say it. I want him to beg for my forgiveness.

The duct tape is ripped from Marcus's mouth for the second time tonight. But like the idiot he is, the first words out of his mouth are, "Please, let me go."

The words earn him a knife to his stomach. I flinch back from the suckling sound combined with his howling. Whether from morbid fascination, a sense of responsibility, or some sick need for closure, I keep my eyes open, staring at the gruesome sight through new tears.

"Apologize," Roman growls, twisting the knife.

My chest tightens. Watching this kind of thing on TV is different from seeing it happen to your foster brother. I wish I had the strength to hurt Marcus the way Roman is, not just for vengeance, but to prove to myself that I can take care of myself in every possible way.

Marcus screams. What if the neighbors hear? What if the police come? What if Marcus lives and tells the police that I was an accomplice, like I know he would?

Marcus's lips quiver, spit and blood flying out as he looks at me. "I—I'm sorry."

I grit my teeth. His apology doesn't make me feel any better.

"You can do better than that," Roman says.

"I'm sorry!" Marcus cries as Roman applies more pressure to the open wound. "I'm sorry. I'm sorry. I'm sorry. I'm sorry," he says quickly. "Please, just let me go."

"Keep going," Roman says.

I dig half-moons into my palms and watch Marcus beg. "Please. I swear—I swear I won't tell anyone. Do whatever you want with that slut—"

I suck in a sharp breath as the blade rips through tendons and sinews before my tormentor can finish his sentence, but the damage is already done. The rage vibrating from Roman is a living, breathing thing I can taste in the back of my throat.

An endless stream of blood pours from the yawning slit across Marcus's neck. The crimson waterfall soaks his chest and rushes down his legs before pooling onto the floor.

I start heaving, but nothing comes up.

Inch by agonizingly slow inch, Roman turns his head in my direction, and I'm frozen in my spot. Dark hair falls over his beautifully vicious face, covered in my foster family's blood.

Electricity cracks in the space between us, and every cell in my body is a live wire under his stare. When his eyes snap up to mine, it's like I'm finally looking at him and seeing him for the bloodthirsty beast he is. And he's found his next kill.

Me.

Pure animalistic instinct takes over with the single-minded need to run from the apex predator. My foot slides backward as he steps forward. One foot back, another forward. Stalking me. Hunting me.

The all-consuming urge to run has nothing to do with his strong strides or the knife fisted at his side. No, it's the glint in his eyes. He isn't warning me not to run.

He's hoping I will.

Reason left me a long time ago. Logic is still tucked away in my bed, oblivious to the chaos below.

You should never run. You can climb, and you might be able to hide, but you *never* run.

Yet, that's precisely what I do.

I run.

CHAPTER 4

ROMAN

8 Years Ago

Roman: 14 years old – Isabella: 12 years old.

"Damn it, Mickey," Bella sighs, dabbing an alcohol-soaked pad to the cut on my face.

I smirk up at her, bouncing my leg on the concrete as I sit on the edge of the deck. "Yeah, but did you see the other guy?"

The glare she shoots my way is enough to make Hell freeze over. But knowing her, I'll say a few choice words here and there, and it'll melt like it's just another day in paradise.

Steve is going to have a field day over this. He'll probably try to get a couple more hits in himself or decide my weekend would be better off spent in the basement. He's figured out that it's far more effective than a belt or a "good ol' fashion beatin'," as he'd say.

"Yes, I saw the other guy." She throws her hands up, but the exasperation doesn't reach her eyes. "You pushed him to his knees and made him beg me for my forgiveness."

I lift a shoulder. "You should have said you didn't forgive him. Make it more exciting for me. You can forgive me by playing tag."

We might be too old to play those types of games, but I just love the way her eyes widen right before I catch her. Screw hide and seek, or hacky sack. Tag is the only game I've ever wanted to play with her.

This time, when she looks at me, she really does seem exhausted, but it disappears when I wince from the sharp sting of the cotton on the open wound on my cheek.

I have to hand it to the kid from before; he didn't look like much, but he could throw a punch. Caught me completely off guard. I almost had respect for him, but then I remembered why he ended up there.

"It was an accident."

She's been saying that all afternoon. It looked like no accident from what I saw. The lunchbox I gave her when we were kids somehow ended up in *his* bag. My Bella doesn't have *accidents* like that.

This was deliberate.

I don't take kindly to that.

Bella and I—not *me and Bella* (she's been helping me with my English homework)—have been playing this little cat-and-mouse game since day one. I'm the cat, everyone else is the mouse, and she's the dog from Tom & Jerry that would try to mediate. Or simply stand to the side and flinch every time someone lands a hit on me.

I like her flinching far more than I should.

I squeeze the stress ball the little princess got me using as of last month. I've already gone through two of them—not that she knows. If she did, she'd probably burst a vein from being overly worried about me. I've just been pocketing them from the department store instead and replacing them before she figures it out.

The stress ball is a handy little gadget that has stopped me from bashing my head into a wall. Or Steve's, maybe even Josh's, too. We have a new kid staying with us, about five years younger than Bella.

At first, I liked Jeremy because he was quiet and kept to himself. Then Bella sniffed him out and decided to take that little shit under her wing. If he's under her wing, then by extension, that means he's under my wing, which gets fucking exhausting when I only have two wings. Half the time, I'm walking myself into the basement before Steve gets the chance to drag me in there.

But it's easier now.

Down there in the cold.

Now, I have the handy dandy stress ball, a pen and paper, and the MP3 player I stole from Skinny—or was it Ugly?—all because they looked at my girl the wrong way.

At least her hair isn't so ridiculously wonky anymore. She means well and tries her damn best, but I usually end up redoing it for her before we walk to school. If not, I just can't stop staring at it in all its chaos.

Every morning, I hold my breath to see if she tried braiding it because, unless she brings a hairbrush, there's no way I can salvage it.

She frowns at me, and I frown, too.

"Maybe you should have talked to him before you punched him," Pigtails says.

If she ever knew I still call her Pigtails in my head, she'd probably be debating whether to disown me or sit in the corner and cry. The last time I did, her bottom lip quivered—God, I hate it when it quivers—and she started getting upset, saying that I thought she was a pig.

I shrug, grinning. "No point wasting time. I was cutting to the chase."

She carefully dabs the wound again. In my entire life, Bella is the only person who has tended to my wounds without being paid to do it. "There are two sides to every story, Mickey. What you did was grievous bodily assault." Her r's come out nice and clear.

Bella's been watching *Law & Order* for the past month, and now she thinks she wants to be a defense attorney—which might actually come in handy for me, so it's all a go from my point of view.

I catch sight of her earring and internally wince. I'm unsure if she still thinks about losing her mother's earrings, but I do. Every day.

"Your side is the only one that counts."

She rolls her eyes. "I'm not sure if that's how justice works."

I can't help it; I roll my eyes too. "Shut up, you're, like, eleven."

"No, I'm twelve, thank you very much." She places her hands on her hips. "Twelve years and three months," she adds matter-of-factly.

I put no effort into hiding my victorious grin. Pointing out her age always gets a rise out of her. She's twelve going on twenty with how much she tries to mother everyone.

Then the first sign starts; the loud wheeze in her breath from the change in season. Bella clears her throat to hide it, but I narrow my eyes at her. Then, as the seconds pass, she turns to the side and lets out a series of earth-shattering coughs.

Reaching for my bag, I tug it onto my lap and ignore the pain from my busted knuckles. I rummage around the front pocket until I find what I need, all while Bella wheezes between coughs.

I sigh as I hold out the inhaler. Her delicate fingers wrap around it without hesitation, struggling to suck it in between breaths. She never remembers to take it like she's meant to. And it's *fall*, the worst time of year for her.

"You lied to me." I *explicitly* asked her this morning, "*Did you take your inhaler?*"

Do you know what her response was? A couple of flutters of her eyelashes and a bashful, "*Mmhmm.*"

Typical.

I'm not falling for that shit next time.

"Do I need to start forcing you to take it?"

Her eyes water from all her coughing as she moves to sit beside me, attempting to calm her breathing. I take the inhaler from her and stuff it back in my bag.

She shakes her head softly. Even without the inhaler, she would have gotten through the worst of the coughs within a few minutes. Still, then she'd spend the rest of the day wheezing until she took the medication. It seems to be getting worse the older she gets.

"Then you better start taking it," I scold.

She tries to play it off by resuming her nursing duties. "It was just the one time."

"This week," I add.

If no one reminded her, this girl would forget to feed herself.

She scrunches her nose. "It tastes bad."

"Don't care. You're going to start taking it properly. Promise me." I know she won't. Isabella Garcia doesn't make promises she can't keep. I can see in her eyes that she's itching to change the subject because this has been a point of real contention for a while.

"*Sarai la mia morte.*"

You're going to be the death of me.

I don't remember much of the language, but Bella is trying to learn it so we can "speak behind the adults' backs," even though her Spanish is better than my Italian. And I don't know any Spanish beyond *gracias,* and *me llamo Roman.*

"Don't forget, I'm going to visit Mitchell's mother this weekend," Bella says suddenly as she plasters on a band-aid.

I groan, but I'm unsure whether it's from the pressure of the band-aid on my cut or from her reminder. I hate when she goes, because she's all alone with no one to watch over her. What if Mitchell, her new foster dad, tries to hit her? He hasn't done it before, but it doesn't mean he won't start. Or, what if she has a nightmare, can't find Mickey Mouse, or has a panic attack again? Or if she forgets her inhaler?

"Why do you have to go?"

It's not like anyone in her foster family has given a shit about inviting her to their family gatherings. At least Mitchell's place is better than the hellhole she was in when we first met.

When Margaret heard all about how she wouldn't get proper lunches—and I may have mentioned a bruise or two—the state swooped in to save the little girl with bright brown eyes. Apparently, she didn't have "attention seeker" in her file, so they believed every word she said and got her out of there.

Mitchell is an asshole, but at least he gives her three meals a day and enough blankets to keep her warm—not like the last house.

Bella pinches her lip between her teeth, then shrugs like it isn't something to worry about. Probably more for my sake than hers. "They told me I have to go. I don't make the rules, I just follow the orders."

"But you should try—"

"Mickey," she says calmly, eying the stress ball that looks a hair away from exploding. "I'll be back at school on Monday, and you won't even notice I'm gone."

She's wrong. I'll notice.

I *always* notice.

Unless I'm in the basement, I'm loitering on her lawn, or terrorizing the neighborhood, which she isn't really a fan of.

If it were up to her, she'd have us both curled up with a book. She's been doing this annoying thing where she likes going to the park to sit down and read, but I hate it. There aren't enough noises, and I like hearing the sound of her voice.

"Isa," Mitchell yells from somewhere inside the house. "Get inside. Set the table up for dinner."

Pigtails steps back with a slight shake of her head, and I jump to my feet. *Two days. She's gone for two days. That's nothing. That's like... Like... Forty-eight hours.*

I can count down or something.

I move forward to give her a hug, but the rejection smacks me in the face as she turns and runs up the stairs, avoiding my touch entirely. I know she wouldn't have done it on purpose, I just guessed—well, *hoped* she'd be a little less scared now.

We never used to be able to high-five without one or both of us flinching, so when she hugged me for the very first time two years ago on my birthday, it was like I saw the light. Then, when she hugged me last year, I'm pretty sure I understood why people find religion.

I can count on one hand the number of times I've been hugged—that I can remember—and Bella takes both places. I wasn't even sure I liked it at first. It felt so claustrophobic, and all her hair was shoved in my nose and mouth, but the second those small arms of hers wrapped around my waist, everything stilled. The noises, the need to move, to burn energy by taking it out on another person. *She* is the only one who has ever been able to calm me. Sometimes she does this special little laugh, and the world quietens, but it doesn't go away forever. Until she hugged me, and for once, everything felt normal.

Peaceful.

Right.

"See you Monday," she half wheezes over her shoulder.

"Yeah," I say. "Monday."

Forty-eight hours.

I can do forty-eight hours.

It turns out I can't count. Either that, or she's been gone for *more* than forty-eight hours. But whatever. I survived. Barely. I'll see her today, and that's all that I care about.

I show up at her house earlier than usual and tug at the bracelet she recently made me as I wait, leaning against the fence. I'm still not used to wearing it and it makes me feel uneasy. Something about the bumps of the cotton strings sends weird shivers down my spine.

Not that I've told Pigtails that.

She was so excited to give it to me—even blew me off for a whole afternoon just to make it.

If I lost it, I'm not sure how I'd react. Or how she'd react—probably cry. So the simple solution is never to take it off, even when I shower. But now the thinning fabric has me on edge.

Bella has what she claims is a matching one, even though the pattern is different, and hers is a mixture of teals and reds, while mine is simply red and black. She claimed it was so I didn't need to worry about getting blood on it.

Well, she didn't use the word *blood*; she used *dirty*, but we both know what she really wanted to say.

Time ticks by at an agonizingly slow pace until it's time for her to come out. Then five minutes pass. Then ten. Then twenty. She never walks through the front doors.

Uneasiness wedges itself into the space beneath my ribs. This isn't like her. This isn't like Bella. She is never late. If she is, she'll stick her head out of the window and wake the neighborhood just to tell me how much longer she needs.

I mutter, "Fuck it," under my breath as I storm to the house.

Mitchell never lets me inside, so I only get to see its interior if he isn't home or if I sneak in. When I go for the lock, the handle doesn't turn. Not caring if Mitchell rips me a new one, I pound my still-healing fists against the door, peeking through the window as I wait.

Five seconds.

Ten.

No sound.

No movement.

The rational part of my brain tells me that her trip has just been extended. She'll be back later tonight, and when I wake up tomorrow, it'll be like she never left. And then everything will be fine. I'll be fine.

But the other part of me has eyes. It knows what I'm seeing. I know what is on the other side of the window, and every inch of me is saying that the *rational* part is fucking delusional.

White-hot rage crawls beneath my skin as I stare at the empty dining room. *Empty.* No chairs, no table, no fake fucking plant. *Empty.*

No.

No.

Bella would never leave me. *Never.* She said she would see me today, and she wouldn't lie about that, would she?

No.

No, she never lets me down in any way that counts.

She's always been there for me—the light at the top of the basement, the first bite after days of starvation, the one who doesn't make me feel like running.

Bella wouldn't leave. She just wouldn't.

I sprint around the outside of the house, checking one window after the other. Empty. Every one of them. But the final nail in the coffin is her room. *Empty.* My drawings aren't on the walls, the bed is gone, and Mickey Mouse is nowhere to be seen.

No.

No, no, no.

They can't just take her away from me. They can't.

My feet take me to the back porch, the last place I saw her, and try the ranch slider, but it doesn't budge. I need to get inside. I *have* to get inside. I have to check. I don't know; maybe she's in there somewhere. Maybe she managed to get away and hide in a closet.

I have to.

I have to. I have to. I have to.

She—

No, she can't be gone. I *refuse* to believe it. I can't—*No.* She has to come back.

I don't feel the glass shattering beneath my knuckles. With each pummel, another shard pierces my skin, and another drop of blood drops onto the floor. It isn't until I *feel* it. Not the pain or the ache. The absence of *it.* The disappearance of the itch.

Then I see it. The one thing I refuse to take off laying on the floor amongst the drops of crimson. The last thing I got from her.

The bracelet.

I broke it.

Bella's bracelet.

CHAPTER 5

ROMAN

8 YEARS AGO

Roman: 14 years old – Isabella: 12 years old.

"Make it stop. Make it stop. Make it stop," I hiss, hitting my head against the concrete.

Maybe if I keep throwing myself against the wall, someone will let me out.

I know they can hear me screaming. I know they hear me banging on the door at night. Or is it morning? I can't tell.

I don't know anything anymore.

You don't know anything anymore. You don't know anything anymore. You don't know anything anymore.

"Shut up! Shut up! Shut up!" I scream. The skin of my knuckles tears against the wall, ripping more and more each time I swing. I can't see the blood through the darkness. Can't see the bone. I need something other than the voices. I need sound or light or taste. I need pain.

My muscles strain. Sweat gathers between my shoulder blades. It's not enough.

I'm as helpless now as I was when I was four.

Useless.

Pathetic.

Piece of shit.

I can still picture the chest freezer, stark white next to heavy brown boxes. The inside, silver in the light, black in the dark. And it was so dark. So quiet. Empty.

My chest still aches from the way my knees pushed against my chest while I clawed at the four walls. I remember wondering if my parents were finally playing with me as they lowered me into the freezer, then *thump* before I was trapped in the coffin. I tried to stand, but my head hit the lid. Tried to move my legs, but they were stuck bruising my ribs. I screamed until I lost my voice, and cried until there were no more tears to shed.

I don't remember what my own parents look like, but I remember the freezer and how the voice in my head screamed over and over: *I want to get out! I want to get out! I want to get out!*

Now I'm back in the dark because of another fucking piece-of-shit *parent.* I can stretch my legs and move, and the ceiling is well above my head. But there's something here that wasn't in the empty freezer: the bone deep cold that starts as a chilling ache, before everything becomes numb.

And I stop feeling anything else. I hit harder and harder, until pain thunders through my hand, but I don't stop. *More.*

Once I'm out, I can see Bella and she'll make it all better.

No.

Wait.

She's fucking gone, too.

She left me like my parents did.

48

She didn't even say goodbye.

No.

She's coming back.

She's going to open the door and let the light in.

She has to come back.

I need her.

CHAPTER 6

ISABELLA

The last thing I see is Roman's eyes flickering with excitement before I spin on my heel and bolt as if hellhounds are snapping at my ankles. A scream claws at my throat, itching to be released, but nothing comes out.

My sock-covered feet slip on the warm liquid splattered on the floor. I try not to think about the fact that it's probably Marcus's as I stop myself from falling at the last second.

Roman stalks closely behind me, moving slowly as if this weren't a chase my life could depend on. Each of his measured steps echoes through the house, creating a haunting melody that pairs horridly with my racing heart.

Roman Riviera doesn't play with his food, but he loves playing with his toys.

My vision tunnels on the front door, cream-colored and covered in greasy handprints. *An escape.* If I can get outside, I can scream.

Just one little scream.

Someone will hear me. The police will come, and this whole nightmare will be over. I'll be free of this house and finally be able to move on. The state will move little Jeremy to a new house, and if Millie is alive, she'll get this god-awful place and the store. I can take what I've managed to skim from the tills, maybe steal a few of Greg's and Marcus's things for extra cash, then go to a new city with no one but myself to look after.

I just need to get past the door and scream.

Freedom is so close, but just out of reach.

Adrenaline floods my veins, ratcheting up the roaring in my ears. "*Bella,*" he sings, and goosebumps erupt over my cold skin.

We've played this game a hundred times before; he gives me a look, and I start running. Back then, it was an innocent game that got my blood racing as the fear of getting caught pumped through me.

It was our own version of tag. He was forever the chaser, and I was forever the one who ran. He'd catch me every single time, no matter how hard I tried.

Back then, it was childish and innocent—even though he never gave up the game when he became legally allowed to vote. Somehow, I don't think he's just going to throw me over his shoulder or wrap his arms around me in a soul-crushing hug.

My clammy hands curl around the door handle, and hope springs in my ribcage for the first time in a long time. But the seed that sprouted withers when powerful arms curl around my waist and up my chest until burning fingers wrap around the column of my throat.

"Got you," he hums against my ear, dragging me back against his firm body and away from any hope of freedom.

"No, no! Let me go!"

I drop my full weight onto him and kick against the door as hard as possible. My escape attempts are futile when all he does is huff and tighten his grip on my throat. A reminder that he can take what he wants, whenever he wants.

"You know better than to run from me. Predators love to hunt." His hot breath caresses my ear as he whispers.

"Roman, please."

Please, what? I don't know.

He buries his head into the crook of my neck, spreading blood from his face and inhaling deeply as he groans. "God, I love it when you beg."

I freeze, feet suspended in the air, when my mind pieces together what the hardness pressing into my back is.

"Do you realize how much I fucking missed you? I was going insane thinking about you."

His teeth scrape against the soft skin of my neck, forcing a shiver from me. I'm not sure where his gloves disappeared to, but he lowers me so only the balls of my feet touch the ground, and I have no choice but to lean into him for support.

I realize too late what his plan is when his hand descends to my lower stomach, toying with the waist of my shorts. I gasp, feeling his hard-on pressed up against my ass, grinding ever so slightly. I know this is wrong, and that I shouldn't be feeling this way, but I can't help the unbridled desire this ignites deep within my core.

He hums in approval, dragging his tongue along the column of my throat, trailing liquid fire in his wake. "You taste like every sinful thought I've ever had."

You need to scream for help, my mind whispers.

I stay silent.

Despite everything that makes this wrong, it has never felt more right. After all these years, I hate that the only thing that has ever felt right is being in his arms. Despite all the blood spilled tonight, I hate that this is the safest I've felt in three years.

Roman's fingers disappear beneath the hem of my top and dip into the waist of the pajama shorts he gave me four years ago. Clawing at his arms only seems to encourage him. Still, I don't stop my desperate movements, even though my body is begging—fighting against my mind—for this to continue.

"Just as I thought," he rasps. "Fucking soaked."

"Don't! Let go of me, Roman." If I don't stop him now, I don't think I'll have the strength to keep fighting.

"Don't let go of you?" He laughs darkly. "Oh, that was my plan. You're all mine now."

I squirm when another finger joins. They do nothing but rest there, yet it's enough for me to squeeze my legs together in a useless attempt to soothe the climbing need for friction. The rumble of his voice, his intoxicating scent, every inch of space where we touch, it's enough for me to almost forget what he's done.

I'm sick and depraved. I haven't accepted it, but I acknowledged it long ago. It's difficult not to turn toward the darkness when I spent my days fantasizing about the boy with a sadistic grin and bloody fists, whose knuckles were always split for me.

"Do you know I was thinking about *you* all that time away?"

My voice disappears with every other thought except one: I was always on his mind. All this time. He *missed* me.

If that were true, then why didn't he come back? Why did he leave in the first place?

"I was going crazy thinking about another guy laying a hand on you." His hold tightens almost painfully. "Do you know what that does to me? Thinking that someone else is touching what's *mine*," he snarls into my neck and demands control over my breathing with the flex of his fingers. "I kept wondering if I consumed your every waking thought, just like you consumed mine." His fingers inch lower. "I kept thinking about what you felt like in my hands, all the little sounds you made. Fuck, and how fucking divine you felt beneath me."

I don't resist when he tips my head to the side to nibble on my jaw. With heavy lids, I stare at the door leading to my freedom while being in the arms of a man who broke me.

"My memories could never compare to the reality of you. Don't you realize you were made for me? We were made for each other." Each syllable from his lips is raw and guttural, like he's hanging by the last threads of his control.

The whimper that escapes me says more than words ever could. We might be a match, but matches burn. Stories end even when the love hasn't died.

"Say it, Bella," he whispers. "Say my name."

I can't bring myself to say it—to call him the name that started it all. If I do, I'll let him back into my life and fall back to the bottom of the pit I've been trying to crawl out of. My traitorous body melts into his hold, only to stiffen a moment later when one of his fingers brushes the sensitive skin between my legs.

Shaking my head, I bite my bottom lip to stop myself from moaning. My nipples harden underneath the thin material of my shirt, showing him exactly what his wicked words and possessive touch do to me.

He gives me the friction I so desperately need, and any attempt at staying silent disappears. My lips form into an 'O' as I try and fail to drop lower to the floor to chase his touch.

I need to—no, *have to* stop this. But just a second longer, maybe two. I can give myself that much. I can feel my mind screaming, but I lock it away. I deserve to feel good. Right?

"So beautiful," he mutters.

A blush scorches my flushed cheeks from the guilt of taking pleasure from this gruesome scene, but my body doesn't care. The gory mess behind us doesn't stop my hips from buckling to his touch. My nails dig into his arms to pull him away and bring him closer simultaneously.

He moves his fingers with expert precision, knowing which cords to play without reading the notes. I close my eyes and imagine he never left, that I'm still whole.

My breath comes out in short pants, living the fantasy of a life I lost as I move my hips to the rhythm of his fingers. He chokes me a little tighter to remind me who is in command.

Knowing how much death he's caused with his bare hands and that I could be his next victim with nothing more than a squeeze is frightening. But the thought only adds to the symphony. The crescendo is in sight, and my hips jerk, chasing the high. Just as I'm about to reach the peak, Roman's touch disappears, and a needy whimper falls from my bitten lip before I can stop myself.

"You're so breakable like this." The smirk is evident in his voice. He wants me to know that only he can bring me pleasure, and he can just as easily take it away. "Completely at my mercy."

His warmth returns. The swirl of his fingers is agonizingly slow, like he has all the time in the world. I know better. Roman is never lazy when it comes to me. It takes every bit of energy I have not to groan and buckle in frustration, so he goes back to the blissful pace he's set.

"Tell me you want me."

"Go to Hell."

His laugh is pure mirth and carnal sin. "You'll be right there with me. You're my favorite sin."

"I'm not going anywhere with you," I bite out while straining my muscles to stop them from moving with his motions.

"Hmm," he muses. "So feisty tonight."

He flicks my clit, and I jump in his hold from the sparks rushing through my veins, making him laugh like the demon he is.

"You seem to have forgotten our promise."

He drags the neckline of my shirt down my shoulder with his teeth, kissing the exposed skin. I keep blinking, trying to remain focused as his thumb rubs against my clit, and he dips his finger inside me. Just the tip. Just enough to send me reeling for more.

I've dreamed about feeling him back inside me for the longest time. I always imagined he would watch me with hooded eyes, a hand gripped in my hair while his expert fingers stole my climax.

That's one thing that hasn't changed. In everything outside of our bubble, Roman is a conqueror, true to his name. He'd take without asking, and any scraps left behind would be a mercy.

"I'll forgive you for forgetting." His gruff voice curls around me. "I'll just have to remind you who you've always belonged to. Let me make it up to you."

I cry from the stretch of my pussy, taking the brutal thrust from two of his thick fingers. Stars dance behind my eyes as I grip his arms tighter to keep upright. The added friction from his thumb on my clit makes any attempts at keeping my mouth shut nearly impossible.

Nothing about this is loving or gentle. This is pure possession, just as he said. He's commanding my body to give him exactly what he wants, and I have no say in the matter. He can have my climax and the knowledge he is the cause for the heat dripping down my legs. But I'm keeping my voice—he can't have everything he wants.

The hold around my throat is replaced by his lips as he sucks the soft skin into his mouth, bordering on pain and falling onto the side of pleasure. He yanks my shirt up, exposing my breasts to him. I've never been well endowed in that area, but he still treats them like they're the definition of perfection, kneading them and twirling the hard buds between his fingers.

I don't see the climax before it hits. The force of my orgasm has me arching back into his body, opening my mouth to a silent scream. He continues to take from me, plunging his fingers in and out of me until I slap his hand to stop.

The chill of the night air against my nipples lessens with my lowering shirt. I'm struck with a feeling of profound emptiness when my panties become free from his intrusion.

"Better than I remember," he mutters against my neck. "You'll regret letting me feel your cunt coming all over my fingers. I promise you, next time, I'm breaking you on my cock."

Then the lust-filled haze over my vision fades away, and my mind suddenly remembers what I was doing before my long-forgotten libido replaced my brain.

"There won't be a next time," I say between pants.

"Don't doubt me. We need to go," he says dismissively.

My muscles wind tighter, walking the thin line of falling from the adrenaline high. As soon as I'm completely free from his hold, my animalistic instinct takes over once more, and I bolt for the door, swinging it open. I can hear Roman cursing under his breath before I break into a run.

I just need to scream.

I just need to open my mouth and call for help.

But neither of those two things happens because I can't bring myself to make a single sound, not even when he catches me. I kick and thrash, and I'm unsure if it's just for show. I'm telling myself the only reason for giving up on my freedom so easily is because I don't want him to get in trouble.

"You're being a very naughty girl, Bella."

The ominous tone of his voice sends a shudder down my spine as he drags me back inside with nothing but the flickering streetlight to guide the way. As soon as the front door shuts, he's caging me against the wood with his body, pinning my arms above my head with a single hand.

"It's like you're begging to be punished." The sentence is laced with hope that I'll fight him again, letting me know how serious he is by pushing his bulge against my stomach.

"What—" My eyes widen when his free hand joins his other, and something soft wraps around my wrists. The door groans as I shift to glance at the black rope Roman is binding my wrists with.

Mouth hanging open, I notice he's not using just any rope. It's not the kind found in a department store, and it's certainly nothing like the abrasive hemp rope he used on Marcus. The realization that he's using *silk* rope kicks me in the gut.

Roman knew I would fight him, knew I would try to run. He planned it all. The mask, the method of torture and death, the different ropes, the message he left when I arrived home yesterday.

I don't know who this man is. Roman never planned ahead when spilling blood was involved. He was impulsive—acting first, avoiding consequences later. Which begs the question, what else does he have planned?

"Don't do this," I beg.

I can see the concentration in his pinched brows as he works to tie my wrists firmly, but not to the point of pain, as I thrash.

"I don't want to do this, Bella. Do you think I want to hurt you?" he asks through gritted teeth.

"Yes."

The muscle in his cheek pulses as he pauses and looks down at me. "Never."

"It wouldn't be the first time."

He tenses, and something flashes in his eyes too quickly for me to figure out what it is.

I look behind him toward the kitchen, where two dead bodies remain. "You shouldn't have done that," I murmur.

He tilts his head, raking his gaze over my face as the corner of his lips curves upward. "You could have stopped me."

"How?"

His eyes soften, and I see the man I used to know for the first time tonight. The one who reserved all his genuine smiles for me and would only truly laugh if it was just the two of us alone.

Roman's voice is dangerously low. "I would do anything you tell me to."

I swallow and hold his stare, hoping he will see whatever I'm feeling so I don't need to admit it to myself. "Let me go."

"Anything but that."

"Roman," I plead.

Any evidence of the man I knew slips away with a flash of hurt, quickly replaced by his menacing grin. "Come on. It's just you and me from now on."

He throws me over his shoulder, knocking the wind from me before I can say anything else.

"Put me down," I hiss, hitting his toned back with my bound wrists.

He chuckles, and I yelp when he slaps my ass. "Fuck, I missed you."

My legs flop against his chest, and my dark hair sways with his movements. What's worse is that I miss him too. I miss his voice, the nicknames, the constant entertainment, and the way he looks at me like I'm the most beautiful thing he's ever seen.

He grabs a duffle bag off the floor, opens the door, clicks the internal lock, then shuts it behind him. I squirm against his shoulder, still beating his back and kicking his front, growling obscenities under my breath.

But if I'm completely honest with myself, it's all for peace of mind that I tried—that I wasn't an entirely willing victim. We both know the truth. It's right there in front of us and undeniable under the cloudy night sky: If I truly wanted to be free of him, I would be.

I could scream, and everyone around would hear. Other than us and the insects of the night, there isn't a sound to be heard in the less-than-safe neighborhood. But still, I stay silent as he carries me through the empty street.

Roman's steps are so leisurely and confident that even the best detective could be convinced he isn't abducting someone. I manage to prop myself up on his shoulders to watch the place I lived for the past four years shrink in the distance until it's hidden behind trees. It's hard to believe everyone is fast asleep in their beds, unaware of the carnage in house number thirty-four.

Roman drops me to my feet beside an unassuming pickup truck, clamps his hand on my arm, and tsks. "Don't even think about it."

I frown at him. I wasn't even thinking about running; I was just waiting for him to unlock the truck so I could step inside. *What is wrong with me?*

The second he opens the car door, I rip myself from his grip and slip inside. The more he touches me, the more my anger toward him wanes, and I deserve to be angry for everything that's happened.

He's breaking my resolve too quickly.

When the door shuts, I'm left alone in the quiet darkness of the car. Suddenly, everything comes crashing down—the adrenaline, the nerves, the ache between my legs, and the tender skin beneath the ropes. A single tear trails down my cheek, and I wipe it away before he can see.

This is really happening.

Roman used to be terrible at chess and sub-par at mind games. He'd prefer inflicting the type of pain that comes from his hand and a well-chosen weapon. But that's part of the problem; he *used* to be that way. The person who smiled at me when I first came down the stairs earlier tonight is all *man*. He's physically changed in ways I can't even begin to describe, with broader shoulders and a sharper jaw. What about on the inside?

Has this man mastered owning the board and come to play with a different type of toy? Something else he can use and discard once he's bored.

The air electrifies when he drops himself into his seat with the same grace as a lion, humming an unknown tune as the car comes to life. Roman drives us away from the neighborhood and onto one of the back streets, tapping the wheel and filling the silence with his sounds.

He's relaxed and at ease.

He's *fucking crazy.*

If it weren't for the evidence of his brutality splattered on his face, I wouldn't believe him if he told me about what he just did.

There wasn't a single secret between us for almost twelve years, and now I don't even know how to speak to him and break the silence. The dynamic between us has shifted. It's no longer the princess and her knight. It's something far simpler: the prisoner and her captor.

"Where are you taking me?" I ask when I can't stand listening to any more of his goddamn humming and tapping.

"Home." He doesn't hesitate with his answer, and his tone has an almost patronizing edge, like his response was a given.

"You just took me from it."

He snorts. "That was a house, but it wasn't your home." Roman adjusts himself in his seat and checks the rearview mirror. I'm guessing it's to see if we're being followed. "Our home is wherever we make it."

Our. We. He's talking like someone who isn't just going to disappear again.

"You went too far."

"No amount of blood spilled will ever be too much for you."

"When will it end?"

He smirks. "When I'm in a grave, and even then, Hell won't keep me from you."

I jump when his warm hand lands on my leg without a single thread to separate our skin. The contact makes me heady in my already delirious mind. I have to squeeze my legs together, because my body hasn't forgotten the state he brought me to in the house. I grab his wrist to try to push him away, but my pathetic attempt does nothing against his brute strength.

I know what he'll find if he dips his hands into my shorts again. No matter how much I tell myself that I shouldn't want this or that I am meant to be angry at him, my body has other ideas. He has the face of an angel and the mind of the devil.

"But you'll ruin me," I whisper.

I watch as his smile turns ravenous, and the desire to run kicks in. "Does that excite you?"

His hand inches higher until it's at the junction of my thighs. My voice hitches when I say, "No."

"Don't worry. If you break, I'll put you back together. If you run, I'm running right behind you. If you burn, I'll burn with you."

When I look down at his hand, I tense for an entirely different reason. Under the fading lights of the city, I spot a black-and-red embroidered friendship bracelet peeking out beneath his long sleeve shirt.

He still has it.

I glance at my own wrist and swallow.

The bindings dig into my skin, and he catches sight of my wince, frowning to himself.

He moves his hand to fiddle with something on the center dash, but the absence of his touch doesn't make me breathe any easier. It isn't until soft chirping filters through the speakers that I stop breathing altogether.

I haven't listened to a nature podcast in years. We had a list of all the podcasts we wanted to listen to, then every day, we would plan which one we'd listen to that night as we fell asleep under a different roof. He said it would be like we were right next to each other, hearing the same sounds and learning the same things.

When he left, I couldn't listen to them anymore, because I was too busy wallowing over someone who wasn't there. And now here we are, listening to the same podcast like the past three years never happened.

I watch skeptically as he pulls a blanket from the back seat and drapes it over my lap.

"Go to sleep," he says, tone filled with the warmth he's only ever directed at me. "You've had a long night. I'll wake you up once we're there."

I know I should protest, and self-preservation requires I stay awake to see where I am going.

His hand moves languidly up and down my leg, lacking any pretense other than comfort. Against my better judgment, the hypnotic touch makes my muscles relax.

Before sleep pulls me under, I hear him ask, "Do you remember what I told you, Bella? Do you remember what I promised you?"

Of course I do. I could never forget his promise.

CHAPTER 7

ROMAN

7 Years Ago

Roman: 15 years old – Isabella: 13 years old.

I'm bad at math, but lately, I've been really fucking good at it.

43 weeks.

301 days.

7224 hours.

That's how long she's been gone.

I'm great at counting now. Bella would be proud.

She used to tell me that she likes to count the marks on her ceiling when she feels like her mind is a little too much for her. I didn't see the appeal in counting anything, because putting a value on something implies a limitation.

Now I get it. I've started counting my steps as I walk, not always intentionally. Still, I count the bricks in the pavement and add another point for every one my shoe touches. Sometimes I count the number of stairs as I go up or down. I lose focus half the time and miscount, but no one is keeping track. No one will know of the mistake but me.

Here are a few examples of my new fondness for counting:

Six. That's how many times Aaron—my new foster father—has scowled at me this morning.

Two. That's the number of times he's hit me since I woke up.

Eighteen. That's how many hours I've gone without food—not Aaron's fault—Because nothing tastes right.

And my favorite: *one*. That's how long until I see Bella again. One hour.

I knew the hell I went through would be worth it the second I saw her again. When she left, I sat in the back of a cop car, bloody and bruised, my voice hoarse from screaming my lungs out, then seeing the vicious look on Steve's face when he picked me up. By that point, I was too numb to the reality of the situation to figure out where I was or why I was there.

Because the voices were quiet, and she wasn't there.

I stared at the darkness for three days. And in those three days, I understood what Bella meant when she said that sometimes the quiet in the brain is too loud. Usually, I had my own thoughts to keep me going, but they left with her. Then Steve got busted for child abuse, and now, here I am with Aaron. He's a total cunt. But Julie is nice enough—when she's around.

Aaron likes to *accidentally* forget to feed me when Julie is away at work. Some kind of hairstylist or makeup artist or something. But it isn't like when I was eight years old and didn't know my way around the kitchen.

So, I just help myself to the kitchen—on the rare occasion there's food.

Whether by blind faith or complete idiocy, I'm still here, putting up with the back of Aaron's hand whenever Julie isn't around. Yes, I tried running away a few times to find Bella, but I always came back. And yes,

Aaron *tried* kicking me to the curb for it, but the government checks kept rolling in.

Plus, leaving for good wasn't an option. How else would she know how to find me?

But she's back.

She's back. She's back. She's back.

God, she's finally back.

I saw Bella last week. Just the back of her head, but I knew without a doubt that it was her. I'd recognize those terrible braids anywhere. She clutched her mom's Mickey Mouse toy in her hand as she climbed up some steps. Walking behind her was little Jeremy and a guy my age. And *man*, if it didn't get my heart pumping. I'm assuming he's her foster brother, but it doesn't matter who he is to her; I don't trust him.

Her new place is just down the street from me, but I haven't been able to go up to her. Not yet. I need to be ready.

Instead, I followed her as she walked to Steve's place and asked where I was. I watched her lip tremble as she shuffled back to her house, defeated. It hurt to see, but it'll all be worth it.

It's the first day back to school after summer break, and I am betting everything I own that Bella will go to the same school. It's the closest school to our houses, and if she isn't there, I'll need to find a way to transfer.

I toy with the broken bracelet in my pocket, my bag heavier than usual. I watch her from a distance, holding Jeremy's hand as she walks toward his elementary school. I'm glad he ended up with Bella so she has someone other than me. Though, I'd prefer it if it was just me.

No, I'm not jealous, I swear.

The little guy's backpack is practically the size of him, coming down to the backs of his knees as he wobbles along, lugging the thing around. Admittedly, it looks empty, while hers is filled to the brim. No one would mistake them as siblings, not with Jeremy's umber complexion and Bella's golden skin.

But out of everything, what has warmth unfurling in the space I haven't felt beat in almost a year, is the wonky, Wednesday Addams braid she's sporting. It's aggravating to look at how uneven it is, with a couple of wrong twists.

But to me, it's perfect.

Everything she does is perfect.

I didn't know it was possible, but somehow, she looks even cuter. I could stare at her all day with her baggy jeans held up by a string and the—what I'm guessing is DIY'd—tie-dyed shirt with some boy band on it.

She's taller than I remember, and I don't know if I like that. I think she might actually be taller than the boys in her class. She better not be taller than me. I don't think my ego can take that kind of damage.

I want to pull my hair out with how slow the walk is, and I know it has nothing to do with Jeremy's little legs. Seeing how hard she's clutching his hand, my guess is that Bella is anxious.

Does she miss me? Is she hoping she'll see me at school? What will she do when she sees me? Smile? Cry happy tears? Freak out about my black eye?

When she gets to the front of Jeremy's school, she turns him around, takes stuff out of her backpack, puts it in his, and then waves him off like a doting mother as he all but skips to class without a backward glance. I guess his nerves are gone because he had the first-day jitters last week when his school started.

Once he's out of sight, her shoulders sag and she curls in on herself, grasping the straps of her bag like she's trying to stay afloat and the bag is her only lifeline.

My blood sounds louder in my ears. What the fuck happened to her when she was gone? I haven't seen her act like that since we were kids.

Bella was never the type to draw attention to herself, but at some point, she stopped acting like she had to ensure she didn't breathe too loudly. Her head would be held up, not too high that she's looking down her nose, but not too low that she's looking up from her lashes.

I pick up my pace, closing the distance between us and easing some of the tension caused by the thing now thumping in my chest. She's too caught up in her own world, threading between the throng of people, focused on getting where she needs to go.

As soon as she passes through the school gate, my patience disappears. Too much time has passed, and I'm not waiting another second.

I creep up behind her and whisper over her shoulder. "There you are, Princess."

Bella whirls around and stumbles back. My blood roars louder when her eyes round with fear, and she throws her arms up like she's trying to block a punch—just like I taught her.

Every cell in my body goes hot and cold at the same time. She doesn't need to say it. Somebody hurt her. Somebody laid a fucking hand on her. I don't care who he is; he's a dead man.

Bella will flinch or yelp and put a hand over her heart, but she *never* pales like her life flashed behind her eyes. The Bella I know doesn't cower, and she sure as hell doesn't look like she's bracing for an assault.

But then everything stops—every bruise on my body, every incessant noise in my head, every buzz in my vein, and every murderous beat of my heart. Because the fear is gone, and the only thing in her eyes is what I've been yearning to see for almost a year.

Relief.

Joy.

Longing.

"Mickey," she gasps.

She lunges for me before another word can make it out, and it's my turn to stumble back. Her arms wrap around my neck, and she crushes me to her so there isn't an inch of space between us. I don't waste a second before curling my body around hers, grabbing and holding her like if I blink, I'll be back to counting without an end in sight.

She's not allowed to disappear again. I won't let it happen.

The feeling of her pressed against me, holding me as if I actually mean something to her... it's nothing like all the times before.

When she hugged me on my birthday, it was a congratulatory hug. Something that came from the heart but was handed out like a simple gift and not something to be treasured. Something that's meant to fade within passing minutes.

This? This is the world colliding and the stars aligning. More than a thousand words are strung together in a thousand different ways. She missed me. She wishes we were never separated. She didn't stop thinking about me for a second. She's back, and she's never letting go.

Like this, the world won't be able to touch her. No one will be able to hurt her, and she never has to worry about a thing ever again.

The top of her head grazes my lips as I pull her tighter and sigh.

Good. I'm still taller than her.

Keep it that way.

She doesn't move away, and there's no way that I'm about to. "I missed you, Mickey."

I close my eyes and lean my cheek against her. That name is for *us*. Roman is who I am to everyone else: The boy whose parents didn't want him the second he was born, and neither did his grandparents. Roman is the one who interrupts in class and can't sit still. The one who's pure mischief and going nowhere in life.

Even after all these years of Bella being able to pronounce her r's, only she says my real name with something other than disgust.

Mickey and Roman are one and the same, but Mickey is just for her. It's the name that has my heart ratcheting because it means I'm her home. She feels safe with me and never wants to lose me, just like her Mickey Mouse. I could die happy knowing she calls me that.

At one point, she became too embarrassed to call me Mickey because someone told her it was cringy. I beat him up and tried convincing Bella not to listen to him, but because I was young and stupid, I didn't realize what the name really meant to her. I'll never take it for granted.

"I missed you too," I mumble into her hair.

"I—" She tries pulling away, but I don't let her go. "I'm so sorry. I had no idea. I swear I didn't know. I *swear*. They told me to pack my things—I thought they were kicking me out, and a truck came. I wanted to tell you. I tried so hard—"

"It's okay."

Her tears soak my shirt as she trembles against me. "I didn't want to go. But they didn't give me a choice. They made me—"

"I know. It's okay, Bella."

"I tried to fight them, but they wouldn't let me leave. I wanted to see you before I left. I promise, Mickey, I had no idea. I didn't want to leave you."

A sob escapes her as she catches her breath. I pull her away from me and cup her cheeks, forcing her to look up at me. "I understand. I know you would never leave me." I thumb away her tears. "None of that matters anymore; you know why?"

Her bottom lip quivers, and I almost lose it. "Because you're back, and neither of us is going anywhere without the other. You hear me?"

Hesitantly, she nods.

"You will never be alone again. I swear on my life. Wherever you go, I'll be right there. We'll always find each other. I'm not going anywhere. It's a promise. We're forever, Princess, and nothing will ever come between us. Do you understand?"

She sniffles. "Yes."

"Say it."

"We're forever."

"Swear it."

"I promise I'll never leave you again."

I grin. "Why?"

She narrows her eyes, but wipes her tears away as she raises her chin. But all I can see is the string bracelets fastened to her wrist. Not one. *Two.* "Because you're a crazy asshole, but I love you for it."

I think I stop breathing. I think my brain has stopped working altogether. I've never heard the word before. Not directed at me, anyway. Is that what it sounds like? Is this the word that describes the feeling in my chest every time I think about her? She said she loves me. The words repeat over and over and over.

She loves me. She loves me. She loves me.

Bella loves me.

"A little overbearing. Impulsive. Kinda frightening," she continues.

"Do I scare you?"

"Never." She frowns. "Not anymore, at least."

I look away dramatically, deep in thought, as I force my fingers to peel away from her skin. "I think we should change that."

I need to see her smile. I need to get my old Bella back—the one who isn't so frightened of shadows.

She scoffs. "I wouldn't say golden retrievers are scary."

That might single-handedly be the most offensive thing anyone has ever said to me, but there's a mischievous grin on her lips I don't want to disappear. *That* is my Bella. The one who snaps and then licks the wound later... Sometimes. Only if I don't piss her off again.

"Hellhound is more accurate," I say as I nudge her toward one of the benches.

As embarrassing as it was, she read *Percy Jackson* to me a few years ago as a way to practice her speech—and because the only way I can sit still long enough to read a book is if she's reading it to me. Greek mythology became my whole ass personality after that. There was some kind of Greek reference in my drawings for so long, I am officially a master at drawing armor.

"Eh." She shrugs and bites the inside of her lip. "You're harmless. You're more like a handbag dog; all bark and no bite."

She's all shit, and she knows it. But Jesus Christ, I'm hooked on every word that comes out of her mouth because *she's finally back*. I've waited so long, and it was all worth it.

Bella, ever the timid princess she is, lowers herself onto her seat far too gracefully. I plop down onto the bench in a heap, which is far more fitting. Especially when a can of spray paint is in my bag—it's my newly acquired hobby.

I shove my hand in my pocket to stop myself from reaching out for her, and my fingers brush against the cotton strings of the bracelet. I run my tongue over my teeth as I pull it out and show it to her. "I, uh." I clear my throat. "I accidentally broke it." She blinks at the red and black tangles in my palm. I'll admit, it's a little worse for wear from living in my pocket. "And you've kept it on you?"

"Of course. It matches my complexion."

Her brows knit together, but it's filled with understanding. "I can make you another."

"No. Can you fix it?"

She shakes her head, and I hate it. I'm not surprised. It's ripped past the point of return. All the edges are fraying, and the knots have come undone. Only a miracle could salvage it.

Her delicate fingers fiddle with one of the string bracelets around her wrist—the red-and-black one that's an exact replica of the one I broke—and she unfastens it.

Time seems to slow as she grabs my hand and fastens it around my wrist. She was *wearing* me.

She was wearing me.

She was wearing me.

She was wearing me.

"Don't break it this time," she says with a playful bite.

"Yeah, yeah," I mutter, reaching for my bag. I've been busy all week, and I can't wait for the look on her face. "I got you something."

She stills. "Wait. What do you mean you *got me something*? How did you know I was going to be here?"

I smirk. "I know everything."

Bella slaps my arm, but it doesn't hurt. She's the only one who could get away with it. "You prick! You knew I was back, and you didn't even say *hi*?"

She's so adorable when she's angry.

I wink at her. "Had to make you work for it."

Bella gives me a look that tells me she thinks I'm insane. Yeah, probably, but she's the only person who makes me feel this way. I'll put all the blame on her for this one.

"As I was saying," I drawl, and take out the crumpled bag. I don't wrap presents—that shit just ain't for me.

Bella once said, *"It's what's on the inside that counts,"* so I'm going to hold her to it.

"I got you something." I hold the bag out to her, and just before she's about to grab it, I snatch it just out of reach. "Manners, Princess."

Those big brown eyes of hers turn into slits. "Please."

"Please, who?"

She sighs, but there's no mistaking the excited tilt of her lips. "Please, *Mickey.*"

God, it's so good to hear her say my name. "That's better."

She holds out her hand expectantly, waiting for the bag, but when a breath passes, her expression turns hesitant, then worried, then scared, all in a matter of two seconds. The heat in my blood returns because that's not something my Bella does. Not if I can help it.

"I've decided to drip feed."

The creasing of her brows is seriously cramping my vibe.

"I want to see each of your reactions." I wink, attempting to lighten the mood.

She bites her lip and looks up at me from her lowered lashes like she's too scared to say what she wants. Which is completely fucked up by my standards. I like Bella whichever way she comes, but I like the real Bella the most.

And *Jesus,* do I want to kiss her.

"First up," I say as I stick my hand down into the ripped paper bag and pull out a book. *Rejected by the Alpha.* She stares at the book, then me, then back at the book with so much bewilderment that I might as well have pulled out a gun.

Jerking forward, she goes to snatch it, but I hold it out of her reach. Bella looks around with frantic eyes before scrambling for me to grab the book.

"Down, Mouse," I tease, putting two fingers on her forehead and gently pushing her back.

This wasn't the reaction I was expecting, but I ain't mad about it. She keeps glancing around like someone might see.

"Remember the day before you left, when we went to the bookstore?" With each passing second, her skin glows redder and redder. I cock my head. Why is she so flustered about the fact I got it for her? She picked it off the shelf, read the back, then checked how much she had in her wallet. Then promptly put it back. "I've held on to it since then."

"You..." She's completely beet red as she blinks a couple more times at my outstretched hand. Bella clears her throat and sits up straighter. "You can't afford it."

"Money can't buy everything."

Translation: I stole it.

My lips stretch into a grin. "But I'll give this to you on one condition?"

"What?"

Her breath hitches, and she leans forward slightly, looking around again like someone might catch us doing something illegal.

"You read it to me."

She blanches, completely mortified, before turning redder than she was before. Whipping her head around, she spots the only person in earshot—one person with headphones—and then she covers the side of her mouth like the guy might hear, and she squeals, "That's an *R18* book."

Oh. *Oh*, this is too good. I tsk and lean back against the bench. "Unrestricted access to written porn will ruin you, kid."

Naughty, naughty girl.

To a bystander, it probably looks like we're dealing drugs with how quickly she snatches *the book* from me and shoves it into her bag.

"Thank you," she says under her breath. An adorable wrinkle forms along the bridge of her nose.

I chuckle and take it as my cue to move on to the next gift—something that won't get her so wound up: a heart-shaped locket. There are a bunch of random ass swirls on the outside, and I know she'll swoon over how "pretty" and "delicate" it is. Which is why the necklace is perfect for her.

"How did you afford—Who does this belong to, Mickey?"

"You."

"Roman," she warns.

I wince internally. She'd never *wear* something special that belonged to someone else, and I only have so much adult money—but my latest *extra-curricular* activities have changed that. I don't make much, but the very first thing I bought was that necklace. I mean, it also meant that I had to skip a few meals, but it was worth it for her.

I'm not the best with my hands—not in the way that I want in this situation. I have my drawings, and Bella has her bracelets and anything else she puts her mind to, but it's not enough.

Bella is sentimental, and I want to give her something that will withstand beating a window or running away from the cops—if she ever needed to. *If* we're ever separated, a part of me will always be with her, around her neck and near her heart.

Though nothing will ever separate us. If she hasn't realized it by now, she's in for a surprise.

"I saved money." Not a lie, but I'm not ready to tell Bella the whole truth just yet.

"Roman—"

"I promise you, no one has ever worn it but you. Now shut up and turn around."

She doesn't listen. Of course, she doesn't listen. She narrows her eyes, completely disbelieving. "When did you get this?"

"Like, six months ago." 163 days ago, to be precise.

Her shoulders sag a fraction. "But you didn't even know if I was coming back."

"I knew. Now, turn around. Put it on."

She gingerly takes the necklace from me, and I admit, I almost keep it out of her reach. *I* should be the one to put it on her. Bella fiddles with the clasp, and my stomach drops. I wanted it to be perfect, and this is less than that. She deserves so much more than the shit I put inside the locket.

All my worries and concerns that she would frown at how terrible it is, vanishes when her lips curve into a smile, and a soft little giggle leaves her.

She runs her finger over the right side of the locket, where there's a picture of Mickey Mouse that I cut out from a magazine. On the left, in small handwriting, it says "*Roman (aka the real Mickey).*" This way, it isn't just me who's kept close to her heart, it's her mother, too.

Bella's obsession with Mickey Mouse started because of her mamá, but she never managed to find any photos of her, just like there aren't any (non-government taken) photos of me.

"Mickey," she breathes as she looks up at me, eyes glistening with unshed tears. "This is beautiful."

"I know."

Her warm smile doesn't disappear when she rolls her eyes or when she hands me the necklace to secure around her neck.

Before she can turn around, I have the next gift out of the bag. A—you guessed it—Mickey Mouse keychain. Honestly, there's this weird trend with Mickey Mouse going on, but I couldn't give a shit as long as it puts a smile on her face. I have no memories outside of Bella that I want to keep alive. Still, I will do everything I can to make sure her happiness is immortalized, even if that means having an excessive amount of Mickey Mouse stickers all over both of our things so she's taken back to Disneyland with her mamá.

Bella claims she's sick of the thing, but it doesn't stop her from pausing whenever she sees that damn mouse like she is now.

Our kids will probably be just as obsessed with the rodent.

"My birthday was, like, months ago." The absolute attitude dripping from her voice right now is uncalled for. She's still a part-time brat, I see.

I cock a brow. "Your point?"

"You didn't know if I was coming—"

"I did."

"I can't accept all of this."

"Who said you had the option not to?" The urge to groan and shake my head in disbelief is real. She does this every time: pretending that her moral compass is in the way of taking something I've gotten specifically for her, even though I can practically smell how much she wants to get her hands on it.

"I do."

"*Signore aiutami con questa.*" Lord, help me with this one. "We can do this the easy way, or we can do this the way that will have you all squirmy. Take the goddamn keychain."

She glares at me as she takes the keychain and clips it on her bag, grumbling, "I haven't liked Mickey Mouse in a long time."

"I'm sure you don't, but I don't make the rules."

Tradition is tradition. Every year that has passed and that will come, she'll be getting a Mickey Mouse item. No ifs, ands, or buts.

"Last one," I say. And thankfully, it has nothing to do with the big-eared rodent.

A little wrinkle forms between her brows as they dip, taking the orange stuffed animal from me. "Foxes aren't my favorite animal anymore."

Of course, they aren't. It changes every year. Last year it was a fox. The year before, magpies. The year before that, wolves. "What is it this time?"

"Bears."

"That's gonna have to change. I'm here, and you aren't going to be a solitary creature."

CHAPTER 8

ISABELLA

3 Years Ago

Roman: 19 years old – Isabella: 17 years old.

Today is always the hardest.

It's the time of year when I remember the life that I had, or more accurately, the life I *could* have had. Not because I think I deserve it, or that it's the path I should be on, but because it doesn't matter how hard I try, the hole in my heart will never be filled.

That's not to say my heart isn't stuffed to the brim. It'll simply never be whole. There will forever be cracks, and shards have gone missing.

One of the cracks—the one glued back together—came when I was born, and my father decided he wouldn't be there.

He also decided he wouldn't be there on my first birthday, second, or even the third. He wasn't there on my first day of school either, or when Mamá got sick and couldn't look after me anymore. I didn't even see him when the state took me in or when they turned Mamá's body into ash.

Mamá said his name is Carlos. "*I told him, Isabella. He'll come find you, and you'll be a family.*"

It was one of the last things she said before she died.

Still, I've never met him.

The biggest crack, the one where no amount of glue or tape will put it back together, happened when I was six. It was ripped off and shattered into a million different pieces. But the hurt wasn't quick, not really. It was slow, spanning months as, piece by piece, another part of me was taken. Until eventually, there was nothing left to take, and Mamá was gone.

The motel she was cleaning at and my childhood home disappeared from under me.

In a single night, the only family I had left, the woman who read to me every night, and did my hair in fancy braids and perfect pigtails every morning, was gone. I lost it *all*.

I would give the world just to be able to sit on the floor with nothing but a blunt pencil and spare paper and watch through the window as Ma rushed around to clean the rooms.

I don't remember much, but I know when she immigrated here, she fell in love with Disney and wanted to give me the childhood she had missed out on.

I still remember the first time we went to McDonald's because she got a pay raise. I can still hear her sing beautiful songs as she pushed me on the swing or danced with me in the living room. Our stereo was broken, but it didn't stop Mamá from entertaining her little girl. Nothing would stop her from being the best mother she could be. She spent years saving up so we could go to Disneyland, and we finally did the year she died. That's when she got me the doll that never left my side and that Mickey keeps saying needs to be washed.

But the hurt didn't stop there.

Another piece broke off when I got moved into Greg's house. With each look Marcus gives me and each word that falls from his lips, another bit of my heart splinters off.

But it's the filling that's keeping the rest of my broken little heart together.

It's when Jeremy comes running into my room because he claims to have invented another pun. Or when Mickey "buys" me art and craft supplies, like candle-making kits or polymer clay. Even when he gets in trouble for hitting the other kids at school for being mean to me or, by extension, if I get upset because someone was being mean to Jeremy.

I haven't told him about Greg and Marcus and everything they do when Mickey drops me off at home. Even if Greg laughs when Marcus calls me a useless whore or pushes things off the table just to get me to clean it, I say nothing. Mickey and I have a plan that doesn't involve getting me kicked out of the house.

Days like today are always the hardest, but like every other day, Mickey makes it easier. I don't need to look out the window to know he's already waiting outside for me. I heard him arrive a while ago—early, like he is on this particular day every year—while I was preparing breakfast for Greg and Marcus. Sometimes Millie helps, but she usually opens the store in the morning, and I never know when she'll get home. Honestly, I'm pretty sure she dreads coming home just as much as I do.

If I were her, I would have filed for a divorce and said a prayer for my son, who is more of a monster than his father. My foster brother needs to be locked up. He's a narcissist, but he's not a psychopath. He gets his kicks from thinking he's superior, which is why he shuts the hell up whenever Roman is around. Mickey may be younger and just as tall, but there's no questioning how lethal he is.

He's basically my personal bodyguard.

I don't hear Jeremy coming until I'm tackled against the kitchen bench in a bone-crushing hug.

"Happy birthday, Isa," he squeals, wiggling from side to side.

I laugh quietly, just in case Greg is still asleep. "Thanks, little man."

He jumps back with a furious look in his eyes. It's adorable because I'm a head taller than him and I actually know my times tables. "I'm not little. I'm the fourth tallest in my class."

"Alright, big man."

He's the fourth tallest *boy* in his class, and there are only thirteen boys. I'll let him have his victory.

"See?" Jeremy thrusts a stick figure drawing into my hands and points to the boy with curly black hair who's double the height of the girl with pigtails.

"Points for accuracy," I quip, smiling at the sloppy, inaccurate spelling of *HAPPY BERTHDAY ISA* in blue highlighter at the top.

"I'm taller than a big kid."

"I don't doubt you for a second." I really should stop feeding into people's delusions. "But thank you, Jer. I love it."

He grins the same type of shit-eating grin he must have learned from Mickey. "I asked Ro if he wanted to go halves on a present with me, but he said no." He shrugs nonchalantly. "His loss."

Jeremy is too smug for a twelve-year-old. I'd boil it down to the fact he thinks he's the smartest kid in his grade (he's the sixth smartest), and he's friends with the "cool kids."

I lean in closer. "Don't tell him, but your gift will be *way* cooler anyway. You're better at drawing."

His eyes light up, but he acts nonchalant as he grabs a slice of toast. "Ms. Terry said I'm a natural at everything I do."

Note to self: teach Jeremy how to be humble.

"Are you sure you don't want me to walk you to school today?"

"Yes," he drawls. "It's weird if you do."

"Your loss." I don't know why I still bother asking. He hasn't said yes in over a year. Jeremy thinks he's too grown up to be walked to school by his foster sister, so it's just me and Mickey now.

Shaking my head, I tuck the drawing away in my bag for safekeeping and head outside. Jeremy barely notices me pat his head before I leave, too caught in his fairy tale of Lord knows what.

My heart skips a beat when I see *him*. It's been doing that a lot more lately. He makes butterflies erupt from every corner of my belly, and the entire world seems to revolve around Mickey. He's trouble on legs, and he's all mine.

I think.

I hope.

I'm all his, at least.

Now that he isn't at school anymore, who knows how many girls he's talking to. Before he graduated, all the girls in the neighborhood would throw themselves at him. He never looked at them once, but people change. He has so much more freedom, and I know the admin girl from his work at the garage, Cassie, always bats her eyelashes at him, especially when he's all greased up, unshaven, and sweaty.

Then she gets handsy. Or at least tries to. Roman pushes her away like he's uncomfortable, but I think that's because I'm there.

In the morning, after school, and right after dinner on some nights, blonde-haired, blue-eyed Cassie isn't around, and Mickey is all mine. When I'm at school, and once I'm in bed, I guess Cassie is all his.

But every morning, the space beneath my ribs blooms from the sight of him leaning against his motorcycle, muscled arms straining against a black t-shirt, with cargo pants belted around his hips.

I didn't believe people when they said puberty does wonders, but Christ, they weren't lying. He's turned into the most handsome man I've ever seen.

Mickey smiles from ear to ear the second he sees me. Not a devilish smirk or a mischievous grin, a *smile*. Does he smile like that at Cassie?

I shake my head internally. There's no point in being jealous. It's not like he's ever made a move that might suggest I'm anything more than just a good friend. Or little sister. *Gross.*

"Morning, sweet Bella."

Another thing I didn't believe about puberty is how deep a voice could get.

The butterflies seem to be activated by voice command as well, because the deeper his voice gets, the crazier they react.

"Morning," I whisper, unable to look into his eyes. They're too hypnotizing, and the last thing I need is for the gremlins in my stomach to make my cheeks heat and for me to become all giggly.

I'm still studying and work at Greg's shop a couple of times a week. I'm practically a child compared to Mickey now. Maybe Cassie is more his style because they both have the same kind of responsibilities.

The wings on those pesky butterflies sag every time I think of her. He hasn't given me a reason to believe he's into her, but who could ever fall in love with a girl who's missing a part of her heart? Not to mention that Cassie is prettier.

Mickey reaches behind him and pulls out a plaid green pencil case filled to the brim with stationary, probably—hopefully.

The answer is obvious, but as I said, I don't know how to function around him.

"I—"

He chucks it in my direction, and I already know I'm going to miss it. I lurch forward to catch it and fumble uselessly as it falls to the ground.

He chuckles, and I turn red. I'm too caught up in the sound of his deep voice and my incoordination to glare at him, though.

He doesn't say anything if he's noticed I'm getting shier around him.

I wouldn't be surprised if the prick likes that I keep getting flustered.

It's so stupid. All I want to do is impress him, when I've quite literally done every embarrassing thing possible in his presence. I drooled all over him when I fell asleep on him two years ago, threw up on him once when I got car sick, went through an acne phase, and tripped over my feet more times than I can count. Oh God, and when I was twelve, I thought I was an amazing singer and tried serenading him by singing *"Love Story"* by Taylor Swift. He even caught me rehearsing it beforehand.

But that's not the worst part. My *rehearsals* involved a complete dance routine.

I want to crawl into a hole and die just thinking about it.

I miss the days when I didn't have a ridiculous, soul-consuming crush on Roman Riviera. The time when I could argue with him day and night because I wasn't yearning for his approval. Now, like some idiotic little girl, all he needs to do is look at me, and I'm a puddle.

"I will hear nothing from you, because the pencil case has nothing to do with your birthday."

"Hmm? Oh, right. Thank you." I swallow as I quickly shove the pencil case into my bag, ignoring the hot blood rushing up my neck toward my face.

Two days ago, I told him I had forgotten my pencil case on the bus when we went on a field trip. This is just what Mickey does; he gets me things I need and things I never asked for.

Like the shirt I'm wearing of a Sumatran tiger, which is *not* stolen from anyone. We listened to a documentary on tigers a couple of months ago, and I decided then and there that they're my new favorite animal. They're the smallest breed of tigers, and there are only four hundred of them left in the world. I tried to hide the fact that it made me a little emotional, but Mickey must have seen right through it because, a week later, he gave me this t-shirt with the *WWF* tag still on it and a card that said, *Thank you for your donation.*

It was probably the first and last charitable thing Mickey will do in his life. "You get your *actual* present tonight."

My heart soars. He's spending less and less time with me at night. He always has some kind of excuse relating to work for why he has to leave early or not see me at all. He also seems to be perpetually bruised and tired. Case in point: his purple knuckles and the patchwork of yellow and green on his cheek.

Mickey told me he's working so much because he's saving up for when I graduate.

That makes sense, but the problem with his argument is that he's a mechanic, and mechanics don't normally work night shifts. Or get bloody knuckles and bruises.

I never knew him to be a liar, but he can be tricky, mincing words so they're only half-truths. All it takes is for another half to disappear, and it's a full lie.

I nod, and the slight twitch of his brow is the only sign he's displeased with my response. If I weren't so woozy and awestruck, I would tease him and say it's because he forgot to get me something or joke that I made plans with Jeremy and he's not invited.

It'd make him all angry and jealous, then he'd throw a little hissy fit and tell me he'd throw me over his shoulder and whisk me away. Then he'd say, *"Tradition is tradition. I wasn't asking."*

Mickey is big on his traditions, even though he only has three of them that I know of.

One, we celebrate every birthday together, because even though there's two years of difference between us, we promised to never leave each other's side.

Two, I can be certain I'm going to receive something to do with Mickey Mouse as one of my gifts. Every birthday, without fail, I'll have another item to add to my ever-growing collection.

Three, rain, hail, or shine, Mickey will be there to take me to and from school. Before I left for a year, he'd sometimes miss a day or two because he woke up too late. Since I got back, I've had to wake up earlier just so he doesn't need to wait outside for so long.

He saunters toward me—well, he's walking normally, but I can't stop staring at how his hips move, so he might as well be sauntering. I watch him through my lashes as he towers over me and tilts my head up with a calloused finger under my chin.

"Happy birthday, beautiful," he whispers.

Beautiful. Not cute or pretty. He thinks I'm *beautiful*.

I move my head to the side and hide my face with my hair to stop him from noticing the blush tinting my cheeks, but it's useless. Especially when I stop breathing because he moves my face back and his lips descend against my forehead.

"Another year of you and me."

The chain around my neck tugs, but I stay completely still as I feel the heat radiate through the cotton as he checks the pendant. He makes a sound of approval that practically melts my insides.

I don't miss how his eyes drop to my chest every time I see him, like he's checking it's still there. The corners of his mouth tilt up, and he does a little nod that I'm not sure is meant for him or me.

But I get it. I have that feeling whenever I see the bracelet around his wrist—a new one because he seems to break it every two years.

Thanks to the advancement of technology and since Mick started working full time at the garage, we both have phones and a decent camera. This means that he spends all day, every day, taking photos of everything but himself, and I have half a million selfies with him. Now, on one side of the locket, I have something to remember Ma, and on the other side, there's a picture of Mickey and me.

"Did you eat breakfast? What do you have for lunch?" Mickey asks.

I stiffen. These questions are worse than random tests at school because at least I have a chance of passing them. Mickey's questions, on the other hand, are an instant fail. Straight to detention (also known as Roman's blistering glare and his huff of disapproval).

If I could sink into the grass, I would. He should just hand me a shovel now if he's planning on asking any follow-up questions.

He shakes his head, reaching for something behind him as he mutters, *"Signore, dammi forza."*

Lord, give me strength.

I bite the inside of my cheek because I can deal with his anger, but not his disapproval.

"I have crackers." I wince the second the words are out of my mouth.

"And?" He cocks a brow.

Please, no more follow-up questions.

"Maybe an apple..."

He sighs again and drops a container into my hands, which I quickly shove into my bag. He's about to say more, but the sound of the front door opening causes his entire body to tense.

I gasp when he tugs me behind him, becoming a makeshift barrier between me and Marcus as he innocently descends the stairs. But Marcus's eyes aren't on me; they're on Mickey, and they're having a stare-off so vicious they could silence the cicadas with it.

Make that four traditions. He always glares at Marcus.

Neither of them breaks eye contact, even when I try to get Mickey's attention.

"I don't like him." His voice is devoid of any softness, something I've only heard seconds before he goes in for the attack. "If he touches you, say the word, and he's fucking dead. You got it?" Those steel eyes dart to where my room is, and he scowls. "I told you to keep your windows closed." Roman trains his attention back on me, and I almost step back with how much ire simmers there. "Do you put the chair under the door handle like I told you to?"

"I mean, sometimes?" I haven't. Not once. What if Jeremy has a nightmare?

I can't very well lock him out.

His eyes darken. "The alternative is leaving the phone on the entire night so I can hear if that fucker comes in. Don't say I don't give you options."

I shouldn't get all gooey when he goes into protective mode, but I do. I don't just *know* that he cares about me. I *feel* like I'm cared for.

"I'll make sure I don't forget," I say, just to ease him. He worries a lot about other males, especially after how much I was bullied when I went away. But mainly because he sees what happens to the wives in the houses he used to get put in.

"You leave your window open at night. Nothing will stop me from checking to see whether you've been a good girl and done as you've been told." If his voice alone could kill, I'd be dead ten times over. "You better make sure you do it."

I bite the corner of my lip. Every sound, every accent-laced syllable coming out of his mouth is sending me and my swooning into a frenzy. "Or what?"

Oh no. I realize right away I shouldn't have said that.

I wait with bated breath as the darkness in his eyes changes from murder to mayhem, and his lips morph into the grin that has every girl around dropping their panties.

"I have a question." He prowls forward until our chests touch, and his scent consumes my every thought. My throat bobs as I stare at his lips. You never look a predator in the eyes. "How much punishment do you think you can take?"

I don't answer. I'm not even sure if I heard him correctly. There aren't just gremlins in my stomach anymore; there's a colony of bees buzzing around in my veins, making tingles creep up my neck to where his skin touches mine. He doesn't mean what I think he means, right? He's never spoken to me this way before.

Mickey hums as his finger traces the line of my jaw. "I think you can take whatever I give you. I bet you'll even ask for more."

Yes, he *definitely* means what I think he means.

I bite my tongue to stop myself from making a single noise, because any sound that comes out of me will deepen my humiliation. I shudder when he leans down until his lips brush against my ears. "One more year and every inch of you will be mine."

My hold on myself disappears as I whimper. He pulls back, lips quirked in satisfaction as he walks backward to his bike. I fix my gaze on the ground, body burning with sensations I've never felt before, and I'm hyper-aware of every breath he takes, every movement, every touch.

A helmet comes down over my head, and he fastens the buckles beneath my chin. He brushes his fingers along the skin of my neck, skimming my collarbones as I finally look up at him.

His helmet is already on, but there's no escaping the weight of his stare on me. He could be watching the movement of his hands, transfixed on the trail of blazing heat he leaves behind. Or maybe his eyes are meeting mine, and he's studying the effect of his touch. I want to know what he sees and what he's thinking. I want to tap into his brain and see what types of ideas are bouncing around in his head.

And what punishment he had in mind.

I pull away first, missing his touch the instant it's gone. As much as I want nothing more than to feel him, it's eight in the morning, and he's quite literally my ride to school.

He taps the top of my helmet twice before climbing onto his bike like he didn't just threaten to punish me and tell me that I'll like it.

Roman will be the end of me. I knew it the day I met him, and I know it now. Maybe I'm a sucker for pain, but I won't fight it anytime soon.

We pull up down the road from the school, and like clockwork, I jump off the bike first, and Mickey follows straight away.

"Helmet off," he orders, even though his hands are already underneath my chin, and he's pulling it off for me as if I'm incapable of doing it myself.

"Thanks," I mumble as my hair catches on the soft inner lining.

For a split second, I cringe at the thought of whether my braids survived the journey. My hair probably looks like a rat's nest right about now.

He shakes his head once he takes his own helmet off, whipping the soft strands of raven-black hair across his forehead. Mickey hardly ever styles it, so some tufts stick up at odd angles to give him even more of a rugged appeal.

My eyes glue to his broad shoulders, trying to stop my shame from showing on my skin. He's so lethally handsome. I don't know how anyone can breathe around him.

"It's cute," he says, stroking my braids. "I like it."

Five words. That's all it takes to make the tension in my muscles relax to the point I almost become a weightless feather in the wind.

I tried extra hard to do my hair this morning—not that I don't do that every other morning, but today is special. My crazy, thick hair is one of the things Mamá and I had in common. Every day she would plait her long dark hair into two French braids, then turn to me and do the most elaborate hairstyles.

She was obsessed with turning me into her own personal Minnie Mouse, giving me space buns or crazy pigtails with gigantic ribbons.

"Here," Mickey says softly, gently turning me around. "Let me."

Roman has many faces. Most of them, he never shows to the outside world. This side of him? It's all for me. The one that evens my pigtails, fixes the many braids I've done, and reties the ribbon so it's perfect. Cassie might see him elbows deep in an engine, but she'll never get to experience this part of him. She'll never know how it feels to have her heart swell with each tug, and her eyes will never well with unshed tears.

He'll never truly understand how priceless that gift is.

I smile to myself, remembering all the times I've walked out of the house with my hair down as he gawks at me like I'm a whole other person. Every time, he'd pull out a comb and get to work on my hair. Each move of his hand is always practiced and precise, and he's careful not to pull too hard or tie things too tightly.

Some kids give us weird looks as they pass, but most don't bat an eye because they've seen this very scene enough times; me, gnawing on my lip while Mickey scowls at the back of my head like he's been personally victimized by my hair.

Simply put, he looks murderous every time he fixes my hair, like he hates it. Yet, every day he does it, and every morning, no one dares to say a word about it—other than Maxim and Mikhail, but Roman doesn't need to know that.

Mickey grips me by the elbow and turns me around, taking my chin between his thumb and forefinger as he gazes down at me. Warmth spreads to every inch of my body when our eyes meet.

This is what being loved feels like.

I sink my nails into the palms of my hands because one day, I'll stop feeling this way. I'll no longer know what adoration looks like. He'll do someone else's hair and call someone else beautiful. I want to bottle this moment up, lock it away, and keep it for myself because the feeling is intoxicating. But the sad truth is that, even if I'm meant to be loved, it will never be permanent.

"You're so beautiful, Bella."

He means it. Every letter and every syllable. Those four words are said from the darkest depths of his heart, not just the dopamine fired in his brain.

"Thank you," I whisper.

I'll never say that I agree. Maybe I am beautiful—even though I've never seen myself that way—or maybe I'm not. Beauty isn't just something you put on or become blessed with from genetics. It's a feeling that doesn't need a mirror or a photo for proof or validation. And Mickey makes me feel beautiful, even on days when I'm disgusted with myself.

The school's warning bell rings through the street, and I can almost hear the collective sigh of every student in the area.

"I've got to go... I'll see you tonight?" I ask, hopeful.

The answer is always yes, but one day it'll be no. I'd rather be prepared and face the anguish now than look like an idiot, standing around waiting for him.

He smirks. "Can't get rid of me that easily." Once he plants another kiss on my forehead, he grabs his helmet. My cheeks burn, and so does the spot where his lips touched. I'm too dumbstruck to do anything but stare at him.

"Don't be late." He winks.

I swallow the lump in my throat and nod helplessly, backing away toward another one of my versions of hell.

CHAPTER 9

ISABELLA

3 YEARS AGO

Roman: 19 years old – Isabella: 17 years old.

The rest of the morning goes by in a blur. Having to spend lunch without Mickey was the biggest adjustment, and most of the kids here knew to steer clear of me when Roman was around.

But at least I have Janelle. She doesn't talk much; we just sit together and read because "girls stick together" and all that.

She's leaning back against a tree, golden brown hair fanned over her shoulders. Now, *she* is beautiful. In the understated, geeky sort of way. It's the kind where with a good haircut and a dash of mascara, every girl and boy would be transfixed by.

We have a couple of classes together and always pair up for any group activities. She's kind of boring, though I wouldn't be surprised if she thought the same about me. The only things we have in common are classes and our love of books and art.

She did give me a birthday hug this morning, which was nice, I guess.

Then we went back to ignoring each other.

Like now.

Fine by me; my book is just getting to the good part. *Finally.* It took about three hundred pages.

"Is that book three?" Janelle nods to the book I'm holding, then takes a bite of her sandwich. We're at Mickey's and my old hang-out spot, another blind spot on the school grounds.

I nod. "The last one in the series."

"Any good?"

"Honestly, I'm just glad it's over."

She snorts. "Say no more."

"My favorite character was killed off, so—"

"I heard a rumor," a rough voice says from behind me.

Janelle and I tense. Two silhouettes stretch around us, and then the shadow falls over me, blocking the sun. Slowly, I turn around and brace myself for whatever is about to happen. I already know who is behind us. Only two people at this school have the guts to talk to me after everything Roman did.

Mikhail and Maxim, the identical twins that started this year. The only difference between the two is the beauty spot on Maxim's cheek.

"Do you know what the rumor is?" Mikhail asks, staring right at me.

We say nothing. Sometimes they get bored and move on to terrorizing someone else. Those who aren't part of a pack always become prey, and to the hunters in our year group, Janelle and I are the wounded rabbits.

I jolt when Maxim snatches the book from my hands. "He asked you a question."

Neither of them pays Janelle any mind, and I send her a mental message to run. She's not about to play hero, and there's no point for the both of us to be victims. Girls stick together, but a herd of gazelles will do nothing to stave off a lion. You run, and only the fastest will survive.

"What rumor?" I say.

If their attention stays on me, Janelle will be able to leave. She must realize this because she quietly stands and gets the hell away.

Satisfaction oozes from Mikhail, and his eyes light up with the same predatory glint I've seen on Roman's face many times. The twins know I'm not stupid enough to try to fight them. I've heard them say enough times that their dad bought them each a gun for their fourteenth birthday. Everyone at school has seen them put another boy in a coma just because he accidentally spilled his water on Maxim.

Once, they threatened to stab me if I told the teacher they pushed me down the stairs. But even if I told someone, nothing would happen. This school doesn't have the resources or the care to do anything.

"A little birdie told me you can't say your r's." Mikhail laughs.

I grit my teeth. "I got over it years ago."

There's no confidence in my voice, and I try my best to keep it completely even. Men like the twins and Roman get off on seeing weakness and getting a reaction. Despite it, there's no missing the quiver when I say the words.

"You hear that, Maxim? She got over it." Mikhail chuckles, lacking any humor, as he hits his brother's arm. His attention trains on me, and every single fiber of my being screams at my legs to run. "Must have been something fucked up with you if you couldn't even say a letter." He bends down so he's right in my face. "One fucking letter. Your mom dropped you on the head, huh?"

I blink quickly. I can't let him see any tears. I can't. Where's Roman? Why isn't he here when I need him?

"What? You mute too?" Maxim sneers.

101

I can't help the sound that escapes when I'm yanked onto my knees by a painful grip on my hair. Maxim shoves my face into the book in my hands.

"Read it," he sings.

My scalp burns from his vicious hold, pulling strands out of my braid. I know the moment my bottom lip quivers, they feel like they've won. Their malicious looks turn smug.

"I said fucking read it, bitch."

I try to do as they say, but I can't make out the letters through my blurring vision.

"Blind, too?" Mikhail laughs. "You gonna cry to your mommy? She gon' knock you on the head even more?"

"Don't talk about her," I cry.

I know my mistake the instant I say it. I showed them my weakness.

One of them whistles. The only thing I can say for certain is that the ink on the page is bleeding along with my heart. Another shard gone, a stab at the hole in my armor.

"Isa's mom is a whore," one of them sings. They're trying to get a reaction from me.

"I bet the apple doesn't fall far from the tree."

"She's not!" I yell, knowing it'll be hopeless. There's no logic to what they do. They want someone to pick on. They don't care what the reason is. If they don't take jabs at my mother, they'll keep trying until they find another way to sink the knife.

"Bet your daddy didn't stick around." More snickers fill the air as Maxim pulls me around again so I'm closer to Mikhail, yanking out hair as he does it.

I try to suppress a whimper. "Leave me alone," I plead.

I've seen how those words affect Roman when someone says them to him. They make him smile as if they're an invitation, rather than a rejection.

"We got it wrong, Mikhail. She's all alone. Orphaned mutt. Neither of her parents wants her."

Hot tears burn my cheeks. It doesn't matter how hard I try to stop it, they keep falling. With each drop, another point is added on their side.

"Hey!" someone else yells, and the hold on my hair vanishes, but the burning sensation remains. I fall to the ground, and pain radiates from the side of my chin from the impact of the concrete.

I don't hear the twins scurry off or notice Janelle and the teacher's hands on me. Nothing seems to exist as they pull me to my feet.

Those boys were right—at least partly. My only living parent doesn't want me. Jeremy will grow up and forget all about me. Mickey will probably fall in love with someone who actually deserves him. A person who can give to him as much as he gives to them, look him in the eye when he speaks, and have a proper conversation without choking up. He's going to be with someone who knows how to love herself and the life she has. She won't have a leaking heart. She won't constantly need his protection.

Once everything—and everyone—is gone, nothing will be left of me. I have no plans for college, no idea what I will do with my life beyond the plans I made with Mickey, where we'd travel around the country.

I've read enough books to know about emotional journeys. The heroine will start off sad, chapters away from breaking. Then she'll learn from every test, blossom after every trial, and she's healed by the end of her story. Whole.

That's not my story.

A happy ending is not written in my book.

Nothing will change the fact that I don't have my parents. Mickey is the only family I have, and I have to accept that one day he will move on to bigger and better things.

I'll be cemented in the same spot, a spot of my own making.

The nurse lets me hang out in her office until the three o'clock bell rings. I spend each minute leading up to it dreading seeing Mickey. He won't even need to see my face to figure out something went wrong today because my messed-up hair is enough of a tell. I won't be able to lie to him, and he knows all my buttons to make me speak.

Then, he'll be angry, and his fists will get involved.

I stare at my feet and ignore the ache in my scalp and the bruise forming on my chin, walking to where Mickey waits. The closer I get, the more the feeling of being vulnerable disappears. When he's around, no one can hurt me. The only one who can is me; as much as Mickey tries, he can't protect me from myself.

Students old enough to know Roman's reputation scurry past him, and they don't dare bat an eye in his direction. I feel the instant he decides that blood will be spilled tonight.

"What's wrong?" His hands are on me within a matter of seconds, tugging my sleeves up and turning my face to check me over. The second he spots the mark on my chin, he erupts. "Who the fuck did this?"

"No one—it's nothing." I try to tear away from his grasp, but he tightens his hold. "I just want to go home."

"Like fuck it's nothing."

Rage vibrates from him in waves, and I stare down at my feet because if his silver eyes bore into mine, I'll crumble. He cups my cheek and angles my face up.

"Look at me, Bella. Tell me what happened."

"Nothing happened." I still can't bring myself to look at him. "Can we just go?"

"Do you think someone can hurt you and get away with it? You should know the answer by now."

I shake my head and blink back tears like the child I am. I don't want to cry in front of him, because it'll become an even bigger deal, and I want to seem like I have my shit together.

"It doesn't matter anymore, Mickey. I just want to forget about it and move on with my day." My face hurts, but my soul is aching. The only thing I want to do is crawl under the blankets and cry into my pillow.

"Give me names."

It's on the tip of my tongue to spill the words he's looking for. "I can't keep running to you to save me."

"You won't need to run; I'll already be there."

"No, you won't be. One day, you will move on, and I'll need to learn to fend for myself. You won't always be there to help me."

"Like fuck, I won't." He looks at me, the promise of death in his eyes. "Names, Isabella."

"No."

"Give me names, and we can go."

"Mickey, no, I—"

"And what's the plan? How are you planning on stopping him if he bothers you again? You gonna hit him?"

I'm about to say yes, but we both know it'll be a lie. I'd do it for Jeremy, maybe even Janelle, but I'll be an unfortunate casualty.

"I'll talk to them."

"*Them*?"

One person, and I may get away with withholding a name. He'd just watch from a distance and wait until I crack. Two? He'd burn the place down to find out.

"Tell me, has that ever worked on me? Has anyone ever talked me out of knocking their lights out?"

No. Maybe I could, but it'd only be damage control. Instead of five broken bones, it might only be two.

"Is this the first time *they've* bothered you?"

I stare at the spot between his collarbones where the skin dips.

"You can fucking set out tea and write them damn letters. There isn't a thing that will make them stop coming for you. They've tasted blood and made you cry. They thought they won, and they'll keep coming back because picking on someone smaller is the only time they feel like men. They need to know they've lost—and they did as soon as they touched you."

I know he's right. I *hate* that he's right. I'm weak. If this were the wild, I would have died a long time ago if it weren't for Mickey. Natural selection would have taken me out. He doesn't just save me or stop the harm from coming. He helps me pick up the parts and put them back together again.

"Mikhail and Maxim Androv. They're twins."

"Good," he says.

I know what will happen when I say their names, and I have absolutely no remorse or guilt. What does it say about me that I won't even beg Roman to go easy on them or not approach them at all? What's wrong with me that when he says "good," I couldn't agree more?

"Where's your phone?"

The sudden change of topic gives me whiplash. "What?"

"Your phone. Where is it?"

"I, uh." Why can I barely string together a sentence around him? What is happening to me? I clear my throat. "In my bag."

"Turn around." He doesn't wait for me to do as I'm told. He grabs my shoulder, spins me away from him, takes my phone out of the front pocket, turns me back in place, and then places the device in my hand. "The next time something happens, you call me. Even if it's just to ask which shirt you should wear or if you're out of snacks. I don't give a shit if I'm working, sleeping, or half-dead; you grab that phone, and you call me. I'll pick up whatever you need, even if I'm six feet under, Bella. There isn't a god in existence that could stop me from getting to you. So you pick up that phone and call me before you even think about calling the cops. Got it?"

I stare at him, dumbfounded. I'm not sure why I'm surprised to hear any of this when those are the only words I'd expect from Mickey. I guess I'm still surprised whenever someone is there for me when I need it, because the only other person who has ever supported and cared for me was my ma.

I nod. Within a split second, the anger in his eyes is gone, shoved beneath the surface, his usual grin taking the scowl's place.

"Come on. We've got a long trip ahead of us."

CHAPTER 10

ISABELLA

3 Years Ago

Roman: 19 years old – Isabella: 17 years old.

Roman is probably kidnapping me right now. Even if it weren't a *maybe* but a *definitely*, I *probably* wouldn't put up as much of a fight as I should.

I have absolutely no idea where we're going. It's not like I can ask him since we're on a motorbike. I don't need to see the dash to know we haven't been going anywhere near the legal speed limit for the past three hours. All I know is that my ass hurts, my hands are cold, and my back aches from gripping onto him for dear life.

We pass a series of back roads and forestry that give my stomach a run for its money, and I almost fall off once or twice.

If this is a kidnapping, I will fight him tooth and nail for the two things keeping me in place: graduation and Jeremy. Because maybe I'll have an epiphany on what I want to do with my life once I walk onto the stage and have the certificate in my hands.

There's not a single thing in the world that would make me leave Jeremy with those horrible people. If I could, I'd take him in and raise him myself, but what type of life would he have? Best-case scenario, I manage to convince state services to move Jeremy to a half-decent home.

I breathe a sigh of relief when we finally slow down, only to groan when he turns us down a dodgy driveway, passing through a busted gate coated in rust hidden behind excessive overgrowth. I can barely see the gravel beneath all the weeds and fallen leaves.

The ground crunches beneath the wheel, and I hold back a gag.

There are probably a bunch of animal carcasses hidden under there.

Yuck.

Maybe he isn't kidnapping me, but skipping straight to murder. I probably wouldn't be surprised if he decided to turn this into a suicide pact.

My only assurance that he will continue wreaking havoc for at least one more day is the fact that Mikhail and Maxim don't have a single mark bestowed upon them by Roman in the name of my honor.

Or maybe it's Mickey trying to avenge me.

Or maybe it's his excuse to punch something. Not like he'd need to use me as an excuse. If he feels like it, he'll just do it.

My grip around his waist grows tighter as the bike maneuvers around potholes and angry-looking bushes. I pray to God I don't see a dead animal. That may just ruin my mood more than the twins did.

We finally come to a stop in front of a rickety old house that looks like it hasn't seen life in years. He kills the engine and doesn't waste any time dismounting, shucking off his helmet, and grinning at me like a kid who is proudly showing off his art project to a parent.

Hesitantly, I unclip the helmet and slide off the bike, landing on the ground with a thud. The muscles in my thighs protest, and I throw my hand back to keep balanced. Mickey has the audacity to look pleased about my suffering.

Ass.

"Do you like it?" he asks in the same voice Jeremy uses when he pretends to seek your approval, but is really just fishing for compliments because he *knows* it's good. Although, I don't think that's a word I would associate with the horror house in front of me.

Cobwebs hang across the deck like layers of chiffon, and darkness hides between the cracks of broken wooden beams, moldy and gray from neglect. Slats are nailed over windows, making the place look even more unwelcoming.

There's no doubt in my mind that someone was murdered here. If I start digging around, I'm sure I'll find some bodies that didn't make it to the coroner's office.

How the hell did Mickey find this place?

Better yet, what on earth are we doing here?

"I know what you're thinking." He sidles up next to me and throws his arm over my shoulder as if he were a top-shot real estate agent. "Wow, Mickey, this is amazing! I can't believe how romantic and perfect you are." Mimicking my voice, he places a hand over his heart. "Thank you for driving me three hours to the middle of nowhere and being so perfect."

I glare at him and his stupidly smug face. It only seems to encourage him.

He cups my cheek and says, "Well, my sweet Bella, to that, I say you are most welcome. Anything for you."

"Right. So are you going to kill me?" I half mutter out of unease, and half grumble out of impatience.

He pinches my cheek as I scowl at him, slapping his hand away. "Vicious princess." Chuckling while entwining our fingers, he pulls me along behind him. "But no, not yet."

"That doesn't bring me any comfort." I glower.

With a wink, he grabs a bag from inside his bike, and starts dragging me behind the house to an even freakier-looking shed. If he isn't killing me, is he killing someone else?

God, what if he has hostages in there?

"Don't worry, I'll protect you," Mickey croons, and I hit his chest lightly. The act seems playful from the outside, but my rapidly increasing heart rate is a whole other story.

"What are we doing here, Roman?" I tense, waiting for another non-answer.

He's good at those.

"Don't call me that." His gaze darkens, and I almost regret saying anything. But I have a right to know what we're doing at an abandoned house, walking toward a creepy shed when the sun is just about to set. He can get over being called something other than Mickey. "Be patient."

Sensing my agitation, he pauses to face me. Just when I think he's going to soothe my worries and give me the answers I so desperately want at this moment, he makes my anxieties worse. I'm not sure what I expect when he pulls something out of his pocket, but it wasn't a black cloth that he proceeds to tie around my head to cover my eyes.

The world around me plunges into darkness, and my adrenaline kicks up a notch, making me hyper-aware of every thread of fabric touching my skin.

"Leave it," he warns as my hands move toward my face.

"What the hell, Mickey! I can't see anything." He's meant to be terrorizing everyone *but* me.

"That's exactly the point."

I growl under my breath, but bite back a smile. This time, when I touch the cloth, a steel grip clamps around my wrist, and I'm hauled toward his hard chest.

I can't see a thing with the blindfold, but all my other senses are heightened. I can feel every one of his breaths that fans my face, the heavy beats of his heart beneath my hands, and the chill of the night air licking my neck.

Goosebumps erupt over my skin, and I shiver when the lightest touch of his lips brushes against my ear. "Are you going to be a good girl and walk with your hands at your sides, or will I need to carry you?" His voice is filled with danger, but with an edge like he's hoping for the latter so that I can be his own rag doll for the rest of the night.

"Tell me where we're going first."

He pulls back as his chest beneath my hands vibrates with his silent laugh. "The shed. Obviously. Stop being difficult."

"*I'm* being difficult?" I all but screech. "You took me to—excuse my language—the middle of butt-fuck nowhere, and then you blindfold me and drag me to some shady barn thing?"

He nudges my side. "Have I ever done you wrong?"

I throw my arms up. "Yes. Many times."

"Like when?" The way he says it is like I've accused him of committing treason.

And they say women are dramatic.

"Let's see. How about that time you wanted to explore a lake, and it turned out to be a landmine?" I put my hands on my hips.

"It was decommissioned," he counters.

I huff. "Or when you took me to see 'some cool art,' and then we had to run from the cops because you were caught tagging?"

"Wasn't a lie. The art *was* cool." I can just imagine him cocking his chin up with a prickly grin.

"What about when you fed me undercooked chicken, and I was out with food poisoning for a week?" I say pointedly.

He's silent for one beat, then two. "But did you die?"

I gape at him. "I was so dehydrated from throwing up, I thought I saw God."

"No, you saw me. And I've apologized." His voice drops a level, and I can feel the guilt seeping out of him.

I bite the inside of my cheek, because it was a low blow. He stayed up with me the whole time, tying my hair back as I threw up my guts, brushing my teeth when I didn't have the energy to, and then he carried me back to bed.

"Now you're a master chef who's taken me hostage," I say with a joking edge.

The week after that, he began using all these cooking terminologies like *sautéing* and *braising*. Mickey refuses to admit it, but I have a hunch he started watching cooking videos. There's no way he went from undercooking boiled chicken to making homemade empanadas without the internet.

A pause lingers between us. "Yet you haven't attempted to take off the blindfold again." I launch into defense mode and twist my arms out of his grip, just like he taught me. "Cut it out. That wasn't an invitation," he snaps, then lowers his voice and says, "But well done. Good technique."

My skin heats from the praise. *Please, Isabella, contain yourself.*

"Walk or carry?"

My breath catches in my throat. "Tell me what—"

"One."

"Mickey, seriously, I—"

"Two."

"Why won't you tell—" My words end with a shriek when strong arms move behind my knees and sweep me off my feet. As it always does when it comes to Mickey, my body betrays me, and without thought, I wrap my hands behind his neck. "No!"

He chuckles. "Too late. You're at my mercy now."

I dissolve into his hold. Even though layers are separating us, we may as well be skin-to-skin. I'm on fire, and the only person who can put me out is him, even though he's what ignited me. But this is a dangerous game. Something so simple shouldn't unwind me so much.

"Put me down right now, Roman Riviera."

I swear I hear him growl. "Do you want to find out if I have duct tape, too?"

My mouth clamps shut.

No... he wouldn't, would he? Surely not...

"Good girl," he muses.

I'm about to say something else. Maybe something snarky, but I really *don't* want to find out if a roll of duct tape is hidden inside his leather jacket.

That kind of kidnapping scenario would be a little too much for me.

Just a little.

Okay, a lot.

The rhythmic thump of his feet along the ground and the soft sway of his movements could lull me to sleep. I admit that I'm disappointed when he lowers me to the ground. I have to pry my fingers apart to let go of his neck, and before I let go of him fully, I miss his warmth. I didn't exactly dress for the outdoors, so the riding jacket doesn't do enough to stop the autumn chill from sinking into my bones.

"Stay," he orders. I lift my hands up to the blindfold, but he slaps them away. "Don't touch."

"I'm not a dog," I seethe.

115

"Mmhmm," he hums.

I grumble under my breath and cross my arms to preserve warmth while a bunch of banging and grunting happens a few feet to my right.

Please don't be a dead body.

Please don't be a dead body.

Please don't be a dead body.

On my next inhale, a low whine whirls at the bottom of my lungs, and I freeze.

Oh...

Shit...

Mickey better not have heard that.

I swallow and quietly clear my throat, even though I know it will do nothing to eliminate the wheeze. It's still worth a try. If he hears me, he's going to be absolutely livid. Not only did I forget to bring my inhaler, but I haven't taken it in at least three days. Which just so happens to be the timeframe for my asthma to kick in if left unmedicated.

Of course, Mickey knows this.

He knows freaking everything there is to know about me.

I jolt when his fingers wrap around my elbow. I didn't even hear him coming, too lost in my panicked thoughts.

"After you, Princess."

I shuffle across the ground hesitantly, attempting to keep my breaths short so he doesn't hear the hitch in each of them. The itch in my lungs grows, and I have to resist the urge to clear my throat every three seconds.

Mickey gently guides me a few more steps before stopping and twisting my body so he has me where he wants me. It's quieter here, the insects' songs dulled. My nose twitches as I try to find any answer about our whereabouts from scent alone, but all I can smell is Mickey, fresh earth, and the lingering scent of hay.

He takes his time untying the cloth around my head as I hold my breath without much thought, too scared to breathe with him so close.

My lungs scream and heave—and holy crap, it's so itchy. They feel like they're filled with the ticklish, crawling insects that sing outside.

There has to be a way to reach inside myself and scratch my lungs.

I blink a couple of times from the burst of sudden light. Then I blink some more to make sure I'm seeing things correctly.

I take one step forward.

And another, spinning in a slow circle to take everything in. Fairy lights twinkle, wrapped around pillars and hanging from beam to beam. Pillows are stacked on top of a thick woolen blanket laid on the concrete floor. Next to it are boxes of blankets and pillows, as well as every single one of my favorite snacks. I turn and spot a white sheet hanging on the wall, along with a projector a couple of feet in front of it.

There's a soft whirring from somewhere—a generator, I'm guessing. It's the only way the light bulb would work unless the abandoned horror house has electricity.

How did he get all this stuff here on his bike?

He must have spent hours here, cleaning and setting everything up. The walls are free of spider webs, and not a single strand of hay can be seen.

I completely forget I'm struggling to breathe as I gape at my surroundings. No one has ever done anything like this for me before. I turn to find Mickey leaning against the door with his hands stuffed into his pockets. "It's so beautiful," I gasp.

He shrugs with his typical confident attitude. "I know."

He didn't need to do all of this for me. This is going above and beyond my wildest dreams. I did nothing to deserve any of it. "You did all this for me?"

117

Easing himself from the doorway, my heart picks up as he closes the distance. I try taking smaller breaths with the purpose of making sure my static chest stays silent. I want to wrap my arms around him and press my lips to his plush ones so he knows how much I appreciate this.

So he knows I see him—all of him—even when no one else does.

I meet his intense stare as he gazes down at me, looking completely lost in whatever he must see in me. "When will you realize there is nothing I wouldn't do for you?"

My lips part, and I swallow a cough. "I can't believe you did all this. How much did all this even cost? How long did it take? When did you have time to do all of this?"

He leans forward and lowers his voice like he's telling me a secret. "I'm a god."

"You'd be a really shitty one. You'll probably do the opposite of whatever people pray for." He's downplaying what he's done, like he always does.

"Who do you pray to?"

I narrow my eyes, confused. "I don't pray."

"You'd get on your knees for me if I asked. Does that make me your god, Princess?"

I choke on an inhale, then the critters crawling in my lungs let loose. The first cough that rips through my throat is a sputter. The second has me hunched over, gasping for air, only to cough instead.

Each one is more painful than the last, and my stomach clenches like I'm about to vomit, but nothing comes out. Tears prick my eyes, and everything is cold but burning at the same time.

I try to slow my breathing while also trying to sit upright, but it's all useless. Dots blur my vision, and I don't notice the hands on me until something is shoved in my mouth. My brain picks up on what's happening—just barely—and I close my mouth around the plastic and push down on the medication.

The puff of medicine doesn't reach my lungs on the first try, but thankfully it does on the second. I try a third time for good measure.

My body is weightless, crumbled on the floor with a hard mass at my back while I focus on breathing.

One measured breath, then two.

Heaving is the better word. Or gasping. Rasping. All the above.

It gets easier as the seconds pass, with the help of the circles Mickey is rubbing against my back. Though his touch does nothing to take away the ache in my ribs or the claws ripping down my throat.

Leaning my head against Mickey's shoulder, he shifts so his arms are wrapped around my waist, rocking us from side to side, murmuring something I can't make out over the rush of adrenaline.

Minutes pass as my breathing evens out, and oxygen slowly seeps back into my brain. I almost wish it didn't so I can escape Mickey's questioning.

"Where's your inhaler?"

Silence follows.

He knows the answer, and I don't have the energy to think of an elaborate excuse for why it isn't in my pocket or my bag like it should be.

"Where's your inhaler, Isabella?" His voice is darker this time, and the tension returns to my tired body.

"At…"

"The next words out of your mouth better not be 'at home,'" he warns, and his arms stop giving me the comfort they did moments ago. "Jesus Christ, Bella. You can't keep forgetting."

I shuffle away from him so we face each other, but my attention trains on my intertwined hands. "I'm fine. It's only mild."

I hear his sharp intake of breath before he all but yells, "Do you realize how serious this is? What if you have an asthma attack and I'm not there, huh?" Roman moves closer, so I can't avoid seeing his anger. "What if no one around you has an inhaler? What then? You could *die*."

We've had this talk more times than I can count, but he's never outright said those words. He's always skirted around the subject so he doesn't upset me. I can't call this an innocent mistake anymore. I can't call it an accident.

Mickey got me more than one inhaler. He got me a goddamn case for it so I can leave it in my bag. He even sends me text reminders to take it. I just... don't. I have no idea why. Maybe for some semblance of control.

My eyes start to water. I'm not trying to be difficult. I want to be able to breathe. To live. I swear I do.

I think I do.

"I'm sorry," I whisper.

God, I'm so pathetic. So this is how it is? I'm going to need a babysitter for the rest of my life? I can't go anywhere without Mickey, just in case I accidentally kill myself, because I can't seem to do something as basic as breathing. How could he want that? Why *should* he want that? He's trying to help me, and I won't even help myself.

He rushes to me, holding my face in the palm of his hands. "No, hey. No, I'm sorry. Breathe. I'm sorry. I didn't mean to upset you; it's just—I—" He closes his eyes and takes a deep breath. When he opens them, they're softer than I've ever seen, yet lined with guilt, grief, and fear. "I can't lose you. You know those cliché sayings that you're the first thing I think about when I wake up and my last thought when I fall asleep? It's true. You're always on my mind. Constantly. There isn't a minute that goes by when I'm not wondering what you're doing, or if you're okay, or thinking about me as much as I think about you. If you were to—" Mickey squeezes his eyes shut again like the words physically pain him. "I need you to take care of yourself. Bring your inhaler with you. I'm sorry for raising my voice; I'm mad because I'm worried."

Sniffling, I shake my head. "Don't apologize. It's not your fault. You're right. It was stupid and reckless and idiotic and—"

"No." His voice is stern, and he lowers himself so he's at my eye level. "Listen to me, Bella, and listen to me well. Here's what you're going to do: You won't apologize. You're not going to cry or say shit like that about yourself. Do you know why? Because you are intelligent and brave and beautiful and kind and fucking perfect, and I don't deserve you one bit. And I want you to see that in yourself every day, too."

My body feels entirely too heavy for me. Too tight.

How many times has he quite literally saved me? Pulling me back when we cross the street, carrying an inhaler wherever we go, or beating up bullies for me. I can't even count how many times he's called the doctor's office for me, taken me to my appointment, then picked up my prescription after.

He feathers his thumb over my cheek, wiping away a fallen tear. Leaning into his touch, I savor the feel of his rough hands.

He'll get sick of me, eventually. It's just a matter of when. He drops his head, pressing his forehead to mine. "You don't take medication or eat breakfast or lunch for me or for Jeremy; you do it for you. Got it?"

All I can do is nod. It isn't fair of me to expect Roman to slide into the role of caregiver. And it isn't right for me to rely on him to keep me alive, fed, medicated, and financed while I sift through my paralyzing thoughts. Any money I make is from working at Greg's store a few hours a week, but even then, he usually keeps my wage.

I have to start taking my life into my own hands and stop blaming my leaking heart for everything. I will never have a mother or father. I've known that for a long time, but I need to learn to accept that.

Mickey shifts his hand down my face, and I forget to stop myself from flinching when he puts pressure on my bruise.

His lips curl back into a snarl. "What did those two shitheads say to you?"

At least we aren't talking about my asthma anymore, but this isn't much better.

I pull back from his hold, drying my face with my sleeve. "Just leave it, Roman." I try not to sound as exhausted as I feel, but I know he sees through my faux resolve. "I don't want to talk about it, because it will mess up our night when you've put in all this effort for me."

"Tell me."

"No."

I raise my head in defiance. We played this game earlier this afternoon, and I lost. In all fairness, I can put on as much bravado as I want, but Roman is worse than a dog with a bone. He won't stop unless he finds the whole carcass.

He narrows his eyes. "Tell me."

"It's stupid high school stuff. Nothing I haven't heard before." I try to feign being unconcerned, but I am very much concerned.

"I don't give a shit if you hear it every day. They made you cry—they *hurt* you. They're lucky they're not dead yet."

"Don't, okay? It's my birthday, Mickey. Aren't you meant to do what I say?"

He leans back and eyes me like I've said something ridiculous. "I do whatever you ask every day of the year. I don't need an excuse for it."

I sigh. I'm definitely not going to win this. "And I'm asking you to forget about it."

"Forget about it?" His thick brows drop, and the chilly air around us turns venomous. "They left a fucking mark on your face, Isabella."

122

As if noticing the attention, pain radiates from my chin. I cringe back at the use of my full name in that tone. In that very, very angry, pissed-off tone.

This isn't going to be good.

"It wasn't really their fault." I try to defend the twins, but the instant I see his face twist, I know I've just made it worse. "He was holding me up by my hair, and when he let go, I fell onto the concrete."

I should have shut up when I could.

He says nothing for a beat.

Oh no.

The atmosphere thickens.

The muscles of his jaw flutter.

"I am going to make them wish they were dead, Bella. I'm going to do it for you."

"Mickey, don't let them get to you," I attempt to soothe. "They're just stupid kids who probably have a really messed-up home life and don't know how to act properly. They need someone to talk to, not to get beaten up."

They need a therapist, which won't happen for anyone who goes to our school unless you're in the system and you're as problematic as Mickey. And by that time, it's usually too late for a therapist to do anything.

If I'm being honest with myself, I couldn't care less if the twins were scared of the sun. So, I don't know why I'm trying so hard to defend them.

Maybe I don't want them to take more of my joy, or maybe I'm only trying to prevent myself from having a guilty conscience.

Maybe it's because this is what Cassie would do. Someone less defective would beg him for hours not to hurt them. Maybe I'm still talking because that's what I *should* be doing.

Slowly, to leave no doubt in my mind, Mickey says, "I'm not asking for your permission, and I am not going to ask for your forgiveness after."

123

I sigh, defeated. "Just... Not tonight."

"Not tonight," he agrees.

"It's just you and me tonight, right?" I ask. "No Mikhail, no Maxim." *No talks about my health.* "Just you and me and any food you brought, because I'm starving."

He watches me carefully for a moment before chuckling humorlessly. "Yeah, yeah."

"Great." I put on my most cheerful smile and ignore my aching lungs.

Fake it until you make it, right?

Or at least lie to yourself until you start believing your own delusions to the point that they sabotage your life.

He doesn't let on if he isn't falling for my act, rummaging through the bag he brought with him and the box a couple of feet away from us. I still can't believe everything he's done for my birthday. Is this what he's been doing at night? A daunting realization hits and settles low in my gut.

There's so much about Roman that I don't know.

He couldn't have found this place by himself, and he's never talked about anyone else other than to complain about people at work. How much of himself is he hiding from me? Have I spent all these years thinking there isn't a side of him that I don't know, but I've been fooling myself the whole time?

I don't take my eyes off him as he lays out all the food: buns, roasted chicken, salad, chips, and fruit. It's the biggest juxtaposition; he's organized the cutest picnic in the creepiest shed and somehow made it romantic.

Once all the food is out on the blanket, he pulls out a little black box that he places right in front of me.

"What is it?" I ask hesitantly, picking up the velvet jewelry case.

"Open it."

I give him one last look before flicking the lid open. I'm frozen in my spot as I stare at it. For the third time today, tears run down my cheeks. I don't think I've ever cried so much.

But this time is different.

This time, the tears don't sting when they fall.

This time, when I cry, there's a smile stretched across my lips.

"Mickey," is all I can say.

He deserves the whole world, and I wish I could give it to him.

They're an exact match to the pair of earrings that Mamá gave me on my fifth birthday that I lost when I was eight. Small, silver Mickey Mouse studs. I cried for weeks when I lost them. I had only two things left from Mamá: the earrings and the Mickey Mouse doll.

He looks back at me with an expression I can't quite name. "How?" I breathe.

"I got them made."

There's no emotion in his voice, but I can see in his eyes that he's battling some demons as he taps away on his leg. I want to know what he's thinking. He usually looks pleased with himself or even excited whenever he gives me a birthday gift. He's never so reserved.

I finally register what he said. "How—You remember what they looked like?"

He nods once. "I'll never forget."

We stare at each other for a long moment before I decide to break the silence. "Thank you, Roman. I love them. You have no idea how much this means to me."

I replace the earrings I'm wearing with the new pair. The silver is heavier than the ones I was originally wearing. I can't imagine how much it would have cost him to get them made.

"Movie or music?" He doesn't look at me when he asks, focused on piling vegetables and chicken into a bun.

There's something about the way he says it that makes my stomach dip uneasily. I swallow and tuck the box away into my pocket. Have I done another thing wrong? Said the wrong words or acted the wrong way?

"A true-crime podcast," I joke, attempting to make him feel even an ounce of my elation.

It's a terrible joke, because neither of us is that into them, but the trick works because his lips tilt up at the corner. "Are you sure you want to give me ideas after discussing the twins?"

"You're right. Movie." I force myself to grin, even though there's still a sour taste in the air.

"As my lady wishes."

I roll my eyes, and he winks.

Enough crap has gone on today, and if one more bad thing happens, I'm calling it quits.

We both get busy with our tasks, him setting up the projector, and me taking over with making the sandwiches—I make them better than he does. Roast chicken, coleslaw, bread buns, and potato chips. If there's one thing we both learned at school, it's that nothing beats a *chip sandwich*, as the Kiwi kid in my class called it.

We eat in silence as the movie starts to play, and like a typical guy, he inhales his food and manages to eat two in the time it's taken me to eat half. He artfully organizes the pillows and blankets and drags me by the waist and into his arms the second I finish eating.

I try to focus on the movie, but I can only focus on Mickey: The way his body is perfectly molded to mine, the kisses he plants on the top of my head every so often, and how he doesn't stop touching me. He's constantly moving, rubbing circles with his palms and writing love letters with his fingers along my back.

He laughs at the movie on cue and blurts out whatever random thing he thinks of as he watches. With the countless layers of blankets hiding our intertwined bodies and nothing but the fairy lights and the projector to light our surroundings, I've never felt so content.

We've both lost our jackets, leaving us in our shirts and pants. He keeps running his hand up and down my arm like he can't get enough of the feel of me. With each touch, the crappiness of everything that happened today floats away.

The credits roll, and I stretch my neck up to find he's already looking at me. I shiver when his hand follows the curve of my waist, leaving a path of fire up along my collarbones to trace every contour of my face.

Warmth unfurls in my chest as the butterflies that have been quiet all night explode in a flurry of short breaths and fluttering lashes. Those gunmetal eyes of his pierce mine, and I can't look away, lost in his scent and the way the shadows enhance his cheekbones and run along his nose. I could live in this moment forever and die happy, never seeing the sun again.

"You're so fucking beautiful, Bella."

His gaze drops to my lips, where his fingers brush them over and over. His eyelids grow heavier with each move, hiding his darkening stare. Inch by inch, his other hand crawls up the back of my thigh, slowing over the arch of my back, eliciting a deep desire in me unlike anything I've ever known. My core tightens as an ache forms between my legs, but I'm too scared to shift my hips in case the movement causes Roman to snap out of his trance.

My pigtails loosen as his fingers move into my hair, threading through the strands as if he owns them. He doesn't need to ask; he can take anything he wants from me. I'm his. It's the only thing I'm certain about in this life.

Roman's eyes glaze over as if he's mesmerized, but he licks his lips like a starved animal, never once moving his attention away from my mouth.

He's looking at me as if I'm the only person in this world who matters.

Like I'm his everything.

Like he's about to kiss me.

"Mickey."

CHAPTER 11

ISABELLA

3 YEARS AGO

Roman: 19 years old – Isabella: 17 years old.

His lips crash into mine, cutting off my words as he drags me to him by his grip on my hair. The entire world lights up on contact. Every bulb grows brighter, every smell becomes stronger, and I can feel the kiss in my soul. The stars could fall, and I wouldn't notice. The room could be set ablaze, and I would be helpless to his possession.

His lips move without waiting for me to catch up. Mickey pulls me beneath him, settling himself between my legs as he dominates every inch of me. Choosing where my legs are curled around him, we become a battle of tongue and teeth that I already know I will lose.

A low growl rattles through his throat as my back arches and my legs tighten around his waist, pulling his hips closer to mine. When he takes my bottom lip between his teeth like he's marking his territory, I can't help but whimper.

It isn't just a kiss. Our lips aren't *just* touching. He's claiming me, body, mind, and soul, and there is nothing I can do to get away from it. Because I want him, too, more than anything else in the world.

Not want.

Need.

I need him more than I need air. If he leaves, I won't survive. There's nothing else in this world that could compare to him.

I'm his, and there's a Roman-shaped hole in my heart that is perfectly made to fit him.

As he pushes his hard length against the part of me that aches for him the most, fireworks dance behind my vision. My body takes over at the sensation, and I grind my hips along him. A guttural moan makes it past our lips, and I try to chase that high again.

But then he stops.

"Fuck," he groans, pulling away from me, and I whimper when his touch vanishes completely.

He leans to the side. One hand disappears beneath the covers to adjust himself. Then he throws his head back and laughs at the ceiling. Looking back down at me, he beams from ear to ear. "God, that was better than I ever imagined. You taste so damn good." He shakes his head. "I don't think I'm going to survive another year," he says, more to himself than to me.

"What?" I shift and try to make myself smaller.

That was amazing, but I don't understand why he pulled away. Did I kiss him wrong? Was that bad? I've never kissed anyone before, and I can't help feeling like I wasn't enough, even though he is smiling at me like I've given him some gift.

He flops onto his back next to me and grabs me before I can escape any scrutiny. Tucking me into his side, he cages me in his arms. Should

I be fighting him? Do I try kissing him again? I don't understand what's happening.

"I'm going to see you every day, and it's going to kill me not to pounce on you." Mickey pushes himself onto his back and raises himself on his elbows so he's staring down at me with a grin. "On that note, no skirts, no shorts, no low-cut shirts, and—I never thought I'd agree with the teachers—no shoulders. For God's sake, you better put away the shoulders. They're too tempting. And those thin little tank top straps? So breakable," he rambles, talking so fast I almost miss what he's saying. I'd believe him if he told me that he was drunk or high.

If the term 'on top of the world' could be captured, it would be Mickey at this moment. He's encapsulating pure joy. I've never seen him smile so brightly before. There isn't a hint of maliciousness or mischief in his lopsided grin. If he started skipping around the room, I wouldn't be surprised.

I wish I could feel what he's feeling. My lips curl into a smile, but it's forced, so nothing happens to the look in his eyes. He's *happy*. Truly happy.

But he stopped. He pulled away from me.

His brows drop suddenly, frowning to himself. "Actually, cover the ankles, too. There isn't an inch on you that doesn't do it for me. I'll control myself, don't you worry. But if someone looks at you?" He whistles. "If you thought I was crazy before, you have no idea what you've just unlocked." Moving again, onto his knees this time, he settles between my legs as if he's done this thousands of times and belongs there. "Do you know how long I've wanted to do that? For years, every single time I saw your pretty pink lips, I imagined what they would feel like between my teeth and whether they were as sweet as you look."

I blink at him. He's not making sense. Why won't he—why did he pull away? "But... a year? Is there—" *Something wrong with me? Someone else? Something else?* Is he waiting for me to be better or more mature?

He chuckles to himself and runs his hands up and down my thighs and waist like the feel of me is a drug he can't get enough of. "A year and one day from today, you're not going to be able to walk. Because once I get my hands on you, you'll be ruined."

Oh, right.

My age.

Two years isn't that big a difference? So many girls at school have older boyfriends, and it's not like I just met Mickey.

What if he's actually waiting for me to be different—better? What if one year is a countdown before he decides whether he really wants me? What happens in the time between? How am I meant to change?

"It's getting late," he says, without even looking at the time. "We should go. There's a long ride ahead of us, and I want you tucked into bed before midnight."

I try to hide my grimace. He wants to get rid of me like he always does at night. He deposits me back into my room before nine and doesn't return until morning to take me to school. What's he doing after this? Will he call Cassie and get her to help with the bulge pressed against me?

"Okay," I whisper. Even though there are a hundred questions I could ask, I won't utter a single one.

Don't ask questions you don't want to know the answer to, and don't cry for help when you're drowning. The only things that can save you are the answers you never asked for.

I can imagine my heart shattering into a million pieces if I ask him where he's going. He'll say he's running into the arms of a woman when he's just been in mine.

He kisses my lips that I pretend I don't feel, even though I kissed him back with the weight of all the questions I never asked.

132

I take his hand and let him help me to my feet, and we pack away the items while Mickey goes on a tangent about all the motorbikes that came into the garage this week. I'm listening, but not really. I feel full and hollow at the same time. It's an awful thing to feel.

I'm barely conscious as I climb back onto the bike and ride for hours until we stop in front of the two-story house with the window open on the top floor.

He kisses me again when our helmets come off. I peer through the curtains once he escorts me inside. There's a skip in his step as he goes back to his bike.

My doubts don't stop swirling as I drag my feet to my room. They don't take a break when my head hits the pillow, and I look up to see the glow-in-the-dark stars Mickey helped stick on.

Eventually, sleep comes.

The next day, I wake with the same thought as I did yesterday: Days like today are always the hardest.

But I know Mickey makes it better. He finds a way by saying something ridiculous.

I pull myself out of bed and go through the monotonous motions of getting ready before the rest of the house makes it out of their rooms. Shower. Dress. Hair. And... and inhaler. And breakfast. For once.

Only after locking the door behind me do I realize there's no bike waiting for me. No Mickey.

I stand there at the edge of the porch, watching Jeremy leave for school. Then Greg and Marcus disappear off to work.

But Mickey never comes.

He doesn't answer when I pick up the phone and call him.

He isn't there when I go to our spot after school, or the next day when I walk out of the house with my hair down.

I call again.

It goes straight to voicemail.

I show up at his home, but no one answers his door.

I go again the next day and the next.

Until days turn into weeks, and weeks turn into months.

A year goes by.

He doesn't show up for my graduation.

He doesn't come when I am hospitalized.

He doesn't say "happy birthday" when I turn eighteen.

A year and one day later, I can't walk, just like he said. I can't bring myself to leave the bed or eat.

I'm not enough.

He ruined me.

Roman Riviera was right, and I was wrong.

I won't die without Roman Riviera.

But sometimes I wish I would.

CHAPTER 12

ROMAN

3 Years Ago

Roman: 19 years old – Isabella: 17 years old.

She's more than a dream. She doesn't compare to my wildest imagination.

I've always known I have the addict gene in me, and I've found my vice. I've been addicted to Bella since the very beginning. Whether just by looking at her or hearing her voice, it fired off little signals in my brain that had my whole body craving my next hit of anything *her*.

I thought I knew what obsession was.

I very obviously did not.

Whatever I thought I felt before is fucking peanuts in comparison.

Now that I know what she tastes like, how she sounds when she moans, and the way her flesh molded so perfectly to me, I'm hooked. This girl was made for me, my own princess. I would give up everything for a single hit—my perfect drug. What she does to me hits like nothing else. And, fuck, if that doesn't drive me insane just thinking about it.

That cute little whimper she made when I stopped kissing her?

The way she clawed at my back like she was as hypnotized as I was?

Don't even get me started about how she was bucking her hips and practically begging me to take her.

Even how she looks wearing what I gave her, the earrings, necklace, and shirt. I wanted to know what the first two would look like against her skin without the last thing getting in the way. Naked, under me, and begging me to ruin her while she wears my marks.

I don't think Bella understands the magnitude of what I just did, and she's not nearly as impressed with me as she should be.

I stopped.

Stopped.

Me? I fought against my urges and let her walk out of there in one piece. I tore myself away from her when I only wanted to consume her whole. If I could live in her skin, I would. I don't think she gets that.

Impulse has gotten me where I am today. Lack of control is the reason why Bella has had to patch me back together more times than I can count. Everything clicked into place when she was beneath me, looking up at me with her beautiful brown eyes. I'm her loyal servant, always have been, and always will be. She's my purpose, my home.

One more year, and she's all mine. She won't have stupid shit like homework and exams to worry about. I won't have to drop her off at home every night and watch that fucker Marcus look at her in a way that has my blood boiling.

I'll probably still have to share her with that little shit Jeremy, but ultimately, nothing will get in our way. Not Maxim or Mikhail. And they're going to know it.

As I drive away from her house, every voice in my head is telling me to turn around and finish what Bella and I started in that shed.

But our first time isn't going to be with that seedy Marcus in the other room, or on the floor in a decrepit, abandoned shed. There will be flowers and candles and pretty things everywhere, like in those romantic movies she's made me watch. She's my delicate princess.

Tonight was meant to be perfect. There were meant to be no tears—the unhappy kind—and the only thing she was supposed to do today was smile, laugh, and be happy. But those two idiots ruined everything.

Mikhail and Maxim Androv.

Never heard of them, and I don't care to know more than just their address. The only thing *they* will need to know is not to be in the same vicinity as Bella ever again. After I'm done with them, they may need to get wheeled out of any place where she is.

I asked Damien for their address, since Lord knows he owes me for all the times I've given out favors for him and the cartel he's running with. I re-check the GPS on my phone. The blood roaring in my ears increases. They only live a few blocks from her.

And she sleeps with the fucking window open. Anyone could climb in.

Fuck it. I'm going to install bars on that window.

The thought only unsettles me more as I park my bike several houses down from where they live. I take a couple of steps away, then glance back at my bike. My only other love. It could be the last time I see her. She might not be in one piece by the time I get back. It's a shitty neighborhood, and she could get sold for parts.

I stole those wheels from someone who owed me money. Someone else might steal the same set of wheels because they need money. It's almost like the circle of life.

I check that she's locked tight one last time, give her a pat, then I'm off on my merry way to fuck up those two pricks.

My body buzzes with anticipation. I can already imagine what their blood will look like on my riding gloves, and I hear the sounds of them begging me to stop. I don't care how old they are; I'm putting them in their place. They didn't pick on someone their own size, so why should I?

After the high of kissing Bella and all the built-up frustration that came with it, this is going to be the cherry on top. I thought I'd have to reach out to Damien, my contact, and find a place to let off some steam tonight, but I guess everything works out for me, eventually.

The street is dimmer with the helmet visor down, but there's no missing their duplex and the two lookalikes sitting on the deck, smoking a joint. They look like idiots.

The twins look like their names sound: short, blonde with a number two cut, and brawny.

Cold sweat gathers down my spine from excitement. I've met their type before. Guys like them wouldn't be sitting outside in this neighborhood without carrying a gun. My lips twitch up at the corners. No one in this area would care if one goes off, but guns mean cops. I'm not in the mood to deal with pigs.

Clad in black, I creep along the side of the house, sticking to the shadows and keeping my footsteps light. I don't do many of these *outings* while wearing a helmet. The anonymity is great, but it fucks with the senses. I won't be able to see or hear as well.

The twins are completely oblivious to the intruder in their midst. I can smell the weed through my helmet, and I might not be able to see their bloodshot eyes this far out, but I'm sure they will be.

Shielded by the darkness, they don't see me coming, too spaced out to hear me stretch my neck from side to side before the first *crack* from my fist carves through the night. Fucker Number One tips to the side, bringing the chair with him. Fucker Number Two scrambles for his gun behind his back, but not fast enough to avoid being hit in the jaw by my riding gloves.

God, that felt good.

His head snaps back, hitting the wall behind him. He groans as his hands instinctively snap up to stop another assault.

"What do you want?" Fucker Number one recovers in time to draw his gun, but it flies out of his hands before he has a chance to use it. Then, someone from inside the house starts screaming, raising my hackles.

An old woman comes running out of the house with a baseball bat, tripping over her slippers and nightie as she goes.

Fuck.

I don't hurt old ladies.

Goddamnit, I have to somehow take her down without laying a hand on her.

"This isn't about you," I yell at her.

Fucker Two suddenly remembers he has a gun, and Fucker One uses the distraction to launch himself at me, hitting me square in the chest. "You cunt."

A laugh rumbles out of me right before I bury my fist into the prick's ribs and swing my head forward, using the helmet's weight to connect with his forehead.

He rears back with blood spurting from his nose, the bottom half of his face drenched in the beautiful crimson.

"Get away from my sons!" their mother screams. I don't get to appreciate the sight of the dark red splatter over his pale skin, because I stumble forward when pain tears through my back.

Helmets are great for anonymity, but fucking shit for visibility.

"Fuck off." I throw my hand back with a snarl and yank the bat out of the culprit's hands. The lady yelps from being thrown off balance. But then her screams turn into words. Only a single word, *Help*.

Fucker Two aims his gun at me. "Don't you fucking touch her."

They can't see my grin as I say, "That's my line." I tilt my head to the side, eying the gun. "You weren't planning on using that on me, were you?"

I swing the wooden bat before he manages to pull the trigger. Those things are great, but they're shit for close combat, which is why I prefer my fists. Using a gun doesn't give me the same satisfaction as pummeling someone's head in until they're an unrecognizable pile of flesh and bone.

He cries out as the weapon is ripped out of his hands and lands by their mother's feet. Fucker One returns, hunched over, charging forward like a raging bull. I lift my leg before he makes contact, sending him careening backward just as Fucker Two swings his arm.

From the corner of my eye, I watch as the woman runs toward the gun on the ground.

And then red and blue lights flash.

Fuck. Fuck. Fuck.

One of the twins lands a hit on my ribs, making me grunt. I grip the bat, raise it in the air and aim it at his head.

"Stop!" she screams.

Bang.

Another scream.

Yelling.

But my arm never moves. The bat doesn't come crashing forward. I'm frozen. I just stare at Fucker Two as he gapes at me. Then slowly, questioningly, he drops his gaze to my chest.

And then I feel it. A prickle at first, like static along my skin.

Suddenly, it's a burn, scorching hot, searing into my flesh as if I've been set on fire, though I never saw anyone light the match. The pain thunders through every molecule of my being, setting every hair and cell in my body ablaze. I feel so cold.

I look down to find my hand already on my chest. Trembling fingers pull away to a liquid sheen that catches the light on my leather gloves.

My body gives out beneath me, and my knees crash against the concrete. The pain is unlike anything I've ever experienced. Pure agony. The basement was better than this. The belt hurt less.

The burning worsens, swirling, until dots dance in my vision. As the world turns bright, something rough hits the back of my head. It's not so dim anymore. The sounds are clearer. But I can't make out any of them. Something presses against my chest. I want to scream, yell, yank this pain out of me.

I can't breathe. It hurts too much. I can't—oh, God. I'm going to die.

No.

No.

Bella.

Who's going to watch over Bella?

Who's going to take care of my princess?

I can't die. I need to take her to school. I have to make sure she's okay. I have to be there for her. What if she forgets to bring her inhaler again? What if she doesn't have enough money for lunch, or has a nightmare?

No. I can't leave Bella. We finally kissed, and in one year, it'll be just us. We'll be going around the country to camp by the beach and see New Orleans, just like she always dreamed of. I'm meant to take her back to Disneyland and give her everything she's ever wanted.

We haven't gotten our high energy dog that's been trained to protect Bella. Or flown to Italy so she can have authentic pizza, and to Greece to relive our ancient history obsession. I'm meant to be putting three kids in her, and we're supposed to have an unconventional wedding, where she'd wear a white dress and start crying as she walks down the aisle.

I can't die. *I won't.*

But I can't fight it.

The last thing on my lips when the lights go out is her name. "Bella."

CHAPTER 13

ROMAN

Three Months Ago

Roman: 22 years old – Isabella: 19 years old.

"Inmate 25963, today's your lucky day."

It takes far too much physical effort to look away from the piece of paper in my hands to Rico's stupid face. I'm not a portrait artist, but I've had nothing but time on my hands to try to draw her. This particular one is my favorite piece.

I managed to get the soft bow of her lips, the sweeping lashes framing big almond-shaped brown eyes, and the little dot on her left cheek. It's the only way I can see her in this shithole, and I don't want to forget what she looks like.

The drawing doesn't come anywhere near the real thing. I could spend a lifetime perfecting my skill, but I will never do her justice.

Adjusting the hand beneath my head, I sink farther into the cot before finally looking at Rico, who's leaning against the bars with his arms crossed over his chest.

I smirk. "Jealous?"

He whistles and shakes his dark brown hair, then nods at the drawing. "Going home to that pretty thing? Damn right, I am."

My lips peel back. "Careful," I warn.

Chuckling, he walks the two steps to the opposite bunk and pulls himself onto the top one. "Two more months, and I'll be back on my shit. I ain't never seeing the inside of this place again."

Over two years and nine months away from Bella almost killed me. I've memorized every inch of this place. I can't count how many times I've thought about breaking out of here. I even planned it all out in my head. I have studied the delivery trucks, the laundry rotation, and when the lazy guards are scheduled.

But each time I'm about to act on it, I stop. I have a higher chance of staying here longer than I do of getting out. No one has escaped this place in over fifty years. I'm cocky, but I don't know if I'm delusional enough to think I could pull off a prison break. In fact, I've been on my best goddamn behavior, which is so unlike me. Bella would be shocked.

I've been practicing what the Shrink Arthur calls 'flat hands.' It's where I *use my palms, not my knuckles*. The only time my fingers curl into fists is when it's wrapped around a dumbbell or a bar of weights to *channel my energy*.

It's some hippy-dippy bullshit, if you ask me. But it fucking works—sort of.

How many fights have I gotten into?

Six.

How many do the higher-ups know about?

One—but I proved I wasn't at fault.

I'm a pillar in this community, an example to the other inmates of what a great prisoner looks like. I took English lit classes—not containing the dirty types of books that Bella reads, obviously—and I even had Arthur convinced I was interested in religion. Not like it was much of a choice. I was bored out of my mind and couldn't use my arms while I was healing, so I had to pick something that made it seem like I was a half-decent person. Once I had full mobility, I flashed my finger at the man upstairs and started breaking my back at the garage they have here.

My religion starts with "Isa" and ends with "Bella," and I'd worship at her altar every night. Blessed be the meal I'm about to eat and all that.

But Arthur buys the whole 'reformed bad boy' thing. He thinks I have "genuine guilt" over assaulting the twins.

Gullible idiot.

The only thing I'm guilty of is getting caught.

And shot.

Getting shot really sucked.

Both during and after sucks more than anyone warns you about.

The bullet was millimeters away from my heart. The doctors weren't convinced I was going to make it, apparently. And the fact I didn't have my Minnie to nurse me back to health was the final nail in the coffin.

The good news? Thanks to the helmet, I didn't have a concussion to go with the life-threatening injury. Silver-fucking-linings.

From the hospital, I was moved to the prison med bay for even longer. I was ready to murder old-man Phil in the bed next to me. It came to the point that if the doctors weren't going to remove his adenoids, I'd remove them for him. I couldn't get a wink of sleep because of the human diesel power generator.

To top it off, I was furious. I *am* furious. Not once did she check in on me while I was in the hospital. After the hell I went through, from recovery to pleading guilty for a lesser sentence, I finally had the chance to call her, and the line wouldn't go through.

She's deactivated her fucking number.

That's not even the worst part.

She hasn't responded to a single one of my letters.

Not a single *one*.

The only thing that pulled me through was the thought of hearing the sound of her voice again. It was the only reason I did every single ridiculous exercise the doctors told me to. Still, she doesn't answer. I have no idea what she's been doing or where she lives now.

The twins had no reason to suspect I attacked them because of what they did to Bella because I never got to tell them to leave her alone, after I beat them black and blue. It wouldn't have been on the news, because shit like that happens all the time. Plus, my registered emergency contact is Margaret, the child psychologist. Margaret probably didn't pick up either.

Not once did I mention Bella's name. It was a conscious decision at the time that I didn't think would have these types of consequences. Having cops come in to interrogate her would only stress her out. So, I told the shrink and the police I had a bad day at work, saw the twins, then got triggered. Arthur slapped my case with an "anger management" label.

Have I learned my lesson? Yes.

Will I stop using my fists? No.

But will I handle all witnesses and look around for police first? Yes.

That still doesn't explain why she hasn't replied to my letters. Unless she moved houses...

Joel scoffs from the bunk below Rico's. "I give you both a month before you're back in here."

Joel's been in the can for twenty years or some shit. In here for organized crime and conspiracy to murder or whatever. Something boring and disproportionate to the sentence time. He's kept being in prison interesting for himself by adding more time to his sentence.

The first year he was here, he murdered a rapist right in front of the guards, then again five years ago. I think he doesn't like his original crime's 'conspiracy' label.

"Old man's already dead. Can't die twice." On the other hand, Rico came in here at eighteen *without* any label other than manslaughter in the third degree. Eight years for killing his father, of all people. "What about you, Tao? You placin' bets or what?"

The bunk creaks as Tao Yang *Junior* shifts before the sound of his Rubix cube starts back up. "Two grand on fourteen months. The court system is slow."

It's my turn to chuckle. Out of all of us, he's the one who will never learn. I can guarantee the second he's out of here, he'll go back to gambling, embezzlement, and money laundering. The only difference is that he'll move back to China and get away with it from now on.

His wife did him dirty during the divorce, and Tao Yang *Senior* dropped over a million on lawyers to get him out of criminal charges.

It obviously didn't do much.

I'm glad he's here, though. Not because I like him or anything. He gets on my nerves with the Rubix cube, and he's constantly droning on and on about stocks. Every other person in this cell *loves* him because he's an absolute fucking idiot who has no idea how to manage his finances. Which, lucky for me, means that there's an extra ten grand sitting in my bank account, courtesy of the Yang family and Junior's shitty bets.

"This pretty face will never see the inside of a cell ever again." Rico's legs dangle over the side of the bed as he shadow punches the air quickly. "I'm too fast; they'll never catch me."

Joel shakes his head and mutters something along the lines of, "I'm too old for this shit."

Rico looks at me, but I don't acknowledge him as I go back to staring at Bella. "Damien's got you hooked up. Don't you worry, my bro will take care of you. I told him about the solid you did for me."

By *solid*, he means looking the other way when he stabbed an inmate from a rival gang. And by *solid*, he also means the drugs I found in one of the cars I was fixing. According to Rico, that is thanks to one of the *other* cartels in the prison—one he's not part of.

I inadvertently started a turf war with Rico's guys ten points ahead, and half a million dollars richer. Needless to say, the Vargas men are *upset* by the whole shipment mishap.

Oh, and I also backed him in a fight. He just thinks I did it for him, but the guy looked at me wrong, and gymming as the only time my fists were clenched wasn't cutting it anymore.

Rico and I are not friends, but I don't hate him completely. He has his uses.

Do Rico and Damien—the Reyes brothers—owe me?

Fuck yeah.

Could I ask Damien to check on Bella for me?

Absolutely.

Will I?

Absolutely... *not*. I'd break out of prison and kill him myself if he went anywhere near her.

"What will you do with your girl when you see her?" From the corner of my eye, I catch Rico leaning on his knees. "What if she's got another man?"

I snap my head in his direction, and his face splits into a wild smirk. *Asshole*.

I keep picturing getting out of here to track Bella down, only to find she has a boyfriend. And then the imagination plays out the same every time: I kill him, then and there.

It wouldn't be the first time I killed for her, either. Mitchell took her away from me for a year, and she got bullied. He should have known better than to do that.

Fortunately, the cops aren't smart enough to catch a murderer who crosses state lines to kill his childhood best friend's foster dad.

"She probably does have a boyfriend," Tao adds.

No one asked for your opinion, Yang.

Because Joel always has to put in his two cents, he says, "Beauts like her don't stay single."

"Three hundred says she does." If Tao doesn't stop talking, he can kiss his Rubix cube goodbye.

Joel doesn't hesitate. "Deal."

"You're going to win for once," I say to the old man. "If she does, I might be seeing you real soon."

"Don't forget what I told you," Rico starts with his shit-eating grin firmly intact. I just *know* that the next words out of his mouth are going to piss me off. "Tie her up, then use your fingers to get Bella's pussy nice and wet before you take that tight little cunt."

White-hot fury flashes throughout my body.

I'm out of bed and on my feet in under a second. He meets me on the floor, in the small space between the two bunks. Red burns in my vision as

I stare him down. "You don't fucking talk about her." My fingers twitch and curl into fists.

I could beat him right now. He might have been here longer, but I'm the one with the experience.

Our chests brush as we square off. He juts his chin out in a challenge. "Maybe she and I should meet up." He licks his lips. "I could have her coming on my cock in two minutes flat."

I'm going to–

"Hey, hey, hey." Joel is off the bed, holding me back before I can land my first punch. As usual, Tao is useless in his bed, fiddling with his Rubix cube like nothing is going on. Asshole better be putting money on me to win.

"Shut the fuck up," I growl.

"I'll leave a mark on her just like I left my handiwork on your chest." He's goading me. I know he is, but if he doesn't stop talking in the next two seconds, I will bash his teeth out. "Isabella," he sings her name.

I spring forward, regretting telling him her name a year ago just because he's good with a needle and ink. Joel's grip isn't as tight as it should be, and I slip away. He yanks me back by the arm, hissing, "Don't be stupid, boy. You gon' let him stop you from seeing your girl?"

An animalistic noise settles low in my throat. Screw him for being right. I didn't put up with and do all this shit for the past two and a half years just to stay back because of Rico.

Sensing that reason has gotten to me, Joel steps back. The smug grin on Rico's face almost makes me question whether it's worth not seeing Bella for a couple more months. Rico and I were getting along, and he just had to say stupid shit like that on my last day.

"Riviera," someone calls. We all turn to see the bored-faced guard. "Hands."

Joel slaps me on the back—not aggressively—and points a finger at my face. "You take care of her. Treat her right."

It's not like I'm going to do anything other than that. I grunt in response and grab my drawings of Bella—I'm not about to leave them here for them to jack off to. That's for me to do.

"Hurry up. I haven't got all day," the guard drones.

He can wait as long as he needs. Fuck him.

I push the drawings through the feeder cap, and he takes them without question, shaking it out to ensure I'm not hiding a shiv.

Tao finally drops to the floor when I turn around. He holds his hand out to me. I take it and pull him closer. "You're going to owe me two grand."

He shrugs. "We'll see."

Prick.

I narrow my eyes at Rico, daring him to say something.

He lifts a shoulder. "See you 'round."

I don't answer and push my hands through the feeder. The cold metal cuffs dig into my wrists, then he unlocks the bars that separate us, and I step out of the cell. I don't understand why we must go through these safety measures when I'm a free man today, but if having the shackles around my ankles and hands means I get to see Bella, so be it.

Back to holding my drawings, I look at my cellmates one last time and nod at them, then begin my walk toward freedom, passing whistling prisoners who bang on the metal bars in celebration. I don't need to look at the Vargas men to know they're glaring daggers at me. The Vargas "gang" is nothing but a bunch of disorganized idiots running around claiming they're Chicago's newest, scariest "cartel", when a majority of their drugs get busted one way or another.

Rico and Damien aren't worried about them, so neither am I.

One presses his head against the bars. "You better watch your back, *boy*," he growls. I think his name is Gonzales? I don't know. I'm bad at names. "Sleep with one eye open."

"Frightening," I deadpan, walking past without sparing him a second glance as I flip him the bird. "I've never heard that line before."

He's in here, and I'm out there.

It's not my fault they didn't pay attention to their shipment. They would have done the same thing if they had found someone else's coke.

Just as I'm about to leave the wing, I hear Rico yell, "Say hi to Bella for me, *hombre*."

Next time I see him, I'll break his nose.

There she is.

Fuck me.

She's even more stunning than the last time I saw her. I didn't think that was possible.

Hell, I thought I was going to die spending all this time apart from her.

She's exactly where I left her, tucked in her bed, cuddling her rugged Mr. Mickey Mouse doll. It's like she was waiting for me.

Bella doesn't need to worry about school anymore. There's no reason for her to still be under the same roof as Marcus and Greg. And yet, there she lies, waiting for me. My girl knew I'd come back for her, because I would never just leave her.

I'm not sure how long I've stood here, staring at her, familiarizing myself with having her bracelet back on my wrist after so long without it. She's so vulnerable like this, tucked under the blanket *I* got her, dark hair fanned around her like an angel, golden skin illuminated by the moon-light spilling in through the slit between the curtains. Her soft breaths fill the room like a siren beckoning me closer.

I'm helplessly drawn to her as I move closer with silent footsteps, careful not to wake her. There will be a time for that, but not today.

I let myself touch her face. Her skin is so smooth, so perfect. I may *make* art, but she *is* art made flesh. Every stroke, every color. *Masterpiece* doesn't come close to describing her.

Even with her asleep with not a care in the world, I'm entranced. There's nothing I wouldn't do for her. I'd die if it would make her happy.

At the risk of waking her, I kiss her lips. I need to feel them, even if just for a second. I need another reminder of how soft they are, and how sweet she tastes.

I can't help myself from pulling her plump pink bottom lip in between my teeth. For most of my life, I've seen her bottom lip quiver. I wanted to know what it felt like to nibble on it, whether I could feel it tremble as I take the rest of her.

I still when Bella stirs. A breathy sound leaves her, just like it did when I had her legs wrapped around me over two and a half years ago. It would have been so easy to slide her pants down her legs and make her shatter around me.

My cock strains against my pants. Every noise in my head tells me to throw my plans out of the window and steal her away now, figure the rest out later.

She's real. She's not just a drawing or a part of my dreams. She's flesh and bone, the only thing that matters. I can see her shape beneath the sheets. The curve of her waist and the arch of her ass.

It's almost painful to look at because of how hard I'm getting, seeing the outline of her body under the cover of darkness and her sheets. I'm pretty sure I wasn't this horny when I was a teenager.

No, actually, I was. I was probably worse. I used to be voice-activated. She'd laugh, and I'd be on like a light.

Unable to resist the urge, I slowly slide the blanket down her body. It's the tail's end of summer, so the nighttime chill is bearable—but not for Bella. I inhale sharply when I see her nipples poking against the fabric of her thin t-shirt.

My muscles tense. Does she walk out of her room like this? Has Marcus seen her like this?

Tearing my gaze from her for just a second, I find something that worsens the ache in my balls tenfold.

I don't think, I just do.

I grab her panties from the top of her hamper, settle over her, pop the button of my jeans, and slip myself free. I bite back a groan the instant the pressure releases, but hiss through my teeth when her pretty pink cotton panties wrap around my cock.

My balls tighten, and I stroke myself once, staring at her sleeping form, completely oblivious to what I'm doing. I grit my teeth and think about something else to stop myself from coming immediately.

Triumph Speed Triple 1200RS, that Italian guy's cooking videos, Bella ignoring me for almost three fucking years.

There's no warmth left on her cotton panties, yet I imagine her wearing them all day, making them all nice and warm as she walks around, goes to work, and makes dinner. Then, just before she sleeps, she leans back against her pillows and slips her hands down her shorts, playing with her pussy. She imagines it's me touching her, that it's my cock filling her tight little cunt.

I pant as I pick up speed.

She could wake up at any second and find me like this, getting myself off to the sight of her with her used panties wrapped around my cock. It almost makes me angry that she isn't waking up at all. She's not even stirring. Anyone could come in here and do exactly what I'm doing, and she wouldn't even know.

My grip tightens at the thought. Maybe I should wake her. Push myself up against her entrance and bite down on her perky tits. I could make her wake up screaming from pleasure or while coming on her face. She'd fight the second she's awake, then smile right before I claim her mouth and fuck her until she comes, crying out my name as she does it.

The very idea of it sets me over the edge. There's nothing I can do to silence my groan as I release myself into her panties.

I hunch over and pant, then hold my breath when she turns over and pulls the blanket over her shoulder. My high doesn't last long.

On her bedside table is the reason why Bella is dead to the world: Xanax.

Why is she taking it? How long has she been taking it? What the hell happened to her that she had to start taking prescription medication?

Annoyance zips through me as I glance at the window. What if it wasn't me who climbed through it? Putting a chair under her door handle will stop anyone from inside getting to her, but the ones on the outside are the real threat.

People like me.

My irritation flares as my lust-blind mind finally clears, and I notice more of her room. There are drawings on the walls, just like before I left.

I tuck myself back into my pants, pocket the panties, and take a closer look. They're drawings, alright. Not mine—*hers*.

Where my pen strokes are harsh, her graphite lines are soft. The proportions of the faces are spot-on, and the shading is blended and smooth. It's realistic—far better than my drawings.

I'm not sure if I should be jealous.

Okay, I am. Just a little.

Before I left, she wouldn't draw anything but the occasional doodle. Now she's out here sketching like she's been doing it since birth? I'm proud, but what the fuck? Who taught her how to draw like this, because it sure as hell wasn't me?

I pull myself away from the drawings and investigate the rest of the room. Other than the art and the supplies, nothing in this room has changed.

Oh, and the Xanax. Couldn't forget about those. I consider throwing the pills away. Though, she could just refill. But that's money she wouldn't spend on food or things for herself.

Later, I think to myself.

Soon, she'll know I'm back and coming for her. Then, I'm going to find out why she's been ignoring me.

And if she has, she's going to regret it.

CHAPTER 14

ISABELLA

THE DAY OF THE Incident

Roman: 22 years old – Isabella: 20 years old.

It's my birthday today.

Not that anyone remembers.

It's not like it matters anyway.

I'm three years older than when Roman left, but I feel I've aged at least ten years. They always said there is nothing worse than growing older, and I will live life chasing my youth, wishing for the day when I could drink as much as I want, party, and wake up without responsibilities.

I never had those four things, so I don't long for them. Sometimes I miss the girl I was when Mickey was around. The one who was delirious and incapable, who questioned everything in the name of insecurity, but nothing that really mattered.

157

It's kind of pathetic that I haven't felt a glimmer of happiness since the day he disappeared, and there doesn't seem to be any joy waiting for me in my future.

What's even more pathetic is wishing he'd taken my virginity before he left so it could be forever immortalized as the day I lost everything.

"Thank you, love," the customer, who has been eyeballing me since he walked into the store, says when I hand him the receipt. He drops his business card and smirks. "You should call me sometime."

I give him a tight-lipped smile. "Thanks."

He nods. When the door rings shut behind him, I drop his card in the trash without reading it. I found that one word works best. *Thanks*. Short, sharp, to the point. Say too much, and they think you're leading them on. Say the wrong thing, and they might kill you.

The joys of womanhood.

Marcus is getting bolder with his advances every passing day. It's only a matter of time until groping doesn't cut it, then he'll take another part of me I'll never get back.

He's developed even more entitlement now that I'm no longer property of the state. I live under his family's roof without paying rent. In exchange, I work at this crappy hardware store while Marcus and Greg work in the garage next door.

I want to leave. With every fiber of my being, I want to escape this horrible family and abominable city and never turn back. The only thing holding me back is the knowledge that, if I leave, there's no one to look after Jeremy. Millie is too busy most of the time, Greg and Marcus won't take care of him, and the state isn't doing jack about it, no matter how much I complain.

I'm losing more battles than I can win.

Scratch that; I don't think I've won a single battle in a long time.

One day, I'll get out of this god-forsaken city. I don't know when, how, or where I will go, but anywhere is better than here. I'll monetize any hobby I have, whether it's knitting, painting, or sculpting. I'll keep building on doing drawing commissions, and hope one day it'll be enough for something.

I may not have any college plans like Roman did with fixing up motorbikes and cars, but I have my own aspirations... of sorts. I want to live a life with a full heart. As immeasurable as it is, I'll know when I get there.

If I don't, I'll be a girl wasting away at a hardware store owned by a predator.

With no one needing me at the counter, I return to stocking the shelves. The place is rundown, with dreary brick walls and linoleum floors. The only good thing about the store is the big bay windows—with safety bars—mainly because of its metaphorical appearance. I pretend I'm outside, under the sun, and not a caged bird.

My days are monotonous. Wake up, make breakfast for everyone, work, make dinner for everyone, sleep, then repeat. But there are good days, too. Those are when someone pays cash, and I manage to pocket some of it without anyone being any wiser. Not much, though; five dollars here and there. Better than nothing when it's the only money I'm saving after buying food.

Stale cigarette smoke and diesel fuel assault my senses, and bile lurches up my throat when Marcus grabs my ass.

"These jeans suit you," he purrs in my ear.

The blood rushes from my body. He puts his arm on the shelf by my head, caging me in.

"One day, you're gonna want me back." He pushes his body against me, and I cringe back as far into the shelf as I can possibly go.

"I need to work," I whisper, forcing myself not to gag.

He disgusts me. Just because I live under his roof—his *parents'* roof—doesn't give him any right to put his hands on me. But I can't do a thing about it. I can't push him or tell him to stop. I can't scold him or give him a piece of my mind.

I slapped his hand away once, so he gave me a black eye in return.

He's a pig. The weakest people are the ones who lash out when they get rejected. That's another thing I've learned now that Roman isn't shielding me from the world. I don't forgive him for leaving, but it was the wake-up call I needed.

"You aren't working tonight." Marcus presses the bulge in his pants against my ass. "In fact, your bed's been pretty empty. You must be getting cold at night; I can warm it up for you."

I'd rather walk naked through the Arctic.

One day, he's going to break the bedroom door down, and my makeshift barricade won't stop him.

I swallow. "I'm okay, thank you."

Why do these men need to be coddled when being turned down? Why do *I* need to be polite when they're the ones who started it? Can't I just say 'no'?

Sorry, I'm alright, thanks.

Thank you for your offer, but I'll have to decline.

Please don't touch me—because you can't simply say *don't touch me.*

I hiss through my teeth when he fists my hair and yanks my head back. "You're going to stop saying no very soon, slut."

I bite my tongue to stop myself from lashing out.

When she wants it, she's a slut.

When she doesn't want it, she's a slut.

The biggest insult men like him can muster is telling a woman exactly what he thinks she is: an object that can be debased to the holes she has.

160

Fuck him. Fuck him. Fuck him.

And fuck Roman for leaving me here to deal with all this shit.

Marcus shoves me away as if I was the one who infringed on his space. I yelp and right myself before I lose my footing. My lungs fill with air, but it feels more like razor blades. And because I don't have a choice, I have to smile at customers and go about the rest of my day pretending I didn't just get assaulted. I have to live with this acceptance. I'm angry, but this is how my life is *for now*. I will get out eventually.

I used to think I was weak because of the stutter in my heart or the way it never feels whole. I thought I was defective somehow, like when God was making me, he shipped me off without putting me together the way he should.

It took losing Roman to realize I'm a survivor in my own way. Because this is what survivors do: they keep walking even if the sun is blazing or the sky cracks with lightning and rumbles with thunder. One foot in front of the other until, eventually, you can't walk anymore.

My heart is still broken, but I've let the shadows take up the empty space and gave it a name: *Rage*.

The phone rings, and I groan internally. I fumble with my mandatory work apron until my fingers wrap around the indestructible plastic brick. "Good afternoon, Barfoot's Hardware Store; how can I help?"

Silence.

"Hello?"

I know this game. No one is going to respond.

"Are you there?"

Nothing.

I shake my head and hang up. I've gotten a call like this almost every day for months. I don't hear any breathing like in the movies, nor weird static. Just silence.

Whenever I consider snapping at whoever is on the other side, I think better of it. With my luck, it could be one of Marcus's buddies trying to mess around and get me in trouble. So, I smile without my eyes and talk softly even when I want to throw up in my mouth and scream.

My own phone starts buzzing in my pocket. "Jeremy, is everything okay?" I say, answering the phone and checking to make sure no one is in the store.

"Yes." The speaker crackles with his sigh. "I'm doing my twice-daily check in."

I heard from him this morning when he wished me happy birthday and promised to make me breakfast once he's back. "Have they been feeding you properly? Are you warm enough? That teacher has stopped giving you a hard time, right?" I ramble on.

"Just like I told you yesterday, *yes*." His disinterest in this conversation is clear. "I'm fifteen, not five. I can take care of myself."

It's the biggest lie I've ever heard from him. If it weren't for me giving him my food portions and bedding, he'd be both starved and cold. Nor would he have a life if I didn't do most of his work in the shop. *Or* deal with Greg's belt on his behalf, and help him with his homework, and make sure he has clothes on his back.

He's fifteen and completely oblivious to everything I do for him. But I wouldn't change any of it if it means he laughs along with friends as he walks home, and he goes to sleep without bruises, not worrying about what the next day brings.

I refuse to end up like Millie, completely dead inside. But I refuse to let Jeremy grow up thinking he doesn't know what it feels like to be safe and loved.

I clear my throat. "What did you do today?"

That question seems to change his tone. "They made us do woodwork, so I made you a birdhouse. I painted it white so you can draw something on it. We also went— "

"Yo, Jeremy, pass the drugs," someone yells in the background.

"Shut up, man, I'm talking to my sister," Jeremy hisses at one of his friends, who bursts into a fit of laughter. "We went—oi, fuck off." I pull the phone away from the loud shuffling noises that go on for a solid ten seconds. "I'll call you later," he pants like he's just been wrestling someone.

"Yeah, okay. Let me know if you need anything, alright?"

"I'll be good, I'll—dude, I'm gonna beat your—" The line goes dead.

I shake my head and continue stacking the shelves. Nothing else of note happens as the hours roll by. Every day that passes seems to take longer than the last. When closing time finally arrives, I clean up, lock the door behind me, and pull the gate down to prevent any break-ins. Then, autopilot kicks in, and my legs take me home.

I pull my coat around me tighter. My feet are aching, and my back is killing me. The last thing I want to do is make dinner for Millie, Greg, and Marcus, but this is my life. I can hear my bed calling for me all the way from here. But even after everyone's plates are piled and tomorrow's lunch is made, I still have a commission waiting for me.

I'm behind on one of my character arts, and I kick myself every time I put it off. It's the only joy in my day, but sometimes I'm too tired to even breathe, let alone draw. It started as a passion project, and now it seems more like a chore on top of everything else.

The sound of scuffed boots, followed by movement from the corner of my vision, snags my attention. I whip my head around, my heart pounding in my ear. A hooded figure decked in black follows from one hundred yards away, partially illuminated by the flickering streetlamp. His stature looks familiar. A customer, maybe? That doesn't make this any better.

I walk faster as my pulse ticks up a notch. I know better than to zone out walking home at night. I'm too scared to turn around and alert whoever's behind me.

What if I'm being dramatic? What if we both happen to be walking in the same direction? But alarm bells are going off in my head, and my gut tells me to sprint. Still, there's that nagging voice in my head, though, saying, *what if you're imagining it?*

Just like I've imagined the feeling of being watched every day for the past who knows how long. Or how my clothes are disappearing—like I couldn't find my favorite shirt two weeks ago, and my good jeans have mysteriously vanished. Even things I swore I put away find themselves on the top of my table.

I fish my phone out of my pocket. I have no one else to call but the police, and they wouldn't get here in time. No one would. I'm on my own for this one. The reality of my helplessness has me picking up my pace as I thread my keys between my knuckles.

The sound of footsteps behind me grows louder. Whoever is following me is quickening, matching my pace. That's my answer. I'm not over-thinking. I break into a run, and so does he. Heavy boots pound down the pavement behind me, and I push myself faster.

No, no, no. I'm not ready to die.

Why was I so stupid? Why didn't I notice him sooner?

Another set of steps joins the first pair, and I push myself faster. Two people are chasing me. *Two.* I don't make it far before my lungs burn from exertion. Not once do I turn around to check how close they are. I don't exercise enough to trust that I won't lose my footing.

I turn down another street. Even though I can't hear them anymore, I don't stop until I'm in front of the house. My wheezing breaths come out in big clouds of smoke. Only then do I glance back at the empty road. Who were they? Will they come back? What if it happens again and I can't run fast enough?

I try and fail to get a hold of myself before I stumble inside, locking the door behind me with trembling hands, and checking it three times. Millie has started on dinner, and Greg is already in the lounge, beer in hand, while zoning out in front of the TV. Marcus is—I have no idea where he is. Locked away in his room, hopefully. Maybe I can get away with not seeing him at all.

Everyone in the house is completely oblivious to what just happened. I should call the cops or tell somebody. But who's going to care? Who's going to believe me?

The world seems to spin as I bolt up the stairs without a backward glance, passing Jeremy's empty room on the way to mine. Nothing makes me feel any semblance of ease until the door to my room is shut. I lean against the wood and force myself to count to ten.

My heart still hammers away in my ribcage, and I'm worried it's going to break bone if I don't get a handle on myself. Adrenaline crashing makes me sway. My exhaustion isn't just bone-deep anymore; I can feel it in my soul. I love Jeremy, but staying here is going to kill me.

I shiver from the cool breeze drifting through the room. With a defeated sigh, I push off the door and flick on the light. I alternate using my hands to rub my eyes and tug my jacket down my arms.

I blink away the fireworks exploding behind my lids, then stiffen.

A heart-shaped locket lies in the middle of my desk. The same one I took off a year after he disappeared. I haven't so much as looked at it since.

I didn't put that there.

I locked that thing away so I'd never see it again.

How the hell did it get there? Who came inside my room?

Rushing to the other side of the room, I yank open the closet door and drop to my knees to rummage around the bottom shelf, searching for the familiar fabric. When I can't feel it, I pull everything out and go through every single article of clothing. Roman's jersey isn't there.

Marcus wouldn't have known or cared that I hid it in Roman's hoodie. Millie wouldn't have been worried enough to do anything that doesn't serve her immediate family, Greg wouldn't have gotten off his ass for anything, and Jeremy isn't home.

If someone broke into the house, surely they'd steal stuff of value? Not... not something this specific, something just in my room. Did I sleepwalk or something?

"Isa, hurry up," Millie yells from downstairs.

I inhale sharply. "Coming."

My body clicks in three places when I haul myself onto my feet. As my back muscles protest, I do my best to ignore the ache. It's easy to ignore when my mind is still reeling from the appearance of the necklace.

I'll figure it out later.

I drag my feet to the door and cast a longing look at my bed. For the third time tonight, every inch of my body seizes.

Because on my bed are two Mickey Mouse plush toys.

One that my mother gave me and one I've never seen before.

CHAPTER 15

ROMAN

THE DAY OF THE Incident

"You did something very stupid." I grin.

The guy claws at my arm, gasping for breath. "I don't know—"

I tsk, silencing him as I tighten my hold around his neck, making the red hue of his face darken. "I think you do know. Should I give you a hint?" He nods, slapping at my arm in a useless attempt to make me let up. "You spoke to a mouse just now. Do you know what else you did?"

He blinks, then his eyes widen in realization. "Look, man, I didn't know she was taken. If I had known, I wouldn't have given her my number. I'm sorry, I—"

"Will never speak to her again," I finish for him, pushing my weight forward. "If you do..." I hum. "Do I need to finish that sentence, or do you understand what I'm saying?"

He nods frantically against my hand.

"Good," I mutter as I let go.

He hunches over and gulps in greedy breaths. I kick him once in the gut for good measure. Then punch him in the face for the hell of it.

"Fuck off. Make sure I never see you again."

A chorus of yeses falls out of his mouth as he scurries away, staggering and limping, leaving behind his shopping bag.

Fucking idiot.

With him sorted, I take my place by the empty house across from the store and wait for the time to crawl by.

My mood sours even more once I look inside the shop. If I thought my blood was boiling before, it's nothing compared to watching Marcus feel Bella up. Every inch of me is screaming to storm inside and murder him with the shit inside his own store. But that would ruin the plan. These past three months have been the greatest exercise of my patience and ability to resist my impulses. Finally, everything is set up for her, and I've found a place for Jeremy.

I mean, sometimes I don't resist at all. Even so, it'll all be worth it because tonight's the night everything changes.

Marcus finally dies.

After years, she will be back in my arms. I'm sick of watching her from a distance and hearing her voice through a phone. I'll get to actually *talk* to her. I want to touch her and have her touch me back. I want to have a goddamn conversation with her. Most of all, I want her out of that house and away from that miserable family.

Tonight, all my wishes are coming true.

I've made one fantastic discovery, though. My princess doesn't have a boyfriend. Never has, never will—other than me, of course. Not like it was an issue in the first place. It just means she won't cry over anyone if I take them out of the picture. There's only room for the two of us from now on.

The light coming from the store gives me a clear view of Bella—she's not Pigtails, because she has her hair down more often than not lately.

She moves behind the till, and my chest squeezes. Out of all the things she's done to scrub me out of her life, the fact that she isn't wearing my necklace hurts the most. She hid it away like I'm a dirty secret she wants to forget all about.

The only reason I haven't slipped it around her neck while she's asleep is because she's still wearing the bracelet. It's one of my few assurances that she hasn't forgotten about me, and she's still hanging on, even just by a thread. It isn't like I'd ever let her forget about me, anyway.

I've been taunting her with reminders of me. I expected her to squirm or dart around with fear burning in her eyes, but she just looks... hurt? Why the hell would she be the one to feel hurt in all of this? She's the one who ignored all my letters. *She's* the one who completely ghosted me. I'm the one who's hurt. Not her.

The lights go out in the store, and seconds later, she's coming out of the front of the shop. Bella starts walking in the direction of her house, head drooping with exhaustion, unaware of any surrounding threats.

I follow behind her, not so close that she can see me, but not so far that I can't see her.

My skin prickles with irritation when I spot someone else following her. It seems that an asshole with a death wish thinks it's a good idea to go near *my girl*.

Bella glances back and quickens her pace. The fucker following her does the same. He's really just trying to make my night, isn't he?

I smile in my excitement. The more violence, the merrier.

My blood runs hot as I close the distance, and Bella chooses that exact moment to start running. So does he.

Fucking hell.

I guess I need to sprint, too, then. They don't exactly have treadmills in prison, and running laps around the yard isn't quite the same as chasing someone into the pitch-black night. Now, I'm working on pure adrenaline. The exhilaration is intoxicating, and every one of my senses is heightened and focused on my prey.

Preys. Plural.

I bound along the pavement, no longer avoiding the light from lampposts. I have to push myself harder. He's fast—probably hearing me behind him—but I'm surprised Bella's even faster. I'd put that to being chased by two people.

When I near him, I crouch lower, and with a burst of energy, I tackle him to the ground. There's no one around to witness the fight. His hood falls back during his attempt to push me off him, and I kick my leg out, knocking his hand out from under him. Gripping his hair, I use the force of his fall to slam his face into the concrete.

I'm mildly disappointed by how easy it is. Why does no one put up a decent fight?

He groans, and I shut him up by slamming him again. Straddling him around his midsection, I lean down to wrap my arms around his throat. He gasps for breath and wiggles as I move closer to him to put him in a headlock.

This was easy. Too easy.

I don't notice his leg move until I'm thrown onto my back with a huff. My hold on his neck doesn't let up until his elbow makes contact with my ribs. Pain thunders through my side, loosening my hold on him. He takes advantage of the opening and breaks out of my grip.

"Fucking cunt," he growls as he turns, lifting his fist.

I laugh and lunge for him before he can punch me, and we both roll around on the ground like prepubescent children trying to get the upper hand. I manage to get him under me once more, laying hit after hit. If his face was bloody before, red is the only color on his skin now.

He doesn't stop trying to block me or push me off. Still, my attacks keep coming, one fist right after the other. Fury fuels each of my movements until his body goes limp, and he stops breathing.

I hiss from the pain in my side as I pull myself onto my feet. "Dickhead," I mutter and kick him in the ribs as payback. Looking around, I try to find a place to stash his body. The last thing I need is a bunch of cops snooping around the area because of him. That would put a kink in my plans.

I spot a rose bush behind us belonging to the nicest property on the block, shrugging to myself. I guess that's good enough.

Keeping an eye out for witnesses, I drag him by his hoodie into the shadows behind the roses. I made a mistake once about not checking for witnesses. I won't do it again. Shoving him under the rose bushes, I try to cover his body as much as possible. Whoever's grandma lives here better not look out the window tomorrow morning. Let's hope someone else finds his body first; if not... Rest in peace, Grandma.

A light layer of sweat clings to my back by the time I have him hidden away, and I'm itching to get back to staring at Bella. I crack my neck and head toward her house. She doesn't realize how long I've been waiting to make her all mine. I stop in my tracks right where I pummeled the guy into the concrete with a sudden thought:

Roses. Bella likes roses.

With the minimal light of a singular streetlamp, I pick the first flower I can somewhat see. I move closer to the lamppost and use my sleeve to wipe the man's blood off the petal. My feet automatically keep taking me in the direction I want to go while I focus on breaking off all the thorns.

I reach my car first, laying the flower on the backseat in exchange for my bag of supplies. I wouldn't be surprised if there's a skip in my step as I make the short trip to Bella's house, where I plant myself across the street.

And now I wait.

I tap my fingers in no particular rhythm on my leg, then bounce my foot on the ground. Bella's going to regret ignoring me, Marcus will regret touching her, and Greg will regret being a useless, perverted piece of shit.

As I stand and wait, the light from the TV flashes behind the curtains downstairs. Right above it, the lamp in Marcus's room is on. Excitement burns beneath my skin and grows the second the lights in Bella's room go off.

What I should do is wait for another half an hour until I'm sure she's asleep. Again, that's what I *should* do. Without a second thought, I cross the street. In a matter of seconds, my feet are on the porch railing, and I'm pulling myself up onto the awning. Her window is wide open; there's no way she won't hear me.

Quietly, I crawl up the side of the house, closer to her room. I'm counting the seconds until she sticks her head out and catches me, but it never happens. I frown, thinking she isn't in there. Peeking inside, I relax when I hear the sound of her steady breaths.

It's too early for her to be asleep. The thought that she worked herself to the bone today and fell asleep an hour earlier than usual unsettles me. From now on, that's going to change. She'll never have to work again if she doesn't want to. If being a trophy wife is the life she wants, then being a trophy wife is the life she'll have.

I help myself inside while keeping my footsteps light once my boots hit the floor. Her face is hidden beneath the covers, so I can't stare at her as I wait for the rest of the neighborhood to go to sleep.

Pulling out an empty duffle bag, I start piling her things into it. I pause after each sound I make, but she doesn't stir. With the bag nearly full, I leave it behind the door and make my way to the empty space next to her.

I don't take my eyes off the back of her head as I unlace my boots and slip beneath the sheets. The single bed creaks and barely manages to fit us both. For the first time, she actually stirs from her sleep. Just not how I expected her to. She turns over and settles herself up against my chest. The top of her head brushes the bottom of my chin as she cuddles into my shoulder. I smile to myself and wrap my arms around my sleeping princess. Her body still knows who I am.

I press my lips against her forehead, whispering, "Happy birthday, Bella."

Over the months, I've touched her face and her arms, but I've denied myself this. First, it was just soft brushes on her arm and stroking her hair. I was worried about waking her up, but I have become more bold over time. It's like she's dead to the world.

If I hold her, I won't stop wanting more. Even now, keeping my hands to myself is impossible when she feels like pure temptation, a sin of the highest power.

I keep asking myself why she didn't respond to any of my letters. Even at the risk of having Greg or Marcus open her mail, I sent them all here. She's not the type to ignore me, so why did she? Did she even try looking for me?

We stay like that even when Marcus starts snoring. I don't peel myself away from her until it's well into the early hours of the morning, ensuring there wouldn't be a soul around that's awake. She follows me as I pull away, and I have to stop myself from lying back down and putting my plans off for another day.

Thinking it'll help me with my resolve, I force myself to turn my back on her and put my shoes back on. My plan backfires when I realize her intoxicating scent is everywhere, making me breathe through my mouth like a goddamn animal. It'd be so easy to crawl back under the blanket and feel her little body pressed against mine. She does something to my head even when she isn't doing anything.

I move through the room so I don't get caught up again, fastening my mask and gloves and throwing the bag over my shoulder. Bella's makeshift barricade scrapes against the floor, instigating a cringe from the sound. I keep pulling on the door until everything she piled up is out of the way. Now the door's open, and there's nothing left to stop me.

It's showtime.

CHAPTER 16

ROMAN

The Day of the Incident

I'm in the master bedroom in seconds. Millie is fast asleep, just like I knew she'd be. She doesn't even flinch when the damp cloth goes over her mouth and nose. She'll wake up tomorrow none the wiser, if not a little disoriented, with a splitting headache.

Too easy.

Oh well.

One down, two to go.

Jeremy is going to be in for a shock when the state picks him up tomorrow after he returns from camp.

Greg's snores shake the house, which is why I don't bother to keep my steps silent as I trudge downstairs. He has absolutely no idea that I'm right behind him as he leans back in the recliner with his hands folded over his beer belly.

I loom over him, just gazing at him as if I were God looking at his creations. Damn, he's so ugly I almost feel bad for Millie. There's no way I'd survive if I had to see his face on top of me or willingly pop out a baby with his genetics. So, what I'm about to do is basically community service, something I, thankfully, didn't have to do along with my sentence. Everyone should be thanking me for getting rid of him and his piece of shit son.

With that thought in mind, I slip behind him on the couch, wrap a belt—the one I've seen him use on my Bella—around his neck, slot it through the buckle, and pull.

From my vantage point, I can see his eyes snap open as he automatically reaches for his neck to wrestle away the item stopping his breathing. His face burns red under the artificial light from the TV. I leverage the angle of the couch and use my weight to keep him right where he is.

I'm so fucking glad I've been gymming. Maybe I should consider going back to prison so I can really focus on my fitness. That would mean I won't have Bella, though, and that simply isn't an option in my book.

He's out within ten seconds, but I don't let up until I hit twenty. I want him unconscious, not dead, not for what I have planned for him.

My grip on the belt loosens as I step in front of him. The only sound in the house comes from the commercials blaring on the TV while I drop my gaze to his stomach and groan silently. This is the part I was dreading.

With a heavy sigh, I grab his ankles and pull. No, "pull" isn't the right word. *Heave* is more accurate. He lands on the floor with an unceremonious thump, and I drag him along the floor, then pause midway to stretch.

Okay, maybe I need to hit the gym more often, because I'm seriously struggling. The guy from earlier has nothing on Greg. The old man has to be at least two hundred and fifty pounds.

Inhaling sharply, I summon more energy for the home stretch. The momentary break from lugging him around is short-lived because I still have to get his big ass onto the stool.

I scrunch my nose and hold back bile when I lean down and basically bear hug him. The amount of body odor on this man is criminal. I'd kill him just for poor hygiene.

It takes me more tries than I care to admit just to get half his ass off of the ground and onto the chair. At this point, I'm more worried about blowing out my back than waking someone up from carrying around this asshole.

I get as much distance from him as I can once he's secured on the seat. What's tragic about this is that I can't open the window to get rid of his stench. Maybe I could hose him down?

No. No time.

Springing into action, I lay all my tools out on the table, tie him up, and slap a healthy length of duct tape over his mouth. Then slap him in general, just for fun.

Marcus comes next. Again, I don't bother keeping my steps silent as I storm up the steps. He'll be far easier to deal with than his father.

Quietly, I open the door to find him shirtless in his bed.

Marcus might be strong, but he's the type of skinny that you worry might fly away during the breeze. Back in the day, he used to be somewhat attractive—at least, that's what the girls would say. I don't see it; never really did, either. But I don't know where his father's genetics went because other than the big nose, they look nothing alike.

That was back in Marcus's youth, at least. Poor posture, crooked teeth, and greasy hair with a topping of predator make up what he is today.

Like I said, community service.

I rinse and repeat the process with him by using one of his own belts to knock him out. Getting him down the stairs is easy. He's so light I could probably throw him over my shoulder to make less noise. It's just so much more satisfying seeing his head bob and his body roll around helplessly when I throw him down the stairs.

I've always wanted to do this.

It doesn't take much to hang him from a beam while frantic noises sound from behind me. As if there's some father-son magic going on, Marcus wakes up before I have a chance to tape his mouth shut.

He gapes at me like a fish while his dad screams under duct tape behind me. "Who—What—"

I slap duct tape over his mouth. "Missed me, asshole?"

I hum to their begging, taking my time to walk up to the dining table where my tools lay on full display. My fingers dance, pondering which instrument I want to use tonight. Hammer? Pliers? Saw? Knife? The options are endless.

Knife, I decide. Can't beat the classics.

I push the blade into the tip of my finger without breaking my glove, glancing back at Marcus. I ignore Greg, who's uselessly trying to get out of his restraints, desperately screaming until his face flushes in rage.

I remove Marcus's tape. "Roman. You're—you—" He stumbles over his words. His attention darts to the knife in my hand, and the color drains from his skin. "You shouldn't be out."

I grin and cock my head to the side. "Shouldn't I?"

Fuck yeah, I shouldn't be. I don't know how the hell Rico's lawyer managed to shave half a year off my sentence, yet here we are.

He gulps, and the rise and fall of his chest becomes more obvious. "You still have three months."

My brows hike up—not that he'd be able to see past the mask. I *may* have left the part about my freedom coming earlier than expected out of my letters. "And how would you know that?"

"The letters you—" He shuts his mouth.

There it is. "Did Isabella share them with you?"

He doesn't respond, but I know the answer is no. Bella wouldn't share them with him—or anyone—unless someone held a gun to her head. I creep closer until the blade grazes his skin. He jerks away from the knife, only to swing right back to me. "Look, man—" he stutters.

"What did you do with the letters?" I ask in a friendly tone, focusing my attention on the knife as I swirl it over his skin.

He squirms. "I don't remember."

I click my tongue. "Are you sure you want to lie to me, Marcus?"

"I swear, I—"

My hand clamps over his mouth while I dip the blade into him. Blood blossoms beautifully against his pale skin, despite his thrashing and pathetic attempts to get away. "Do I need to ask you again?"

He shakes his head and mumbles something. Greg continues his fruitless struggles to save himself and his son behind me. If I don't wrap this up soon, they're going to wake Bella.

"I'm going to move my hand, and you're going to be a good little boy and not make a peep unless I tell you to. Isn't that right?" I say as if I were speaking to a child.

He nods like a blubbering mess.

"Where?" The one word makes him shudder.

"Under my bed," he whimpers as crimson drips from the wound on his stomach.

I stiffen. *Excuse me?* Is he saying that he took my letters away from her or that Bella never received them to begin with?

"Tell me, Marcus." I speak as if I'm amenable enough to reason, like there may be a possibility he walks out of here alive. "What are the letters doing in your room? And I wouldn't lie if I were you." I wave the blood-stained knife in front of his face as a warning.

Tears well in his eyes while switching his attention between me and his somewhat unharmed father. "We, uh." He takes a ragged breath. "We saw Isa got mail, and we, um."

I don't need to turn around to know that Greg is shaking his head. "Yes?" I graze the tip of the blade along his chest.

"We—we were going to throw them away, but we decided to keep them," he says quickly.

I cut an inflamed glare at Marcus before turning my attention to Greg. "Is that true?"

When he doesn't answer, I press the blade against Marcus's chest, and he nods quickly.

My pulse pounds relentlessly in my ears. After all these years of thinking she threw me away or forgot about me... *she never forgot about me*; she never got my letters. I can't help but laugh. She wasn't ignoring me. She doesn't hate me. She isn't mad at me. She just had no idea where I was. Bella's waiting for me.

The two men glance at each other while I continue laughing. The sound dies in my throat when I look at Greg, my eyes narrowing on the belt wrapped around his throat.

I left her unprotected, and she was hurt because I wasn't there.

Because of them, she thought I left her.

I grit my teeth and rip off a piece of duct tape from the roll and slap it over Marcus's mouth. "You two?" I chuckle, lacking any humor. "Oh, you two fucked up real bad." They both start screaming when I tear Greg's shirt open. "Do you know what you did?" The two men thrash and mumble as I grab the belt from around Greg's neck, pulling my arm back and swinging down so the buckle comes down on his bare chest, splitting his skin in two. "You put your hands on her." I bring the belt down again with an audible whip. "You kept her from me." *Again.* "You hurt her." *Twice this time.* "You treat her like a slave." *Three times.* "You talk down to her." *Four.* "What do you have to say for yourself?"

He sobs and says something behind his tape.

"I can't hear you." I cup the back of my ear. "Nothing? Alright." I keep beating him with his belt, alternating between the buckle and the tail. "Does that feel nice, Gregory? Do you like the way your belt feels?"

He cries out in pain and fear as he shakes his head.

"You know what I think? I think you like it." I turn to Marcus, saying to Greg over my shoulder, "I think your son might like it, too." I laugh at the tears streaming down Greg's reddened face. "Come on boys, the show is just getting started."

They shouldn't have touched Bella.

They shouldn't have looked at her.

They shouldn't have fucking breathed near her.

Marcus swings away from me, but there's nothing he can do to get out of my range. There's nothing anyone could do to stop me as I slice each and every one of Greg's fingers and Marcus's dick off, or as I buckle the belt around Greg's neck. I step back and look to make sure that Marcus is watching as Greg—his father—dies, slowly losing oxygen.

"Don't worry," I say to Marcus with a shrug. "You're next."

He sobs as my knife pierces into him, leaving another trail of blood down his body. The sound of floorboards whining behind me rips me out of my blood-crazed haze, back stiffening in anticipation. I jolt back from Marcus and spin around with the knife raised and ready to attack.

Bella.

Dropping my arm and the knife to my side, I rip off my mask. Even with her hair standing at odd angles and her brown eyes puffy from sleep, she's gorgeous. I move closer, wanting to feel her. Now I know she wasn't trying to hurt me; she wasn't trying to pretend I didn't exist.

But she isn't looking at me; she's looking at *them*.

Is she admiring my handiwork? Is she happy they'll never be able to come near her again—that I saved her?

"I'm sorry, Princess," I say softly. "I didn't mean to wake you."

She looks at me for a fleeting second, instantly looking away, causing a pang to go through my chest. There's not an ounce of surprise or happiness on her face, nothing that could suggest she's even remotely glad to see me.

I step in front of Marcus's hanging body, so she has no choice but to look at me. I want to know exactly what she's thinking and why she looks like she's wishing I weren't here. Easing closer to her, I decide that I want—no, *need*—her to know I'm real, I'm here for her. I'm never going away again. First, her bottom lip trembles. Then, the tears well in her eyes, and a sob rips through her little body.

I would get shot in the chest again just to stop her tears.

She's in my arms before I realize I'm moving. "No, no, shh. It's okay. Don't cry, alright? I've got you." My girl is too beautiful to cry over those pieces of shit. It's all over now. Red smears across her cheek from my thumb, and the sight of her covered in my favorite color makes me feel more deranged.

She shoves me. "Don't touch me," she pleads.

"You were always a heavy sleeper." I chuckle even though it hurts. Bella missed me as much as I missed her—I know it. She's only reacting like this because I'm a little dirty now. I mean, the number of times Bella has seen me covered in blood is well over double digits, so it's nothing new, but the substance covers me more than usual.

She loves me, and she's glad I'm back.

Marcus screams, ruining our moment. Her eyes snap away from the smile on my lips when I nudge the handle of the knife into her hand. "Would you like the honors, Princess?"

After everything that piece of shit did to her, she's the one who should have been beating Greg with the belt he used on her, the one carving into Marcus until he bleeds out. It's infuriating contemplating how much they might have done that I haven't seen. I've watched as Bella barricades her bedroom door just to get changed, thinking, '*What the fuck did they do to her to make her listen about the chair?*'

She has every right to take from them when they've taken from her without asking. She deserves their blood and so much more. I did this for her.

Her vengeance.

Her liberation.

Her justice.

After this, she'll know what freedom feels like. She'll know what it means to never be alone again. We'll be *together*. We can do this together.

Bella sniffles, looking anywhere but at me. "Where—Where's Millie?"

That wasn't the answer that I was hoping for, but I realize she has a soft spot for motherly figures, even if said figure is a bitch. "She's okay."

"What does 'okay' mean?" I reach for her, but she steps back, shaking her head from side to side, taking in the room. "What have you done?"

Not once have her almond-shaped brown eyes focused on mine. I just want her to look at me. Why won't she look at me?

Wait. No. Why is she fighting me, resisting everything I'm doing—and have done—for her? I've spent every day of the past three years trying to get back to her. I thought she'd be happy to see me. She's *meant* to be happy to see me.

183

"What have you done, Roman? What—what is this? What are you—I can't do this. *I can't do this.*"

Roman.

Roman. Roman. Roman.

That's not my name, not to her. It sounds wrong on her tongue—feels wrong—like she's talking about a stranger, not the person who hasn't left her side in fourteen years. The very same person who has made sure she was warm and fed and never felt alone or afraid. The one who would do *anything* for her.

I try to hold her still and reason her with my stare, but she still won't fucking look at me.

Just fucking look at me, Bella.

"Deep breaths, Bella. Don't look, alright? Just focus on me."

"No. *No!*" she screams. "You're crazy. You're fucking *crazy.*"

"I prefer the term 'artist.'"

She's shocked. I get it now: this is a lot for her to take in. I've kept this side of me hidden from her, so it's only natural.

Bella blinks and leans back like she's just been hit. "What is your fucking problem? Why are you here? You left, so you should stay gone." Each word drips with malice.

I run my tongue over my teeth. I'm telling myself this is a completely normal reaction to have, and once all the bodies are out of sight, she'll realize that it's me: her Mickey. The love of her life.

"Go back to bed. I was hoping to finish up without disturbing you." Another half-truth. I was hoping to kill them without her witnessing all the steps I took to get there. Only after I was done cleaning myself of the pigs' blood would I wake her so we could drive into the night, pretending I hadn't just killed her foster dad and brother or that I had "left" her for years.

Bella's expression turns seething, and she finally looks at me. "Fuck you, Roman. I hate you."

No, this is wrong.

This is all wrong.

This isn't how any of this is meant to go.

Shocked. She's just shocked.

Bella just needs a couple more minutes, and then she'll run into my arms and ask me to take her away.

"You don't mean that—"

"*Leave*. I don't want you here. I don't want you here. You're a monster," she hisses, not a single doubt in her voice.

I rear back, but I'm never going anywhere again, regardless of what she says. Cupping her cheeks in my hands, I wipe away her tears. "It's me, Bella. It's your Mickey."

Say my name, Bella. Just say my name. I need to hear you say it.

She doesn't say anything, keeping up her futile attempts at fighting me off, throwing weak punches and kicking her legs like she has every intention of injuring me. "I don't know who you are anymore," she growls.

"Bella—Bella, please. It's me. Mickey. I'm *back*. I'm going to get you out of here." My lungs contract, and it's getting harder to breathe.

No, no, no. She doesn't mean it. She doesn't mean it.

"You abandoned me!"

I didn't. I didn't. I didn't.

Those fucking letters. If they gave her the letters like they should have, we wouldn't be having this conversation right now. This is their fault. Marcus and Greg, the fucking pricks. I wish Greg was still alive so I could kill him all over again, bloodier this time. "I know. And I'm sorry, I—"

"Sorry," Bella echoes breathily. "*Sorry?* You're sorry? *Sorry?* You don't get to be sorry! You don't get to come here and act like everything is alright.

Do you know what they did to me? You left me for *dead*, Roman. You're a coward. A fucking coward!"

Bella, please. Bella, you have to understand. Bella, fuck—I can't live without you, Bella.

My skin burns. My lungs burn. My heart *burns*. I didn't want to leave her. She's mine, and I'm hers; that's all there is to it. Doesn't she understand that I didn't want to leave her, and all I'm doing right now is my apology to her for hurting her—us?

Her words sting more than the bullet did. When she cries and pushes me away, it's like she's taking a knife and twisting it right through my ribs and into my heart.

It's like she doesn't believe me.

It's like she doesn't *want* to believe me.

"I can't believe I trusted you and gave you all of me. I regret ever laying eyes on you. I regret speaking to you. I regret ever meeting you."

I feel sick to my fucking stomach. I was wrong. This wasn't Greg's or Marcus's fault; this is *my* fault. I caused all of this. I'm the reason for her tears and the anguish in her eyes. Even though she doesn't want me right now, I pull her into a hug. It's nowhere near enough, but I'm not giving up on her.

"I hate you, Roman. I fucking hate you. You're the worst thing to happen to me. I hate you. I hate you. I hate you."

Bella doesn't mean it. She can't mean anything she's spewing in her rage. We've been through too much together, and I'll spend every day of the rest of my life convincing her that she *doesn't* hate me.

"I'm sorry. I didn't want to leave you. I'm back. There's nothing else that will separate us now." I mean every word. She has to know that. I never had another option but to follow her wherever she goes. Slowly, Bella calms, and I kiss her forehead. "Wait here. I'll be a second."

It kills me to leave her downstairs, even if it's just for a minute. I was separated from her for too long, and all those years when we were kids living under two different roofs made me hungrier for her.

I run up the stairs and to the bedrooms to get everything I need, moving as fast as I can to get back to her. I'm not worried about leaving Marcus with her because if what she wants is to set him free, then so be it. I've marked him enough to make him regret the day he was born.

When I get back downstairs to find Marcus tied up and bloody, pride fills my chest. My baby girl is as murderous as me. She knows what will happen unless she steps in, and Bella's permission to have my way with Marcus is all I need as I taunt him and destroy his skin before I take his life.

Pure adrenaline thrums through my veins as a crimson waterfall pours from his throat and splashes against my clothes, soaking the black fabric through until I feel the warm liquid on my skin. The sensations spur on my natural, animal instincts, and the smell of iron heavy in the air turns me into a savage monster. Maniacal laughter bubbles in my throat, and I want to let it out. My muscles itch with pent-up energy.

A shuddering breath sounds from behind me, and it's as if my ears perk up in interest as my body becomes attuned to the prey in my midst. My heart thumps rapidly as I slowly turn toward her. My sweet Bella. Mine, all mine.

Our eyes meet, and electricity lights up between us, setting the primal beast clawing inside my chest on fire.

And like the perfect little prey, she runs.

An ear-to-ear smile creeps across my face. *Tag.* Oh, this ol' game. How I've missed it. I've always loved a good hunt. But this chase sends a thrill through my taut body that I've never felt before. I know this catch will taste especially sweet.

Her fear permeates the air as I stalk her through the house. It's the most intoxicating scent I've ever smelt. *"Bella,"* I sing when she rounds another corner, slipping and scrambling on the blood-slick floor like her life depends on it. My cock strains from the sight, imagining all the ways her smooth legs could wrap around me.

I keep a few paces behind her so she thinks she might actually get away. I can already picture the way her eyes will set aflame when I catch her, and the sound of her whimpers when I take what is mine.

My smart girl manages to get to the door before I close the distance between us, clicking my tongue as she tries to fight me. "Got you."

I pull her against my body, wrapping my fingers around her slender throat, feeling it vibrate as she begs, "No, no! Let me go!"

A snarl rumbles through my bones as a match sparks inside my soul. Every cell in my body is telling me to mark her, lay claim to her, sink my teeth into her soft skin, and never let her go until she's a willing victim in my trap.

Her pulse races against my fingertips, matching my own speeding heart. "You know better than to run from me. Predators love to hunt," I whisper against her ear, relishing how a violent shudder racks through her body.

"Roman, please."

I could come right now, just from the sound of her pleading. I want to find out all the ways I could make her cry out.

"God, I love it when you beg," I groan, pulling her hips against mine so she understands exactly what she does to me. I can feel her soft ass through the thin material of her shorts, and there's nothing I wouldn't do to rip them off her and sink into her tight little cunt. "Do you realize how fucking much I missed you? I was going insane thinking about you."

I scrape my teeth against her skin, licking and lapping because I can't get enough of her. I feel like I haven't eaten in three years, and she's my first meal. How did I survive this long without her? No rehab could get me away from the hook she has on me.

My hand descends along the smooth skin of her stomach, pressing my aching cock against her tight ass. She shivers against me, and I almost groan into her neck. "You taste like every sinful thought I've ever had."

Bella knows how to get out of this—she could scream for help, but she wants me as badly as I want her. I can smell her desire for me just as I can smell her fear.

Fuck.

I can't do it anymore.

I can't wait any longer.

I need to feel her.

Bella buckles when I dip my fingers inside her, and for a second, I think I'm going to finish in my jeans then and there. She claws at my arms like she's begging for more, and I'm only too happy to provide.

"Just as I thought," I rasp. "Fucking soaked."

"Don't! Let go of me, Roman," she cries.

Never.

"Don't let go of you?" I laugh sadistically. "Oh, that was my plan. You're all mine now."

She squirms, moaning when another finger slides into her. She can fight me all she wants, but she's drenching my hands, squeezing me like she doesn't want me to run away.

She wants me.

She wants me. She wants me. She wants me.

"Do you know I was thinking about *you* all that time away?" I lick her skin, curling my fingers inside her needy little pussy. I could die happy inside of her. "I was going crazy thinking another guy laid a hand on you. Do you know what that does to me? Thinking that someone else is

189

touching what's *mine*," I snarl against her hot skin, heady from how she clenches around me as I move my fingers. "I kept wondering if I consumed your every waking thought, just like you consume mine. I kept thinking about what you felt like in my hands, all the little sounds you made. Fuck, and how fucking divine you felt beneath me."

I nudge her head to the side, and she doesn't fight me. *Good girl.*

"My memories could never compare to the reality of you. Don't you realize you were made for me? We were made for each other." My voice comes out hoarse, because it's taking everything in me not to push her against the door and fuck her while I'm wearing someone else's blood.

She whimpers, moving her hips against my fingers, chasing her needs like she knows only I can fulfill.

"Say it," I whisper. "Say my name." I need to hear her call me Mickey so I know I have her—that I haven't fucked up beyond repair.

She shakes her head like she wants to deny me, but rides my fingers like she wants to own me.

I rub her clit, pushing my cock against her grinding hips. "You're so wet for me. Does your cunt miss me? Do you need me to get on my knees and taste you, so you can see the evidence of how much you want me all over my lips?"

Her lips part, and her heavy breaths fill the air, along with the sound of her desperate pussy taking my fingers. Fuck, she feels better than anything I could have ever imagined.

"So beautiful," I murmur.

Her flushed skin reddens beneath me, but she doesn't fight, sinking her nails into me like she's trying to root me into place. My hold around her neck tightens in answer, promising her that I will never leave her again. I chuckle inwardly; Bella is wearing a collar made of my hands.

"You're so breakable like this." I smirk, flexing my fingers around her neck so she knows she will always wear me. "Completely at my mercy."

I slow the movement of my fingers and watch her set on fire as she growls in frustration.

"Tell me you want me, and I'll let you come."

"Go to Hell," she bites out.

Fiery little thing. "You'll be right there with me. You're my favorite sin."

"I'm not going anywhere with you." She sounds so certain. Her body knows better, though, as she angles her hips like she's trying to chase my fingers.

"Hmm," I muse. "So feisty tonight."

The little princess jumps when I flick her clit, making me laugh. But it doesn't stop her from coming right back to my fingers, jerking around like she's trying to get friction so she can come all over me.

My chest rumbles against her back. "It wasn't a suggestion. You seem to have forgotten our promise."

The tip of my finger dips inside her, and she throws her head back with a moan as I sink my teeth into her tender skin. She squeals in pleasure, squirming around in my arms, grazing her ass against my aching bulge in the process.

"I'll forgive you for forgetting. I'll just have to remind you who you've always belonged to. Let me make it up to you."

She cries out when I sink my fingers inside her again, squeezing her eyes shut as her chest rises and falls like she can't breathe. I circle her clit with my thumb, making her arch into me, grabbing at my skin like she needs me to keep upright.

Suddenly, the walls of her pussy spasm, and warm heat pours over my fingers, dripping down to my wrist and coating my sleeves. The feel of her is enough to kill a better man. "You'll regret letting me feel your cunt coming all over my fingers. I promise you, next time, I'm breaking you on my cock."

"There won't be a next time," she says, panting.

"Don't doubt me, Isabella."

I'm going to make you come on me every day for the rest of your life.

But before then, you're going to say my fucking name.

CHAPTER 17

ISABELLA

PRESENT

The vibrations from the car and the steady caress of a warm hand keep lulling me back to sleep. My consciousness stirs when his hand disappears, and I peel my eyes open when I hear the sound of something flickering. I angle my head to him just as an orange flame lights Roman's face and the embers of a cigarette come to life.

I scrunch my nose. "Why are you doing that?"

He gives me a sideways glance and lifts his shoulder. "Something I picked up."

I shift my legs to point toward the window, stopping midway to fix the blanket draped over me before I remember that he tied my hands. Right. *Dick.*

"It's gross." I try to inch my legs as far away from his as I can as a small act of defiance.

"Keeps my mouth busy." He takes a long drag and lowers the window to exhale. "Don't you like it?"

I look at him, dumbfounded. "Didn't I just say it's gross?"

Amusement is written all over his face. "You never used to be this snarky."

"Abandonment and betrayal do that to a person," I snap.

I'm not sure whether it's exhaustion, trauma, or character growth, but I'm not in the mood to deal with his shit. Day in and day out, I've kept my mouth shut at work and at home. The rage and frustration have built until it's overflowing, and I don't want to hold it back anymore. Especially not toward the person who helped create me.

I was nice to him and every other male I've encountered, and look where it got me? Harassed, assaulted, and tied up in the front seat of a beat-up car. If my *snarkiness* shocks him, then great. He's been taunting and playing mind games with me for how long now? Add that to the fact that he *left me* right after earning the title of 'my first kiss' on my birthday—of all days—*upset* is an understatement.

Oh, let's not forget that he *murdered my foster family* while I was asleep upstairs.

He's always been great at avoiding the consequences of his actions, but here I am: *consequences*.

Unfortunately, anger and frustration are an ugly look on me, as I'm just now learning that the combination of all my bottled-up emotions makes me cry. Not the pretty, dainty cry, either. No, it's the ugly kind of crying where you can't breathe, and snot is running from your nose and into your mouth, so you'd rather no one is around to see.

Fuck him.

Roman's throat bobs and his lips thin. The cigarette goes flying out the window and he grabs a stress ball, pretending like the car doesn't reek like Greg did.

"I tried getting back to you." He sounds tired. Good. He deserves to be. Jerk.

I sniffle. "Whatever."

It's freeing, not living life with the sole purpose of pleasing him. I have no desire to impress him or seek his validation. That ship has long since sailed, and the only thing that's worth my time is my own opinion.

"I started reading." I can see his lopsided grin out of the corner of my eyes. I don't want to give him the satisfaction of looking at him properly. Or seeing my silent tears. "By myself," he tacks on.

"Good for you," I bite out.

It wasn't like I was planning to go back to the *good ol' days* when I'd read to him. *Or* talk to him like we're the bestest of friends and sit in the middle of the field while he braids my hair.

I angle myself even farther away from him until my knees hit the door. Droplets of scorching tears fall onto my t-shirt as I force myself to stare out of the window to focus on the gloomy trees.

My nose chooses that moment to sniffle and give me away. Tension crackles in the air between us. "After everything that's happened, you must feel—"

"I feel nothing."

He makes a noise at the back of his throat that tells me he *definitely* believes me. "Then why are you crying?"

I whip my head to face him and meet his stare. "Fuck you."

"Tell me how you feel."

Like the pieces of my heart—of my life—I put back together after he left have shattered all over again. "That is no longer any of your concern."

"It is my concern, and it will *always* be my concern. Now answer the damn question. How do you feel?"

"Fine."

The car screeches to a halt on the side of the road. His calloused fingers grip my chin, so I don't have a choice but to look at him. "Never lie to me."

"Why?"

"Hit me, scream at me, fucking shoot me if it makes you feel better—at least I know that feeling. But you don't keep your feelings in, and you sure as fuck don't lie to me. Got it?"

"Fine."

Slowly, he says, "I understand you're confused about—"

Is he fucking kidding me?

"*Confused?*" I echo. "I'm not confused. I'm devastated. I'm angry. I'm hurt. I have every right to be! And I'm not going to apologize if that upsets you."

"Good."

I stare at him blankly. "Excuse me?"

"You shouldn't be apologizing for your feelings."

And yet, all my emotions have given me is more pain. "I wanted to feel less. Then I did. And I realized that feeling empty hurts more than feeling full." Maybe the problem wasn't having emotions. It was caring too much.

I hate that I care about Roman.

I hate that I'm not even sad that Marcus and Greg are dead.

I hate that I'm not more upset that I've been taken away from the only life I knew.

"It'll get better," he says, with too much certainty.

"I don't believe you."

The look Roman gives me is full of promise. "Question whatever you want, but don't you question what I would do for you."

I scoff. "Yeah, like *leave*? I believe that."

"It's late." He puts the car back into drive and gets back on the road, effectively dismissing me. "You're tired. You need rest."

Here I thought we were almost getting somewhere. "That's what you say to a toddler, Roman. I'm an adult—a woman."

"You can't even drink yet," he mumbles under his breath.

My mouth opens and then closes. *Asshole.* He has a point, even though I'm furious about it. You know what? At least I'm not crying anymore. Nothing smart or snarky comes to mind, and the best move I have is to give him the cold shoulder. I lift my bound wrists and throw out, "Congratulations on the child abuse, then."

His knuckles turn white on the steering wheel. "Get used to it, because one day you'll be begging for me to tie you up."

Heat flushes my cheeks.

Actually, no. Fuck him. He can't just barge back into my life and start with the innuendos. My bound hands unbuckle my seatbelt before he can realize what I'm doing. Just as my hands reach the door handle, a steel grip yanks half my body to face Roman and over the center console, yelping when his warm lap meets my face.

I grunt and huff frustratedly, attempting to wrestle out of his grip, but he holds me in place effortlessly. The handbrake digs into my ribs, and the angle he has me in makes my hips ache.

I thrash harder, the car swerving when I bump the wheel. Roman rights the car with a single hand, his other one moving from holding my bound arms to tangle in my hair, chuckling to himself as if almost dying amuses him.

"I like you feisty." He tugs at my hair, but keeps me in place. "It makes me feel all...hot and bothered."

My breath catches in my throat when my body's awareness turns on, and suddenly, I really wish I didn't stupidly think I might be able to escape. Something solid and hard, hidden beneath his jeans, presses against my shoulder, right by my face.

"Gross," I squeal before stilling. I wish I did find it gross. I really wish I could. But the combination of our compromising position with the memory of his fingers inside me hours ago is still fresh in my mind. My body feels like I'm waiting for the main course after a satisfying appetizer.

He laughs. "Why'd you stop?"

"What?" The viciousness I was hoping for is nowhere to be found in my voice. *Worse*, I sound like the sixteen-year-old version of me who lost all reason when he was around.

His fingers curl tighter in my hair, moving my head around like he's testing out his grip and my compliance. I try to jerk away or push against him, narrowly avoiding the wheel and *very much* touching the hard *thing* that I should *not* be thinking about.

"That's my girl," he rumbles. "Keep moving around like that, and I'll have to pull over."

He lifts his hips so it's pushed closer to my face. "Roman," I warn.

"You tried doing something really fucking stupid. This is your punishment."

Against my will, my body relaxes the second he starts massaging my scalp.

Traitor.

I wiggle around to throw his hand off, but stop breathing altogether when his dick twitches by my cheek, followed by his deep grunt.

"This Bella is so much more enjoyable," he says, more to himself than to me. "We're going to have so much fun together, you and I."

I bite my tongue from the rush of heat throughout my body from his words. Anything I say will make him talk more, and the subtext of his comments might be the reason I implode.

Even though I don't respond—not a grunt or a nod—he keeps blabbering about anything and everything. Current events, music, his exercise routine, and the latest bike models he has his eyes on.

My non-existent abs strain and my hands are asleep by the time the windy roads turn to gravel, the car tipping from side to side, vibrating and shuddering from the uneven terrain. My attempts at keeping still are proven useless as my body is jostled around in his lap. I'm stuck between a wheel and a hard place, with Roman holding me in a way that guarantees I hit the latter every time I'm bumped around.

The car stops, and he removes his hand from my head. I try to clamor away from him using my bound hands, reaching for the door handle before he can change his mind about letting me go.

"Ah-ah," he taunts, grabbing my arm. "I hope you weren't thinking of running." The gravel in his voice sends my blood soaring.

Groaning, I try and fail to pull my arm back. "Did you think I would just stay with you?"

He drops his head to the side, a slow, saccharine smile spreading across his face. "I don't *think* it, I *know* it."

Looking out at the window behind me, I breathe in sharply. Indigo light covers our surroundings, casting an ominous glow onto the gnarled trees and overgrown greenery.

Familiar gray weathered boards stare back at me. Though the abandoned house looks completely different from the one in front of me, I remember coming here three years ago. Spider webs and mold no longer decorate the outside, the broken wooden planks are fixed, and the windows are exposed without any slats covering them. Insects buzz, cutting through the crisp morning air and my stupor as I stare at the house, then back at him.

"Let's get you inside, Bella."

I can't say anything as he comes around to my side of the car with a duffle bag over his shoulder. He wraps the fallen blanket around me—as I remain mute and stupefied—and leads me to the entrance. He's taking me into a creepy farmhouse... I should be yelling and screaming right now, begging him not to make me go in there.

I can barely get enough oxygen to my lungs, let alone say anything.

The boards beneath my feet have been scrubbed clean, the silver handle of the door glinting in the dawn as the key glides in smoothly, and Roman pushes the door open without a single squeak.

My feet follow as he guides me deeper into the place and plants me onto a chair. But my brain is struggling to comprehend what I'm seeing. There isn't much furniture, just a couple of kitchen appliances, a dining table with two chairs, a love seat, and a pile of wood beside the fireplace. A few bottles of soda and energy drinks are scattered throughout the space, and empty takeout packets squeeze into the black plastic bags. The place smells like him: sandalwood and cinnamon.

It smells like home.

Although it's what *isn't* here that speaks volumes. Just like outside, there aren't any cobwebs or dust. Patches of plaster and cut-up boards dot the walls, covering holes. The place isn't just repaired; it's lived in.

The cold settles into my bones, and a violent shiver tears down my spine. Perhaps it's from the realization that this is where he's been the whole time. Three hours away from me in the place where I last spent time with him.

The edges of my vision blur with tears. I've spent the last three years bitter, sad, and hurt while he was out here, living his life as a—what?

Lumberjack? *Farmer*? What the hell was he doing out here all this time? What made him decide to become a hermit?

Honestly, I wasn't sure where I thought he might have disappeared to, but I had some ideas: He left to live in another city with a baby momma or Cassie, or maybe he joined the mafia. I even thought he went for a ride and got lost or crashed and died.

Whatever it was, I didn't deserve the radio silence that I received.

"I'm sorry, I didn't want to do this," Roman whispers, voice veiled with strain.

I snap my attention down to him, scowling at him on his knees in front of me, untying my bindings. He's still the most attractive man I've ever seen, even covered in my foster-family's blood. The screwed-up part of my brain *likes* that there's blood on his face. Blood that's only there because of me.

"But you did it anyway."

Being in this place is messing with my head. I don't know when he started fiddling with the ropes or when I decided to talk to him, but now I'm starved for answers.

He moves the ties from my chafed, burning skin, making me hiss.

"Sorry. Does it hurt?" he mutters again, undoing the knot. When I don't answer, he says, "You left me no choice."

I snatch my arms away and finish untying myself. The skin isn't as raw as I thought, but there's no missing the divots the rope left behind. "Don't give me that crap. Do you know how many choices you had other than the ones you made tonight? You could have talked to me, sent me a text, oh, or I know, not ghosted me for three years."

Roman twists a jar open, and I narrow my eyes at it.

He gives me a smile that I can't quite decipher the meaning behind. "You're talking a lot more now than you did before I left, so I'm going to say you're a lot smarter now too."

"Don't patronize me."

"I'm not," he says like it's obvious. He reaches for my arm to apply the balm, but I don't let him. "You and I both know you're a different person now. I'm exactly the same, and you know goddamn well there was no way either of those two fuckers would continue breathing after the shit they did to you."

"Oh, I knew if you were around, you'd do something about it. But don't go telling me that you haven't changed. The Roman I thought I knew wouldn't have waited three years to step in."

"I couldn't," he says through gritted teeth. "And I wasn't ready yet."

"You know what?" I take the balm out of his hand and drop the ropes onto his lap. "I don't want to hear it."

He grabs my hand when I sidestep him. "Bella, wait."

"What?" I snap.

He digs into his pocket and drops my inhaler into my outstretched hand. "Two puffs, morning and night."

I bite the inside of my cheek. After three years, he still remembers. "I can take care of myself."

"Can you?" He says it playfully, but all I see is red.

"I'm still here, aren't I?" It comes out sharper than I intended, and his flinch makes me feel bad about it. Regretting my words should be the last thing I do after what he put me through, but I've always hated seeing Roman hurt or upset. Especially when it's over something I've said or done, when he's only ever tried doing right by me. At the start, at least.

I can't let it get to me. I've come too far and been through too much to be thrown back into the hole where I couldn't live without Roman and his approval. Three years without him, and I'm physically better than ever. My mental health is another question.

This time, when I pull away, he lets me take a couple of steps. "Bella—"

I spin on my heel. "What now—"

His arms close in around me before I have a chance to jump back, fingers threading into my hair and face nuzzling into the crook of my neck. I go stock still, engulfed in the smell of iron. What the hell am I meant to do, pat his back? Tell him it's alright? Knee him?

I should be doing the latter, but it's taking every ounce of strength not to dissolve into his hold and hug him back. I know that if he keeps holding me, the ugly tears will come back.

"I'm so fucking sorry for hurting you. It was never what I intended. I'll make it up to you, I promise." Sincerity oozes from every word, and I'm not sure if I'm a fool for believing him.

Silence blankets us as the seconds tick on, his warmth seeping into my very core. There's more to the touch than just a reprieve from the cold; it's every night we spent together, curling beneath the covers, watching random videos, leaning on his shoulder as he draws while I read to him, and cuddling up to him as he talks about everything and nothing.

It feels like everything I lost three years ago that I never thought I would get back. I'm angry at him for ruining all of it, and I'm angry at myself for wishing we could go back to the way we were. But I'm not that girl anymore, and I never will be again. He made sure of that.

I let myself enjoy his hold for one more second, then I take a step back.

"I need to shower." What I'm actually saying is I need to feel warmth that isn't coming from him. I'm also hoping that he has plumbing set up so I don't need to take a bath in a stream or something.

"Your stuff's in our room."

My stuff? What stuff?

Wait. *Our* room?

I walk faster, deciding that investigating is more important.

The room in question is nothing like the rest of the house. Where the lounge was barebones, this place is covered in drawings. Some are by him. Some by me. Some *of* me. The dates on his drawings of me span the last five years. He has too much pride in his drawings to write the wrong date.

Mismatching side tables sit on either side of the bed. On the right, closer to the door, an energy drink, knife, bottle of cologne, and random screws and bolts are strewn on the bedside table. On the opposite side, an inhaler, a single unopened box of tissues, my favorite hand cream, and a stack of romance books.

His and hers, just like the two dressers in the room. One with clothes sticking out of drawers and body spray on the top. I move closer to the other, where a mirror, hair ties, and ribbons are stored away in glass containers.

Tentatively, I open each drawer, one by one, until my heart sinks to the floor. When I get to the bottom row, I pull out the pair of jeans lying at the very top of the pile—the very pair I couldn't find this morning.

With shaking hands, I search both drawers for everything I need to shower, but come up empty. Grumbling, I grab the first t-shirt and sweatpants I find, then dart into the bathroom next door. The faint smell of smoke wafts through the house, but it doesn't overcome the smell of sandalwood and cinnamon clinging to the walls of this place.

How long has he been here? Why the hell did he bring me here? He doesn't seriously think that keeping me prisoner will work out for him, right?

I don't like that last question. I'll fight and argue with him, but how long will it last until I'm back to the girl from before who looked at Roman with rose-tinted, heart-shaped glasses? My mind is at war between the memories of the last three years and the eleven before them, while my body craves his affection, a slave to his touch.

The only upside I'm letting myself see right now is that there seems to be plumbing in this horror house. The downside is that there's no shower, just a ceramic bathtub that looks as old as time itself. Steam fills the room within seconds of me turning on the faucet.

I use the time waiting for the tub to fill to do a double take at the shampoo and conditioner under the sink. He got the same brand I use. It's clear Roman has planned his kills and my stay. I'm scared to know what else he has in store for me.

There's no window I can climb out of to make a run for it. Even if I got out of here, where would I go? The first time I came here, I didn't see any houses for miles. It's not like I can get the car keys off him, either. Plus, in my t-shirt and shorts, I'll probably die of hypothermia before I find any sign of civilization.

The heat of the water thaws my muscles and makes my eyelids grow heavier, but I still feel cold. Fool's hope is thinking this is all a bad dream. I'd be lying to myself because the only good dreams I've had in the last three years have all involved Mickey.

The feeling only gets worse as I slip into the clothes I grabbed in my hurry to get away from him.

My fingers trace the cold metal handle of the bathroom door, and I count to three, summoning as much strength as I can, because all I want to do is lock myself away and pretend that nothing beyond these four walls exists.

Steeling myself, I turn the handle and open the door into my new hell.

CHAPTER 18

ISABELLA

"You brought me everything except a bra," I snarl, hands on my hips as I stare Roman down in the kitchen. Any evidence that he was just covered in another person's blood is gone.

His grin spreads from ear to ear while he shrugs playfully. "Did I? That's unfortunate." Red burns my cheeks as he licks his lips, dropping his gaze to my chest, then back up. "If you need someone to hold them for you, I have two *very* capable hands right here."

I clear my throat and fold my arms like it might make his hungry gaze disappear. "A bra, Roman. I need a bra because it's cold."

The fireplace and thick hoodie are nowhere near enough to compensate for how aggressively my nipples are pushing against the fabric from the chill.

His smile falters, but he recovers by shooting me a wink. "I can tell."

"You're not allowed to look at them." I make myself as small as possible, wishing I sounded more assertive.

The corner of his lips hikes up. "Is that so?"

"Yes." I raise my chin and look him dead in the eyes in defiance.

He stalks closer, and a slow, mischievous smile crawls across his face. "Careful, it would be so unfortunate if your panties were to go missing as well."

I narrow my eyes. "You wouldn't."

It's useless trying to ignore how close he is and how small I am compared to him. I'm caught in the web of his ravenous stare, the brush of his chest against my folded arms, freezing me in place.

He could bend down and kiss me or pull me into his hold for the third time today. The worst part about this is that my brain will scream at me, just like it is now, to run away from the predator in the black hoodie, but my body will develop a mind of its own.

"Try me."

A lump lodges in my throat. There's one thing that hasn't crossed my mind since he came back: what he said to me three years ago. He was waiting until I was eighteen to seal the deal.

I'm twenty now, and they aren't empty threats or mindless sexual jokes. He means everything that comes out of his sinful mouth.

I breathe a sigh of relief when whatever he's cooking in the pan starts hissing, releasing me from my trance. My freedom is short-lived when I become transfixed with watching him move through the kitchen, opening cupboards and dishing plates. Tension lines his jaw, but there's an ease to his motions, as if he has finally let his guard down.

"I promise you that you will never go hungry again." I catch a glimpse of the well-stocked pantry, but I don't say anything. "Sit." He nods to the bacon and eggs on the table.

My protest drowns when my stomach grumbles. Eyeing him warily, I plant myself on the seat. The ire in my veins soars to a new high as he drags the chair from across the round table to sit by my side.

I narrow my eyes at him as he plops down and pretends like he isn't so close that our chairs are touching. "What do you think you're doing?"

"Eating," he says with a full mouth. "You should too."

Whatever. I'll allow this because I'm hungry.

My hand stills when it's halfway to my mouth, a sudden terrifying thought coming to me. Who's to say he didn't slip some poison into my food? What if he knocks me out, and I wake up chained like a dog?

Not missing my hesitation, voice low, he says, "Eat the damn food, Bella."

I drop my fork onto the plate. "You could have poisoned it."

His brows hike up to his hairline. "And you think I would ruin perfectly good food by doing that? It would be easier to just use a rag or syringe."

"If you're trying to convince me that you haven't tried to poison me, it isn't working."

He grins, only making me feel worse. "Just eat the food." When I don't, he rolls his eyes. "Do you think I would try to kill you after everything?"

"I don't know. Do I need to give you a recount of the past twenty-four hours?" Tugging up my sleeves, I show him my wrists and the faint outline of the rope.

He exhales loudly and reaches over and helps himself to my plate. "See," he says, bringing the fork to his mouth, chewing quickly, then swallowing. "No poison. Now, eat."

Satisfied I'm not about to get drugged, I eat my breakfast, all too aware of his body close to mine. Every time I try to scoot my chair away, he drags me back to where I was. Even when I'm on the very edge of my seat, trying to put as much space between us, he smirks and shuffles closer until we're practically sharing a single chair.

"Stop it," I snap.

"Just let me love you," he teases.

He meant it innocently, something for the both of us to laugh at or for me to fume over while he giggles to himself. But I'm not laughing, and fuming doesn't begin to describe it.

"Love me? What a fucking joke, Roman. You *left me*." I was compliant and complacent, letting my emotions bubble and boil. Now I'm exhausted and infuriated. There isn't an excuse in the world to justify what he did.

I jump to my feet while glaring at him, hoping he can see that I want him to get up. I want to yell and scream. He has said many things tonight, but none of them answered anything. I want him to know that my soul hurts, and I don't forgive him.

"Do you know what they did to me when you left? All the shit I had to put up with because I didn't want to leave Jeremy alone with them? Marcus would grope me. I'd stand in the shower and hear the bathroom door rattling because he was trying to break in. I'd drop a plate and Greg would beat me. And that's not even all of it!" I yell. "You promised me, Roman. You fucking promised that you wouldn't leave me—that I'd never be alone. You said no one would hurt me. You told me no one would touch me. You're a liar, *Roman*. I can't believe I trusted you."

I wish I could want him to suffer for everything he's done, but I can't. The reality is that hurting him will only hurt me, too, because I feel the sorrow that flashes through his eyes, and I can taste the guilt pouring out of his heart as if it were my own.

I want to hate him—I even said I hate him—but looking at him right now, sitting at eye level with my chest, what I'm feeling isn't hate; It's something much worse.

"I didn't have a choice. I tried so hard to get back to you." He's already said this before, but it still means nothing to me. If he meant it, he would have done as he wanted and stayed with me. "Just sit down and let me explain."

"I'll stand."

"Sit down, Isabella." The sudden burst of rage vibrating from him has me flinching and doing as I'm told.

Even though his anger isn't directed at me, my life of obedience replays through my head; every time Greg told me to get a beer, every time Marcus told me to sit by him, and all the times Maxim and Mikhail have laughed as they ransacked my bag, or when other kids would tell me to say certain words back when I still had a speech impediment.

'No' was never an answer because 'No' meant that I was asking to be struck.

I'm so tired of living like this, with my tail between my legs, scared of loud noises, and grateful for any scraps thrown my way, but I don't know how to heal myself.

He rakes his hand through his hair. "I was in prison."

Everything around me stills. "What?"

"After I dropped you home, I paid those twins a visit. I got shot and went to prison for two and a half years."

I stare at him, mouth ajar. There's no humor on his face, nothing to suggest he's lying. "But... I tried calling you the next day?" are the only words I manage to form.

"I was in the hospital for a long time."

"I... And..." I shake my head, my labored breaths making it harder to think. "This place?"

"I had a lot of time to plan what to do."

Everything should be clear, but I don't understand any of it, like I'm looking through a window on a cloudy day. "You never got in touch."

"I sent you letters, but Marcus hid them, the fucker."

"You never forgot about me," I whisper.

"I could never leave you. There is no me without you."

I keep waiting for the punchline or the joke, but it never comes. "You never called."

"You changed your number."

"You had a lawyer." They—or the police—could have told me.

"I didn't want to get you involved during the investigation."

I gawk at him. "So it was better that I was kept in the dark?"

"You never looked or tried to find me." It's his turn to make the accusations.

"I didn't think you'd be in *prison*!" I all but scream. "I checked your house, your work, everywhere! Your bike was nowhere to be seen—I thought you rode off without me."

"I wasn't *just* in prison, actually." He shrugs. "I was in the hospital."

What he said earlier finally sinks in. "You got shot," I echo, staring at the patched hole in the wall in front of me.

"Mmhmm. In the chest." I snap my attention back to him, and he has the audacity to look smug about it.

"You could have died?" I don't know why I can't string together more than a few words. He can't be telling the truth, can he?

He nods, looking even prouder of himself. "They thought I wasn't going to make it, but the thought of leaving you alone pulled me through."

No.

This is a lie; he's a liar.

He could have done so much to make sure I was okay. I spent days thinking he was dead, crying and suffocating under the weight of my guilt for being so angry at him.

Wait... the twins were away from school for a couple days after Roman disappeared. They looked worse for wear when they came back, but I didn't think anything about it.

Two and a half years for assaulting—wait, would they have been minors? That can't be the whole time.

My eyes widen. "Did you break out of prison?" I hiss under my breath as if someone might hear.

Throwing his arm over the back of the chair, he grins. "I got out early on good behavior."

Bullshit. "You don't know the meaning of that word."

"I had good incentive." Out of nowhere, under the dim light, his face hardens. "You left me too. Don't forget that."

Oh, *now* he's angry? I bet he's been holding on to that for a long time.

"I didn't have a choice!" I was twelve and had to follow my guardians wherever they wanted to take me.

"And I did?" he counters.

I throw my hands in the air. "Absolutely, you did."

"I love you, Bella. I never wanted to leave you, and I sure as fuck didn't want to go to prison." His livid stare sears into me, and I can't look away.

"I don't know what you told yourself, but you don't love me, not really. You care about me, or maybe you're obsessed, but you don't love me." *Not in the way I love you*—or did.

There are many kinds of love, and I loved him in every single way. *Loved*. Past tense. Although, I don't think I know the meaning of the word, anyway.

213

"If you did, you wouldn't have done what you did. You would have thought about me before going to the twins."

"You're the reason I went there. *You're* all I thought about." He speaks calmly, but there's no missing his barely restrained frustration.

"No," I bite out. "Don't put that on me. You went there for yourself, too. You needed something to get off on, and you wanted to feel like you were doing something right. You did it because you wish someone was there to do it for you."

He stays silent, which is somehow worse than his anger. If we were both screaming, maybe I wouldn't feel bad for cutting into him. There would be something to make both of us bleed and become casualties of our own making.

But I shoved the knife in, and for the first time in my life, I'm going to twist it. Even if it hurts me too. "Actually, I should be thanking you."

His brows lower. "Why?"

"Because I realized I don't need *you*. I needed to learn how to be myself and be thrown into the water without anyone saving me. I learned I can survive without you."

I don't pull away when he reaches for my hand this time. "It was never about needing someone to save you. Everything has always been about having someone else there to make living a little easier." He pauses before continuing, "You never needed me. You needed someone to love you for who you were. I love you—all of you."

I swallow, not wanting to acknowledge *those* words. "I survived the past three years without you."

"It's about more than just surviving."

"We need to go back, Roman," I whisper. "There's no one to look after Jeremy, and I have all my commissions I need to do."

214

The smile he gives me is almost sad, but hopeful. "I organized for a decent family to take him in and packed all your supplies into your bag. We're staying here."

"I want to call him. He'll be getting home from camp and he's going to freak out."

"I'm sorry, Bella."

"I *have* to call him. I need to make sure he's okay," I insist.

He takes a deep breath. "The police will be monitoring his calls. They could start looking into him or take him out of his home."

I feel stuck between a rock and a hard place. I don't want Jeremy to worry about me. "Where is he? How did you manage to get him a place when I've been trying to get him out of there for years."

"An old woman I know named Margaret has a free room and an endless supply of Pop-Tarts," he explains, even though it doesn't make any sense to me. "Just give it a couple more weeks and I promise you can call him, okay?"

"Fine." I stare at the space between us, counting the grooves in his wooden chair. This conversation isn't over, but I don't have the energy to deal with this right now.

The chair groans and skitters back across the floor when I get up. "I'm going to lie down. Please, don't come into the room."

Because I know he came into mine these past few months. The mornings smelled of sandalwood and cinnamon, and I thought my mind was playing tricks on me. I know better now; like I know that every morning I'd wake up hoping it wasn't my imagination.

CHAPTER 19

ISABELLA

AMETHYST LIGHT POURS THROUGH the slit in the curtains, casting long shadows across the room. Objects take shape, clearing and solidifying the more I blink.

Faces come alive in the sketches lining the walls, staring down at me as I sink deeper beneath the covers. The heavy blankets aren't enough to keep my lungs from burning with each inhale of frigid air.

A loud whack clears away any prospect of going back to sleep. My muscles groan as I peel away from the warm bed, examining the room.

I'm not sure what the logic behind my thoughts is, but ever since I got here, I haven't needed assistance to get to sleep. I never took Xanax religiously. There was just an added comfort of having it beside me to take whenever I thought I'd need it. Yet, when I got here, it didn't even cross my mind. Instead, I've caught up on three years' worth of sleep in two days.

Roman didn't come in after breakfast yesterday, or when he dropped food and snacks in front of the bedroom door today. There was also a single red rose that showed up. It had a weird stain, but I still left it on my bedside table.

His scent is woven into the fabrics all around me. Though he's not in the room, one thing in this room is his tell: the heater in the corner.

Roman's respect for my personal space usually ends where my physical well-being begins. Any attempt at abiding by my request for privacy—or even pretending to abide by it—would be thrown out the window the second he sees I've turned off the heater.

Another whack forces me out of bed. I angle my head toward the noise beyond the window and muster the emotional and physical strength to tear myself from any semblance of comfort. Goosebumps erupt on my skin when the blankets fall away, and I've never moved so fast to shove on more layers.

The frigid air makes my lungs rattle in my chest, so I reach for the inhaler waiting for me on the bedside table, and inhale two deep breaths of the medication.

I trace my fingers over one of Roman's jerseys I've kept for the past five years. The tag has been cut off, as he does with all his clothes. Tracing the bleached orange lines, I still remember how he bit his lip and huffed and puffed about painting his favorite black hoodie with bleach.

Sucking in my cheeks, I tamp down the memories and look around the rest of the room, my shoes lining the bottom of the wardrobe floor, the rose on my bedside table, and the drawings of me all over the walls.

Suited up, though far from mentally prepared for whatever the rest of the day has in store for me, I leave the room. The fireplace rages in the living room in front of a mountain of pillows, cushions and blankets. A plain white sheet now hangs on the wall above a projector.

I open the door with one last solidifying—and maybe dignifying—breath. The frozen air assaults every inch of exposed skin, almost causing me to tuck my tail and run back inside. Winter is a few months away, but I could be convinced it's here now.

I am many things, but I am most definitely not built for the cold. I am wearing four layers, and I still think I might die.

And then there's Roman in a thin, form-fitting long-sleeve.

Fuck him and his warm blood. And his thick forearms and defined shoulders, along with his slender waist, how the veins in his hands move as he grips the wood, and how his inky black hair whips around his face. Or how he grunts with each swing. And—oh God, why does he have to look so good chopping wood?

I've seen him elbows deep in grease, head in an engine, breaths heaving as his muscles ripple and tense, and—images of blood splattering across his face ruins whatever fantasy I had playing around in my head. For good reason. The last thing I need right now is to be lusting after him.

Mickey looks so out of place here. He's got that bad boy biker thing going on, and he's also a piercing short of falling into the rocker category.

Another cut of wood joins the pile on the ground, making the pieces tumble over. Butterflies erupt in my stomach when he looks up at me, eyes shining as he smiles. That's the thing about Mickey: his eyes will meet mine in a crowded room every single time.

Wrapping the jacket tighter, I rock on my heels. "I don't know much about fireplaces or natural heating, but I'm pretty sure you've cut enough to last an entire year."

It's too easy to fall into how we once were and forget everything that came after. Though his response pulls my head back into reality.

"That's the point."

Roman Riviera isn't a flannel and overalls type of man, and I sure as hell am not a gumboots and chicken coop type of girl. I am *not* staying out here for a year.

"So what? I'm meant to just live here? Live off the land?"

Amusement is drawn all over his face, but he averts his gaze back to the wood. "I have a car if we need something, and my bike's in the shed. No one is coming back for this house. The world is ours," he says coolly, as if there is no other possible answer.

"I can't live with you. I can't share a bedroom with you. I can't—"

"Why not?" he asks, lining up another chunk of wood.

"We're just—"

The ax comes down, splitting the trunk in two, then his searing eyes snap up to mine. "Call us friends. I dare you."

My heart ricochets against my ribs. "I have a life." Another whack thunders through the clearing, and I flinch.

I look at the ground, hearing how weak I sound. What life? The only person who *might* miss me is Jeremy. There's nothing there—in that town or home—for me.

"Do you want to run?" The deep tenor of his voice rattles my bones.

I match his steps. He moves forward, and I move back until there's nowhere left to go with the house pressed against my back. I'm prey, falling perfectly into the predator's trap.

"Run, Princess." His breath fans my face. "Don't let me catch you."

Falling victim to his snare, I'm unable to do anything but stare into crystal eyes. Ones that have gotten me through countless meltdowns and filled the space my parents left behind. I'm enraptured by the shape of the same lips that have told me how beautiful he thinks I am and filled the silence so I don't need to listen to my own screaming thoughts.

Tender hands wrap around the back of my neck. Not to hold me in place, but to remind me just how helpless I am to him.

The warmth emanating from Roman is better than any fire, and he could make me burn hot with a single word. Just like he has with the reminder of the last time I tried running from him.

Frigid air kisses my skin, and a shiver travels down my spine. "Honestly..." I say breathily. He leans forward, lips tipped upward in excitement and satisfaction. "I've run more in the past forty-eight hours than I have since high school P.E. Please, not right now."

I expect him to manipulate me into a cat-and-mouse game or make my insides swirl as they did when his fingers were inside me. Instead, a different type of heat unfurls in my belly as he throws his head back and laughs.

It's a stunning sound that ripples through me like a poison, one that hurts every level of my being. I never thought I'd hear that sound again.

Ruining the moment, my body spasms from the onslaught of cold, and I duck out from under him before he gets the chance to fawn over me.

I'm a grown woman. I can deal with a little cold.

Or a lot.

Whatever. My point still stands.

"What do you think you're doing?"

I roll my shoulders back and bend my knees, piling as many pieces of wood as possible. "Whatever I want."

The heat of his stare burns into my back. "Okay, Miss Independent, pile half of it over there, then get your ass inside and out of the cold."

As much as I want to prove myself to him and keep piling up, my ass very much wants to get inside. Scrambling to stack the wood, I all but run inside and start another pile next to the fireplace. I hiss as the last one falls to the very top. This is why I can't live off the land. Stupid things happen, like getting a splinter while cleaning up.

I'm pulled onto my feet before I can inspect the damage.

"Let me see," he says as he grabs my hand.

Miss Independent in me curses as I surrender control to him. Having someone else look after me feels so foreign, yet familiar. I shouldn't like it, but I do.

By what has to be magic, he gets the splinter out on the first go, and then looks up at me with so much concern—as if I was the one who got shot.

"Thanks," I mutter and pull away from his orbit. Shoving my hands in my pockets, I stare at the pillows stacked on a fluffy rug. Where do we go from here? I can't live this type of life when there's so much I haven't seen. I refuse to exchange one prison for another.

"Are you okay?"

The look on his face says that he's asking about more than just my finger or if I've defrosted from my short rendezvous outside.

Sighing, I sink down onto a pillow, and he follows suit, stationing himself directly across from me at an arm's reach.

"No, Roman, I'm not." He cringes at the name. "You can't expect me to forget the last three years."

The vermillion light from the fire colors the sides of our faces, heating our skin. I shed my jacket and fold it to the side.

"Let it out."

I suck in a breath. "I was hurt, and I felt betrayed. But most of all, I was so angry at you. *Furious.* I knew you would leave me eventually, but I didn't expect you to do it when you did." I stare at my empty hands. "I spent so long being angry that I realized I was actually feeling grief. In my eyes, you died, Roman. But in my heart, you were living a life without me." My vision blurs as I look up at him. "I thought the sadness would last a lifetime."

We all have demons. He happens to be mine.

"Why would you think I'd leave you, Minnie?" His voice wraps around me in a tight embrace, and the nickname wedges itself inside my heart. I'm sure I would tell him anything that he asks at this moment.

"Isn't it obvious?" I laugh dryly to myself. "Everyone leaves me."

"Not me," he says. I fix my attention to our intertwined hands. "Never me."

I don't want to tell him all the other reasons I thought he'd leave. If he's the type of person to discard me for another woman or something as trivial as age, then I should be glad he left. No one deserves that sort of treatment.

Do I tell him that, deep down, I know he'd never leave me—now, at least? Part of the reason he was in prison was because of me. Then every second since he's gotten out has been dedicated to me. From my favorite snacks in the cupboards, to the soaps, and my Mickey Mouse doll that appeared on the bed after my shower. Hell, even doing up a whole house just for us.

"I should be grateful for becoming stronger since you left," I start, because he needs to hear it too. "But am I supposed to be happy that I lost a part of myself to become that way?"

He squeezes my hand. "I disagree." Frowning, I look up at him. "You didn't lose yourself. You found the part of you that was built to survive. The part you thought you lost is still there; it's learning and waiting for you to let her out again."

The voice that usually screams at me to fight is silent when he pulls me onto his lap and wipes away a fallen tear. When did he become such a therapist, anyway?

"I've grieved so much; for my mother, the father I never had. I kept thinking it wasn't right, that they should be here by my side, keeping my heart full. But life gives, and it takes." My bleeding heart hates the truth,

223

and it aches every day. But maybe saying it out loud will make my heart understand the real world. "It wasn't right, but it's what it's meant to be."

Slowly, he rocks us with his arms wrapped around my waist. He's heard me talk about my missing parts before, but he's never been one for words. Not really, at least.

His soft breaths ruffle my hair as he says, "There's no point living if you don't feel alive. I'm going to make you a promise; you're going to wake up every day knowing that your heart is full and you have someone who will never leave your side. It'll be my life's goal to make you so happy that you shit rainbows and eat butterflies. You'll never live feeling like you need more."

"Please, don't hurt the butterflies." We both chuckle half-heartedly, and a sad smile curls across my face. "I always knew you would carry a part of me with you wherever you go." I bite the inside of my lip and continue, "Because you took it from me. I knew you cared about me and lent me every piece of your heart that you had. But there's a quote I once read: *Even if it is full of love, all a ghost can do is haunt.*"

He rearranges us so that his eyes bore into mine. Calloused fingers wrap around my wrist to bring my hands to his face.

"Do you feel me, Isabella?"

I nod.

"I am skin and bone, living and breathing. I am not a ghost. Most definitely not to you."

My fingers move on their own. At my touch, his eyes slide closed as he shivers. Stubble prickles the skin beneath my hand, traveling up his cheek and over his jaw.

Opening his eyes, he says with a pained whisper, "I missed you so much, Bella. I woke up every morning, counting down the minutes until I could go back to sleep so I could see you." Soft, dark hair brushes against me as he lowers his head to mine, taking all the air from my lungs. "In prison, I couldn't keep anything physical. No pictures, no bracelets, or drawings. But everything reminded me of you, and I finally understood the meaning of *looking under the same moon*."

"*What?*" Roman Riviera doesn't quote classic literature.

Wearing a grin, he shrugs innocently. "I told you I started reading."

That's life with Mickey: easy. He gets into the deep end and always finds a way out. But there's one thing I almost forgot; he's always kept me afloat.

"R-18 books?" I ask, plucking at the carpet.

A smile cracks across his face, and the old wooden floor creaks beneath our weight. "We call that contraband in prison." His hot breath feathers against my ear, sending a shiver down my spine. "But maybe those books of yours taught me a thing or two."

My red cheeks greet him as he pulls away with a mischievous grin, running a hungry eye from my chest to my unblinking eyes. Rising to his feet, he offers me his hand.

"Come on, let's make dinner."

I hesitate. Just for a second, but it's enough for him to notice. The tiny flicker of hurt morphs into a place where only darkness lies, making me question whether I made the right choice by taking his hand. But how could something bad make my heart feel so light? It's beating without sound, pumping blood without pain. It's freeing.

We move around the kitchen, completely in sync, knowing who's cutting, cooking, or seasoning without needing to say a single word.

This time, when Mickey pulls my seat next to his, I don't try to move away. Not when he cups my chin to face him, either. I'm starved for his touch and willing to accept whatever crumbs he's willing to give me.

"They deserve what they got," he says suddenly, expressionless.

225

I breathe in slowly and nod. He doesn't need to say exactly who he's referring to because the answer is everyone he's ever hurt in my name. "They did, but what will I ever learn if you keep fighting my battles for me?"

His expression turns into one of disapproval. I snap upright, not expecting when he grabs my legs and drapes them over his thighs, acting like this is a perfectly natural thing to do at the dinner table. I shouldn't live for simple things, like touching each other under the table.

"You shouldn't be in a battle to begin with. Wars aren't fought alone."

I shouldn't like a lot of things about Mickey, but when he says words in a way that seems like I'm the only thing that could ever matter to him, I'm ready to be any girl he wants me to be.

Even if it hurts me.

I can't let myself be that person anymore.

Metal clinks against porcelain, and I mutter, "I'm broken, Roman."

It doesn't matter what he says about being this amazing, beautiful person in his eyes, I don't see it. And I'm tired of living inside of a shell.

"But you're not fragile," he says pointedly, lacking the somber tone I feel in my heart.

"Despite everything I've gone through, I'm still a girl missing her mother." I narrow my eyes at him. How can he pull me from my emotions with the curl of his lips? Try as I might, this man still owns me. "Why are you smiling?"

"Because you know you're not *just* a girl."

I shake my head, hiding behind a curtain of fallen hair. He's doing it—wearing down the walls I built around myself to keep me safe. Each time he speaks, he reminds me why I fell in love with him to begin with, and why I've only ever felt alive around him. These past three years, I wasn't just longing for freedom; I wanted to feel like I had a life that's worth living.

Roman has always made the hard days easy, and the good days great. And... and I don't want to lose that—*him*.

"I thought so much about what's happened; I'm not sure I want to understand anything anymore."

"You don't always need to understand it; you just need to know it's there." He tucks the hair behind my ear and flicks my nose.

My lips part, and I poke his chest. "When did you get so philosophical?"

"I saw a shrink. When did you become so self-aware?"

"I was left alone with my thoughts," I say matter-of-factly. You know what? I like that I don't have to live in the darkness anymore. I shouldn't be tormenting myself over liking the feeling of being happy.

"You've always been mature for your age—and don't give me that biology, brain development bullshit." He throws a cushion at me with a grin, and I bat it away.

I huff a breath and pick up the utensils. "Biology doesn't lie. Plus, I didn't ask to be mature. I didn't have a choice. I had to grow up faster than I wanted to, constantly dreaming of another life where I wasn't me. It sucked up all my energy."

Silence blares around us, and then he says, "You and me both." He nods at my plate. "Finish up, then I'm going to read to you."

My eyebrows rise. "You mean that you want me to read to you?"

"I said what I said."

He did, in fact, say what he said, because later, he tucks me into bed, lies right next to me, holds me in his arms, and reads to me.

...An R-18 book.

CHAPTER 20

ISABELLA

"WHAT DO YOU WANT for breakfast?" If *breakfast* is even a term that can describe the current hour. *Lunch* is more accurate.

If we had to live off the land, we'd probably die of starvation from waking up too late. Neither Roman nor I have ever been morning people. We're both night owls through and through. I guess prison didn't change his habit of sleeping in, either.

Other than a muffled groan, followed by soft snoring, there is no answer, so I answer my question for him. It's my apology-not-apology for making him sleep on the floor instead of in the bed with me. The silver lining is that he has no shortage of pillows to make himself comfortable.

Just as I'm about to move, my feet keep me in my spot. Silver reflects the faint light of the living room like a beacon.

Keys.

Car keys.

My ticket to freedom is right there on top of the fireplace, and he wouldn't know until it's too late. I could be all the way back at my old house by the time he wakes up. Hell, I could probably be in another state.

I told him I wanted to go back. I've been fighting him at almost every turn, but I can't move, unable to bring myself to grab those keys and run from him. I can't leave him behind.

What was the point in all that fighting, then? What was I trying to achieve? I wasn't fighting for the sake of fighting, was I?

Roman's muttering of nonsense spurs my body toward the kitchen, but my eyes are still glued to the keys. I thought everything I wanted would be mine if I could outrun him. I guess I was wrong.

The same thoughts repeat themselves as I make brunch. I believe Roman when he said Jeremy will be looked after, and he wasn't lying when he said all my art supplies were in the bag.

"What are you thinking about?"

I jump out of my skin and slap my hand over my heart, sending little bits of omelet flying. "Crap, you scared me."

Leaning a hip against the counter, wearing a cocky grin, he folds his arms over his chest, lifting his long-sleeve slightly so a sliver of olive skin peeks out above his sweatpants. The deep V of his hips points to the place I've only ever imagined—and bumped my head into far too many times. I look away before I get caught, but his face doesn't make it any easier to handle his presence.

The closest word to describe Roman's bedhead is drool-worthy. The bad-boy persona is in full swing; anyone can tell he's trouble by just the twinkle of his silver eyes.

Seconds pass, and I still can't get my eyes off him. More specifically, the way the veins in his hands move when he squeezes his bicep, like he's trying to rein himself in. I still remember how those skilled fingers drew pleasure from me and made my body addicted with just one hit.

He pushes off the bench, and the distance—or lack thereof—between us becomes suffocating. Not because we're touching, but because all he needs to do is reach for me, and I'd be at his mercy. "What's that saying? Think of the devil and he will appear?"

I square my shoulders. "I wasn't thinking about you."

"Mmhmm, is that why you're blushing now?"

"I'm not blushing." I most definitely am.

"Right, and you aren't distracted by me at all."

"Not at all," I say in agreement, fixated on the curve of his lips. I still remember how soft they were and how much he said against my mouth without needing to utter a word.

"Is that why you're burning breakfast?"

"What?" I spin around and yank the pan off the hotplate.

Sure enough, the eggs are past well done. What do country people do with inedible food? Feed it to the pigs?

The reasons why we could never live here keep piling up. There's absolutely no way I could kill any animals or even eat the eggs because they could hatch into cute little chicks.

He chuckles as he takes the handle from me and dumps the remains into a black bag. I blink quickly, unsure of what to do when Roman kisses my forehead before pushing me aside to start on another batch of eggs.

Neither of us mentions the wasted food as we eat, even though, with the way we grew up, wasting food is the most cardinal sin. Mickey blanches when he accidentally drags his fork along the porcelain, creating a high-pitched noise. He shudders, then goes on about everything he did around the house and how he's mastered the art of Google. As he talks, my eyes drift to the keys on the fireplace mantle.

What is there left for me? It's not like I have the money to afford a roof over my head and food in my stomach. I get a commission every few weeks, which is better than nothing. Millie probably wouldn't want me working at the store after what's happened, and it's not like I'd want to.

"Do it," he challenges me, gesturing to the keys. "But remember, there isn't anywhere you could go where I won't follow." His promise sends my heart galloping, and fire ignites in my veins.

I open and close my mouth, willing words to come out, but I have nothing to say—*No*, not nothing. I don't know *what* to say because the words on the tip of my tongue will seal my fate, and I'm not ready for that.

Silence reigns over us, making the tension between us electrify as the fireplace crackles. "Run." His chest rumbles while his deep, darkened gaze locks with mine, descending goosebumps along my skin. "I'll give you a head start. But know, I *will* catch you. Every time. You'll scream, beg, and fight, but there will be nothing stopping me from claiming you." I draw in a shuddering breath when his lips brush the shell of my ear, his voice a silky whisper. "*Run*. I *dare* you."

Then he gives me the look that tells me what time it is: *Tag*.

The chair tumbles back and clatters against the floor as sparks ignite through my blood, alighting my skin with a flush of fear and excitement. Thunder erupts through the house to the beat of my bounding steps as I bolt past the keys and for the door.

Fear and rapture flood my senses, making me lose all thought as I aim straight for the trees, not feeling nature's assault on my feet. Cold air stings my face as I go bounding through the forest while I hear the door slam open.

"Oh, Bella," he calls in a singsong voice.

As my heartbeat roars in my ears, I don't dare look behind me to see how far away he is. His voice seems close and a world away at the same time.

My thundering steps sound too loud in my ears as pine needles stick to my clothes and branches tear at my skin. The pain doesn't register beyond the need to keep running and the desire to meet the hunter when I'm caught.

It's fucked up and thrilling. Pure exhilaration surges through me; feeling like I have injected some kind of drug straight into my veins.

Tag. It's been years since we've played it; I've forgotten how the euphoria of that hunt feels.

He'll trap me. His claws will sink into me, and he'll claim his territory like a savage.

Even though I can't see him, I can feel him and his scent everywhere, overpowering the smell of the fresh earth.

He starts whistling a cheery tune somewhere, as if the chase doesn't tire him. The eerie melody spurs me on, heightening my sense of panic.

My muscles burn as I push myself to run faster, each unsteady step threatening to send me tumbling down. I glance around frantically, aiming for something that helps me hide my tracks. Luckily, it's not long before I spot rock formations on the horizon, covering a good portion of the forest floor.

I didn't expect Roman to give me so much time to run, but I know he's playing with me, giving me the false sense of security that I might have some semblance of control in this situation.

Climbing onto one of the rocks, I jump to another, then another, finally sprinting for a low-hanging tree. I duck behind it, breath ragged and wheezing. Even as I try to muffle my greedy lungfuls of air as I move, I may as well be screaming for him to find me with how loud I'm breathing.

"Come out, come out, wherever you are." His coo echoes through the forest, so I can't pinpoint where he is.

Nature stills, and the birds' and insects' songs go quiet. I hold my breath. Waiting. Listening.

One heartbeat.

Two.

Nothing happens. No sound, no movement, nothing.

The cawing of a bird booms overhead, and I jump back, colliding with something solid before a hand clasp over my mouth.

"Tag. You're it."

I shriek against his hands, and he releases me. Spinning around, I stumble to the ground, before scrambling to escape him.

Roman's laugh bounces through the forest as he stalks forward, never more than a couple of feet away. The wide red smile of the mask—the one he wore to murder my foster parents—glows tauntingly.

I would bet my life there's an animalistic grin plastered over his face.

Every one of my senses screams at me to run away from this predator. I keep crawling away from him, slipping in the sodden earth.

He pauses, and I do too. A head tilt is the only warning I get before he lunges. A cry rips through my throat when he seizes my ankles with his strong hands and drags me back to him. I thrash around, clawing at the ground with all the strength I can muster up, but everything is in vain.

His hips press against mine, and I cry out again, switching tactics by unleashing my hands on him instead to find purchase with my nails. He's quick to react, and my wrists are shackled above my head by his long fingers before I can do any damage.

"I told you I'd catch you." His dark laugh sends a tingle down my spine, and he grinds our hips together. I want to squeeze my legs shut to stop the building ache that only grows damper with each second, now that the predator has trapped his prey, and all that's left for him to do is play with his food. "I hope you're ready to be devoured."

I bite the inside of my cheek to stop the moan wanting to break loose. "Please," I whimper, wiggling around without actually trying to get away, but all it does is add friction to where our hips connect.

He pushes his hand down my panties, and I buckle beneath him, breath rasping and lids heavy. Rough fingers sink into my core and curl up. There's no way to hide the evidence of what his words and commanding touches do to my body.

I don't remember tag being like this. But I think it's now my favorite kind. Nothing I do frees my hands. He isn't going to let go, and I don't want him to.

"God, you're fucking wet. Does my girl like being chased?" He clicks his tongue tauntingly, making my breath hitch. "Dirty girl."

His fingers move, and his palm digs against my center. With my nerves soaring and the anticipation of being caught rushing through me, his touch feels better than it did at the house.

I'm sure I'm possessed. I must be. That's the only reason to explain why I start grinding my hips.

"*Fuck*. Your cunt is drenching my hand."

I moan at the sensations unfurling low in my stomach, kindled by his sharp thrusts. I shouldn't want him like this when I haven't fully forgiven him for what he's done. Especially not when my wounds are still fresh. But it feels so good to have him here, above me, like he was three years ago.

This is exactly how it should be, with both of us panting and sweating, so starved for each other that candles and refinery mean nothing. It's always been raw and primal, so full of passion that it's sometimes hard to breathe.

I never needed the grandeur of fairy lights and picnics. I love them, but as long as I had Mickey there, it could be a real haunted house and it wouldn't matter.

I want him in his element, and now he's here before me. This is who we are; predator and his prey; Mickey and his mouse.

"Roman," I plead, staring into his gray eyes, hoping he can read my mind without me saying what I want. My blood grows hotter because I can't see his face or how he's reacting because of the mask.

My teeth sink into my lip as he works his fingers faster. Just like he said, I'm drenched. Some sick, depraved part of my mind begs for more when my body is already shuddering and stretching to accommodate the intrusion.

"Say 'Roman' if you want me to stop." He doesn't stop plunging his fingers into me as he says it, and there isn't a single cell in me that wants to be left on edge.

His fingers slide out of me.

He's giving me a chance to back away, but I can't deny that I want him to keep going. I'm showing both of us that I want all of it—all of him.

"Please," I beg again, shaking my head.

Thick fingers circle around my entrance, dipping in—just the tips—and pulling out. I lift my hips, trying to guide him where I need him to fill me.

Then he removes his skillful fingers. My eyes snap completely open, and I have to bite back the frustrated groan rising in my throat.

Roman lifts his hand to his mouth and licks me clean from his fingers, letting a heady noise reverberate from his chest. "I knew you'd be my favorite meal."

His masked face lowers inches from mine as a strong hand digs into my waist, holding me steady. Air rushes into my lungs with a gasp when he rubs himself against me.

My eyes widen. The layers of fabric between us do nothing to disguise his size.

He grinds his hips again, pushing against the very part of me that his fingers abandoned. "Say my name." The command reverberates through my body.

"Mickey," I moan, moving my head from side to side against the fallen leaves. "Please..." I can't find the words I want to say. I want him to take all of me, but I'm frightened to give him more than he's already taken. My heart has already felt too much pain.

He shoves his hand under my shirt, grabs my breast like he owns it, and has the deeds to prove it. "I warned you, Isabella. I *promised* you," he snarls. "I'll be claiming you once I catch you. You ran, Princess. You. *Ran*. You thought you could leave me? You thought I wouldn't hunt you down? Now, I'm going to claim my prize."

I hesitate, then say, "But I'm a virgin." It might just be a word, but I wish he could say the same.

A strained sound comes from his throat. "Good girl. You waited for me."

I can't help but blurt, "And you didn't." It's not a question, but a statement. There's no way he hasn't gotten around.

"Who said that?" he hums, rolling his hips in slow, languid motions. "What? You think I've ever had eyes for anyone else?"

I gape up at him, breath ragged. He...He can't be serious. Not when he looks like that.

"How many times do I need to tell you that you're the only one for me?"

It's a feat to believe he hasn't been with anyone else when girls would bat their lashes and throw themselves at him.

"I don't want this," I mutter, acknowledging the lie in my own words. I've wanted this for longer than I could have realized.

He pinches my nipple, causing me to arch my back. "*Liar.*"

With one word, one name, I could end this game and save what's left of my heart.

But just like the other night, I don't make a sound.

He briefly lets go of my hands, but I'm too slow to react before the cold air kisses my bare skin. My top lands in a heap on the forest floor.

Goosebumps erupt all over my body. Before I know it, my hands are stuck again, and my pants join the pile, leaving me completely naked beneath him.

He hisses beneath the mask. My body heats, feeling him brand the sight of me into his memory, from my puckered nipples down to the wetness coating my inner thighs.

Red blossoms across my skin, and I wiggle around to try to cover myself. No one has ever seen me this vulnerable and bare. And he's there, fully clothed and leaving everything to the imagination.

"Fucking hell," he groans and releases my hands so that he can knead at my breasts like they're the most precious things in the world. "Just look at you. Jesus—Fuck," he mutters gruffly, shaking his head. "I can't believe how stunning you are. Look at how perfectly your tits fit in my hands. Your pussy is going to be so fucking tight. I just know it."

I whimper as the rough material of his jeans rubs against my clit as he continues exploring my body, slapping my hands away every time I attempt to hide from him.

He keeps me in place by holding his hands on my hips while pulling himself out of his pants and teasing at my entrance.

I squirm as more arousal pools between my legs. "Mickey," I gasp.

He slides himself up and down my center, coating himself in my slick. I can't look away as he does it over and over, the head hitting my clit each time.

"Beg me to fuck you," he growls, pulling my head back by my hair. When I do nothing but squirm against him, he says, "That wasn't a question, Isabella. It wasn't a fucking suggestion, either. Beg me to fuck you until the only name you remember is mine."

The air is so charged with angst and desire I can practically taste it. "Mickey." I shiver from the cold and anticipation.

"Mickey, *what*? Leave you like this, alone in the woods, all horny and wet?" he muses, purposefully bumping my clit with the head of his dick.

"Please," I whimper.

"Do you want me to shove my cock into you and fuck you hard like the dirty little girl you are? Huh, is that what you want?"

"Yes," I pant.

My entire body buckles and spasms when he rams his fingers inside me, thrusting fast and hard. I scream, and my eyes roll to the back of my head until I see stars. My nails sink into his arms while my legs squeeze around him. Still, his vicious assaults don't slow.

Pressure builds in my core, tightening my muscles. I writhe and chase the high, but he pulls his fingers out right before I find release.

I whimper, completely delirious, as he snarls, "Then fucking say it, Bella."

I shake my head but cry, "Mickey, please fuck me."

The words are barely out of my mouth before he drives his dick inside me until there's nothing left to give. My whole body convulses from the intrusion, and I scream out. The stretch causes pain to thunder through me, followed by mind-numbing pleasure.

"Shh, you're doing such a good job." He gives me a second to breathe, then pulls back and sinks in fully.

Then, a second time.

Drawing himself out to the very tip, he slams into me. His hands stay on my hips to stop me from sliding on the soggy ground.

"That's it. Take my cock," he hisses through gritted teeth. "God, you're bleeding all pretty, Princess."

He does it again, and again, and again, until it doesn't hurt as much anymore.

"Fuck, I need to kiss you."

First, he pulls off the smiling mask. Then, with one hand, his shirt lands next to my clothes, and my breath catches in my throat. My eyes widen as I see the bare skin of his chest and arms for the first time in three years.

Almost every inch of him is covered in tattoos. Different animals and designs were painted on his figure in dark ink, some that looked like he had drawn them. But that's not what my attention is fixed on.

It's the only one I can see where the black has turned gray with age.

A single word is at the center of his chest, just above his heart.

Bella.

His lips meet mine before I can process the tattoo.

"You're mine." *Thrust.* "Fucking mine." *Thrust.* "You're not getting away from me." *Thrust.* "You're not going *anywhere.*"

With each thrust, he's marking another part of my soul. And it frightens me. I'm unsure if I can give myself to him in the way he wants—the way he is to me.

I don't realize I'm shaking my head until he stops.

"Scream if you want me to keep going. Tell me you love me if you want me to stop." The muscles in his arms flex like he's trying to hold himself back.

My eyelashes flutter as I try to get my bearings and ignore how his cock is twitching inside me. "That—that doesn't make any sense."

He lowers himself so his lips brush mine. "If you can still speak while I fuck you, I don't deserve to have you."

I stare up at him, unable to do anything but glance at the tattoo and then back at his face. I could call him Roman. He's given me an out.

Mickey allows me precisely three seconds, then pounds into me, savage and merciless, squeezing my flesh in his hands. This isn't love-making or sex. He's fucking me. And it's perfect.

Roman might be his name, and that will forever be a part of him. But buried deep down in the softest part of my mind, I know he'll always be my Mickey. They're the same person, but completely different at the same time.

It's brutal, yet tender. Claiming and commanding. His mouth latches onto one of my nipples, and he sucks, lathers, and bites. But he doesn't stop there.

He keeps trying to ruin me.

His fingers strum against my sensitive skin, sending electricity to every atom that makes up my being. The stimulation is almost too much, and I can barely make out the top of his head from the haze over my vision.

I pant and screech and beg, but he doesn't give up. My body cannot fend him off as pleasure explodes in my core, wild and unbridled. It sweeps through my bones and sends my mind into a faraway plane.

Shoulders tense, jaw tight, and abs rippling, he never once looks away from me. He never once stops touching me. Whether it's my ass, my breasts, or fisting my hair, every bit of his attention is given to me.

Silver catches my attention, but it isn't his eyes. A coin-shaped pendant swings and hits his chest in time with his movements. I try to make out the writing on the necklace, but I'm struggling to even make out my name on his skin from the mind-bending sensations he's bringing me.

"You're fucking addictive. Do you feel your cunt milking my cock?" he pushes out between pants as he continues his pace, stealing more pleasure from me than I can give. "I'm going to fill this little pussy of yours, and you'll feel me dripping out of you all fucking day. And you know what's going to happen tomorrow? I'm going to fill you all over again."

He doesn't give me a chance to respond before he slams into me more forcefully than before. Warmth pools inside me as he empties himself, eyes squeezed shut before he collapses on top of me, more relaxed than I've ever felt him.

My body is slack and sore. I need a shower. What I wouldn't give to be in bed right now, so I could nurse my aching muscles instead of needing to trek all the way back to the house.

Vibrations rumble through his chest as he chuckles against my skin. "You were perfect, Bella. Like I said, you were made for me."

CHAPTER 21

ROMAN

I STILL COUNT.

1,096.

That's how many days I've been waiting for this. Bella curled up in my arms as I carry her to my—*our*—house.

The memory of being inside her plays on repeat. I'm pretty sure the first wet dream I had was about her. Thirteen-year-old me would be high-fiving myself and patting my back. Shit, I'm even walking with my chest puffed out.

Is this the post-sex glow everyone talks about? Bella looks exhausted, flushed and freshly fucked. I bet I look like a god right now.

I'm surprised that I lasted as long as I did, actually. The second I was in her, I was ready to finish. I had to start thinking about things *other* than Bella.

Luckily, she came when she did; if not, I wasn't sure if I could have held it any longer.

I don't think she realizes how stressful being a virgin in a men's prison is.

Twenty-fucking-two years old, and my girl and I lost our virginities in the middle of the woods. This will go down in the history books.

Frankly, I could go again. Round two: see if I can make her scream louder... and if I can last longer. It's unlikely, but I'm up for the challenge.

I was ready to go the second I saw my come leaking from that sweet pussy of hers. *Fuck*, that was everything I wanted and more.

Best game of tag we've ever played. I almost fucking lost it when she became sneaky and tried to throw me off her scent with the boulders. God, she's perfect. I can't get enough of her, can't even pull my sights away from her, half asleep, nuzzled up into my chest.

Her thick lashes dust her cheeks, and her pouty lips are parted ever so slightly. Dirt is smeared across her face, and an assortment of leaves and twigs have made a home in her hair—it's going to be a bitch to clean. Her hand rests between my ribcage on the spot where her name is permanently marked on my skin.

I wanted to pick her brain apart and figure out what she thought when she saw it. There can't be any more doubt in her mind that everything I've told her is the truth. She's the only one there is for me, and there's nothing else to it.

Hands down, these have been the best three days in my life, even though she's ignored me for the majority.

The floorboards squeal beneath our weight, stirring the princess from her nap.

"Shh, keep sleeping. I've got you."

A soft crease forms between her eyebrows, and she keeps her eyes wide open but makes no move to get away.

Which, obviously, goes straight to my ego. There are only two reasons I'm willing to accept why she's happy to stay in my arms. Firstly, she loves me and never wants to leave me. Secondly, I fucked her so well that she, again, never wants to leave me. I'm not even going to entertain the possibility that it's just because she's tired.

I'm a pessimist by trade but an optimist when it comes to her. She called me a name for it once: "*delusional.*" I called it being a "*realist.*" We agree to disagree and all that. I don't like labels, whether from her, Margaret, or Arthur, the prison shrink.

"I can walk," Bella argues.

The bubble bursts.

I hold back a sigh and the retort on the tip of my tongue and settle with, "Shut up."

She's still a bit sensitive about the whole murder and kidnapping thing, which makes sense, I guess. So I have to go easy on her and shower her with pretty words so she doesn't see blood in the foreseeable future.

Unlikely.

But as I said, I'm an optimist when it comes to her.

How long would it take for someone to get over that? Like, two days? Three? She never used the safe word; at least she isn't mad at me anymore. Which makes her constant need to fight irritating—

Oh.

I chuckle to myself as I open the door. So this is how she feels whenever I get us into trouble using that beautiful word starting with 'V.' Not vagina, *violence.*

"Don't tell me to shut up," she mumbles, lacking the usual anger she carries around with her nowadays.

"Hmm? I seem to recall you being pretty compliant just minutes ago."

Her cheeks redden. "I wasn't."

245

Again, with the combativeness.

I head for the bathroom and will my cock to settle because the big guy knows that we're about to see our princess naked again. What a sight that is.

"Would you like me to refresh your memory on what a good girl you were for me?" *Shit.* This is just a recipe to make me harder. "You ran when I told you, moaned my name, begged me to fuck you, came on my—"

"Okay, okay. I get your point," she interrupts my list. I finish saying the rest in my head.

Slowly, I lower her onto the bathroom floor, her clothes ripped and muddy. The newly installed faucet—thanks, Google—hisses and sputters for a few seconds before water fills the tub.

I turn back to Bella and the weary stare she's sporting. "Strip," I order.

Her big doe eyes turn to saucers. "What? No, I can bathe myself."

"That wasn't my question? In fact, I don't recall asking one. Now *strip.*"

She crosses her arms over her chest protectively, rather than in defiance. A blush pairs with her discomfort. Maybe that's her new nickname, *Blushing Bella.*

No, I don't like it. The alliteration doesn't sound right in my head. I'll stick with the ones I already gave her.

I smirk. "Don't get shy on me now. I just had you naked with your tits in my mouth."

I'm not sure how Bella became a prude when she grew up with me by her side. I didn't expect her to splutter like she's trying to find the right words to scold me.

"If you need convincing about whether your body is quite literally the hottest thing I've ever seen, I suggest you look away from my eyes and farther south." There's no point trying to hide the bulge; it's not like I can get it down anyway.

Now that I know what she feels like, being alone with Bella anywhere will make it hard to function.

She stills when she does exactly what I suggested. "Aren't you tired?" she gasps.

"Spread your legs and find out."

Bella shudders like the thought physically pains her. I don't have a virgin kink, but fuck, seeing her blood on me was enough to do me in.

Deflating, she says, "You're not going to leave, are you?"

"Did I give you the impression that I might?"

It irks me that she doesn't grace me with a response—like she's not just physically tired, but also tired of me.

She mutters something under her breath and starts undressing. By some unknown power of inner strength, I manage to stop myself from pulling up the stool just to watch her remove her clothes and instead rummage around the cupboards for something that says serum or bath explosion—I don't know. Whatever they call the stuff they put into bathtubs to make it all bubbly and shit. Is it just soap? Fuck if I know. It's not like I've had the fortune to take a bath with Bella before.

I find a little bottle of oil I stole from Millie and put a couple of drops into the water. Followed by soap.

Bella barely gives me a chance to admire her naked body before she practically jumps into the tub, hugging her knees to her chest. The water sloshes around her, a thousand tiny bubbles popping against her tan skin.

Reaching behind my head, I pull my shirt off and shuck my pants to the side. She whips around, eyes almost falling out of her head as she shrieks, "What are you doing?"

"What does it look like?" The hot water burns my skin when I step in, but I grit my teeth and pretend it's just right.

"No! You can take a bath after." She goes to the other end of the tub, where the tap water runs down her back, so she's as far from me as she can possibly go. When will she learn that fighting me is useless?

"You're not the only one who had some fun in the dirt."

I'm not sure if she heard what I said because her jaw has dropped, and her full attention is on the big guy, who is *definitely* getting a little too excited at our proximity to a very naked Bella. She clamps her mouth shut as her throat bobs, really doing wonders for my ego.

"You can touch him. He doesn't bite." I smirk. "*Much.*"

She snaps her attention away and proceeds to wash herself, ignoring me completely. No, that won't do.

"Hey! Stop that!"

Her weak little hits to my arms do nothing as I pick her up and settle her between my legs, but I admire her tenacity. Plus, all her squirming is making my dick harder—which she is getting a first-hand feel for because, in my infinite wisdom, I have managed to get her ass perfectly lined up against me.

Bella stills when I start twitching. "What is—" She slams her mouth shut.

I smile. She noticed the rager downstairs, after all.

Pigtails hasn't changed on the squeamish front. When she turned sixteen, it was like she was a different person around me. I put it down to the fact that she realized she was madly in love with me, but it could also be hormones, biology, and shit. I don't know. I mean, *I* definitely got hotter around that time.

"I won't complain if you move around again. Just know I will hold no responsibility over how sore you are after."

She squeaks. That's the only way to explain the sound she made. It's something like a swallowed gasp and a tiny shriek that can barely be heard above the sound of the tap.

"Good girl."

Like in the woods before, she visibly relaxes from the praise. I can't wait to see what else will get her going.

I scrub the dirt from her skin and de-nest her hair, and it pleases me more than it should that she hasn't tried fighting me again. But that doesn't mean I've gotten any softer. Nope, I am very much still hard and prodding around areas that I *very much* want to sink into.

It isn't until I start massaging her scalp that she relaxes into me. It makes brushing her hair difficult, but I'm not about to ask her to move. It feels far too nice having her against me, especially when she grabs a cloth and returns the favor. But I don't quite like the frown she has as she does it.

"What? You—"

"Don't ruin it." She silences me with three words without so much as a glance my way, frowning harder as she scrubs the marks on my forearm.

I don't have the heart to tell her she can scrub all she wants; it isn't dirt she's trying to get off. I paid good money to make sure that ink wasn't going anywhere.

I see the exact moment Bella realizes what it is. Her cheeks go red, and she looks at me from the corner of her eye and pretends she didn't spend the better part of a minute having a go at trying to rub off the fine-line tattoo of a drawing she made me when she was seven. The *first* drawing she ever gave me.

Either way, I still take the interaction for what it is: a win.

Deciding her work is done, she drops the cloth onto the corner of the tub, sighing as she relaxes onto my chest.

My heart beats steadily as I watch her and how she curls into me when I wrap an arm around her waist. There are so many things I want to say and do, but I know I'd ruin this moment if I did.

I know she thinks she has changed, but to me, she's the exact same person. The only difference is that she's come out of her shell. I always saw hints of her snarkiness and fighting spirit, but she never let it out. Not even in the three months I've been watching her.

"What's this from?" I trace the three little scars on her stomach. One below her belly button and another on either side of her stomach.

"My appendix burst. I was hospitalized."

I still. "When?"

"Two years ago."

I can't think of what to say. I should have been there for her. Millie and Jeremy wouldn't have sat by her side or waited when she had surgery. I want to kill Marcus all over again for keeping the letters from her. She must have felt all alone.

"Are you okay?"

She lifts a shoulder. "I just don't have an appendix."

Bella's brown eyes fix on the ink covering my skin. She purses her lips as she runs her nimble fingers over the bear standing on its hind legs on my thigh, to the snake coiled around my wrist, then the tiger crawling down my shoulder, to the mouse on my chest, and finally, the bullet wound just under her name. She ends on my inner bicep, where I have a mouse wearing a tiara, her signature on any street art we'd do together.

She traces each one she can reach, even the pieces I've drawn, like the one of the barn house, the design on her locket, and the trip we did to Yellowstone—which she hated because of how much walking we had to do, but loved because she was stalked by a stray cat for three hours. She called herself a cat mom for a solid month after.

"Do they have meaning?" she whispers as her hand skates over a fox.

"Yes."

She looks up at me through her lashes. "Why did you get them?"

"So when you look at me, there isn't an inch of me you don't like."

Realization unfolds behind her brown eyes. Everything she's ever liked is marked on my skin for the rest of my life: her favorite animals, the trips we've done, things that matter to her.

Her bottom lip trembles for the briefest moment before she tears her eyes away from the tattoos and to the chain around my neck.

Fingering the pendant, she turns it over, narrowing her eyes to read the date engraved into the silver coin.

"My first day at Woodside Elementary," I say before she can ask.

She looks at me in question.

"The first time we met."

Her lips form into an 'O,' and she slowly settles back against my chest so I can't see her, stiff with tension. Did I do something wrong? I'm pretty sure I didn't say anything to piss her off.

I turn her around and settle her between my legs. "While I was in prison, I also learned how to play guitar," I add, to lighten the mood.

"Oh, really?" There's an air of disinterest in her response. Seriously, what did I do wrong now?

"Yeah," I say coolly. "I can play *Mary Had a Little Lamb* with my eyes closed."

Her chuckle is half-hearted at best.

Fuck it, we're going in for the kill. What's she going to do? Get madder? That's fine. She's still stuck with me.

Grabbing a cloth, I say, "Oh, that's right, how silly of me."

"Huh?"

"I missed a spot." She all but lurches out of the bathtub when I *gently* press the cloth against her pussy. Squealing, she tries to push my arms away, but she isn't sure which one to focus on; the one squeezing her nipple or the one getting nice and *thorough* with the cleaning.

She clamps down around my fingers, making me groan. "Settle down. You don't want to get me excited."

"Mickey," she gasps. "I'm serious! I need a break."

"I'm not doing anything." I chuckle as she bucks her hips, practically grinding her ass against me as I slowly move my fingers in and out of her. "What type of person would that make me if I didn't make sure you're squeaky clean?"

Bella whimpers and digs her nails into my wrist, but she's hardly trying to push me away. Ribbons of red are drawn all over my arms and chest. If I wasn't already tattooed, I'd get her claw marks permanently etched into my skin.

"Oh, I think I missed another spot." I curl my fingers, and she moans—God, I can't get enough of that sound—pushing farther back against my cock. I may potentially die from blue balls, but it'll be worth it if I can feel her choke my fingers.

I twist her nipple between my fingers, watching how her chest rises and falls and the outline of her sweet pussy through the rippling water.

"Mickey." She draws out my name on a whimper when I thumb her clit.

"I'll be gentle. I promise."

She trembles. "I'm sensitive."

"Then tell me to stop." Other than her hiccupping moans, she doesn't make a sound. "That's it. You like it, don't you? It feels too good. Do you know why, Bella? Do you know why your cunt isn't letting me go?"

I tip her head up by her chin and brush my lips against hers, smiling when she leans forward to chase my touch.

"Your body is made for me. It knows only I can give you what it wants—what it craves. You belong to me. *All* of you. And you know what the best part is?"

She stares up at me with heavy lids without responding.

"Answer me," I growl, plunging into her faster.

"No," she pants, gripping onto my arms.

A smile drags across my lips, eliciting a glimmer of fear in her eyes. "You're going to come on my fingers because I fucking say you will."

I don't give her a chance to argue before I pinch her nipples and latch my mouth onto the soft skin of her neck. She cries out, tightening around my fingers as I increase my speed, keeping them curled and my thumb on her clit.

Bella releases a beautiful, guttural cry as her entire body spasms against me. But I don't stop fucking her with my fingers—not until she's screaming and pushing away my hand like I might kill her if I keep going.

My balls are so tight that it's painful, but I try to keep distracted by massaging out her muscles even though she's practically shattered against me.

Fuck, for the first time in years, I feel like I can finally relax. I'm out of prison, Bella is in my arms—reluctantly, but she'll be volunteering soon enough—we've got a house, food, and nothing but time on our hands.

"We should get out before we prune," Bella says, pulling away from me.

"In a second." I draw her back, even though the water is going cold.

"But I want—never mind," she finishes with a whisper.

"You do mind. Tell me what you want."

"I'm hungry."

Well, that's enough to convince me to get out. Come to think of it, I'm starving, too. "Okay," I say, slowly releasing her, even though I really don't want to.

I help her out of the tub and let her get dressed herself, because I'll jump her if I have to look at her naked again. She locks herself away in our room while I fix our late lunch, and pop a packet of Plan B next to a glass of water—I'm down for kids, but after three years without Bella, I'd rather have her undivided attention.

As I put food on the bench, movement catches my attention from outside the window. My senses kick into overdrive. Keeping my steps light, I creep toward the coat hooks next to the front door and grab the gun from my jacket.

Walking past window after window, no one comes into view. Then I see him, some brawny fucker who looks like he could crush my head with his bare hands. White-hot rage burns through me when I realize he's heading toward the bedroom.

I don't think twice before sprinting to Bella. The door swings open, and she jolts back with a gasp, crossing her arms over her bare chest. "What—"

Her words die when I clamp my hand over her mouth and drag her back into the bathroom. She kicks her legs out and the start of a scream vibrates against my skin.

"Someone's here," I whisper. As I push her down into the corner, she freezes like a deer caught in headlights. "I need you to stay very silent for me, okay?"

Removing my hand, she nods.

"You don't move from this spot, no matter what you hear."

Her breath comes out in ragged bursts as she bobs her head up and down.

"There's a knife hidden in the second drawer." I nod to the vanity and rush onto the porch, gun ready.

My pulse hammers away, roaring in my ears. This asshole must have a fucking death wish coming around here when Bella is in the house. The cold air stings my bare chest, and the ground is no less vicious on my feet as I stalk to the back of the house.

I snap my head toward every sound I hear, waiting for someone to jump out of the shadows or step into the house while I'm outside.

"You owe us money," a deep voice growls from behind me.

I whirl around, gun raised. The monstrosity in front of me has his weapon raised, too, except his is one of those flashy gold and marble pistols. He doesn't look like the usual city gangster, more like the cowboy rendition of one with his hat and a pair of boots.

"No, the fuck I don't."

I could. I have no idea. Usually, when someone tries to rig a game, I don't do as they say. Then they get pissy about it and claim that *I* owe *them* money when I never agreed to their terms.

Who is he and what money does he think I owe them? And most importantly, how the fuck does he know where I live, and who else knows?

He turns his safety off. "Don't play dumb with me, boy."

This is only going to end with him in the dirt. Bella's inside, and there's no way he's coming out of this alive. "I don't know who the hell you are, but you better get off my property."

"You lost some friends of mine a great deal of money. I'm here to collect."

"I don't owe you or your friend shit," I spit. "I'm going to give you three more seconds to fuck off."

"You seem to think you're the one in power—"

They always seem to doubt my seriousness. Older guys like him always think they're smarter and better, but the fact that he's twice my size only makes me more trigger-happy.

"One."

"If I were you, I'd shut up and listen before your girl—"

The trick is never to get to 'two.'

A loud *bang* echoes through the forest, shaking the trees and making my ears ring from the sound—kind of like screaming. I've fired before, and it's never sounded like this.

"Mickey!" I whip toward the sound of Bella's shrill cry, and I see *red*.

Another guy—one I *didn't* fucking see—has his hands around Bella's neck and a gun aimed at her head. Tears stream down her ghastly pale cheeks, and her bottom lip quivers violently.

"You stupid motherfucker!" he snarls, throwing Bella to the side and aiming straight at me.

I drop to my haunches and lunge. A shot fires, missing me completely. Half a second later, my shoulder collides with his gut. He brings his knee up at the same time, kneeing me in the stomach, but his lack of balance has us both on the ground, grappling for the upper hand. A-fucking-gain.

First, the fucker who followed my Bella, now *him*?

The guy's bigger than me, so he has me under him before I can do shit. My head swings to the side as pain splits through my jaw from the force of his punch. But he made a big mistake. He brought a fist to a knife fight.

I grab the switchblade from my pocket and bury it into his side just as he lands another punch. The bigger ones are always slower to react.

He rears back, grunting in pain, but he doesn't stop trying to hit me. Removing my knife, I jam it into his side again.

Crimson warmth pools on my stomach, but I don't get the chance to stab him a third time before he's whipped to the side. Standing beneath the fading light of the sun is my very own saving grace, holding a spare wooden plank in her hands.

He reaches back to grab her, but she swings again, this time making us both grunt as a splinter lodges itself into my arm. She screams when he attempts to grab her in his disorientated state. Then I'm on him, ignoring the pain in my arm as I sink my blade into him over and over again.

I lost count at six stabs. I can still picture the gun pressed to Bella's head—*my* Bella—and the fear in her eyes that she might be the next one to have a bullet in her.

The asshole falls onto me, limp, but I'm not done.

"He's dead," Bella cries.

I shove him over and keep stabbing and slicing. Chunks of flesh peel away from this pathetic man's body. All there is—all I see—is red. Blood. Rage. It isn't enough.

He put his hands on her. He was going to kill her. He was going to take *my* Bella away from me.

"Mickey, stop," Bella sobs, dragging my attention away from the carnage.

Her big brown eyes dart around, from the blood all over me, to the knife, to the two men and the fallen gun. Over and over and over. Each time she does the rotation, the air grows thicker with her terror. She steps back when I step forward.

No. Not this shit again.

She keeps stepping back, though I don't let her get far. There's no way I'd let her out of sight after what we did today. She accepted me. She *chose* me. I'm not going to let her forget that.

I can't lose her. I won't.

The knife clatters to the ground as I grab her hand and root her to the spot before she can go any further.

"Bella." I grip her chin and force her to turn away. "Look at me, okay? Not at him. You did such a good job hitting him."

"You—" she gasps for breath, glancing down at the blood covering me with wide, frantic eyes. "You—you *slaughtered* him. Just..." Her eyes dart around like she's trying to figure out what to say. "Just like you did to Greg and Marcus."

I sink to my knees before her, feeling the wet earth seep into my pants as I tug her hands to my chest, ignoring the way the splinter digs deeper into my skin. "Do you see what I'd do for you? You drive me crazy—*I'm* fucking crazy. For you. Only you. Tell me you get that. *Tell me you get that?*"

She shakes her head slowly.

No, no, no, no. She can't look away from me. She has to *see* me, *see* that there isn't a line I wouldn't cross for her.

"I did this for us, Bella. For *you*." I try to pull her down with me, but she refuses to move. Refuses to pull her attention away from the corpses. "Look at me."

"How many?" she shudders out. "When will people stop dying around us?"

"No one else was meant to die." *That you needed to know about.* "I don't know how they got here or why they were here. You have to believe me. This wasn't part of the plan. I didn't tell anyone about this place."

She tries to snatch her hands away, but I don't let her. "What is the plan then, Mickey?"

"To stay here." Just until we figure out what we want to do. The place needs a lot of work, and I didn't have time to fix everything before I got here.

"And then what?" she snaps.

"We'll figure it out." Leave, go somewhere new, get a fresh start.

She looks at me blankly, fear gone from her eyes. "*We'll figure it out,*" she echoes. Closing her eyes, she takes a deep breath. "So you're telling me that you planned to do up a house, break into my house, torture and kill Marcus and Greg, then tie me up *and* kidnap me, but *not what to do afterward?*"

I can't help it, I grin. Those were all greatly executed things she listed. "Well, I didn't *plan* on tying you up. That was just an added bonus."

Wrong thing to say.

That was *definitely* the wrong thing to say.

I'm pretty sure there's steam coming out of her ears. She's so cute when she's angry. Her face goes red, and she does this little scrunch with her nose, always cocking her hips, all sassy. The best part? Her attention is completely on me. *Score.*

"An added bonus," she says slowly, wrapping her tongue around each syllable like she's making sure she says it right. "An added bonus?" There's a flare with how she says the words. And now, cue the fireworks. "*An added bonus?* You—"

"Baby, you're so good at repeating things."

At this rate, she might shoot me. I could blame my stupidity on the combination of post-coital bliss, blue balls, and bloodlust. I said she's cute when she's angry, right? Because shit, even the way her eyes light up is adorable. Bella's like a mad little puppy that, though she can be mad all she likes, she's stuck with me.

For the second time, she closes her eyes and takes a deep breath, muttering to herself, "No, nope. I'm not going to go there."

I nip her finger, and she snaps her eyelids open. "Let's go there, baby."

"No, Mickey, we will not be going there. So, pray tell, what did you see as the exit plan if and when someone came knocking on the door, and you had to kill them." She's practically vibrating with barely restrained anger.

It's kinda hot, but I don't like the tone she uses. It reminds me of a teacher telling a kid off.

Rising onto my feet, I attempt to wrap her arms around my neck, but she refuses to comply. So instead, she stands there, stiff as a board, while I hold her waist. *But* she doesn't lean back when I close the distance, so there's only an inch between our faces.

"I guess we're going to Mexico, baby."

Her jaw drops, completely floored by my response, and suddenly, she's all wiggle-and-fight-Mickey again, slapping my arms and shrugging out of my grasp.

Fine, I'll let her have this little victory.

I let go, and she goes flying back, crossing her arms with a crazed expression. "My mother almost *died* trying to get out of that country, and you want us to go there *voluntarily*."

I squint at her, considering her point. "You're right. Well, I hope you like maple, mooses, and mountains then. Canada, here we come."

"Moose," she corrects. "The plural of moose is moose."

"You're so sexy when you get all nerdy on me." I wink.

Narrowing her eyes, she does that cute nose scrunch. "How do you expect us to go there? I'm probably on the missing persons' list right now—there's probably an ABB on me! Not to mention, we have no money."

"It's APB. And, Bella, you can question a lot of things, but don't doubt my ability to make you happy."

She doesn't look convinced. "Happy would also mean that we aren't starved and homeless."

"I've got money and a car. We can drive around until we figure it out." It's obvious Bella isn't a number one fan of this place, with the crease that forms between her brows every time the house creaks or whenever she looks at the patches on the walls.

"We can't just live out of a car, Mickey. What about kids?"

I pause, checking that I heard her correctly. "You want to have kids with me?" I smile.

She flutters her eyelashes and looks anywhere but at me. "What? No. I mean—um, it's just not the right type of living conditions."

"Mmhmm." I'll pester her about that later. For now, we need to get the fuck out of here before someone figures out these two guys are dead.

Whoever the fuck they are.

CHAPTER 22

ISABELLA

ROMAN'S WHISTLING.

Why is he whistling?

He's acting like setting fire to two mutilated bodies is an everyday chore for him. It must be because he didn't hesitate when he took a photo of their IDs, stole their cash and a couple of coupon cards, and then doused gasoline on it along with the rest of them. All while whistling.

I can still feel the cold barrel pressed against my temple and how the man's hand felt wrapped around my neck. The safety went off a second before the other man went down. *Click*. The sound plays on repeat.

When Mickey pulled the trigger, I thought I was done for. I was certain the man would call an eye for an eye and take my life.

I guess I should count myself lucky that the person who found me in the bathroom had some qualms about hitting women because he was gentle until he threw me aside.

Less aggressive than I'm used to is more accurate.

The moment he stepped into the bathroom, I froze. My drive to fight disappeared, and the only thing I did was whimper when he pointed the gun at me. I thought I was better than that. Stronger.

It's mortifying, and both settling and unsettling that Roman can be so calm while committing several felonies after almost dying. It almost makes me feel like I'm the crazy one for being upset by all the gore I've witnessed in the past seventy-two hours.

Oh, lord. Has it only been three days?

I should be more upset by the fact I'm becoming the old me who followed him along and jumped when he said jump. But at least I'm sort of fighting him at every turn, and that must count for something.

I hope.

Even though I'm amped up, I bite back a wince with every step I take around the house. I'm now intimately aware of what everyone meant about not being able to walk after. It feels like my insides have been rearranged, and my poor lady parts are throbbing in a good and awful way. I both never want it to happen again, and simultaneously want it to happen on a daily basis.

The whistling stops, replaced by humming. Dear Lord, now he's singing *"Another One Bites the Dust"* while washing up in the bathroom. How is he not more stressed about the situation? More freakishly intimidating men might come. Who knows, maybe next time we won't be so lucky.

I'm moving faster than I have in my life, packing the essential clothing into bags, food, blankets, towels, basic utensils—Christ, what else would we need when we're running from outlaws *and* the law?

Running back inside after stuffing more things into the trunk, I find a freshly washed Roman pulling a t-shirt over his head.

Momentarily off balance by the sliver of abs, my eyes focus on the splash of red on his arm, spanning a centimeter. "You're bleeding," I gasp. "He cut you? Let me check."

He wipes it away with his thumb like it's nothing. "That's why you shouldn't roll around on the ground. You get splinters." He grins.

I narrow my eyes at him, then glance out the front door and to the car. "I've packed."

He looks at me, sticks his head into the room, and says, "Not well enough."

First whistling, now he's smirking? Is this what a sociopath does?

"What do you mean?" Following him into the room, I start prattling, "I've got food, water, some clothes—"

"You forgot Mr. Mickey Mouse." He holds up the doll my mother gave me and sticks his bottom lip out in a pout. "I can't believe you were going to forget about me, Isabella," he mimics Mickey Mouse.

I snatch Mr. Mouse from Roman and hug the toy to my chest. "Well, I didn't say I was ready to go."

Roman hums in disbelief, grabs a duffle bag from the closet, and starts dropping all the hair accessories he bought inside.

"Those aren't essentials."

Without looking at me, he says, "You've had your turn packing. Now it's my turn, and you didn't have me breathing down your neck while you did it."

I can't believe we're having this conversation after I almost died.

I huff like a petulant child and storm back into the living room, doing a once-over of everything we could possibly need.

Oh wait, I forgot the first-aid kit and toiletries.

Five minutes later, I'm stepping into the car while Roman slaps the roof, hooting, "Road trip, baby."

I'm not sure whether I should be upset or happy about leaving the horror house. I guess I'm pleased that I'm no longer at risk of needing to cultivate my own food, but I don't like that I'm only leaving out of fear of being murdered—a worse fate than dying from starvation.

Roman's expert fingers massage my neck while he drives, and his calm—not calm, *normal*—exterior is the whole reason I'm not hugging my knees, repeating the moment in my head, over and over. The *click* of the safety, the *bang* of the trigger, the terror in Mickey's eyes, because he thought it too.

He thought I was going to die.

Yet, it's been half an hour, and he's strumming the wheel, screaming along to whatever plays on the radio as if there wasn't a threat to our lives an hour ago.

Would I stay with Mickey if I constantly had to look over my shoulder to check if a gun is pointed at me? I mean, it's only been this one time; he's never placed me in danger like that before. He even left me for years so I wouldn't have to deal with the police. He's been a pretty big advocate of protecting me from danger.

Plus, I heard the conversation Mickey had with that man, and I believe Roman when he said he didn't know who the man was. Which begs the question, how did they find us to begin with?

I've seen Mickey on the phone several times since those guys turned up. Could whoever he's texting have something to do with it? Wait, who is he even texting? Prison buddies?

Turning down the stereo's volume, I yell, "Where are we going?"

He drops his hand to my thigh and squeezes. "To get some extra cash."

I throw my hands up. "That raises more questions while simultaneously leaving my first question unanswered."

He grins at me. "You turn me on when you use big words."

"Everything turns you on."

"Only when it comes to you." He winks.

"Back to my question. Where are we going?"

"It's a surprise."

I roll my eyes. "The last time you surprised me, you committed double homicide."

"Don't worry, baby, I'll outdo myself this time. Make it triple." He taps my thigh. "Actually, that's standard. Make it quadruple, and then we're talking."

"What do you mean, *standard*? Have you committed triple homicide?"

He just grins. *Grins*. He's meant to be reassuring me. None of his answers calm me in the slightest. How many people has he killed? Do I even want to know the answer to that?

"Mickey," I say cautiously. "What do you mean by standard?"

He turns to me and blows me a kiss like we're love-drunk teenagers, then goes back to belting it out to the music, leaving me stewing. I promised myself I would start asking questions, but maybe I'll leave that to rest. Plausible deniability is in my best interest this time.

An hour later, the sign for Chicago illuminates under the headlights as we turn onto a main highway. "Seriously, where are we going?"

"Just trust me, Princess. Would I let anything bad happen to you?"

I stare at his profile. "Do I need to remind you what happened two hours ago?" And just because I'm in a mood, I add, "I trust you so much, I haven't jumped out of the car yet."

His face hardens. "It won't happen again. And you aren't fucking going anywhere."

"How can you be sure about that?" He was so certain that we could stay at the Horror House, but obviously, that's not the case.

"Because after this, I'm done."

"What do you mean?" My heart picks up its pace. After what? Done with *what*? Does he mean done with me? Is he going to leave me again like he—

No. I'm not entertaining those kinds of thoughts. If I can accept that I'm enough for me, then so can he. And if he leaves after getting my name tattooed, then good riddance.

My insecurities got the better of me last time, and I won't let that happen again. The past three years have taught me if there's anything that would separate us, it would either be someone else's doing or if I manage to run fast enough. The former seems more likely than the latter.

"You'll see." He grabs my hand and kisses it. "I promise you, just a couple more days, and I'll go straight."

I let the silence hang in the air, with the occasional "mmhmm" I send his way when he starts back up with his chatter. I can tell he's uncomfortable because his rambling doesn't make any sense, along with his use of movie quotes in his conversation with himself.

I want to fix all this, but I don't know how to. I want to know the next steps, but I don't want to make the decisions. Maybe it's because I'm scared, or maybe I'm just hoping something will land in my lap and the rest of my days will be all happy-go-lucky.

A few hours later, he's stiff and silent, and I'm sick of sitting in a car. It's pitch-black outside, and I'm seriously ready to find a bed to crash out on for the next two days.

Mickey pulls us into a rest stop and cuts the engine.

"Why are we stopping?" I'm basically speaking in questions tonight. But it must be asked when a glance around tells me that the only building around us is the dodgy-looking bathroom. Other than that, it's nothing but woods for miles.

I wanted a bed, not Horror House 2.0 minus the house.

"We'll rest here for the night. We're still too close to the house to get a hotel."

I groan internally and get out of the car without responding. He follows me to the bathroom, standing guard wordlessly. It's not until we get back inside the tin can that I use my inhaler, then recline my seat to lie down with my back to him.

"No, that's not happening," he says the second I shut my eyes.

There's a violent edge to his voice that I promptly ignore by grabbing a blanket from the back seat. What's the worst that will happen? He'll kill me? Tie me up again? I don't think so.

"Either look at me, or we're sharing a seat. And I don't give a shit how uncomfortable that is."

Actually, I stand corrected; that can go on the list of bad things that could happen. The issue now is whether I play the stubborn card or give in to his demands like the old Isabella. I'm about to choose the former when my nether regions remind me just how sore I am and how much worse this whole lap-sitting thing will be.

"Too late." Mickey hauls me over before I get the chance to utter another word.

"No, no, no, stop," I plead, hitting his arms as he arranges my body on top of his, careful not to hit the steering wheel. "You're hurting me."

He freezes. "Where?" His gaze is filled with concern and his voice is laced with panic. It makes me feel unnecessarily warm inside.

Damn him.

"Umm." I'm not about to tell him where. My heating cheeks should be answer enough.

"Where, Bella?" he warns.

When he shifts his leg, I yelp and nearly leap off him from the sudden ache the contact causes.

"Bella," he muses, walking his fingers across my thigh until he dips between my thighs, where I squirm strategically so my core doesn't rub against anything. "Is my baby girl sore?" He makes a pleased sound in his chest, skimming his fingers over the part of me I've been trying to keep *away* from him.

"Mickey, I'm serious. It hurts."

"Fine." His chuckle brings me anything but relief. "On one condition."

"There shouldn't be any conditions to this. I don't think I'll survive another round." My voice rises an octave or two.

"What's that saying? You break it, you buy it," he teases. "Well, that only works if I don't already own it."

"You do not own it *or* me, Ro—Mickey Riviera." I bite the inside of my cheek for the near slip-up. I could say it, and he'd stop with his advances. But what else will stop?

"I disagree." He places the tiniest bit of pressure on my center, and I push back against his chest to escape his touch. "Do you want to know what my conditions are?"

I burn holes into him with my glare. "What?"

"Kiss me."

I narrow my eyes. Mickey is never that simple. "What are the caveats?"

"There are none. Kiss me, and I'll let you go back to your seat." He's smirking, and I don't know if it's a mischievous smirk or a cocky one.

"Okay." I quickly peck him on the cheek and scramble to get away, but his vice-like grip around my waist becomes steel.

He presses his lips to my ear and lightly circles my sensitive nub through my tights. The friction is enough that I can feel the heat of his fingers through the thin material. "It was *very* generous of me to give you such an easy offer. So I will say it one last time, and you'll give me a kiss like the good little girl you are. Or else I might decide that your pretty lips would be put to better use...*elsewhere.*"

His threat vibrates through my body. Somehow, someway, despite how beat up my *nether regions* are, Mickey manages to make me throb with pleasure.

"Okay," I whisper, a tremble in my voice.

"Okay, what? You want me to come in your mouth, baby girl? Fuck, I can just imagine what those eyes of yours will look like when you gag. I bet you're wet—"

"I'll kiss you," I blurt out to cut him off.

I don't need him to know that he is one hundred percent correct about what's happening downstairs. His praise only adds to my downfall. And waterfall. What would he feel like in my mouth? I never got a chance to feel him, but he looked like he would be silky to the touch. How would—

I shake my head to clear my thoughts. *Kiss Mickey,* that's all I need to think about right now. Nothing else. No distractions. Just... Just focus on those very kissable lips and keep our hips a healthy distance away from each other.

He raises his brow, eyes alight with amusement. "I'm waiting."

Here goes nothing.

I lower my lips to his. At first, he doesn't kiss me back. Then, my breathing stutters to a stop with the force of his kiss. It's as brutal as the way he fucks. His hands move to thread in my hair, holding me hostage as his tongue dominates my mouth.

Kissing him here feels more intimate than what went down in the woods and the bath—intimacy without the sex. I want this, right? I want Mickey, just under different circumstances and at the right time? I... I don't know why I'm feeling this way. I haven't had time to sit in my corner of the world and sort through my thoughts and feelings. But I have to focus on the now.

"This is more than a kiss," I try to say through his refusal to break it.

"Shut up, Bella." His gravelly tone curls down my spine.

He bites my lip and angles my body to deepen the kiss, but it *hurts*. Not my lips, but my goddamn abused *bits,* rubbing up against the harsh material of his jeans and solid muscles, making me want to scream.

I tense with a pained whimper, and he stills.

"Did I hurt you?"

That's a loaded question. "Yes. I kissed you, like we agreed. Now, can I please lie on my side so I can attempt to make a full recovery."

Mischief gleams in his eyes. "On two conditions—Three."

If looks could kill, the one I'm giving him would be considered second degree homicide. "I swear to God, Mickey—"

"Keep your claws to yourself until you hear what I have to say."

Sighing, I cross my arms and lean away from him. "What?"

"You can stay on your side of the car *if* you face me while you sleep *and* hold my hand." Mickey says it with his deep voice and that unhinged sparkle in his eye, but all I can think about is how I used to make the same request to my mother. "Do we have a deal?"

I nod hesitantly.

"Shake on it." Mickey holds his hand out.

Narrowing my eyes, I take his hand before he can pull it away and turn this into a germaphobe's nightmare. I still have trust issues after he quickly spit on it and slapped our hands together when I was twelve. It was the most disgusting thing I'd ever felt.

"Good." He releases me, motioning to my seat as if I've been dismissed. *Such a little shit.*

The journey back to my side of the car is less than graceful. A whole bunch of awkward positioning of limbs and less than ceremonious grunts. Oh, and a brutal slap to my ass.

Once there's no pressure on my backside, and I'm protected by the blanket's warmth once again, I try to pay attention to something other than Mickey. But there's nothing else to look at but him because condensation coats the windows, so there's no way to know if anyone is standing outside.

There isn't a doubt in my mind that if anything were to happen, Mickey would risk his life to save me. That kind of knowledge makes falling asleep easier, but the longing in his stare chases the prospect of rest away.

"Hand, Bella," he scolds.

"But it's cold."

I shook on it, and it's a cardinal sin to break what has been shaken on.

He mutters something under his breath and drags another blanket to the front seat so it covers both of us. Without waiting for me to give him my hand, he shoves his arm beneath my blanket and fumbles around until our fingers are intertwined, and then he grunts his approval.

We've been through Hell together, and like he promised, he came back for me. I'm giving him a hard time, but I still want to be wherever he is. As I stare at his profile and let the sound of breathing calm my racing nerves, I realize something; he feels like cocoa in the winter and the first sign of color in the fall. And when I'm around him, I feel like sangria in the summer and daffodils in the spring.

We're polar opposites, but work so perfectly together.

Or maybe so tragically.

"Goodnight, Princess."

"Goodnight, Mickey."

CHAPTER 23

ROMAN

"I'M JUST SAYING, IF we were ever in a *Mad Max* and *Aliens* situation, we'd be sorted. I'd set us up a nice ride—maybe steal a Tesla, go electric—and we'll be crusin' around the country, just you and me. I mean, it would suck because there probably wouldn't be any radio, and we'd have to hunt our own food—lucky we have the house—but I think we have a serious chance of survival."

Bella mumbles a non-committal "Yup," while reading the back of a chip packet, which she follows up with a cute little frown. "The Tesla would be useless without electricity."

So she *was* listening to me. Good. "We'll head to South America, so I can be a cooler *Indiana Jones*, and you can be *Jane*."

Bella still doesn't look up from the packet she's been reading for the past ten minutes.

The great news is that her hair is back in her signature pigtails—but she didn't want my help. So that pissed me the fuck off this morning.

Fuck baby steps. Why isn't she madly obsessed with me yet?

"Jane's from Tarzan, and please don't compare yourself to Indiana Jones. You'll never win."

Test number two: Passed.

Wait, actually, no. Now I'm a little bit jealous. What the hell does she mean that I can't win against Harrison Ford?

That's it. She's banned from watching movies with him in it.

All morning, Bella has been either ignoring me or giving me her very obviously distracted attention. I'm inclined to pull over and *make* her give me her full attention, but she's lucky that we've got an appointment to make, and we're already late.

It's time to change tactics and say something that will really get her going. *Pull out the big guns*, as they say. "Oh, I forgot to tell you. While in prison, I read this book that said that when snakes lay eggs, you should always spin and tip the eggs a couple of times to help them grow strong."

I bite back my grin and wait for her to *explode*.

She drops the bag and looks up at me with crazed eyes. "You'll kill it if you do that!"

Bingo.

Yes, Princess, I very painfully remember the YouTube phase you went through. I had to sit and watch *hours* of egg-hatching and snake breeding videos. *Weirdo.* I'm practically traumatized—but I still didn't hesitate to get the Mojave ball python tattooed on my wrist.

Christ. The things I'd do for this girl.

And *to* this girl.

Note to self: Once we pull over, Google how long she needs to recover so we can go another round or two.

"The book also said that if you see mold growing, run it under hot water and use a toothbrush to clean it." I'm trying so hard to hide my grin, but damn it, I'm failing. She's just too easy to rile up.

Over hypothetical snake eggs, of all things.

"Mickey!" she gasps, like I killed a dog or something. I'm not sure why she's acting like either of us will be breeding *or* raising a clutch of snake eggs anytime in the foreseeable future, but I guess she's preparing for the unlikely event it does happen. "No! You can't do that. You'll damage the shell and risk hurting the snake. *You could kill it,*" she says with haunted eyes. "You have to sprinkle antifungal powder to try to save the egg."

So much passion in such a little body.

I pinch her cheek, and she slaps my hand away—as expected. So I send her a wink. "I'm just *egging* you on. No baby snakes are being harmed. Promise."

"Snakelet. Not '*baby* snake.'" She scoffs, doing a cute nose scrunch. "It's like saying baby dog instead of puppy."

Out of everyone, I find Bella the easiest to read. Glaring and nose scrunching usually means she's angry. Red cheeks and fluttering lashes mean she's feeling flustered. Who knows what the fuck the rest means. She usually gives me a piece of her mind and fills in the blanks for me.

My phone buzzes for what has to be the tenth time in the past half hour. I check the GPS and slow down to a stop in front of a block of decrepit apartments.

Damien sticks out like a sore thumb in this shitty neighborhood, leaning against his bike like an A-class predator. I'd say we're pretty equal on the hunter scale, but at this moment, I'm envious of the prick; I want to feel the wind around me as I ride my goddamn bike.

But, I gave it up for Bella.

I'm driving a 2006 Toyota pickup instead of the other love of my life, my BMW GS.

"Why are we here?" the *main* love of my life asks.

"To get IDs."

She stares at me, mouth ajar. "This was the surprise? You seriously couldn't have told me this last night."

I shrug, grabbing my gun from the glove compartment. "It didn't seem like a big deal."

"Are you kidding me? We're on the run because someone almost *murdered* me, then you started driving us to God knows where *at night*, and you didn't think telling me where we were going was important?" I pause with my hand on the door, glaring at her because the reminder of the fucker holding a gun to her head sets me off. I should have kept stabbing him, or beaten his sorry ass up before he died.

"Sorry. Well, now you know." I'm out of the car before she can blow up. Unless I cool my shit, we'll probably have another murder on my hands.

I still. Wait, I was meant to Google something. Shit, what was it? I remember it's something really important. I narrow my eyes at Bella, hoping she'll inspire my memory.

Oh, that's right.

I pull my phone out and type my question into the search bar. Pursing my lips, I tip my head from side to side. Three to four days until she's recovered. I can live with that.

Barely.

Bella doesn't waste time running to me, darting her watchful gaze up and down the street until she settles on Damien. Other than him, the only people around are the kids biking and playing farther up the street.

Rico's brother nods at me. It's a good thing Damien looks nothing like his annoying ass brother. Different mothers or something like that.

Damien's all slicked-back hair and dead eyes. Whereas Rico's got a buzz cut, and he's like a dog that doesn't know how to shut the fuck up.

I stand up straighter when Bella grabs onto me, leaving no more than a foot between us.

"Who is that?" she whispers under her breath.

"An acquaintance." I'm sure as shit not about to call him a friend. I doubt he'd call me anything other than a person he knows. But I've got to admit that I still trust Damien more than his punk of a brother.

I've known Damien for five years. He's a runner of some kind (I like to call him *bitch boy*, which he doesn't appreciate) for the Alvarez Cartel, traveling over state lines for one thing or another. Damien got me doing some jobs for him on and off for extra cash; get money from this guy, fuck up that guy, win this thing, drop that thing off.

In principle, I don't fuck with gang business, and he knows I have no loyalties with the Alvarez, but there's no questioning that it pays damn well. It's the only reason I've been able to spoil Bella.

And because I wouldn't trust the cartel with two-week-old pizza, let alone personal information, until yesterday, I'd never mentioned Bella to him. Rico probably told him, though, and Damien strikes me as someone smart enough to do his research before getting into business.

Damien makes no move to greet us as we approach. He doesn't need to take his glasses off for me to know he's staring at me blankly. The man only has two settings: bored and angry.

"Riviera." Even his voice sounds bored.

"Reyes."

He looks at Bella for a beat too long, so I glue her to my side by an arm around her shoulder.

Actually, hey, that's an idea. Maybe I could cuff us together so she can never leave my side (aka, she'll have no choice but to shower with me). I'm a genius. Why didn't I think of that earlier?

"Your contact?" I grind out when Damien continues to stand still.

Typical fucking criminals refusing to share their contacts so they can get a cut. I mean, Damien won't expect anything, but he'll want the person to know he referred me to them.

Without another word, he walks toward one of the three-story apartments. The guy unnerves me with how quiet he is, but at least he doesn't run his mouth like Rico. And Damien can actually throw a decent punch. I've been in the ring with him a couple of times and became intimately aware of how good it feels to have my nose broken by his fist.

Bella sidesteps the trash and random shit on the stairs as we climb up the three-story building. Laundry hangs over balconies, and people sit on plastic chairs next to their open doors, smoking and having their morning beer.

On the third floor, Damien removes his glasses and leads us down the walkway to the second apartment from the very end, which happens to be the only apartment with a camera in front of its door. Whoever owns it painted the camera the same color as the walls, but it's hard to miss when a single, black, beady eye is staring right at you.

I tug Bella behind me to get her out of view. Damien tracks our movements but, as expected, he doesn't say a thing.

Before his knuckles hit the door, it swings open, and I instinctively reach for my gun.

"You're late," the little thing behind the door snarls, hands on her hips, teeth bared, looking more murderous than I feel.

She's a five-foot-something package of loathing, with bleached white streaks at the front of her hair, glaring daggers at Damien. Bella's pretty tall for a girl—small compared to me—but Damien's contact must come to Bella's chin. Hell, she looks about our age, too.

Her freakishly blue eyes snap to me, and her scowl deepens. The fuck is her problem?

"Come in," the aspiring demon snaps. "I've got better shit to do than wait around for you two assholes." She narrows her eyes at my girl, who's stepped out from behind me. Her scowl drops, and she dips her chin at Bella. "The name's Connie."

Oh. So the Oreo-haired girl knows how to play nice, after all?

My princess gulps. "Isa."

Connie steps back to let us in, sneering extra hard at Damien as he passes. His only reaction is a dismissive glance her way.

The door locks behind us, causing Bella to jump and huddle closer to my side. The mouse is eyeing Damien and the dark room, where the only light comes from the locked computer monitors. Connie pushes a button, and a photography setup in the corner of the living space comes to life.

Connie crosses her arms and stares me down while Bella shifts her weight. "So what do you need?"

"IDs." I almost jump when Damien answers for me. Since when the hell does this guy speak voluntarily?

She whips her head to him. "I wasn't fucking asking you, now was I, Reyes?"

His eye twitches, but he doesn't say a word.

"Passports, driver's licenses, and birth certificates. For the both of us," I say, because fuck that guy for talking for me. I was planning on just a driver's license, because decent fake shit is expensive, but the guys from yesterday made me realize that we need some extra precautions.

"What grade?" Connie's expression is all business.

"The best."

"Can you pay?"

I pull out a fat wad of cash from my pocket.

She nods, studying the stack like she's trying to count how many bills I hold. *A lot*, that's how much I'm handing over. Inflation hurts criminals, too.

Which also means I have to make up the money somehow.

Connie unlocks her computer, and one of her five monitors lights up. "Name?"

"Michael Key." I grin at Bella, waiting for her to get the joke.

Connie types the name and raises a brow at Bella.

She gives me an *are you kidding me?* look. "Um." Pigtails bites her lip and looks around like she's trying to find inspiration. "Alice." *In Wonderland*—one of her favorite movies. "Uh, Benson?"

"Key," I correct.

Connie jerks her head from the computer. "What? Are you siblings or something?"

I glower, and Damien shifts forward. "Put her down as my wife."

Bella scrunches her nose. "What?"

Connie glances from Bella to me, then back to Bella. "So you'll need a marriage certificate *and* a name change certificate as well?"

"No." What we're already getting is expensive enough.

Connie shrugs. "Figured if you're starting fresh with a good product, you'll need a solid cover."

Little shit has a point.

"Fine, Alice Benson," I say.

"Alice *Olivia* Benson," Bella says.

So *that's* where she got the last name. "You are not naming yourself after a character from *Law & Order*."

Pigtails frowns and crosses her arms, feeling emboldened by the glare Connie is giving me. "Why not?"

Christ, the attitude on this girl.

"Don't you support her on this." I point at Connie and direct my attention back to Bella. "If you're trying to have a convincing cover, you don't name yourself after a TV show."

She narrows her eyes at me and looks at Connie as she confidently says, "Alice Rosa Benson." Then she mutters, "Rosa Diaz is just as cool."

This woman. I shake my head internally.

The silence that follows grates as Bella and I take turns standing in front of the camera. Damien never once takes his eyes off Connie as she moves around the apartment, checking photos and writing the names and ages we want.

I tap my leg as we wait for Connie to do whatever it is that she needs to do when she finally says, "Give me two days. I'm low on ink."

I don't fucking think so. "I came here because I was told I'd get *quick* results. Either we get the IDs today, or we're walking out that door."

Connie steps forward, and I don't miss the way Damien stiffens. "Then leave. By all means, run along and find someone else. Then, you can cry your little baby tears when you get pulled over and a cop sees right through the ID, and then your Bonnie and Clyde gig is over. You asked for the best; I *am* the best." The mismatching ball of crazy pokes me in the chest. "You don't come to *my place* and talk to me like that. So you can either shut up and wait two days, or you can get the fuck off my property."

"We'll wait," Bella says, surprising us all.

Connie softens a bit and nods. "Good choice." Turning her back on us, she starts doing something at a bench. "Drop the money on my desk and close the door on your way out."

My heart sinks as I slam the cash on the table. My pockets feel lonely already. Then both Bella and Damien glare at me as if I just kicked a child. Why the hell am I being picked on right now?

"Don't piss off the lady making our illegal documents," Bella hisses as we walk out the door. "I'm not." Excuse me. When did she get confident calling out my shit in front of other people anyway?

She scoffs and storms ahead. What is going on?

"Women," Damien mutters from behind me.

I turn to catch him shaking his head as we walk down the stairs. Right, well, whatever, back to business. "I need another gig. What have you got? It looks like I'll be in Chicago for two more days." It physically hurts me to drop a couple of grand on fakes.

Damien is part of the reason I could afford to do the house up and still have money for everything else. I wouldn't say I owe him anything, but he hasn't done me wrong in the five years I've known him.

"A match tonight. Do it well, and you've got a spot tomorrow." He says nothing for a moment. "Bring the girl."

Fuck no. "I'm not bringing her." It isn't the place for Bella, and if any guy looks at her for a second too long, the fighting won't happen inside the ring.

"Then leave her by herself and see what she'll do."

What the fuck does he know about Bella? I wish I could say with absolute certainty that Bella wouldn't run. I want to believe that she wouldn't, but I don't. Not completely. I could tie her up, but I have a feeling she wouldn't take kindly to it.

Fuck.

I'm going to regret this.

"Send me the details."

CHAPTER 24

ISABELLA

"Where are we going, Mickey?"

He's been twitchy ever since we got into the car after seeing Connie. The shower did nothing to calm him, and I started talking about random things to fill the silence of our motel room. Even when he laughed, the corners of his eyes creased with unease. Whenever I asked him what was wrong, he'd shut off or start pacing without saying a word.

Now we're back in the car, and it's hard to breathe with all the tension in the air. My question turns his silver eyes into steel, and he twists his white-knuckled grip on the steering wheel.

Something is wrong, and I'm trying hard not to let my insecurities get the better of me, but all I am thinking about is the worst. What if someone else puts a gun to my head? The guy from before—Damien, Mickey called him—doesn't exactly look like a friendly, law-abiding citizen. My radar went off when I saw him, and my brain recognized him as a threat. I'm not stupid; I know he's part of a gang.

Mickey gave me the backstory of their relationship and the CliffsNotes version of the jobs he's done for Damien. Basically, he's bad news whichever way I look at it.

Wherever Mickey is driving us has the hair at the back of my neck standing on end. I mean, we're literally going somewhere so he can do a job, and none of the jobs he's told me about seem like anything I want to be involved in.

Taking a deep breath, I place a delicate hand on his lap. "Mickey, where are we going?" He blinks a couple of times and drops his attention to my hand. "It's not fair that I don't know where we're going."

The tension in his muscles relaxes ever so slightly. He licks his bottom lip, then grits his teeth.

"We're about to go somewhere dangerous. You are not to leave Damien's side. Do you hear me? Not even if you need to go to the bathroom."

"You're leaving me with *him*?"

Molten silver eyes bore into mine as he squeezes my hand. "I'll be right there, baby. I just won't be able to look out for you as much as I need to. Nothing will happen, I promise."

The lethal edge to his voice slices through me, and the lump in my throat doubles in size. I guess staying in the car isn't an option. Staying at the motel wasn't an option either, apparently, in case some guys manage to track us down. But I don't know if this is much better.

I'm pretty sure anything would be safer than whatever we're heading into.

I saw the stack of cash he pulled out of his pocket earlier today. There's no number of commissions I could do that would make up that amount of money, so following Mickey into Hell is my financial contribution to our relationship.

"Don't talk to anyone. Don't look at anyone. If you see anything happen to me, don't scream. I mean it, Bella, don't you dare leave Damien's side if I'm not there. Promise me."

My breath catches. "What's going to happen, Mickey?"

"Promise me, Isabella."

"I promise," I whisper. "Why do we have to go?"

"It's the fastest way to make money."

For some reason, his answer reminds me of the men from yesterday. "Do you owe someone money?"

He shakes his head. "The money is for us, baby."

Part of me believes him. The other part reminds me of what a fool I was for believing everything he says.

Roman lived a double life I had no idea about. It explains why he was so unphased about all the deaths he's caused and how lighting bodies on fire wasn't a big deal to him. What else is he hiding from me?

I've seen the movies. Guys always have ladies crawling all over them, and the men in those movies never hesitated about finding a dark corner to have their way with them. Mickey might have said I was his first, but I don't believe him. Not when he's older than me, had this other life, and then went to prison, of all places. And *especially* not when he pounded into me the way he did.

He didn't move like a virgin.

I mean, it's not like I'd actually know, but I'm fairly certain no virgin could move like that, have magic fingers like he did, *or* last that long.

Either way, I don't believe him.

He's hidden so much from me. Now that I know his other side, all those missing nights make sense.

I should be angrier about it, not just *upset*, but the more I think about it, the more I realize he never really lied to me about it. He simply kept it a secret. Which might be better, but it doesn't stop it from hurting any less.

My selfish side is glad he never told me what he was doing all those nights, because I wouldn't have slept, too busy worrying myself sick about him. But the tired part of me is too exhausted to give a shit about anything that happened over three years ago. The broken part of my heart doesn't seem to feel much anymore, so used to having shattered bits break more each day.

Mickey parallel parks on the street of an industrial area. There are a few cars around, but apart from it being ten o'clock at night, nothing is setting off my alarm bells. Or maybe my fight-or-flight senses are fried because sleeping inside a car is incredibly unpleasant, and I'm very much ready for bed.

Mickey kills the engine, then turns to cup my face. "Remember your promise, okay?"

All I can do is nod.

Don't talk. Don't look. Don't scream. Stay by Damien, even though he looks like he could kill me with his bare hands. A man who looks like he carries a gun.

Click.

I can still hear the sound of the safety turning off as if it were happening again.

I'm not ready to die.

Mickey kisses my forehead before grabbing the bag from the back seat. He flicks off a text to God knows who and tugs me beneath his arm as we walk down the poorly lit street. He's rigid, but there's almost a bounce in his step and a slight smirk on his lips, like he's excited.

What the hell is going to happen, and where on earth are we going? What if we're going to a strip club or something? Or like an underground lair with a bunch of naked ladies? I don't think I'd survive. Not because I'd stick out, or because I've grown up feeling men's leering gazes, but I'm self-aware enough to know that I'm a damn jealous person.

I'm heating up enough at the thought of half-naked women looking at Mickey, or worse, of Roman looking at half-naked women... it wouldn't be envy or jealousy I'd be feeling, it would be unbridled fury.

My heart works double time when we get to what looks like an abandoned warehouse, not exactly screaming strip club. But there was a brothel on the same street as Greg and Millie's house, so who knows.

The streets in the vicinity are deserted except for the singular burly man standing next to an entrance off to the side of the warehouse. The place where he's standing is illuminated by a single droplight. Shouting and music spill through the gaps in the door, growing louder the closer we get. Is it a club?

Damien steps out of the warehouse. "They're with me."

The bouncer puts a hand on Roman's chest when we step toward the door. "Security check."

An annoyed grunt leaves Roman's throat, but he reluctantly peels himself away from me, lifting his arms from his sides. Jaw tight, brows low, lips curled, his disdain toward the man's pat down is a living, breathing entity.

The bouncer checks the bag next, then turns to me.

"Don't fucking touch her," Roman warns.

Unfazed, the bouncer continues moving toward me, only to stop two feet away. "No check, no entry," he says simply. There's nothing untoward about how he looks at me, but it doesn't stop my nerve endings from screaming.

"Touch her, and I'll—"

"That isn't necessary." My new babysitter comes to my rescue at the same time I say, "It's fine."

I hope Mickey sees the plea in my eyes. I want to get this over with so I can crawl into bed and pretend my life is normal. "We need the money. It's okay. Let him."

There's no mistaking the internal war unfolding behind Mickey's steely eyes. "Do it." The resignation is loud and clear in his voice, and I send him a silent thank you.

The bouncer is a lot more delicate with me than he was with Roman, which I put down to the fact that I'm a woman and I look like a grunge child in pigtails, wearing Mickey's bleach-dyed hoodie.

He doesn't hesitate to usher me through the doors, shooting the bouncer a scathing look. Damien's I-don't-give-a-shit demeanor isn't adding to my comfort in the slightest when all I can hear is yelling.

My focus is on Roman and the tension lining his face, deepening the further we descend into the basement. With an aching heart, I reach for his hand and give him a reassuring squeeze. As the sounds grow, the taut muscles of his shoulders relax with predatory ease, head tilting up with the confidence of a man who owns the place.

It isn't just one or two people making some noise in the basement; it sounds like a whole crowd. The second we make it to the bottom of the stairs, I hate how right I am.

The putrid smell of sweat, booze, and cigarettes singes my nostrils. Bodies clump together, jumping up and down, fists pumping the air as they jeer. Scantily clad women move between the throngs of men, some holding drinks, others hanging off a man or two's arm.

Two temporary walls cage me in, so the only choice is to move forward into the throng or back the way we came. I arch my neck, squinting my eyes to get a better look at the people poking out just above the wall.

Suddenly, the underground basement comes alive. Everyone jumps to their feet, roaring and screaming their heads off. The men and women closer to the entrance turn and give us their backs, joining in with the cheering.

My blood heats while my skin turns cold. I can barely hear my thoughts over the mixture of people and music... and the *smell*. This is almost too much for me to handle. There's too much noise, too many people. I need air.

The bodies part as Roman pushes me forward with a hand on my back. Then I see it: the stage.

No, not a stage; a platform.

A fighting ring.

That's what Roman is here for. That's why he packed clothes and cash into his bag. He's going to fight.

In the ring, a man as big as the bouncer straddles another equally large man. His fists fly, one right after the other, landing on the other person each time. His hands are up in an attempt to block his face, but it isn't enough to stop the assault.

Fingers wrap around my hand, making me jolt back. But I can do nothing to stop Roman from dragging me behind him. My mind is running a thousand miles per hour, and it still isn't fast enough to comprehend the fact that Mickey will be in there.

He's going to fight someone.

And he's going to get paid for it.

How long has he been doing this? When I returned to Mickey after I was taken away as a teen, I thought he seemed a little calmer. I explicitly remember thinking he wasn't itching for a fight every few minutes and brushing it off as puberty. He must have been around fifteen years old.

Oh God, is this how he paid for all my gifts?

How did he keep this from me? How did I not know? I can't count how many times Mickey has picked me up, bruised and bloody, and I barely questioned it because he would give me the same answers each time.

They deserved it.

You should see the other guy.

Don't you worry your pretty little head.

My stomach churns and I focus on the back of Roman's head. I'm mildly aware of the strange looks I'm getting and the occasional scowl, but I'm reeling too much to fully pay attention. We go down a corridor, where the deafening noises are muted, and I can't help but wonder if he's been here before. I'm not sure when he might have had the time to drive to Chicago, but he's moving around the place like this is his home.

Damien and Roman stop before a set of doors, where a man leans against the wall beside the entrance. He's shorter than Mickey, with slightly smaller muscles and a tattoo of a rose peeking through his faded buzz cut.

He's another gangster, if the teardrop tattoo and the skull on his neck are any indication.

"Hey, Bella," he purrs.

A shiver rips down my spine. How does he know my name? Not Isa, but *Bella*? Only Mickey calls me that; no one else.

The way he's looking at me isn't leering. It isn't ogling, either. The only word I can think of to describe it is *challenging*. He's looking at me like he's waiting to start a fight... with Roman.

"Isabella," Roman corrects, squeezing my hand and pulling me behind him. I'm all too happy to oblige.

The man with the buzz cut raises a shoulder and drops it in a non-committal shrug, clearly not caring what Roman wants me to be called. Pushing off the wall, the guy stuffs his hands into his pocket and moves closer to me.

"Did you like my handiwork on your boyfriend's chest, *muñeca*?"

Doll.

Even after all the comments I get from random men because of my childish hairdo, I can't bring myself to retire the pigtails.

His question slowly registers. What does he mean about *his handiwork* on Mickey's chest? When I look at Roman in question, he's grinning from ear to ear like he's pleased with something I said. Or didn't say.

Wrapping his arm around my shoulders, he says, "This is Rico. He's the fucking annoying cellmate I told you about."

"I thought that was Tao?" I whisper.

Rico's laugh bounces across the concrete hallway, and I feel self-conscious more than anything. Today, Mickey told me stories about his time in prison, but he'd get distracted and jump to another topic, so I never really got the full picture.

"You didn't tell me that she's funny, *hombre*. But no, *bella*, we like Tao." He says the word with an accent, like he's calling me beautiful, rather than my actual name. "Yang makes us money. We like money."

Roman ignores him and turns to me. "Remember what I said about staying by Damien?"

I nod skeptically.

"That does not include Rico. You are *not* allowed to be alone with him. And you—" He whips around to Rico "—If I see you talking to *Isabella*, you're a fucking dead man."

From where I'm standing, I don't think his threats are empty. Rico apparently disagrees. He must have a death wish because he gives Roman a big, goofy smile that says that he's going to go out of his way to make sure we're left alone together.

But it's odd... I've never seen Mickey act so... *civilly* with another person after being taunted. Death threat aside, this is the first time I've seen him interact with someone else for more than five seconds without using his fists.

I never thought I'd see the day Roman Riviera has friends. I'm actually... proud of him. Now that I'm thinking about it, I don't think he's threatened Damien about anything, *and* Mickey clearly trusts him enough to be my part-time babysitter.

"And, Bella?" I chew the inside of my cheek and make a strained sound as Roman tips my chin up to him. "Eyes on me the whole time. I'm going to win the match for you."

I can't focus on his promise with how close his lips are to mine. I don't want him to leave, and I don't want him to fight. Even if it is for me.

"Alright, *hermano*. Get a room." Rico claps Mickey on the shoulder. "Time to get you suited."

Roman grunts and kisses my forehead. "Remember our promise."

I nod and watch as the two of them walk down the hall to one of the doors. Their chests are both puffed, as if trying to out-posture one another. It's kind of cute to see.

Mickey looks at me one last time and winks. Then Rico does the exact same thing and says, "*Chica*, you and me are gonna be the *bestest* friends."

Front-row seats are meant to make you feel like the top of the food chain, but I feel anything *but* good about this. The beer Damien brought me is making me feel *worse*, but that could also be because it tastes like crap.

The ring is more daunting up close. With the arena-style seats, everyone here has a clear view of what's going down on the platform.

Men pass money to other men, who then give them a ticket of some sort. I can't hear who everyone is bidding on. I've heard *Ares* a couple of times, and the name *Copper* thrown around even more. I know for a fact Roman wouldn't be caught dead with having *Copper* as a stage name.

It's the calm before the storm. The atmosphere is buzzing with booze, nicotine, and anticipation. Everyone is high off the last match because one of the fighters had to be dragged out of the ring unconscious.

"Your boy's good. He'll be fine," Damien says from beside me.

I glance over at him to find him staring at the hands I've been wringing since the second I sat down.

"Is Copper any good?"

He nods once. "The best."

How the fuck was that meant to make me feel better?

His eyes narrow slightly. I would have missed it if I weren't paying attention. He seems to communicate in micro-movements. Even though he doesn't speak much, he misses nothing.

"So is Riviera," he explains. "They're both fast and agile. Same height and weight group. Both arrogant, with just as many wins."

Again, I do not see how this is supposed to bring me peace.

"This is Copper's crowd. Over there." He nods toward the group of men in suits on the other side of the room, all with half-naked girls on their laps.

I don't need to move closer to know they have money spilling out of their wallets. Golden chains hang around their necks beneath Armani suits that match their bulky golden watches and diamond rings.

"The Bratva," Damien explains. "Copper's on their payroll. To the Bratva and every other person in this room, Ares is a nobody. Copper will think he has the upper hand because this is his territory."

"I don't understand." Is Roman being set up to lose? Is that how he makes money?

"They're both cocky, but Riviera is smarter. No one in this room knows he's already won. We've got the key that will *make* him win."

"What is it?"

"You."

My brow line flattens at his answer.

"People fight for all sorts of things: money, power, glory," he continues. "Copper will fight for money and to add another win to his belt. Riviera will be fighting for *you*. And *that* is why you, me, and Rico are going to be rich tonight."

I down the rest of my drink, willing the night to move faster. Or better yet, come to an end.

I'm not sure what to make of what Damien said. Like any person who's told they're a lucky charm, I feel special. But at what cost? I want Roman to win, but I don't want to watch him get beaten to a pulp just to get there.

"And what are you?" I ask when the alcohol hits my bloodstream. "They're Bratva, and what does that make you? Cartel?"

"Who said I'm part of anything?"

"Deflection doesn't answer the question."

The corner of his lips tip. It's barely noticeable, and I'm not sure if my alcohol-addled brain is making it up. "Alvarez Cartel."

"Never heard of them." It's a stupid thing to say, because I've never heard of *any* of the cartels. The only cartel I know about is the El Chapo Cartel that had all those exotic animals at their mansion. Or is El Chapo just a person? I can't remember.

"Keep it that way. The less you know, the better," Damien says, his attention only partially on me as he glances around. "You see the man with the scar on the top row to your left?"

I look at where he said, and sure enough, there's a man clad in black, sporting a scar from his forehead to the other side of his cheek.

"What about him?"

"Pay attention to everyone sitting around him. Never cross paths with any of them."

"Who are they?" My blood roars in my ears as I subtly try to ingrain each one of their faces into memory.

"Riviera lost them a lot of money. And people like us hide our weaknesses so someone else doesn't hit us where it hurts."

He doesn't need to say what he means.

I think I need another drink.

"*Muñeca.*" Rico plops down into the empty seat next to me, sandwiching me between him and Damien. He shoots me a lopsided grin. "Your man is fucking insufferable when you're around. It makes pissing him off easier. Thank you."

Words die on my tongue. What do I say to that? Men who want to have casual, non-creepy conversations with me are few and far between. What would I say to Mickey if he said that? Am I meant to laugh? Say you're welcome?

"You never answered my question before."

I inhale sharply. "What?"

"The tattoo on his chest, *Bella.*" He purrs my name in a joking way.

My brows hike up my forehead. "You did that?"

He nods proudly. "Thought it was fuckin' weird that he wanted *'beautiful'* tattooed on his chest. Gave him shit about it for a few months. Then I saw him drawin' you. Connected the dots after that." He shrugs.

The lighting changes before I respond, then Rico pulls me onto my feet without warning.

Copper comes running in wearing a red silk robe when the MC calls out his name. True to his name, Copper has copper hair. *How original.* The crowd goes wild as he waves his hands and beats his chest like a neanderthal. Girls giggle, and men cheer, some chanting his name. There isn't a single person here other than the two men beside me who isn't eating up his performance.

His face is riddled with the evidence of his battles. Scars mar his porcelain skin, cutting through his lip and splitting his brows. Another sits on his crooked nose. What's more daunting is the patchwork of tattoos covering his fingers and arms, especially the Oskal tiger baring its teeth on his neck. The man is a full-blooded criminal.

I think I'm going to throw up.

How is Mickey going to win against him?

There's no grandeur or cheering when Roman—*Ares*—comes out. No one is jumping up in their seats, the air not buzzing with electricity or excitement the way it did for Copper. Because Ares isn't walking out from the shadows. He *stalks* out of it. The darkness seems to follow as he moves, reaching for him and blending into his obsidian robe. The air around him vibrates with danger; not even a knife could cut through it.

Copper may command the room, but Roman owns it.

Like an apex predator, he prowls toward his prey, eyes narrowed, lips peeled back into a sinister grin.

His focus doesn't shift when he bends beneath the rope and into the ring. Not once does his attention stray anywhere other than on Copper.

Until it does.

In a split second, the air vanishes from my lungs because his predatory stare falls onto me. His eyes immediately notice the arm wrapped around my shoulders.

Rico plasters me to his side and taunts the beast in the ring. "I got your girl, *chico*."

The key, the winning ticket. The men sandwiching me are handing it to him.

And they're showing everyone here where to hit Roman to ensure he gets hurt.

Murder flashes in Roman's eyes. Gone is the hunter playing with his prey; he's ready to go in for the kill.

Rico leans down to my ear, keeping his eyes on the man who's a heartbeat away from tearing his throat out, as he whispers, "Like I said, *best* friends."

Roman barely reacts when the referee introduces him or when Copper goes to the corner to get ready. His stare belongs to the madman beside me.

"He's gonna kill you," I mutter.

Rico's chest shakes against my shoulder with his chuckle. "No, *bella*. He's gonna kill Copper while wearing your li'l bracelet."

I'm not sure whether I should feel sick or elated by this knowledge. Right now, I'm feeling both. Maybe my stomach is turning because I feel chuffed. In the ring in front of at least a hundred people, to Roman, having me marked on his chest isn't enough. He wants to win while he's holding a part of me. He's going to beat a man while showing everyone who he belongs to.

Roman breaks his stare off with Rico and hulks to his corner, where a stool and bottle await him. When he removes his robe, all I can see is the scar between his shoulder blades, half concealed by ink. I can just imagine how much shit Rico would have given him if he knew that he was shot by an old lady.

I'm barely aware of what's happening, when a minute later, fists wrapped in white bandages meet skin. The crowd erupts into madness because the men don't waste time circling each other first. They're here to do one thing: annihilate.

My eyes are on Roman, not because he told me to, but because I can't look away. He's hypnotic. He's... *smirking*.

Roman's muscles ripple with each motion, hitting, blocking, side-stepping. Each move is practiced and executed with perfection and vicious grace. There's no hesitation, no regret. This is his element, and we are in *his* arena.

He's beautifully fit for his name. *Ares,* God of War.

The slick sheen of sweat coating his skin makes the scene all the more entrancing. The defined V-line above his low-hanging shorts is distracting. I wish I could have felt it in the woods. I know Mickey would let me do what I want if I just asked, but I can't bring myself to do it.

Rico is losing his mind beside me, screaming instructions at the top of his lungs.

Block.

Fuck him up.

Uppercut.

Get him, motherfucker.

Roman staggers back from a blow to his face. Blood flies from his mouth, but he recovers faster than I can blink, sending Copper backward with a kick to his chest. Mickey is on him a second later, laying punch after punch, making crimson explode from Copper's face.

It doesn't take long before the other man is on him. More red colors the scene, splattering onto the platform and onto sweat covered skin. Then Roman hits the floor.

I wrap my arms around my middle, regretting the beer.

He's back on his feet before his opponent can pounce, swerving away from each attack, letting a hit or two land like he isn't trying to avoid them. Why isn't he moving out of the way? Why isn't he hitting him back?

Over and over, they throw punches and the occasional kick at each other. Roman's arms are up, attempting to block the hits, but he's waning. Even his punches are weak, barely stirring Copper. Roman's hunched over, focused on retaining this balance, cornered against the pillar.

The crowd's elation is potent, and Copper must taste it, too. A slow, victorious smile etches across his pale skin.

We're going to lose. Roman is going to lose.

"I told you he's going to win."

I startle, forgetting Damien is there. What the fuck? "How?" They're both covered in blood; I'm not sure whose blood is whose. And Roman looks like he's barely holding on.

Damien nods. "He's putting on a show."

Rico leans forward until his breath tickles the side of my face. "He's fuckin' with the *pendejo*'s head."

Roman's eyes flicker my way for a split second. Out of nowhere, and with energy I thought he no longer possessed, he delivers a clean blow to the other fighter's jaw. Copper's head whips to the side, and an audible gasp rips through the arena.

The boys weren't kidding.

This is a game, and Roman has Copper right where he wants him; tired, shaken, and delusional.

That's my man up there.

"Go, Mickey!" I yell with every bit of energy I have.

Roman's smile isn't slow or weary; it detonates across his face. But he isn't looking at his opponent like he's the prey. He's looking at *me* like I'm the one he wants to ruin.

Before Copper can recover, Roman uses the momentum to send him careening back. Gone is the fighter who took the blows. Ares is a god here to remind Copper that metal is nothing in the face of the divine.

Murderous energy vibrates from Roman as he lands hit after hit, after hit, until the Russian is backed into a corner. Ares is acting like a madman. An absolute lunatic.

"If Copper loses, he doesn't get to fight tomorrow," Rico says.

"Tomorrow?" I squeak. He means I have to go through all this again? I have to witness Roman getting his ass kicked *again*?

I can practically smell the Bratva's anger from here. A fight means money. Roman is making them lose money.

Oh God.

This isn't just a fight anymore. This is a death wish. What if they retaliate for losing? What if the next fight kills him?

Copper doesn't tap out, even though he can barely block Roman's punches anymore. One right after the other, Roman descends his fists onto his prey. People with eyes filled with bloodlust wince, but they don't look away from the massacre.

And I realize in an instant, as I avert my gaze from the fight, the Bratva aren't the only ones who are pissed.

Ares is a nobody around here, and he just proved everyone wrong.

CHAPTER 25

ISABELLA

My stomach knots as I watch Copper drop onto the floor. Another man falling unconscious inside the ring.

A quarter of the crowd roars with victory. The brothers beside me join in, but I can't bring myself to do the same. The people who've bet on the underdog are few and far between. Only a handful of the men's eyes are burning with excitement, their lips pulled into smiles stretching from ear to ear.

I'm frozen in my spot as Roman winks at me and slinks back into the darkness, leaving behind the crowd to collect their winnings or mull over their losses, and for the very pissed-off Bratva to drag their fallen man out of the ring in shame.

A prickle of awareness heats the side of my face, but I can't spot anyone looking at me when I turn.

I'm running on an adrenaline high like some junkie. My veins are buzzing from the fight, turning my blood both hot and cold. The brawl was vicious, but it doesn't feel like it's close to being over.

Rico's arm curls around my shoulders, crushing me against him as he leads us to the same door Roman went through. "How good was that, aye? You know, I was thinking, if you want a tattoo too, just give me a call. Imma set you up with a real good deal."

He slips a piece of paper into the pocket of my hoodie, and his older brother mutters, "Fucking idiot."

Rico smiles stupidly and continues, "Promise I'll be gentle with you, *chica*. I have what some people call magic hands." He winks as he rakes his gaze up and down my body.

"Because one day they'll disappear." I force a chuckle at Damien's response.

"I'm too fast for that."

I roll my eyes without meaning to.

Rico scratches my head like I'm a dog. "What? You don't believe me? Come to one of my matches and you'll see your pretty boy ain't shit. I'll win every match just for you, *bella*."

It's odd, but I kinda like it. The only person I've had this dynamic with is Mickey, which makes me feel compelled to say, "I don't know how you're going to fight if Roman cuts off your hands."

He smirks as he pushes the door open. "I can take Riviera. How does the saying go? Win the fight, win the girl?"

"I'm not an object."

"Don't need to be an object to be a prize, *muñeca*."

The idiot with the death wish doesn't let go of me as we round a corner into the room where Mickey is wiping his body with a damp towel. His eyes brighten when they find mine, only to turn pitch black when they go to the arm wrapped around my shoulders.

The smile he draws on his lips is easy, but there's no mistaking the deadly intent radiating from him in suffocating waves.

"Bella and I have been getting real close." Rico curls his arm so I'm pressed even closer to his body.

He's going to die today.

Roman's lips peel into a smile that's all teeth as I try to wiggle away. "Do you know what's going to happen in ten seconds?"

Rico leans his head against mine. Surely there are easier ways for this idiot to die—ones not involving me.

"Enlighten me, *hermano*."

I look at Damien, hoping—praying—he'll step in. But apparently, his phone is more interesting.

"You have four more to get your hands off my girl, or I break them," Roman says with deadly calm.

Rico—oh, Lord, help me—shoots me a lopsided grin and lifts his hands. "These magic hands? My Bella over here was just learning about how good they are."

My Bella.

Oh no.

I shriek as Roman snaps, lunging across the room faster than lightning. Rico rips away from my side just as quickly. Neither lands a hit because Damien is there in a flash, throwing his brother through the open doors like a rag doll.

I press myself against the wall, trying to blend in with my surroundings—not like it does anything.

Rico, the fucking lunatic, laughs as Roman roars, "I'm going to fucking kill you, *somaro*."

Donkey.

His limited vocabulary would be laughable if he didn't look like he was possessed by a demon, held back only by Damien's hand wrapped around his throat.

"You should ask Bella what's in her pocket," Rico goads.

"Shut the fuck up, Rico," Damien growls and turns his attention to Roman. "Chill. You're scaring your girl."

I'm not scared. Not of Roman, at least.

Of the conflict? Yes.

Of accidentally being caught in the center of it? Yes.

Am I still on my adrenaline buzz? Yes.

Roman's piercing eyes turn on me, and I try to melt into the wall to escape it. He holds his hand up in surrender and ignores Rico when he says, "We're going to share a seat tomorrow."

Mickey winds me when he practically slams my chest against his. Strong arms encircle my rigid body, and he flattens his palm against the small of my back so there isn't an inch of space between us.

The room is quiet, filled only by the sound of my racing heart and Roman's rough breaths against my hair as he desperately gasps in my scent as if I were a drug.

"Did you doubt me?"

I peer up at Roman through my lashes. Splaying my fingers over his damp skin, I lightly trace the hard ridges of his muscles.

He shudders slightly. "I told you I'd do anything for you. Don't you ever doubt when I say I'll win for you."

Rico wolf whistles behind me. "I'd win for you too, *chica*," he pipes.

"Shut the fuck up," both Damien and Roman bark.

Rico scoffs. "Anyone ever told you that you're an asshole, Riviera?"

"All the time."

Mickey lets me pull away from his hardened body, but he doesn't let me get far, slipping in front of me to act as a makeshift barrier between me and the guy he called donkey. Out of nowhere, three near-naked girls and a man wearing a cheap suit pour into the room.

"What a fight, am I right?" the lanky guy bellows, waving several wads of cash in the air.

The girls giggle in unison as the guy throws a couple wads at each man in the room, all catching it with practiced ease.

"Good show, good show. Let's aim for double tomorrow, aight boy?" The man throws Mickey the remaining bills. "Same time tomorrow. More blood. Make it messy. People eat that shit up, eh?" He tilts his chin at Roman with a shit-eating smile. "I'm headin' off. Gonna go make some more people rich."

Then the man exits the room, winking at a blonde as he leaves the women behind. Rico snags one of the girls before she sets her sights on the reigning champion. The other girl latches onto Damien, but he couldn't look more disinterested.

The last girl has the most stunning golden hair I've ever seen, trailing down her back in big, luscious waves, which pair perfectly with her glittery, backless cami. Her bright blue eyes train on Roman, and she stands straighter, pushing out her breasts and elongating her neck like an animalistic mating ritual.

She's a breathtaking peacock or a flamingo with her long legs and delicate curves proudly on display. In comparison, I'm a common, everyday, trash-living pigeon; loose-fitting jeans, an oversized hoodie, and red chucks.

My insecurities fly out the window when a red-tinted film drops over my eyes. The blonde bombshell sidles up to Roman's side and feels up his abs, completely ignoring my existence.

But I say nothing.

Do nothing. I bite my tongue and watch. She doesn't owe me anything. It's not my job to stop her.

"Need a hand taking the edge off, handsome?" She doesn't get to finish her sentence. Roman's hand is on her forehead, pushing her back until she's a full arm's length away.

"Not interested." A missing blotch of makeup the size of Mickey's thumb marks the middle of her forehead. She blinks up at him in shock, but I have to hand it to her, she recovers quickly, plastering a saccharine smile on her irritatingly pretty face. Whether desperate or stupid, the woman reaches for Roman's arm again.

This time, his lips crash into mine instead of moving her away. Like always, there's nothing gentle about his kiss. It feels less like a claim and more like he's making a pledge. He isn't just declaring that I'm his, but he's also mine.

Roman abruptly pulls away, leaving me breathless and my lips bruised. "Don't touch me again. This is your only warning." He levels her with a blistering glare that makes her rock back a step.

The blonde gasps before tucking tail and scurrying away to leave me with an amped-up Roman. Rico's tongue is too preoccupied to notice the turn of events. As for Damien... well, he checked out the second he got paid.

"You can't hurt her." My voice is a combination of a plea, order, and scolding.

"I wasn't," Mickey says, offended. "If she tries anything stupid again, I'll dump water on her head or something." He angles my chin so his lips brush against my cheek. "We better get your sexy ass out of here before I fuck you while everyone watches."

My eyes widen as heat instantly unfolds low in my belly.

"What? You think I wouldn't have the energy to make you scream after I almost kill someone? Baby, that was an appetizer. You're my whole meal."

I breathe in short bursts against his face. "But..." I gulp. "I'm still sore."

He rakes his teeth along my jaw. "Who said I need to fuck you to make you come?" He chuckles darkly and grabs a handful of my ass. "If only you knew about all the depraved things I've been dreaming about doing to you."

I bite my tongue when he pulls away with a devilish smirk. It's impossible not to let his hungry eyes affect me. Especially when said eyes are paired with a bare chest, deep V, and a bulge tenting his boxing shorts.

Really, I'm fighting a losing battle over here.

He adjusts himself and throws on a top and jacket. None of the men acknowledge each other's departure as Roman pulls me in the opposite direction of the arena to a set of stairs leading to a fire exit.

Before I realize what's happening, he throws me over his shoulder. "You're not walking fast enough."

I shriek, but I don't fight him. I can't believe he's real and this is happening. This man has survived prison, worked for a cartel, walked into a ring to fight *the best,* and came out victorious. He killed the people abusing me, took me away from a life that wasn't leading anywhere, and set up a house just for us, all so we could have our own slice of paradise. Above all of that, he chose me.

Every single time, he chose me. He does it all *for me*. How many times has he risked his life, just to spend the money on something that would put a smile on my face?

He's real, and he wants me—not my flesh, *me*. He could have anyone and anything, and he still chose me.

I'm breathless with the weight of the knowledge when he buckles me into my seat. Mickey goes on, recounting the fight and reliving every moment of it, but I'm still stewing in my disbelief.

"Tomorrow, I'm going to win again," he says with confidence I don't feel. "And when I do, I'm dedicating my victory to you."

Tomorrow.

Another day, another match.

I don't need him to fight for me or for us. Not if it means that I could lose him.

"It's not just a fight, Mickey."

He squeezes my thigh. "It's business, Princess. Those men walk into the room knowing they could lose money. I'll be okay." He bites the inside of his lip, smiling to himself. "I like it when you worry about me."

I sigh. "There has to be another way to make money without putting a target on your back."

"Didn't I promise you this will be the last one? I'm going clean after this."

"You have an itch that always needs to be scratched."

He can dream all he wants about keeping his fists to himself, but the liquid pumping through his veins is ninety percent bloodlust. He can't just *quit*. Because then he'll realize that a starved lion will eat anything. Someone will set him off, and we'll end up in the same place, amongst the same crowd. And maybe he'll end up in prison again, and I'll be alone. Again.

"How will you stop it from festering?" I add.

He taps his fingers on the steering wheel as tension gathers in the air. "Do you know what happens when you fight in prison?"

I shake my head.

"They put you in a box," he starts. "Four walls. Six feet wide, twelve feet long. One bed, one toilet, one sink. There's a blurred window the size of my hand, so I can't see out of it. You don't talk to anyone, don't see anyone, don't have anything in there to make the time go by. You just sit there. Sometimes it's cold, and sometimes the air conditioning is conveniently broken. Then the lights go out." He laughs half-heartedly to himself. "What do you do when you have nothing to do all day? You sleep. What do you do when the lights go off and there's nothing but silence and you can't sleep anymore?"

My fingers tremble as I wrap them around his hand.

"I thought at twenty years old, a basement would be nothing more than a room. But some basements are rooms, and some are prisons. The only difference between the two is what I bring inside."

Tears gather on my lower lashes. Squeezing his hand, I bring it to my lips and press a kiss to his bruised knuckles.

"I went in the box once, then never again. Any fight I got into, I didn't start. Any energy I needed to burn found an outlet that didn't involve anyone else. *Flat hands*, my shrink called it." He turns to me so his silver eyes can sear into mine. "I won't go back into the box, Isabella. I stopped once; I can stop again."

"I believe you," I whisper, brushing my thumb over the top of his knuckles.

"I'm not leaving you again. I promise you. This is it. Tomorrow's win will set us up for the whole year. Just trust me, okay?"

"I do."

CHAPTER 26

ISABELLA

HEAT LICKS AT THE base of my spine, seeping desire into my bloodstream. An ache grows slow and needy in my core, building faster with every second and spreading along my every inch like wildfire. It's a blinding spotlight within the darkness, calling me closer.

I'm chasing it, but it's not enough.

More.

I need more.

My body moves, searching for release while debauched noises escape past my lips. I'm too delirious to figure out what sound I made or to be embarrassed.

I know it's cold—the type of cold that makes my nipples hurt. But it's confusing. I don't know how or why, but the bottom half of my body is warm, and my blood is on fire. I can't stop moving. It feels too good to stop. The light is right there. It's so close. Just a little more and I can reach it. I have to reach it.

My body takes over, attempting to move my hands to my center and take what I need. Yet, I... I don't move. I try again, but my hands, they're... stuck?

Pleasure curls through me, forcing me to shiver, even though my hands are still fixed together.

Frowning, I twist my wrist to try to get free. But the more I twist my wrists, the more they burn. Not the pleasant kind of burn. It's more like the pain that came from the ropes Mickey tied around my—

My eyes snap open. I try to sit forward, but I'm yanked back in place by my wrists. With labored breaths, I blink back the lust-filled haze over my vision, focusing on the shapes hidden within the darkness. Out of pure reflex, I start tugging at the ropes, pulling this way and that, but my hands are still fastened to the wooden headboard.

"Don't bother," a gravelly voice rumbles from the shadows. It's the type of sound I'd imagine coming from the monster hidden in the corner of the room. "You're not getting away from me now, Bella. You're mine to do with as I please."

I gasp, whipping my head toward the sound, blinking once, twice, three times. It doesn't matter how long I stare; the sight in front of me doesn't change, but my body does. The rose-tinted film falls back into place and my veins thrum with desire because it isn't just any monster waiting to devour me whole. It's *my* monster.

I'm completely bare from the neck down, covered only by the arms curled around my thighs and the head nestled between them. His tongue circles my clit, and I can't help the guttural moan that leaves me as euphoria edges closer. "Mickey, what are you doing?" I pant into the darkness.

"I couldn't wait anymore. I'm starving." The sound of Roman's strained voice sends a jolt of electricity to each atom of my being.

Light streams through the curtains, casting a hazy glow over his deadly features, highlighting his strong nose and glistening eyes. Light catches on his stubble and the wet glaze covering his chin and mouth.

Ares, Roman, Mickey, whatever he wants to be called, is absolutely stunning.

"You're my pretty little toy, aren't you?"

"What?" I gasp. The degradation should be upsetting, not making me wetter with each word that comes out of his mouth.

A shiver rolls through me when his tongue descends upon my entrance. I arch into his touch, my body set on chasing the high.

"I could do whatever I want to you, and you'll be soaking wet, begging for it. Do you know why?"

Shadows fall across his face, accentuating the lethal edge of his sharp cheekbones. My hips chase after him when he tugs my soft flesh between his teeth. The sensation is unlike anything I've ever felt before, a whisper of pain, followed by a flicker of pleasure. His tongue plunges into my entrance with so much brutality that I feel the splinters of his sadistic movements all the way to the back of my throat. Then on the cusps of his torment, when I think I can't take anymore, he kisses me like I am the most delicate thing on earth. As if I'm something to be cherished, but broken. Loved, but hate fucked. Pretty, but ruined.

"Because you're mine, Bella. Perfectly made for me. My personal little princess to fill, to fuck, and to... eat." He drags his tongue along my center, forcing me to shudder. "This pretty pussy of yours belongs to me."

If he keeps going, I won't have control over the sounds I make. My inner thighs are begging me to close them for a reprieve from Roman's relentless attack. It doesn't matter how hard I try to wiggle my hips away or move my legs to lessen the pain. He has me in an iron grip. Even if he didn't, I'd still be stuck, legs spread wide and at his mercy. A pair of silken ropes wind around my ankles and the bedposts, baring my pussy to him and the cold air at all times.

The scene before me is concerning on so many different levels. The first is how he managed not to wake me while arranging me like a rag doll. The second is how hot my blood runs at the thought of him tying me up like an object designed to fulfill his desires, then eating me like I'm a delicacy to be savored. The third concern? The fact that I want none of this to stop, even though every part of my rational brain is telling me to say the word that will end this.

Even more messed up is that I might start getting excited for bed because of what might happen while I sleep. I'm his for the taking. He knows it, my body knows it, and it's just my mind that hasn't gotten with the program.

For years, he lived another life while I was fast asleep and oblivious. Whether it's his intention or not, it feels like he's telling me that he'll always keep my bed warm. He's shared the other side of him with me, and it's as if he's promising that we'll do everything together. Maybe it's all wishful thinking, but I truly believe that promise is our new reality.

Mickey's hot breath fans my center as he groans, "Fuck, you taste so good." I yelp when he bites the inside of my thigh. "I told you I'd make you scream again."

"I'm sore," I whimper as he continues lapping at me. It's nothing more than a dull ache, but if he fucks me, the pain will outweigh pleasure.

"I'll make you feel good, baby," he mumbles against my wet heat, peppering soft kisses that are so unlike the vicious way his tongue moves. "Tell me what you like."

I don't need to say a thing because he figures it out himself, throwing me into a world of bliss. He doesn't just lick me. It isn't just foreplay. This is a ritual. He's a god demanding servitude from his loyal subjects. He's a puppeteer, pulling all the right strings to make me dance beneath him. And I am a willing victim caught in his net.

It's not rough or gentle, but it's consuming. My breathing labors, hiccupping and moaning in time to each flick of his tongue. He works his tongue in and against my pussy like I'm his death row meal; like he's been starved his whole life. Mickey's hands leave my hips, groping and searching my tender flesh until he finds purchase on the oversensitive tips of my nipples. I moan at the slightest touch to them, feeling the pleasure zip down to every corner of my body.

Then he perfects his rhythm.

And I'm a goner.

If I was in heaven before, the plane I'm descending to is a place no god or man could survive. There isn't a higher being that could save me from falling from grace and into Mickey's grasp. I scream while pressure blooms at the pit of my stomach until colors explode in the backs of my eyes. The sensations keep blossoming and erupting until it's too much for me to handle. "Mickey, please!" I cry, pulling at the ropes.

"Again," he grunts. "You're going to come on my mouth again. And this time, when you scream, you'll scream *my name.* If you don't, we'll start all over again. Do you understand?"

A muffled sound leaves my throat in answer, unable to form a coherent thought because his thumb takes over from his devilish tongue.

My entire body seizes when he slides a finger inside me. "Good little fuck toys answer questions."

"Yes," I sob as his fingers slide in and out of me. It isn't as painful as I thought it would be, but it aches unlike anything I've ever felt. It's the hungry type of need that could never be sated.

"Has my girl been good?" He drags his teeth along the inside of my thigh.

"I've been good, I swear, Mickey." The words tumble out of my mouth before I can stop them. It's like he's dragging the answers out of me with his fingers.

"Oh." Delight wraps around the single word. "I know you have. That's why you get to come again."

I nod my head and wiggle in the bindings holding me in place.

His tongue resumes its tortuous rhythm, circling the part of me that begs for friction. Only this time, he's giving me what I was missing from before: being filled.

The single finger is enough to have me panting and moaning like I have never been touched before, and I never want it to stop. I scream his name and dig my nails into the ropes like it might keep me from crashing into a blubbering mess of moans and curses.

"Again."

"What?" I say on an inhale.

"Say my name again."

He isn't asking me. He's telling me. He's *making* me with the curve of his fingers. The light comes closer with each push of his fingers on my G-spot. I cry out his name over and over when I reach my peak, legs spasming and back arched. He keeps pumping into me, dragging out my orgasm for longer than I thought was humanly possible. Even though I'm completely spent, and my entire body is overstimulated from his greedy touches, my attention fixates on each of his minuscule movements as he rises to his feet. The light casts dark shadows across his abdomen, high-lighting every inch of hard muscle and deadly grace. I'm drunk at the sight of him.

He climbs up my body with slow, predatory movements, trailing a path of mind-numbing bliss with the kisses he leaves behind. My body arches against his lips and he doesn't hesitate to pounce onto my waiting flesh to leave his mark on me. And just like he did when he was on his knees before me, he latches onto my skin ruthlessly before planting a tender kiss in its place. Then finally, his lips meet mine and our tongues move against each other as if we were long-lost lovers reuniting under a starless night.

Suddenly, he pulls away and I stare at his retreating frame. The glow from the window catches the rough skin on his chest where the scar sits. He looks every bit the danger that he is. Perfect muscle formed in the darkest pits of hell, with eyes that could rival a siren's luring stare. I can still picture how hypnotically he moved in the arena and how the sweat dripped from his body.

"It's my turn now."

My trance fractures. "What do you mean?"

Mickey's fingers move to undo the ropes around my ankles. "I can do whatever I want to you, Princess. If I want to fuck your face, I will."

My heart hammers against my ribs. I don't know how to do what he's asking.

Mickey climbs on top of me in all his naked glory, and my gaze hooks on his hard length that's grazing against the hard pane of his stomach. "I've wanted your pretty pink lips around my cock for *years*." He brings my face to his. "You came on my tongue, so it's my turn to coat yours."

I try to squeeze my legs together. I don't know how my body thinks it could handle another orgasm, and I'm pretty sure I would die if I tried to find out. The muscles in my arms sigh when I'm freed from the headboard, but my wrists are still being held hostage by the silk ropes.

"I don't..." I start, unsure how to say the words, as he leads me off the bed, using the ropes like a leash.

Roman lowers me onto my knees, holding onto the length of the rope as if I might try to run. "You don't what, baby? Know how to suck cock? If you did, we would have a big fucking problem because someone else would need to die."

My breath hitches. "What if I'm not good at it?" *Stupid, stupid, stupid.* I'm meant to be over my self-doubt.

"Open your mouth," he orders.

My eyes widen at the monster in front of my face, standing big and proud, pointing right at me. There's no way that's going to fit in my mouth. I know from experience he barely fits between my legs.

Still, I comply hesitantly. He fists himself a couple of times before a shiver runs through him the instant his pre-come slick head brushes against my parted lips. He curses. "Wider."

I swallow, then open my mouth as wide as I can, gaze glued on his to take my mind off the sheer size of him. He slides into me before I can take another breath, completely filling my mouth. There isn't enough room to move my tongue or breathe.

My throat contracts with a gag as he hits the back, and it takes every bit of my focus not to move my jaw as I push against his thighs. His sharp hiss reaches my ear just as his hand clamps into my hair to keep me in place. Heat spreads from my chest as my burning lungs beg for a whisper of air.

"Fuck," he groans and withdraws suddenly so I can breathe. "There's nothing you could do that wouldn't feel good."

The power in his stance as he towers over me could end a lesser woman. Shadows flicker across his abs while the image of pure bliss takes over his face. Heavy lids and parted lips. The rapid rise and fall of his taut chest.

I did that.

I made Roman look like he was about to crumble to his knees.

I shouldn't be as wet as I am by seeing him like this, but I want to commit it to memory.

He rams his hips forward with his fist still in my hair, not letting me escape. My hands move each time to try to push him away when he breaches the back of my throat.

"That's my girl," he moans.

There's no stopping the tears streaming down my face, or the soft moans that fall from my mouth as I lick him tentatively when he pulls away long enough for me to do anything.

Letting go of my hair, he says, "Hold it."

He grunts when my bound hands wrap around his girth. Carefully, I move my hands up and down his length like I saw him do moments ago. I flick my tongue out to lick his head before wrapping my lips around it, and he snarls like he's holding back a beast. Somehow, Mickey keeps his hands to himself as I explore him; licking the contours beneath his head, and using my tongue to follow the veins on his cock. The sharp breaths he takes only fuel my exploration. When I scrape my teeth along the underside, he cracks.

His fists descend into my hair, and he moves his hips like a maniac. I can barely keep up. There's spit everywhere, and my lungs are close to giving out. I can't even see him through the tears blurring my eyes.

"Look at you taking me like a good girl." He forcefully stops my attempts at a moan with another savage thrust down the back of my throat. "Are you my good girl?" The way he delicately cups my cheek is at odds with the vicious way he moves. "I asked you a question."

"Yes," I choke, even though I can't make out the word.

"Say, yes, Mickey, I'm your good girl." He doesn't let up. His grip on my hair keeps me from pulling away to say the words he wants to hear. All of my attempts come out as a jumbled mess of mumbling and gagging that makes him grunt up at the ceiling. "You feel so fucking good."

He keeps going until he hisses out a curse. The muscles beneath my hands stiffen before he pulls out of my mouth. The cords in his neck strain as the room fills with the sound of his guttural groan. White hot ropes of come hit my cheek and blanket my tongue.

He came.

He came because of me.

He's marked me because of what I've done to him.

Roman pants as he lets go of his cock and grips my face between his thumb and forefinger. "Show me. Stick your tongue out."

I do as he says, feeling the creamy texture roll around my tongue and drip down the sides of my lips.

He hums in approval. "You look so beautiful with me all over you, Princess." He caresses my cheek.

My skin reddens at his approval.

"Swallow. You're not allowed to miss a single drop."

It's so salty, but I'm committed to pleasing him. Despite its strong taste, I would do it again in a heartbeat. It's intimate in a way I didn't expect. Mickey seeing a part of him on me is like laying claim to me without any words or more action on his part. For me, it's like owning a part of him.

With my bound hands, I make a show of using my fingers to wipe the come from my face and into my mouth, licking each drop clean.

Mickey curses and helps me to my feet. "You make me crazy, Bella."

I stagger forward, but his hands are there to catch me. He carries me into the bathroom, wipes my face and the inside of my legs clean with a wet cloth, and brushes my hair before braiding it, all while humming an unknown tune, slowly lulling me back to sleep. I'm physically and mentally exhausted, but I force my eyes to stay open to track Mickey and the upward slant of his lips as he takes care of me.

"I think the neighbors know my name now." Mickey winks.

My only energy left has me shaking my head with a soft smile. I'm weightless in his arms as he takes us back to bed. Mickey refused to get a room with two single beds, and right now, I'm grateful that he did. The last thing I want is to feel cold in the same spot where he set me aflame.

He arranges us so our legs are tangled, and the blanket reaches up to my chin. Even though I'm fighting sleep, he kisses me senseless: my forehead, cheeks, lips, shoulder, the top of my head, anywhere he can reach without moving me.

There's one question weighing on my mind, and I know once I ask, the post-orgasm delirium wrapping around us will end. But it needs to be asked.

"Damien told me you lost some bad people a lot of money."

He grunts, and as I expected, the warmth in the air evaporates. "I've lost a lot of people a lot of money. He needs to be more specific."

I shift my head to look up at him as unease rolls through my stomach. "There was a man with a scar on his face."

"The Vargas Gang—or cartel, depending on who you ask." He tucks my hair behind my ear. "Don't worry about them. Everyone thinks they're a joke. No one will lay a hand on you. I'll keep you safe."

"It's not me I'm worried about. It's you." He's the one who steps foot in the ring and becomes an animal under the spotlight.

He smiles smugly. "I like it when you're thinking about me."

"This is serious, Mickey. You'll be front and center, taunting them each time you take a breath. You have to be careful."

He holds me tighter. "I am. They won't get to me, Princess. We'll get out of here before they get the chance."

"I still don't like it. You're a target in the middle of the arena." I shake my head slowly.

He turns us so he's on top and our gazes tangle. "They won't take me away from you. I promise."

The boulder in my throat doesn't get any smaller. Roman is just one person against an army. Despite his fighting name, Ares, he's not the god he thinks he is, and he sure as hell can't take on a whole cartel by himself.

"What did you do to piss them off?"

He sighs like it's a distant memory. "A car came into the prison garage. I was the first one there that morning—and the rule is, first in, first serve. The form said there was something wrong with the suspension. I started working and noticed a tire was a bit fucked and needed to be replaced. I found a kilo of coke glued to the wheel."

I brows pinch. "Did you tell the guards?"

"Shit, no. I'm no snitch." He laughs. "Rico saw and claimed it as an *Alvarez* import. Guess it belonged to the Vargas." He shakes his head, chuckling to himself. "It wasn't even the first time someone else claimed their shipment."

"Then shouldn't they be mad at Rico, not you?"

He kisses my forehead and pulls me back on top of him, with my head on his chest. "It isn't Rico's name on the form."

"Is there anything you can do to fix it?"

He scoffs. "Hand myself over to them and let them beat the shit out of me so they feel better. Or give them the half a mil they lost."

"But isn't it their fault for not getting to it first?

He winks. "My thoughts exactly, baby girl."

"Just promise me you'll be careful, Mickey," I sigh.

"For you, anything."

"Say it."

"I promise."

"And you better mean it. Don't be stupid tomorrow, okay? We go in, you do the match, and we get out. Which means no getting into fights with anyone else."

"Okay, I can't promise that."

"Mickey!" The definition of staying out of trouble is not starting beef.

"I get a free pass to punch Rico."

I'm on board with that, actually. "Just *a* punch?"

"Good point. *Punches*, plural. I can kick him as many times as I want as well." He holds his hand out, and we shake on it. "You, Miss Garcia, have yourself a deal."

I smile and settle back on his chest, feeling the way his chest rumbles as he talks. Mickey tells me about the Cadillac he got to work on in prison, as well as all the other types of cars that came through the garage. He also tells me about his English classes and how boring he thinks Shakespeare is. Yet, I don't have it in me to mumble any response.

"What's wrong?" The heaviness in his voice wraps around me like a blanket.

"I'm too tired to talk."

"That's fine. The silence is alright if you're there."

CHAPTER 27

ISABELLA

THE NOISES AND SMELLS of the arena aren't any easier to handle the second time around. I'm sure my eardrums are a hair away from bursting with how loudly the guys behind me are yelling.

To make matters worse, the blonde from yesterday keeps shooting me dirty looks before sucking on someone's face. Maybe she thinks I'm the reason she couldn't get rich off yesterday's victor. Or maybe she just doesn't like rejection—an odd trait to have in her line of business.

Or, the blonde—along with every other freaking person in this arena—can see the three giant *fuck-off* hickeys on my neck. I'm not sure whether I look like a girl who had a very satisfying sexual encounter, or a girl who has been mauled by an animal.

When Roman and I arrived here and met Rico in the changing room, Roman pointed at the dark blue, borderline abusive looking bruises, then pointed at Rico, and said, "*She's mine*. Touch her, and I'll show you how artistic I can get with a knife."

It was charming, if not embarrassing, until Rico said that he'll give me another. Roman *obviously* reacted very maturely to the provocation.

"You know, one time Riviera said my name while sleeping, and I never felt so special in my life." Rico has been regaling me with prison stories ever since my butt hit the front-row seats. I've zoned out for half of what he's said because I honestly don't believe that twenty-eight different girls were writing to him, wanting to be his slutty pen pal.

This guy is growing on me like a freckle. He's there even though sometimes I don't want him to be, but I'm stuck with him for the time being.

I glance away from the empty ring and to the ugly purple bruise forming on his cheek. Mickey showed Rico how good his right hook is (again) after the idiot said he'll *keep me company* in the wrong tone.

To be fair, I felt the urge to do the same after all the shit he's been talking. But I have a feeling the brothers planned it that way.

A riled-up Roman is a dangerous Roman.

"I wouldn't get your hopes up. It probably wasn't a good dream for you," I slur—maybe I've drunk a bottle or two. Maybe three.

Rico crosses his fingers. "Riviera and Reyes are tight. Everyone knows. Two peas in a pod, causin' trouble in B Block. My man would never hurt me."

I nod toward his cheek. "Really?" I say blankly.

He waves his hand dismissively. "A one-time thing. He wouldn't do it again."

Damien grunts beside me, then sips his drink like he isn't listening to our conversation.

"Did you share bunk beds?"

Rico whistles. "He wishes he could get all this."

I roll my eyes, settling my attention on the empty platform. "Let me guess, you were too fast for him?"

His eyes twinkle. If he tells me how fast he is again, I'm going to punch him myself.

"You and me, *chica*, we're the real pair. Riviera ain't got shit to what we got going."

I hum in patronizing approval.

With beer in my bloodstream, there's no stopping my hand from slapping Rico's chest when he tugs at my hair. "Ow! What was that for?"

"Don't touch me. And don't be a baby; I didn't hit you that hard."

"Here I was, innocently trying to make conversation and ask you what's with the pigtails, and you attack me. You're breaking my heart, *bella*."

I let Roman do my hair today. He tried to act chill about it, pretending it was no big deal, like his offer was as mundane as asking if I wanted a tissue after sneezing. But the psycho started humming while getting all the accessories and items he needed. His step even had a tiny little bounce as he moved through the room. Then his forehead crinkled with concentration while he brushed my hair. Mickey went so far as to ask me what I was thinking of wearing so he could match the ribbons to it. But then he decided he would pick my outfit for me: his red shirt, my black jeans, red ribbons and black lace in my hair, and his zip-up and leather jacket. He also made me wear his studded belt.

I had to put my foot down when he tried to make us match. That's too much, even by my standards. He reluctantly agreed, then shoved a red shirt into his duffle bag when he thought I wasn't looking. *The little shit.*

"You could have ruined my hair," I growl at Rico.

"Why didn't you say so earlier? It would be my pleasure to ruin you, sweetheart." He winks.

I fake a gag and swear I hear Damien snort beside me.

The conversation drops when the MC walks into the ring, calling out *The Unseen Destroyer*, one of the fighters who won yesterday. I have no idea how Roman's going to win this one. The guy is double his size.

Rico barely notices the crowd growing wild, and honestly, neither do I. The second we walked in here, I made a conscious effort to unplug myself so I wouldn't wind myself up to the point of nausea again.

This is a job.

The last one.

Then we're getting our IDs and doing God knows what. No more cartels, no more fighting, no more guns to my head. It'll just be me and Mickey.

Plus, I didn't want to ruin the high I'd been running on all day. I didn't leave the motel at all, so I got to spend the entire day drawing and working on some commissions. It was one of the best days I've had in a long time. Hell, Mickey even got me a new phone to message all my customers.

So, after the two a.m. wake-up sex, the drawing, and the food coma I fell into after dinner, there's no way I'll let this fight ruin my otherwise perfect day.

This means, the only way for this whole affair not to get to me is by downing beer like water. Luckily, I'm not drinking for taste. But unluckily, my bladder is suffering for my crimes because I desperately need to go, but the line was a mile long last I checked.

The air magnetizes as Mickey forms from the shadows after the MC calls his name—Ares. This time, the crowd sees him for the threat he is. People roar as he walks onto the stage.

"Time to get rich." Rico grins. Then the lunatic wraps his arm around my shoulders and whistles to get Roman's attention. The cherry on top of this mess? When Roman looks our way, Rico kisses my cheek.

Rage blasts through the air. Roman twitches forward like he's about to lunge across the ring and tear Rico's head off. But I can't let that happen. We need the money the fight will bring, and Roman needs to keep laying low—well, as low as he can.

Without thinking, I let my reflexes take over. I slam my elbow into Rico's ribs. When he keels over—*no hard feelings, Rico*—I straighten my arm and ram my fist into his groin. It isn't hard enough to do any real damage, but it's enough for Roman's eyes to brighten with pleasure.

Rico's too busy cupping his manhood and groaning in pain to see Roman's scathing glare, but I don't miss the wink he throws my way. My cheeks heat like I'm back to being a teenage girl who doesn't know how to handle being shown affection in public.

Oh *God*.

My entire body is on fire when he taps the tattoo of my name, *blowing me a kiss*.

Roman—*Ares*—blew me a kiss.

Not at home. Not at a game in high school. No, he did it in front of Chicago's biggest mafia family, the freaking *Bratva,* a cartel, *and* Lord knows how many other criminals.

I think I might die from renewed nerves. From the looks of the people around, even they're confused by the whole scene.

Surely, street fighting 101 is *not* to look weak in front of your opponent?

"Loverboy Ares won last night's match against Copper," the MC continues his introduction, and Rico hobbles off somewhere. To ice his balls is my guess.

Damien doesn't look up from his phone once, not even when Ares and *The Unseen Destroyer* square off, and the MC trades places with the referee.

What even is the point of the referee anyway? I haven't seen him step in once, and I don't think there's a single rule in this underground version of sport. Shit, I don't think murder is off the table, for that matter.

I take another swig of my now empty bottle of beer, and my bladder reminds me that it exists and is in dire need of a reprieve.

Damien tucks his phone into his pocket when the Destroyer lands a blow to Roman's face. I wince and scream Mickey's stage name, which may as well be a magic trick or spell, because Roman lands three consecutive punches to the Destroyer's stomach—which counts for something, even if it barely made the guy flinch.

"I need to pee," I yell at Damien.

He nods, uncaring about my bodily needs, and I scurry off to where I saw the ladies' room. It's down one of the creepy corridors, but it could be in the middle of the woods, and I wouldn't care right now. I'm seconds away from combustion.

I breathe a sigh of relief to find the bathrooms blissfully empty—disgusting, but empty. I know I'm in trouble the second my behind hits the toilet seat.

How much did I drink? Like... four bottles? Or was it six?

I think I'm substantially drunker than I thought. The alternative to my inebriation is that the world is moving, and I'm the one that's completely still...which seems unlikely.

I'm not sure how long I sit there. Maybe a minute, maybe twenty. I'm dead to the world, attempting to take deep breaths and ground myself physically, mentally, and metaphorically.

How the hell did I get here?

Not the bathroom, but *here*, in a goddamn underground fighting ring? I thought the wildest thing I'd do in my life is be an accomplice to an after school fight involving Roman or maybe break into a place or two because he convinced me to tag along. But now I'm hanging out in an arena filled with every shade of criminal in existence.

Mickey said this is the last time. I believe him.

I think.

As long as he comes out of this alive, I'm willing to move on from this criminal chapter of our lives and pretend to be Alice and Michael, not Bonnie and Clyde.

Taking one last steadying breath, I force myself to get up. I stumble a couple of times before I make it to the sink to wash my hands.

If Roman saw me like this, he'd probably kill me.

Actually, I'm pretty sure he'd love having a drunk Isabella to himself. But a drunk Isabella alone in the bathroom of an underground fighting ring?

Wait, not alone.

There's... is that a man?

Am I imagining things? Did I accidentally go to the men's bathroom?

The man narrows the space between us, taking up all the oxygen. He's the size of a mountain, maybe bigger. With long black hair tied back into a ponytail at the nape of his neck, sides shaved to show a massive scar. He smells like danger and looks like he wouldn't hesitate to turn my lights off. Permanently.

Oh God.

Oh God. Oh God. Oh God.

I broke my promise to Mickey.

Oh no. Oh no. Oh no.

"What's your name?"

He creeps closer. Every cell in my body screams at me to get out of there. I need Damien. I shouldn't have left his side.

My heart rattles in my chest. He was one of the men from the Vargas Cartel that Damien told me to look out for because of the stolen cocaine.

His words ring in my head.

People like us hide our weaknesses so someone else doesn't hit us where it hurts.

I'm trying to rationalize my safety with myself. The bouncer would have taken his gun off him, right? So I won't get shot. Not like any of that matters. He and I know he won't need a weapon to kill me. He has to be at least triple my size.

I push myself against the sink and try to inch toward the door, but he reads my thoughts. The next thing I know, he's standing in front of the exit and staring at me with an excited glint in his eyes that raises the hairs on my body.

"Isa," I whisper.

I chant Damien's name in my head, thinking—hoping—he'd be able to hear me and come to my rescue. Roman would be too busy, and the last thing I want is for him to start a fight with *this* guy.

"Isabella?"

My throat seizes. How does he know my name? What else does he know about me? Could he know about Jeremy?

I was wrong. I was so, so wrong. Mickey isn't the one I should have been worried about. I am.

I'm the weakest link. I am Roman's weakness.

He owes the cartel money. They want to make him pay.

To destroy him, they only need to look at me.

I shouldn't have had anything to drink, shouldn't have gone to the bathroom alone, shouldn't have left Damien's side.

"What do you want?" I squeak.

He takes a step toward me, and I match it back. "Our money. But we'll settle for you."

My heart stops for a split second.

Everything stills.

Then I open my mouth to scream.

CHAPTER 28

ROMAN

SWEAT TRICKLES DOWN MY back.

Every inch of my body burns.

I glance at the wall behind the big fucker's head, where the time stares at me in big, red, blinking numbers.

Fourteen minutes and thirty-six seconds since the match started.

Another three minutes and twenty-four seconds, and another two grand will be added to my wallet. If we last to the twentieth, five grand will be added.

They want a show, not a quick knockout. But if one of us is still standing by the twenty-fifth minute, people get bored, and the money stops coming. This isn't boxing. There's no break every three minutes. So we're tired and sloppy, but it still makes for a good show.

Vargas's fighter looks even shittier than me. The guy is probably the best fighter that gang has. He's strong but slow. His right hook is deadly, and my head is still swimming after failing to block one. But I'd wager that Bella has better endurance than him.

The bigger they are, the faster they burn.

He swings, narrowly missing my nose. With his arm suspended and flank open, I pivot on the balls of my feet. My kick flies into his ribs. It isn't enough to make him stumble, but it takes him by surprise. I use the shock to land a punch to his cheek.

That's the beauty of street fights; there are no rules.

Big guys like him prefer boxing, all hands and no feet. Until now, he thought I was a boxer, too, just a slippery one. Hopping from foot to foot, dodging more hits than I'm throwing to tire him out.

After fifteen minutes, he's just found out that I am a slippery asshole who can kick. Guys like him are the same, all about smashing with zero tactics. Muscle and brawn, but no brain.

Spittle explodes from his mouth guard, and he blocks the next kick in time. None of my hits are doing anything but annoy him, but I'm just doing it so he finally moves, and I can go back to seeing Bella behind him.

My stomach sinks even further to my feet when he does move.

She's not there.

It's been four minutes.

She's still not back.

Where the fuck did she go with Damien? Did they get a drink? Go to the bathroom? Are they in my changing room? I told Damien I didn't want her leaving the building without me.

For the first time since the fight started, I look at Rico. Unease settles low in my gut. His annoying grin isn't plastered on. He isn't even looking at the action.

Something is wrong.

I can fucking feel it.

I go back to our dance, keeping one eye out for Bella. But as the seconds crawl by, the rock in my stomach grows heavier. And when Damien comes back to his seat, shaking his head at Rico, the rock sharpens and pierces my skin.

Bella isn't with him.

He isn't with Bella.

The second they glance at me, I know. I just fucking know it.

Something's wrong with Bella.

A demon takes over me. A beast. I don't see anything else anymore. I don't know how I do it, not even sure if my limbs moved or if everything unfolded through willpower alone. I barely see *The Unseen Destroyer* fall to the ground beyond the red haze over my vision. The referee calls my win, but I couldn't care less.

One second, I'm in the ring, and in the next, I have Damien in my clutches. Rico tries to pull me away, but it's useless. Bella is the one thing I'll never let go of.

"Where the fuck is she?" I roar. Damien—the fucking asshole—is calm as ever. "She said she went to the bathroom. But she's not there."

Nothing else he says registers because, from the corner of my vision, I notice someone looking at me. Not just anyone. *Him.* Vargas in the flesh. The man smiles ear to ear, staring straight at me.

I lurch in his direction, but someone holds me back. I swing my elbow and twist my body to try to break out of their grip.

"Don't be stupid. They'll fucking kill you," one of the brothers hisses in my ear.

Vargas doesn't look away, challenging me to take him on. He watches everything play out like this is going according to his plan.

If she's hurt, I'll fucking kill him. I'll kill *all* of them.

If she's dead—

It hurts to even think about it. There's no story where Bella ends, and I don't go with her.

Bile rises in my throat. I lunge for the asshole, only to be held back. "You better not have fucking touched her!"

"Shut the fuck up and go find her," Damien growls.

Vargas just laughs. *Laughs.*

My chest tightens. My blood is no longer red and hot; it's black and electrified. There's one thing on my mind, and it has everything to do with Bella.

Damien—the *useless fucker*—is right. Attacking Vargas will do nothing. It won't help me find her, and I'll have to get through his men to get to him.

One of his men walks toward me, but Damien steps in front of me before I can rip his head clean from his fucking body. "Call off your dogs, Vargas."

The cartel boss just laughs, as if this is all a fun game to him. He opens his mouth to say something, but I turn and start running without listening to the words. He's stalling me.

Someone's hot on my heels, but I don't care to see who. Because if it's one of Vargas' men, there would be no running; I'd be fighting like my life depends on it—because *her* life depends on it.

I don't know my way around this place. I shouldn't have brought her. I shouldn't have thought she'd be safe if she came.

Damien yanks me in a different direction from where I'm going. "Not there, I've checked." He points to another corridor. "There's an exit over there."

I check inside every door I pass, yelling her name over and over again. Energy that didn't exist during the fight rages through my veins, and I sprint for the stairs. I don't know how long ago someone got to her, or if she's even still in the building. How many men did Vargas bring? How many were sitting with him? When did he get the balls to pull something like this off?

Fuck.

Fuck. Fuck. Fuck.

"Bella!" I yell when my feet hit the first step of the stairs.

This hurts more than being shot in the chest. I'd rather take a bullet a thousand times than for Bella to get hurt. In my head, I keep hearing the same thing, over and over again.

Bella is going to get hurt, and it's all my fault.

I knew Vargas was there, and I still brought her. I knew Vargas's base is Chicago, and I still came. I underestimated them. I knew Vargas could be a threat, and I did nothing. I practically handed Bella over to him.

I fucked up. I fucked up so bad.

I didn't even tell the cops about Bella, just so they wouldn't bother her, and twenty minutes ago, I claimed her in front of Vargas and every other fucker in the warehouse. How stupid can I be?

The emergency exit door swings open. I don't feel the cold, or the glass digging into my bare feet, or my pounding heart. My entire body is attuned to her and the sound of her muffled screams in the distance.

But I can't figure out which direction it's coming from. "Bella!" I roar.

Then she lets out another scream.

Damien isn't behind me anymore. We're both racing through the empty streets toward the noise, using her blood-curdling screams and moonlight to guide us. I push myself harder, and so does he. The closer we get, the clearer the sounds become.

Grunting. Scuffling. Crying.

Then she comes into view, body half dragged along the ground by the fist in her hair toward the rugged van. She isn't making this bastard's job easy, clawing his arms, kicking at his feet to trip him, mouth snapping against the gag to try to bite him.

Then he hits her.

And I explode.

I fucking lose it.

"Bella!" I roar.

The asshole hurting Bella snaps his attention to me. He throws her to the side, and she lands with a scream, just as someone else comes running out of the van. My heart rattles in its cage when she looks at me with tears streaming down her face, a concoction of emotions swirling behind her red eyes. Hurt. Anger. Betrayal. I want to put a bullet in myself for it.

The fucking cunt who hurt Bella snarls as he charges forward. I meet him halfway. I need this asshole to pay. For a split second, pride blooms at the sight of Bella's art on his skin. Three bloody slashes run diagonally along his cheek.

He's bulkier than the guy in the ring, faster too. I don't dodge his first hit in time. He doesn't miss my throw either.

Behind me, Damien grunts as he exchanges blows with the driver while a gun lays abandoned on the street.

Then the light from the streetlamp glints against metal, flashing through the air and onto my forearm. I snarl from the pain that thunders across my flesh as I collide my own fist against his jaw. We dance around a couple more hits, but there's nothing that will save him from me.

He's fighting to stay alive. I'm fighting for Bella.

There's no strategy or tact in my punches as I knock the knife out of his hand. My muscles move in pure rage. I can't feel the pain in my arm anymore. Every hit lacks its usual thrill, and it doesn't matter how many times I kick him or feel his bones crack, the surging, white-hot anger doesn't dissipate.

He made Bella bleed.

He tried to take her away from me.

He hurt her.

The driver pulls me off him, but someone tackles him a second later, leaving me to continue with my assault on the man who hurt her. He reaches for the gun, but Rico grabs it before he can, going to help his brother.

I yank the man back to me by the collar of his shirt and descend my fists on any part of him I can reach. The fire isn't doused when he's on the ground, and I'm seconds away from killing him with my fists alone.

I put Bella at risk. I got her hurt. I failed her. I need to kill them all.

"Roman, stop!" Damien tries dragging me off. The mother fucker isn't conscious, but I'm not finished. He needs to die for what he did. They all need to fucking pay. "Take your girl and get the hell out of here."

My girl.

I whip around to find Bella sprawled on the ground, leaning against Rico for support. *Why the fuck is he touching her?*

The harsh moonlight isn't enough to see the damage clearly, but what I can gather makes me want to keel over. Tears stream down her face, tangling with the red droplets falling from the split in her soft cheek. The delicate skin of her hands is bloody and bruised, too.

Bella is hurt, and it's all my fault.

Bella is hurt, and it's all my fault.

Bella is hurt, and she's leaning on Rico.

"You're bleeding," Bella says to me, voice hoarse.

I'm on my feet, taking long strides toward them. "Get the fuck away from her."

Rico leaps up, hauling Bella with him before holding up his hands. "Chill the hell out, bro."

"I'm not your *bro*. This happened because you two fuckers left her alone," I snarl, as I pull Bella to my side. Exactly where she's meant to be. Where she will *always* be.

"Stop treating me like a child," Bella snaps and crosses her arms. Her voice lacks genuine anger with her shuddering breaths... She sounds broken instead.

Fuck.

"Not right now, Bella."

"Fuck you, Roman," she sneers, breath shuddering.

Roman.

She said Roman.

No. *No*, she wasn't thinking about it *that* way. She's just saying the name because it's what she calls me when she's angry. She doesn't want to end this. *Us.*

"We need to get your inhaler. If they hadn't fucking left you alone, you wouldn't be hurt." She doesn't believe my words. Neither do I.

I can't blame them when I'm the one who should have known better. This is the second time I've put her in danger.

"No. This happened because *you* brought me here," she cries, then steps back to cough. "And look at you." She waves at the gash in my arm, but I don't feel the pain.

In the distance, the sound of a door crashing open has the two brothers snapping their heads. Bella doesn't seem to notice or care. She's too busy staring me down.

Rico throws my duffle bag at me, somehow getting into my locker while everything else was turning to shit. "Cash is in there."

"Leave before more shit hits the fan," Damien growls, already walking away with Rico.

I curse under my breath and reach for Bella's elbow, but she yanks herself out of my reach. "I know where the car is." With that, she spins on her heel and starts running, leaving me behind in the darkness. I follow behind her, fumbling with the bag to get her inhaler as the sound of her ragged breaths fills the night air.

If she thinks she can run away from me, she's wrong.

If she thinks that one word will make me leave, she's fooling herself.

I made her a promise, and I intend to keep it.

CHAPTER 29

ISABELLA

1) The romance authors lied. Real-life mobsters are scary, ugly, the bad kind of dangerous, and should *not* be romanticized.

2) I am beyond sick of getting kidnapped and all the emotional and physical bruising that comes with it.

3) Fuck Roman Riviera.

I REALIZE THERE'S SOMETHING off-kilter about my current state of mind, but I think it's highly justified.

My face hurts. My throat is raw. My lungs burn. My ribs are probably an unnatural shade of purple.

In the span of three days, Roman-fucking-Riviera almost got me killed *twice*. No guns were involved this time, but the prospect of all the horrifying things the cartel could have done to me is far more terrifying than getting my brains blown out.

And it's all Roman's fault.

Sure, I'll take part of the blame. Yes, I should have had Damien accompany me. Yes, maybe I would have heard the man come in if I didn't drink so much. Yes, I should have *insisted* not to come. But I'm not the catalyst for all this.

Maybe I should be distraught about thoughts of what ifs. Like, what if Roman didn't save me? What if Vargas sent more than one man? But I can't bring myself to truly feel the anxieties regarding the *what ifs* because what's done is done, and tomorrow is another day where Vargas and his men still live.

"*Riviera killed two of our men. And now, he gives us a pretty, breakable gift,*" the man said.

Me.

The Vargas Cartel put a gun to my head two days ago because of Roman. And tonight, the Vargas Cartel almost took everything away from me *because of Roman.*

I even talked to him last night about the Vargas Cartel, and he *still* brought me to the arena.

Maybe I deserve all this for being a bystander in countless deaths and beatings. It could be the universe's way of getting retribution for all the depravity I've inadvertently participated in. So maybe I'm not mad at

Roman that it happened, but I'm *pissed* that he could have prevented it, and he *didn't*.

After every trauma, I've experienced a different reaction. When I found Marcus and Greg, I was shocked about what I saw, but angry that Roman was back. Then, at the Horror House, I was scared and sad, and I only became angry when he started talking. Now? Sure, I'm shocked. Any person would be. But that's not the emotion pumping through my veins right now. What will I feel the next time Roman puts me in danger? Acceptance?

I'm done. I'm not letting myself get to a point where I'll feel nothing when a gun is aimed at my head. I can still recall the *click* of the safety, but in my messed-up reality, my brain has already decided that the sound is something to expect in my everyday life. I always thought Roman's recklessness would get him killed, but I was wrong; it'll get *me* killed.

"Bella, talk to me."

By my count, this is the third time he's said those four words in the past five minutes.

He also rotates between a couple of other sentences.

I'm so sorry, Bella.

This is the last time, Bella. I promise nothing like this will ever happen again.

Bella, baby, please speak to me.

I wouldn't have let anything happen to you, Bella.

I relented and helped him bandage the cut on his arm that probably needs stitches. But other than that, I've refused to even look in his general direction. Instead, my entire body is angled outward, and my lips are sealed shut. My heartbeat is still thundering, the blood in my ears still roaring, and my lungs are still squeezing and burning for oxygen.

The pain in my cheek isn't improving, and I can already feel a whole bunch of nasty bruises forming on my face and body. I'm convinced that the cut on my cheek will open back up if I look at him, and I'll bleed all over him and his goddamn clothes.

But, of course, he came to save me, like always, with his fists and a damn inhaler.

I've slapped Roman's hand away every time it comes near me, but my hand hurts from hitting the shit out of my abductor, and I think I pulled several muscles trying to get away from him. But ultimately, Roman's hands still ended up on me, and, if I'm being honest with myself, they're the only thing stopping me from bawling my eyes out.

Before Roman went to prison, I—the Isabella from before—probably would have found a corner to cry in and clung onto Mickey like a lifeboat on a sinking ship. She was a scared, traumatized, and weak little girl.

I used to only feel fear when Marcus looked at me in the leering way he did. I would toe the line of hyperventilating when I'd get groped or hit on by strangers. The fear was and is alive and well. But my terror made friends with rage, which makes a toxic combination.

I'm still weak; I admit that. If it weren't for the support his hands are bringing me, my head would be between my knees as I struggle for breath as the shock and rage takes over. If Roman hadn't found me when he did, who knows what sort of nightmare I would be experiencing. But the fact remains, *he* is the whole reason something happened to me.

I wouldn't need a lifeboat if he hadn't set the ship on fire.

The difference between directing my anger at him or having Mickey as a lifeboat is that one has the paddles in my hand, and the other has them placed in someone else's, someone who might jump overboard at any second. Paddling will wear me out, but at least I'll have control and can rely on myself.

We pull up in front of our motel room, and he locks the doors when my finger touches the handle.

"Let me out, Roman," I grit out.

I need to wash away the feel of that man's hands on me and all the dried blood beneath my nails, crusting on my hands and face. Then, I'm going to scream into a pillow while letting it soak up all my tears.

And after that...

Well, I need to put my safety first.

"Talk to me."

Silence.

"Fine, we can stay here all night, then." I hear him settle into his seat. "I can't help you if you don't talk to me."

"I don't want your help," I snap.

So much for staying silent.

"You're right. That was the wrong choice of words. I'm sorry you got caught in the middle of my shit; it never should have happened. I'm going to make it right," he promises.

I shake my head. "There's nothing you can do to *make it right*. It happened. It's done."

"Look at me, Bella."

"No." His hands move, and I quickly add, "If I look at you, I'll remember what his hands felt like around my neck and what his body felt like against my back. So, no, Roman, I won't look at you right now."

Roman promised nothing would happen to me, and I promised I wouldn't leave Damien's side or talk to strangers. I guess we're both liars.

The air turns cloying. My words will cut him. And he has a point. He can't do anything unless I talk. Actually, now that I think about it, I *do* have things to say. So here we are again: actions meet consequences.

I look him in the eye, and just like I thought, I'm picturing what it felt like to scream Roman's name through a ratty gag. "It's my fault I didn't stay with Damien. But it's *your* fault I was there to begin with. *You* put me in danger. Not me."

The muscles in his jaw feather. "He needs to pay for what he did."

Too many people fall under the word *he*. Vargas, Damien, Rico, the asshole who took me. Roman will go on a warpath with no end in sight, and I don't plan on being a casualty of it.

"And so will you."

His brows dip. "What is that supposed to mean?"

"It means, if you go after him, I'm gone. And I will spend the rest of my life making sure you never get me back. You can tie me up, but you'll never have me. I'll never be yours."

"This is the underground world, Isabella. Each person you meet is more fucked up than the last."

I flinch. Hearing him say it makes those *what-ifs* bubble back up like molten lava. "Do you honestly think I don't know that? When he dragged me out of the bathroom, I knew they could pass me around to every single one of his men, and there would be nothing I could do about it. I knew they could torture me the same way you tortured Marcus and Greg. And I was *terrified*."

His lips tighten as he swallows roughly. "I wouldn't have let that happen."

This again? "You keep saying that. Stop being so delusional." I flail my bloody hands and point a finger at him. "You can't do *shit*. Do you remember what you told me last night?" I don't wait for him to answer. "That no one would lay a hand on me because you'll keep me safe. *Look at me*, Roman. Does it look like *nothing happened*? Do I look okay to you? No, absolutely fucking not, Roman."

"I thought you'd run."

I stiffen. "Excuse me?" I expected him to give me a grocery list of excuses, or a thousand and one different ways about how sorry he is or how he thinks he'll make it up to me. Not this.

His throat bobs. "I didn't want to leave you in the motel because I thought you'd run."

I stare at his profile for a long moment. The only sound coming from the harsh rise and fall of our breaths. "So, you would rather put me in danger and risk losing me for good?" I can't be bothered screaming anymore.

He turns to me, and his expression is a twisted mix of guilt and anguish. It's wrong, but I want to kiss it away and make it so that only one of us has to feel the hurt. But I'm not going to be that for him right now.

"I didn't think they were a real threat." He twists his hands, rubbing his fingers and shaking his leg. "The worst thing they did in prison was try to trip me up."

I drop my head against the backrest and sigh. I believe that he truly thought they would be harmless. But how can I be with someone who attracts danger but can't see it when it looks at him right in the face. "Well, you thought wrong, Roman."

"Stop calling me that."

"How many times do you have to hurt me before you lose the right to another name? You disappeared on me for three years, and so much has gone wrong since you've come back."

He swallows. "No more matches, Bella. No more fights." It's not just a promise; he's pleading with me. "I'll say and do anything you want."

I huff, because it sounds ridiculous to my own ears when I say, "I couldn't care less about the fighting. As unhealthy as it is, it's your release. What I care about is how I'm the one facing the consequences of your actions."

"I didn't mean to hurt you, Bella."

I inhale sharply, staring straight ahead at the door to our room. "I know you didn't want to cause me pain. But that doesn't mean you wanted to help me. Or keep me sane."

"Of course, I wanted to help you!" Roman taps his finger on the steering wheel. I can hear the cogs turning in his head. "You have to understand, unless I take him out, Vargas will keep coming. Look at what he did to you. That asshole can't live, knowing that he made you bleed. He needs to die, Bella. They all do."

I give up.

"Do whatever you want, Roman. You always do."

He's like a dog with a bone. If he smells his chance for vengeance, he'll chase it down whatever road it leads. Even if it ends up killing him.

And me.

If I have learned how to care for myself, Roman can learn how to save himself.

From my periphery, I see him turn his entire body toward me. "No. No, don't say that. That's not fair. Everything I've done was for you. Everything I *do* is for you. You are the only one I think about. Am I impulsive? Yes. But I'm trying. I'm working on it. I swear. I'm doing this for *us*."

"That's not enough." My stomach churns as my tongue rolls around each syllable. Roman Riviera was my everything once, and I never thought I'd want more. "And if you were really working on it, you wouldn't entertain the idea of going after Vargas."

"The fucker—"

I cut him off. "Unlock the door, Roman. This conversation is over."

"We aren't done." His piercing stare heats the side of my face.

"It's *over*." I don't deserve his kindness, and I don't deserve this torment. I try the lock myself, and it opens. "Do whatever you want; I won't try to stop you. Just remember that I gave you an out, and you chose not to take it."

Chapter 30

ROMAN

It's silent.

I focus on the sound of her breathing to remind myself she's alive and here—*safe* is another question entirely. It doesn't matter what I say or how many times I say it, she doesn't respond.

The only form of communication I've gotten from her is a scathing glare that could end a nuclear war when I slipped into the bathroom with her. But I barely noticed it. Or the wound on my arm that's bleeding through the bandage. She can look at me however she wants because all I see is the patchwork of blue and red coloring her cheek. A chill strips another layer of warmth from me every time I see it.

I'm not letting her out of my sight for a second. From this day on, there will never be a moment where we aren't breathing the same air. I'll never make that type of fuck up again.

I'm tempted to step into the shower, carry Bella to the car and get as far away from Chicago as we can get. But first, we are in a silent agreement that she needs to wash that fucker's scent off her.

Just thinking about that asshole's face makes my blood boil.

Vargas.

I can't believe I was so stupid. The warning signs were right there, and I ignored them. I can't for the life of me think of excuses for why I did. I'll never forgive myself because Bella has paid the price for it.

Vargas needs to be taken out, but I won't do it at the expense of losing her.

The shower tap turns off, and the curtain opens, showing off her naked body, dripping in water and steam. She doesn't acknowledge me when she steps out of the shower, wrapping a towel around her body.

"Bella," I say, standing from the seat.

She passes me without a second glance.

Fuck.

"Please, talk to me."

She doesn't, getting dressed in a new change of clothes as if she's decided we're leaving the city tonight.

I sigh at her back. "Damien will be here in ten minutes to drop off our IDs."

Nothing. No response.

"Bella, I love you," I whisper, reaching for her chin while holding a bag of ice. "Please, just look at me."

Without turning, she elbows me in the jaw when I touch her. I let her hit me. I'd let her kick me and punch me all she likes. I deserve it for putting that bruise on her face. I don't let her move far away from me. After several careful maneuvers on my part, and several hits on hers, I manage to get her on my lap until her wiggling stops.

She winces every time the bag of ice moves on her face, and I feel every flinch like her pain is my own. I'll spend the rest of my life making it up to her—making everything I've ever done wrong up to her.

My heart sinks below the earth when her stare grows blank, as if she found a spot within her consciousness to disappear into where I can't follow her. I hold her tighter, both wanting her grounded back with me and wanting her safe, wherever her head is at.

I kiss her forehead and inhale her scent, rocking us slowly, which does nothing to make her relax. We stay like that until a knock on the door has Bella leaping to her feet and scurrying behind me. The guilt that hits me hurts like a motherfucking bitch.

A knock made her jump out of her skin. A single knock.

"It's just Damien," I assure Bella.

Her gaze bounces to mine, giving me a single, tense nod. I open the door and Damien holds out a brown paper package.

"It's all there." He nods behind me. "How is she?"

What the fuck do I say to that? *It's none of your business? She'd be alright if you actually watched her? She was scared of your knock because of how badly I fucked up?*

"Fine," I settle on.

"The rest of your cut is in there."

We both stand in silence, then I ask, "Vargas?"

"I'll deal with it," he answers simply.

"How?"

He crosses his arms. "Word is they hijacked Alvarez's shipment last week. Boss is waiting for proof before taking Vargas out."

I raise a brow. They've been around, what? Three years, and they're already going to be wiped off the map? What kind of idiot thinks he can steal from a cartel triple its size? Bella shouldn't have been dragged into any of this shit.

"There's a kid," I start. "His name's Jeremy. Lived with Bella." I don't need to explain any more than that. Even though it's a closed adoption, Damien would be able to dig up information.

He nods. "He's under our protection." Damien gives me one last look. "Keep her safe," he says before disappearing down the street.

I look inside the bag he handed me, ignoring the sour taste in my mouth. This is blood money. I've never had an issue with it before, but that was when the only blood on it was mine or another person willingly signing up for it. This has Bella's blood on it now, too.

If we didn't need the money and Bella didn't go through hell just to get here, I would get rid of the cash without a second thought.

But this is us now, on the run from everyone and everything. As long as I have Bella, I don't care where we go or what we do. She may not feel the same about that right now, but she will. She doesn't have a choice.

When I'm back in the room, she goes back to doing everything possible to avoid looking at me. I want her to let all her frustrations and anger out on me. I want her to cry, scream, or sob—anything other than this grating silence.

Maybe we just need a change of scenery. Maybe getting some sleep and food will get her to actually look at me.

We pile everything and ourselves into the car without a word, and then get the fuck out of Chicago.

What a load of shit.

Maybe some sleep and some food will fix it? That's the biggest bullshit I've ever told myself.

Bella has had plenty of sleep; I heard her little snores while her back was to me in the car. At this rate, I will know the back of her head better than I know my own hand.

I dragged her to the grocery store—*yes, dragged.* As I said, I'm not letting her out of my sight, which, in hindsight, was a terrible idea. She's still all bruised up and didn't wear any makeup to cover it, so the sight of me forcing her somewhere would be enough for someone to call the police.

I got her all her favorite snacks and takeout food—I even got her a teddy bear hugging a pillow that says, *I love you.*

Bella happily took what I had to offer her, then *shoved it in my face.* She accepted the teddy bear, but not without mutilating it first. She literally ripped out the cotton from inside with her bare hands and threw it in the back seat, then turned onto her side so her back was to me. *Again.*

And people call me a psychopath.

If I weren't driving and we weren't trying to get the hell out of dodge, I would've pulled off the road and put her over my knee for being such a little brat.

Yes, she's traumatized over what happened, but keeping it bottled up won't help any of us.

It's been twenty-four hours, and she hasn't said anything other than, "I need to go to the bathroom." I saw it as an opportunity to blackmail her into speaking to me; talk, and I'll pull over in exchange.

Did it work?

No. The stubborn princess held it in for almost a goddamn hour before *I* was the one who relented.

This girl really does have me by the balls.

I even tried saying things I knew would piss her off. Did she take the bait? Absolutely fucking not. Talk about giving a guy the cold shoulder.

Now we're here, in a shitty motel. She's still giving me her back—which is fine, because she's trapped in my arms, and her hips are pressed against mine like the perfect little spoon. She still hasn't said another word—not even when I stepped into the shower with her—but I've decided that she has another twelve hours before I go down the extreme route.

"Bella," I say into her hair.

Silence.

Fucking hell.

"You better start talking real soon, or else you might regret it."

Nothing.

"This is me giving you space. If you think I can't get any worse, you have a whole other thing coming for you, baby girl."

Zip.

Nada.

I sigh and pull her tighter to my chest. "Don't say I didn't warn you, Isabella."

Soft light filters through the curtains, illuminating dust motes specked through the air. The stale air is aggravating my nostrils, but the faintest scent of something sweet is settling my nerves.

Jesus Christ, what time is it? I feel like I've been hit by a truck. Based on how bright it is, it's too early for me to be a functioning human. So, like, eight or nine o'clock in the morning, maybe.

I groan as I stretch my arms, reaching behind me to pull Bella into my chest. Instead of warm skin, my hands touch the flat cotton surface of the *very* empty bed.

My heart lodges into my throat as I snap upright. "Bella?"

I don't wait for a response before throwing open the bathroom door. *Empty.*

"Bella!" I yell, running to the front door and onto the walkway of the motel. The parking lot is empty; besides an old man, I can't see anyone else.

Rushing back inside, I finally notice her shoes and coat are missing. So is Mr. Mouse. She's on the run—*she ran from me*, just like I was scared of.

Fuck.

Fuck. Fuck. Fuck.

I spot her phone on the bedside table and our IDs exactly where I left them last night. My wallet is open on top of my jacket, but it's still brimming with cash like she opened it and changed her mind, or only took a few bucks so I wouldn't notice.

Throwing on a random pair of pants and shoes, I shove all our shit into the car and fire up the engine. I barely look back as I reverse out of the park and head onto the main street. The frost covering the windows slowly melts away from the blaring heaters.

My heart hammers erratically against my ribs as I speed down different roads. It's a small rural town with two motels and a single grocery store. I park and check each and every building she might be in; she couldn't have gotten far.

Unless she left earlier this morning and caught a bus.

I press my foot on the gas and fiddle with my phone to locate the station—any fucking station, bus, train, radio—I don't care, as long as I find her.

I barely pay attention to the actual road, speeding along and heading to where my phone tells me to go. The tires screech to a stop in front of a brownstone building with only two bus stops in front of it. Bella isn't in front of either one of them.

Running inside, I stop in front of a graying lady who looks like she's never stepped out of the building in her life. She peers up over her glasses at me as I approach the counter.

"Tell me what buses left this morning."

She scowls and opens her mouth like she's about to protest.

"Tell me!" I roar.

She jolts in her chair, but raises her chin. "Manners."

My lips peel back in a snarl. "Are you fucking kidding me?"

The old woman looks at me defiantly in an almost grand-motherly way. "Boys who don't mind their manners don't get what they want."

"Fucking tell me!" I snarl, slamming my hand on the counter.

She blinks at me, bored and waiting.

For fuck's sake.

"Tell me what buses left this morning," I grit out. "*Please.*"

She scoffs. Without another word, she drops a pamphlet onto the counter and returns to reading her book. I snatch it up, running my finger and eyes over the information, matching times and dates with the route.

Only two buses have left this morning; one is heading to Chicago, and the other directly to Denver.

"A girl, pigtails, yay high. Which bus did she take?" I leave no room for negotiations with my question.

The lady stares at me for a moment. Just as I'm about to bark at her, she raises her hand to silence me. "Who's she to you?"

I narrow my eyes. "Everything." What is this *girls stick together* bull-shit?

Sighing, she shakes her head. "She could only afford to go to Cheyenne."

Where the fuck is Cheyenne?

I grunt and run back to my car, hearing the lady mutter, "No wonder she left you."

Punching the place into my phone, I refer back to the pamphlet. Doing the math, I figure she's got at least twenty-five minutes on me. *Jesus fuck.*

I can barely breathe as I speed onto the highway surrounded by nothing but greenery, a cold sweat covering my skin. Irritated and desperate, I tap my fingers on the wheel, trying to contain my scattered breaths and rapid pulse.

The silence in the car makes the voices louder, question upon question piling on top of each other. What if she catches another bus before I get there? What if Vargas somehow knows where she's headed? What if she never went on the bus and hid in the city? What if that lady lied and Bella is on a bus to Chicago?

God, *Bella, Bella, Bella. Please.*

I can't lose her. I can't live without her. Fuck, what if I can't find her once I'm there? I'll spend the rest of my life looking for her if I don't get to her in time. There's no version that ends without Bella by my side.

I'm going at least ten miles over the speed limit. I'm not sure; I'm not paying attention to it, focusing on the arrival time dropping on my phone and the traffic. The minutes seem to drag on like hours, the drive going by in a blur. By the time I reach the exit for Cheyenne, I think I'm going to have a heart attack with how tight my body is.

I'm not sure how I make it in front of the Cheyenne station, but I do, parking illegally on the side of the road as I run inside. I don't feel the chilly air on my bare arms or the drizzle slowly soaking my t-shirt. Bella would have arrived five to ten minutes ago, and who knows where she might have disappeared to in that time.

The sound of my thundering footsteps echoes through the station, but I can't spot her anywhere. She isn't lined up for another ticket or waiting for another bus.

Fuck. Fuck. Fuck.

I run back outside, searching left and right for even a glimpse of her. She couldn't afford to go farther than Cheyenne. Did she even take enough money for a motel? Food? Fucking hell. I throw the car door open and slip inside, starting the truck without buckling my seatbelt. I'm on the road again, driving up and down street after street as the piercing pain in my chest amplifies to the point that I can barely breathe.

Twenty minutes later, pigtails catch the corner of my eye. I pull into one of the quieter streets and park in front of a driveway. A lump builds in my throat as I run in the direction I saw it as the rain falls harder, turning the air frigid.

Then I see her. Bella.

My Bella.

Walking along the street, staring straight at the ground, not noticing the boutiques and offices she passes. She looks so sad. Broken. *I caused it.*

I narrow the distance, pulling her into my arms and beneath the awning of a cafe, nuzzling my head against hers to inhale her scent. At once, all the voices quieten. *I found her.* She yelps and tries to fight me, but I ignore all of it because I can breathe again. My heart no longer feels like it will be ripped out of my chest.

"Fuck, I thought I lost you." I wrap my arms around her tighter, ignoring the people running past who are trying to get out of the rain. "Don't you ever do that again." I'm meant to sound stern, maybe scold her a bit. But all I sound is desperate.

She can't leave me.

She's never allowed to run away from me.

"Get off of me!" the princess hisses, pushing against my chest.

I don't listen, squeezing her against me. "I was so worried." I should be angry at her for sneaking out when I was asleep, but I can't bring myself to care beyond the fact that I have her back. "I almost lost you twice this week. I won't let there be a third time."

She shakes her head against my chest. "Let go of me, Roman!"

Bile lurches in my stomach from the sight of her red-rimmed eyes and the fading bruises when I let her pull away.

"I'm not going back with you," she says, choking back a sob as a tear falls down her cheek.

"Either I follow you, or you follow me. There's no version of this where we go our separate ways."

Bella tries to squirm out of my hold, while also gripping onto my shirt like it might kill her if she lets go.

"Miss, are you alright?" We both snap our attention to the cop standing a couple of feet away, who has his hand conveniently close to the weapons at his hips.

It kills me to step away from her, but I do it, keeping one hand on the small of her back. I'm not going back to jail, but I can't tell him that she's fine when she very clearly looks like she's not fine. In fact, my ruined knuckles probably make it look like I'm the one who caused her bruises.

"Sir, I'm going to ask you to step away from her," the cop says slowly, wrapping his fingers around the taser.

I grit my teeth, but do as I'm told, staring at Bella, pleading with her not to send me away like this when we haven't talked about what happened. The only thing I can imagine that's worse than being put in a box, is if Bella is the one who sends me there.

"Miss, I ask again, are you okay?" The cop slowly inches forward, muscles tense like he's gearing up for a fight.

"I..." A shiver rips through her and she hugs herself tighter, glancing from me to the police officer as her bottom lip trembles.

Please don't do this, I think, even though she can't hear me.

The silence stretches for a long moment. She can tell them that I kidnapped her and held her against her will, that she had nothing to do with any of the murders. They'll send me away for a long time, but I'll still do everything in my power to make sure nothing bad happens to her. Then once I'm out, I'll come crawling back to her, because since the day I met her, the only thing I've known for certain is that I'd die for her.

Her throat bobs with her swallow. "It's fine," she breathes out, staring straight at me. My shoulders sag in relief. "He's... a friend."

I curl my fingers into fists, but keep my mouth shut.

"Are you sure?" the cops asks.

She nods and gives him a forced, reassuring smile.

"Okay." He narrows his eyes at me and gives Bella a comforting smile that she doesn't need as he backs away to the other side of the street, out of earshot, but perfectly in his line of sight.

"I won't come with you," Bella whispers.

"Princess—"

"I was so scared, Roman," she cries. "I was scared all my life, and you were there to protect me, but what if you're the one I'm scared of?"

I reach for her, and she steps away. "I would rather kill myself than intentionally hurt you."

"You got me out of the life I know, and however shit it was, I still had Jeremy. Now? What do I have? A life where I'm constantly at risk of getting killed? Where I don't have Jeremy? All I have is the unknown, and you don't know what we're doing. Hell, you don't even know what you're doing."

I shake my head. "Neither of us has known what we are doing ever since we were kids. When have we ever had a solid plan on anything? Everything we did was spontaneous, but we didn't give a shit because we had each other."

Tears fall down her face and I want so badly to hold her again. "I don't want to go back to hiding and being scared. What if something happens to you while you're fighting or going around killing people? What if you're dead? What am I going to do then?"

"What you've always done, Princess. Survive. And I told you, there's going to be no more fighting, no more gangs, no more killing—unless absolutely necessary."

Bella hugs herself tighter. "I'm not safe with you."

She's right, but she's also never been more wrong.

I reach for her again, and this time, she doesn't fight me when I pull her into my arms. "You're safer with me than without me." Her chin trembles, wiping her tears away with her shoulder.

"That's clearly not true. Should I list all the times I've ended up hurt with you around?" She looks at me with a mixture of sadness and fury, like she wants to curse my name and then kiss me after.

"I have a better idea; how about you list all the times you were hurt when I wasn't around." She shakes her head. "That wasn't a suggestion, Isabella. Look at me and tell me every single time you were hurt because I wasn't there, and the people who will never hurt you again because I stepped in." I cock my head at her silence. "No? Alright, how about I start with the ones I know about—because I know you like to keep quiet about what happens."

"Roman, don't—"

"Greg. Marcus. His friends."

"Roman."

"Maxim and Mikhail. Mitchell."

"I get it."

"Skinny and Ugly. Those fucking customers at your work. The fucker that followed you from work the night you found me," I list.

Her eyes widen. "That wasn't you?"

"I stopped him before he could. Should I keep going?"

She shakes her head, and I watch the heavy rise and fall of her chest.

I continue anyway. "Troy from biology, who kept putting dead animals in your bag. Maddy from Phys-Ed, who would cut your bra straps. The postman who kept pressuring you for your number..." I tilt my head to the side. "How weird that he suddenly wasn't interested anymore? Last I heard, he's now mute." Her eyes widen. "Aaron, who slapped your ass whenever he did his weekly trips to the store—you hadn't seen him around lately, had you? Pity what happened to his house." I continue, my gaze locked on hers. "What about that guy who works at the grocery store who likes to corner you? I wonder how he broke both his hands."

She's completely frozen, teeth chattering and staring at me with her mouth ajar.

I lean forward until our foreheads are a hair away from touching. "Now riddle me this, Bella; why did all those people stop hurting you?"

She sucks in a sharp breath as her lips quiver and drops her gaze to my feet. "I hate you." She sounds like she's trying to convince herself.

"That's fine, Princess. You can spend your life searching for a reason to hate me, but the truth is, you hate that you can't live without me. And you know what? I would rather die knowing you wish I were dead than for you to feel nothing toward me at all." I tip her chin to get her to look up at me.

"Maybe I haven't made this clear: You have never been just a phase to me; you've always been the whole picture. Without you, I am incomplete."

"But your heart is already full," she whispers, searching my eyes for something I can't see. "My leaving won't change that."

Wiping away her tears, I kiss her cheek. "My heart has only ever belonged to you, little Bella. You. Are. It."

"What if..." She wets her lips. "What if something happens to me again? We'll be spending the rest of our lives running from them."

"It won't," I promise. "I'm going straight."

"But... you want to get back at Vargas?" Her voice breaks as she talks.

"What happened once Damien dropped off the envelope?"

Bella chews the inside of her cheek. "We left."

"That's right. You and me, we drove off and got far away from Chicago. Far away from Vargas and Damien." I cup her cheek. "Do you see what I'm trying to tell you?"

More tears spill from her beautiful brown eyes. The cop behind her shifts, crossing his arms as he watches us. If he tries to ruin this moment, I'm going to lose my shit.

I answer for her. "Ask me to give up anything, and I'll do it for you, Isabella. As long as I have you, I don't give a shit about the rest."

Her eyelids fall close as another shiver racks through her tiny body. "Then prove it," she says as she opens her eyes.

My lips tip up at the corner. "Always. For the rest of my life."

"What about Jeremy?"

"Damien will keep an eye out. And once things settle in a couple more weeks, we can go see him."

Taking a deep breath, she nods and doesn't run when I drop my hold to her elbows. "Where'd you park?"

Bella's coming with me willingly.

371

Bella trusts me to keep her safe.

Bella wants to be with me.

"On the road."

She sniffles, wipes away her tears, and starts moving in the direction that I came.

"Hey, no, get your ass back here."

"What?" she frowns, looking back at me.

"I'm mad at you, too."

Her eyebrows hike up her forehead. "Excuse me?"

"It's cold." I pull her hood over her head, button up her jacket, and wrap her scarf around her properly, all while she gawks at me. "And for God's sake, Bella, if you're going to run, at least take some money and the IDs with you. This isn't amateur hour."

CHAPTER 31

ISABELLA

ROUGH COTTON SCRATCHES AGAINST my cheeks as I turn over in bed. My back hurts. My ass hurts. My goddamn eyes hurt. I'm so sick of sitting in a freaking car.

Even with Roman and I's fickle truce after he picked me up from the station, things are still tense. I'm not ready to go back to where we were before he went to prison or even before I almost got kidnapped.

But he's trying to make it up to me; I know he is.

After a lot of arguing last night, he respected my wishes to let me have a bed all to myself. Trying to fall asleep while he watched me from his spot on the chair was unnerving, but I managed to, eventually. Part of me thinks he only agreed to keep his hawk eyes on me to ensure I don't run again.

I honestly wasn't sure how I got away yesterday morning. He's a light sleeper, and he's become worse since he came back. I guess prison changed him after all.

Peeling my eyelids back, I survey the room, searching for Roman. The bathroom door is open, and all our stuff is still here. He probably went off to get breakfast. I guess he thinks leaving me is a show of trust or something.

But I admit, it's unlike him to be out of bed before nine-thirty in the morning.

Whatever, he'll be back whenever he's back.

Yawning, I rub sleep out of my eyes as I crawl out of bed, ready to use all the hot water. I reach for one of the duffle bags on the floor—they all look the same, so it's a guessing game to figure out which is mine.

Kneeling on the floor, I stretch and click out my rigid joints before unzipping the bag to get a change of clothes. Various shades of dark clothes spill out of the bag as I search for a pair of underwear and a fresh shirt before I realize that I'm looking through Roman's bag.

Just as I'm about to place the contents back in, my fingers wrap around something solid. Frowning, I pull it out and inspect the stack of envelopes tied together by rubber bands. Needles prickle my throat as nervousness fills my body. It's addressed to me.

Tentatively, I remove the bands and pick up the first letter, seeing it ripped open already. Right in the corner is a stamp: *UNITED STATES PENITENTIARY*. Every single letter has the same return and sending address.

My heart slams against my chest, unsure if I should pull it out. Why does Roman have this? Why is it addressed to me? Who opened it?

I glance around as if he might have materialized out of thin air to answer my questions, but it's just me and the stack of letters calling my name.

Swallowing the lump in my throat, I pick up the first envelope and unfold the letter, reading the scratchy handwriting.

Dear Isabella,

What's up Princess,

Ignore the first line. I didn't realize how hard it was to figure out how to start a letter. Shit's too formal. I should warn you that this is the first time I've written without auto-correct in over a year so if you see any spelling mistakes, no, you didn't.

And ignore the shitty handwriting because if you didn't know, I got shot (like, literally, with an actual gun and bullet). Don't freak out though, I'm alright. Now. I wasn't for half a second there. I had a half decent doctor and a couple decent nurses. And don't get jealous, I've been waiting on you to give me a sponge bath (I didn't realize how much I used the winky face emoji until now).

Anyways, you've probably been wondering where I've been (and I refuse to believe that you know where I am but you're intentionally ignoring me). Just know that I haven't left you, and I'll be back to being your loyal bodyguard/ man-servant/ chef/ hair stylist/ guinea pig/ art supply dealer/ soulmate/ human heater/ sexy taxi driver in three years.

There's no easy way to say this, so I'll just say it:

1. Those fuckers Maxim and Mikhail know how to fight.

2. Their mom has a solid aim.

3. I got arrested.

4. Surprise! I'm now in prison.

It fucking S U C K S in here. And my chest hurts like a bitch all the time. But what sucks even more is that I don't have your pretty face and your sweet voice to make my day anymore. Which leads me to my next point. You changed your phone number? What the fuck? I expect a letter ASAP with your new number.

Okay, my chest is starting to hurt too much to write. I expect to see your cute little butt on Saturday when we can have visitors.

Congratulations btw, you now have a prison pen pal.

From your one and only,

M.

P.S. Marry me? We can have conjugal visits.

A lone tear drops onto the paper, making the rough black ink bleed all over the page. He really did try to get in touch with me. He didn't forget about me.

I suck in a sharp breath. Roman told me Marcus and Greg took the letters he wrote, and I never thought twice about what he said. I could've asked about them, or checked if he took them so the police wouldn't connect the dots to him so easily. But as always, I've been too caught up in myself.

I pick up the next letter.

Hello Isabella,

I'm mad at you, so you don't even get any nicknames right now.

Firstly, what the fuck? I've sent you four letters now and you haven't responded to a single one of them. No, "Hi Mickey, I missed you so much. Can't talk right now!" or "My darling Mickey, oh dear! Are you okay?" from you? Literally nothing.

Nada.

Zilch.

Come to think of it, there's no 'secondly'. You haven't answered my calls or visited me. Even this fucker named Damien came to visit me. I almost turned down his visit in case you showed up, but guess what? You didn't.

WHY.

WON'T.

YOU.

ANSWER.

ME?

Someone tried to stab me today, and they came real fucking close to killing me because I could barely move my arms. Do you even care?

Oh, and in case you were wondering, I'm healing great after my wound got infected. Thanks for asking. Really appreciate that, Isabella.

I'll probably forget about how mad I am at you if you respond. But you better have a really damn good reason for the radio silence.

The only time I get to talk to you is in my dreams, and that's not good enough for me anymore. I want the real thing. I want the real you.

I fucking miss you, Bella.

Respond to me. Please.

Yours,

Mickey.

*P.S I'm still serious about the conjugal visits. Say the word and I'll get it arranged **ASAP**.*

There's no stopping the tears streaming down my face.

We both suffered. I haven't stopped for one second to think what it was like for *him* for the past three years. I'm not the only one who felt like life was ripped away from me, and I'm so unbelievably selfish for being so goddamn self-absorbed.

The next letter I pick up is dated earlier this year.

Are you okay? Thunderstorm was really bad, and I know how scared you get.

Please reply so I know that you're alright.

He never forgot about me. He didn't even try to move on, and here I was, spending the past three years trying to forget about him.

There's no order to the letters, because the next one I open is two years old.

Someone thought it was a good idea to play Disney on TV in a room full of thugs. We watched Mickey Mouse. It made me think of you.

Everything makes me think of you.

Why didn't Mickey give me these sooner? Why didn't he remind me about them?

I just won two and a half grand in a bet. Where do you want to go? I'll take you anywhere as soon as I'm out of here.

I chuckle through my tears as I pick up the next letter. My heart crumbles, the padding falling out and the cracks splitting wider.

8160 hours.

365 days.

52 weeks.

That's how long it's been since I've seen you.

Happy birthday, Isabella.

I've been learning how to sketch portraits. It's not much, but the drawing at the back of this page is my gift to you.

I love you, Princess.

I wish I could hear your voice. Or that you'd write to me. That would be my birthday wish. That's the only thing I want.

I choke on a sob, giving up on trying to keep my tears from spilling onto the parchment. He's bled for me while I've cried for him. We're nowhere near even. I know, without a shadow of a doubt, he's willing to bleed for me until the day he dies, and he'll spend the rest of his life keeping the tears out of my eyes.

I have an idiot cellmate who gave me an early birthday present in the form of a prison tattoo. Can you guess what it is?

That must be Rico.

Why didn't I try harder to find him? Why didn't I even consider the possibility that he might be in jail?

That was stupid. I don't know why I asked you to guess.
I'll just tell you the answer: I wanted to carry a part of you.

It hurts.

It all fucking hurts.

There must be at least a hundred letters in this pile.

I don't even know why I still bother sending you letters. You probably don't even read them. You're eighteen now and most likely far away from Greg's house. I've been lying in bed wondering what you're doing now, which colleges you applied to, and what you're planning on studying. Or if you are still deciding what you want to do.

You're so smart, I know you'll be amazing at whatever you put your mind to.

I knew you'd worry about paying tuition, so I've been saving for when you decide if you want to go. And if you don't want to go, that's fine too. I just want you to know that it's there when you need it.

Just respond whenever you can, I guess.

I miss you.

M.

Hidden in the corner behind the bed, I stop breathing as I read the next letter.

They put me in the box yesterday.

As soon as they put me in there, my first thought was, "At least I can see Bella after this." Then as the minutes—or maybe hours—went on, the voices got louder. They wouldn't stop. No matter how much noise I made, they made more.

It's worse than I remembered.

I wanted to die, Bella.

Thoughts of you were the only thing that pulled me through. But I couldn't stop thinking about this one question. Do you think about me anymore, or have you forgotten?

I tried telling myself that there will be a letter from you waiting for me once I crawl out of Hell. But I should have known better, because I know the answer.

You've forgotten about me.

Pulling my knees up to my chest, I sob into my arms.

I don't deserve him. I never have. I never will. I've taken him for granted; he should never forgive me for how terribly I've treated him.

I want you to know that even if you don't miss me, you have been the only thing on my mind since I met you. Bars will never change that.

"Bella, what's wrong?"

I snap my head up to the door, and a second later, I'm on my feet. Nothing else registers until I crash into his arms. Sandalwood and cinnamon soak into my skin, but I need more of him. My fingers find a home in his hair to draw him closer until there isn't an inch of space between us. "I'm so sorry. You must hate me. I've been awful to you. Mickey—Oh, God, I'm so sorry," I cry against his lips.

Pulling away, deep gray eyes bore into mine, the corners creased with worry. "Bella, what happened? Talk to me."

I nod frantically. "I will. Whenever you want."

I lean into his touch when he cups my face, and I hold his gaze. All he's ever done is support me, and it's time I support him too. "Why are you crying? Who do I need to kill?"

I bark out a breathy laugh, sniffling as I wipe my cheek. "The letters."

He pales. "You..."

Pressing forward, I thread my fingers through the silky strands of his hair as my broken heart beats for the man in front of me. "Why didn't you show them to me sooner?"

His forehead leans against mine, and I hug him tighter. I just want to hold him so he knows how sorry I am for being so selfish. All I've done is look out for myself when he looks out for me every day. But who takes care of him? Who makes sure he's alright?

The answer is no one, and I promise to never let him feel that way again. Because I know what it feels like, and I wouldn't wish that upon anyone.

"I didn't want you to feel bad."

"You could have shown it to me back at the Horror House," I insist. I probably would have fought him less or gone with him more willingly. I think.

"The Horror House?" he questions, then shakes his head. "The letters aren't important."

"How could they not be important?"

He lifts a shoulder. "What we have can't be simplified down to a couple of letters, Bella. I want you to want me because you're everything I need."

My skin prickles along with the hot tears. "I can't give you anything." I've never been able to. Mickey has always been the one to provide for me, chase the monsters away so I can sleep easier at night. All I've ever been able to truly give him is my fractured heart.

"You're all I want." His soft lips brush against mine, and I don't hesitate to chase them. But it hurts because, even though I know he would never leave, I could have been so much better to him.

"I can't give you dinner at six. I can't wear a pretty dress and be as beautiful as you think I am, when all I want to do is disappear underneath the covers. I'm not this sensual goddess that can give you sex appeal." Gesturing to the fraying bed behind me, I say, "I can't even give you clean sheets." I don't know what it's like to live when I'm not under a thumb, scared of the creaks in my own home.

"Who said I want any of that?"

"Everyone wants that," I whisper, suddenly doubting why I'm still fighting him, when all I've ever really wanted to be is complete and by his side.

Hands curl around the backs of my thighs, lifting me so I wrap my legs around his waist. The stiff bed groans as he lies me down, towering over me as he runs the back of his knuckles along my jaw and whispers against my lips. "I want every single thing you are willing to give. I want takeout with you at midnight. Sleep-ins and sleepless nights. I want you crying, and I want you smiling, no matter the reason for either of those two things. I just want you, Isabella, whether it's on an unmade bed or the forest floor. You're all I need." He kisses my wet cheeks. "You don't know what I want, even though you've already given me everything I need."

CHAPTER 32

ISABELLA

My lips meet his, and I give him everything I have to offer. My soul, heart, and body. All of it swells and explodes, feeling too big for my little self to take.

That's one thing about Mickey. We were never made for the silent type of love. We were made for the kind that shatters windows and breaks the earth's surface. It's fireworks and dancing and lime juice mixed with absinthe.

This time, he isn't the one claiming with our kisses. I'm his just as much as he is mine. Our lips move in sync, labored breaths filling the space in between.

I claw at his t-shirt covered back, needing to feel his bare skin against mine like it's the only thing that could keep me alive. He chuckles darkly as he rips his shirt over his head, tearing mine off before my heart can take another beat.

The cold air prickles my skin, pebbling my nipples into sensitive points as they ache under his heated stare. He doesn't give me time to acclimatize before my shorts and panties disappear into the corner of the room.

His gunmetal eyes turn pitch black, as if possessed by a demon, descending on my core, devouring me like I'm the closest thing to food he'll ever find.

Holy shit.

By my count, he's only done this once, which doesn't explain how he's so good at this. Every time he licks along my entrance, my breath catches. Each time he takes my sensitive clit in his mouth, I see stars. He's playing me like a professional who has done this for years.

"You're stunning, baby girl."

My back arches into his touch, begging for more. He licks and kisses and sucks like he's never tasted me before, and he's starved for seconds. The darkening gaze of his predatory eyes holds me hostage as two fingers slip inside me.

"Mickey," I cry, my body arching from the bed as my hands latch onto his hair.

He doesn't let up, sucking my clit while pumping his fingers in and out of me until the evidence of my arousal covers his face and hands. He keeps hitting that spot.

That spot.

The one that sends a thousand fiery butterflies fluttering through my veins, lighting me up like a firework. Hundreds upon hundreds of blinding sensations zip through my marrow. Tension builds and multiplies in my stomach, tightening around his fingers, layer upon layer of pleasure and pressure bringing me a taste of heaven as I scream out his name.

Until suddenly, it disappears.

"Holy fuck," Mickey gasps, taking his fingers with him when he stands back.

My eyes widen, and my muscles wound tight as I snap upright. "What?"

Did I do something wrong? Does he find me... gross? Maybe it's too much for him in the light, or he needs more time to get used to being between my legs? Or... it could just be a cramp. I mean, he's been going at it pretty hard, right?

My gaze trails over the moisture covering his face and dripping down his chest. A splatter of dark wet patches stains his jeans. Slowly, I look down at the sheets between my legs. Soaked.

Mortification colors my skin bright red. Oh, God. What have I done? Why did I have to do that? Oh, shit, shit, shit, he must be grossed out. I can't even look at him. What does he think about me now? This has to be at the top of my list of the most embarrassing things I've ever done in front of him.

I jolt out of bed. "I'm sorry. I'm so sorry."

"Where do you think you're going?' he all but growls.

I swallow and inch back from the bed. "To get a towel?"

"Get your ass back here. You're doing that again."

I blink. "What?"

"That was the hottest thing I've ever seen."

By some divine power, my skin turns an even deeper shade of red. "But you're all wet?"

"I came on your face, and I know you fucking loved it." He grins. "It drives me wild just thinking about having you all over mine." The muscles in his shoulders ripple as he hunches over the bed, fists on either side of the space I filled moments ago. "Get back here. *Now.*"

I hesitate, watching fury blaze in his eyes for a moment before the inferno morphs into desire that melts my insides. With slow, uncertain movements, my hands hit the bed, then my knees, feeling the springs dip and squeak as I crawl toward him with big, innocent eyes. His gaze stalks each of my motions until he's close enough for me to reach forward and run my tongue over the hard contours of his abs.

"Good girl." A low sound rumbles through his chest. A hand shoots out, keeping me in place with tense fingers gripping my chin. Possessive lips crash into mine, showing me that he belongs to me, just as much as I belong to him.

Fisting my hair, he yanks my head back. "I'm not done with you yet," he snarls, voice filled with gravel and shadows.

Every inch of me is completely at his mercy as the world turns in a series of colors and lights until the darkness hits. The cotton sheets press against my face, making each breath harder than the last.

Warmth overwhelms my core in a vicious drag from my entrance to my clit. My body reacts to his call with an arch of my back and pushing my raised hips against his face. Strong fingers slip into me, and I throw my head away from the sheets to scream.

Oh, God, I can barely take him. The burn from the stretch is as blissful as it is painful. His vise-like grip around the back of my calf stops me from running away from his commanding touch.

"Always taking me like the needy little girl you are." Roman chuckles darkly, biting the soft skin of my thighs while his three fingers work me over.

"Please, Mickey," I whimper as I dig my nails into the sheets to try to find purchase to get away.

"You can take it."

The hand around my ankle winds its way around my hips, holding me in place while he rubs circles over my clit. With the compounding sensations, it doesn't take long before the pressure builds, growing stronger and stronger, and like boiling water, I overflow. The release rips through me, bone deep.

Mickey continues his punishing pace until the world around me goes blurry, and another orgasm shreds through me, from head to toe, until there's nothing left of me but a panting pile of skin and bones. A kaleidoscope of stars burst behind my eyelids to rain molten desire all over my body.

My legs give out beneath me, and I tumble onto the bed. He flips me over before I get another chance to breathe.

"That was fucking glorious." He chuckles as he peppers kisses all over my chest and face.

I need a second.

I'm pretty sure I just saw another dimension.

When he positions his hard cock at my entrance, I have absolutely no idea how I'm going to survive if he makes me orgasm again. An idea festers in the darkest part of my brain, and I put a hand on his warm chest to stop him from using me for his pleasure.

He pulls back, concern etched deep into every crease, pinching his face. "What's wrong?" It's only two words, but I can feel the concern dripping from them into my soul.

Newfound energy finds a life in my racing heart as my plans solidify. With unsteady movements, I shuffle my legs away from him and lift myself onto my elbows, crawling back like the mouse he thinks I am. My face doesn't betray my emotions as his remains in the same worried stare while he tracks my movements.

My chest aches from making him feel this way, but I know it'll be ancient history to him in a matter of seconds.

All my life, Mickey has catered to my every want and need, sacrificing himself just to make me happy. He gave me bliss; I want to give him something in return.

"Bella, baby, what's wrong? Did I hurt you?" Mickey reaches out to me with a tentative hand, but I'm gone before our skin can touch.

"Tag," I squeal. In a flash of white and black, I take off for the bathroom, leaving a trail of barely contained giggles for him to follow. "Catch me if you can," I throw over my shoulder.

I'm unsure when he caught on to my plan or when he started moving. One second, my bare feet are flying over the carpet. The next, my body is sandwiched between a wall and a hard body.

A hand curls around my neck, placing the slightest pressure, just enough to make my lungs work harder for air. His bare chest vibrates against my back in a warning growl. "That wasn't very smart of you."

Fear and exhilaration light up my nerve endings. Whether by sheer stupidity or pure masochism, I say, "What are you going to do about it?"

The deep, rolling laugh that follows my words makes my hair stand on end. "Are you challenging me, Isabella?"

With a single move, he fills me with his cock, stretching me more than his fingers. My head falls back onto his shoulder without choice as he forces me to curve my back to take every thrust of his bruising pace.

"It's like you don't want to be able to walk."

A scream works its way out of my throat when his skilled fingers find my sensitive flesh. No amount of clawing or begging adds the term *mercy* to his dictionary. Roman is ruthless through and through.

Dots dance in my vision as the unbridled and uncontained moans leave my lips. Then, suddenly, he stops. I bite back a groan. I didn't *actually* want him to stop.

"When I let go of you, you're going to run for the door." The dark cadence of his voice sends a shiver through my bones.

My eyes widen. "But I'm naked."

"Then you better learn how to hide, because I'm killing every person who lays their eyes on you."

He means what he said. It isn't a threat; it's a promise. "Mickey," I plead.

He lets go of me.

"Run."

One word and the earth shifts.

My axis spins as I scramble away. The fractured heart in my chest beats loudly, roaring in my ears as every one of my senses narrows onto the front door, just like he told me to.

I want God to hear my prayer for once in my life. *Please* don't let anyone be outside.

Just like the game of cat-and-mouse we played a week ago, my freedom is in sight. All I need to do is *open the damn door*.

But he stops me from reaching civilization when my hand touches the handle.

He yanks me back with a fist in my hair and crashes me into his chest when a scream breaks past my lips. "You can't outrun me," he hums. "You'll never get away from me."

My feet have no choice but to comply as he walks me back to the bed. It's useless to throw my arms out when he shoves me face-first into the mattress, because his torso is right behind me, forcing me to fall into submission.

He drives into me without warning, making pleasure and pain thunder to every corner of my body. The cotton sheets muffle my moans and cries, and the pressure building in my core is unstoppable. This time, I'm confident I won't survive. When my climax rips through me, everything goes black, and all I can hear is the sound of Mickey snarling his release, spilling his seed into me.

The hard muscles of his body crush me against the bed as he topples over, rasping his tired breath against my sweat-stained skin.

My heart swells as Mickey rolls us over, positioning me on top of him so there isn't an inch of space between us. Then he kisses me like there is nothing else in this world or the next that he'd rather be doing.

We hold each other, letting the moment stretch on. I realize another truth: we bring out the best and the worst in each other, but the only time we can breathe is when we're together. With all the darkness in our past, our love story is as cheesy as it is cliché, because nothing else matters as long as we're with each other.

CHAPTER 33

ISABELLA

"I want to show you something."

I blink up at Mickey, wanting to stay like this for an eternity. "What is it?"

A lopsided grin splits across his face. "It's a surprise."

I groan.

"Hey," he argues. "When have I ever done a shitty surprise?"

He has a point; I'll give him that. "Remember when I was eight, you caught a mouse for me, and I needed a tetanus shot because it bit me."

"I was ten years old," he protests, then says under his breath, "I can't believe you still remember that."

I bite the inside of my lip and plant a kiss on his chest. "You should have been more specific in your question then."

"Here we go."

Hitting his chest playfully, I let him slip out of the sheets and into his pants. I follow suit, running across the room to fight the chill and jump into some warmer clothes. "No blindfolds this time," I say.

He curses. I snap my head around to him, and he winks at me with a smirk drawn across his face. "I'm willing to negotiate."

Taking Mickey's outstretched hand, he leads me into the motel's corridor with peeling wallpaper and spiderwebs decorating the edging.

"Should I be scared?" I ask, hugging his arm.

My body flushes with warmth when he kisses my forehead. "Never."

"Not even a little?"

"Shut up, Bella."

I giggle as I squeeze his arm tighter, refusing to let go when we reach the stairs.

Mickey smirks. "About the blindfold... how off the table is it?"

My skin blazes when someone walks past, and I hiss, "We're in public."

"Are you trying to change my mind? Baby girl, the thought of fucking you raw in front of other people makes me crazy."

"What?" I squeak, hiding behind my unmade hair.

"Then there's no doubt about who you belong to." He winks and says under his breath, "And who's going to be the death of me."

I give him a nerve-racking chuckle that grates against my bones. Dear Lord, what does this man have planned?

I mean, what's the worst it could be? My immediate thought is a dead body, but I *really* don't know how much that fazes me anymore, despite how much I hate the thought. And there's no way Mickey would show me a dead animal.

Christ, what if he made a super impulsive purchase and bought a cramped little sports car? Or like that time he bought three bikes because he couldn't decide on one.

394

"Please, no blindfold," I whisper.

Looking up at the ceiling, he groans. "I really can't say no to you, can I?"

"I think you can."

He squints, then bobs his head from side to side. "You're right, I can." As soon as we make it through the front door, he slides in from behind me, covering my eyes with his warm hands. "You said no blindfolds. Nothing about hands," he says pointedly.

I make a noise of frustration, but my nerves are buzzing beneath my skin, so I can't find the words to say as Mickey guides me forward. Pavement changes to gravel beneath my feet, crunching with each step we take until we come to an abrupt stop.

"You ready, Princess?"

No.

"Yes."

I hold my breath as he removes his hands. My lips part on a gasp before I can hold it back.

A quaint sage caravan hooks onto the back of the pickup truck. Buttery cream and lace curtains peek out from behind the silver-trimmed windows. It's the type of caravan you'd see on retro magazines and vintage-inspired mood boards.

I can already picture it nestled next to a tree by the beach while we both lounge on fold-out chairs. Or hidden away in the forest with fairy lights draped from the trimming as we picnic on the damp earth.

"Surprise," Mickey whispers in my ear.

"Mickey," is all I manage to say.

This is what I always wanted without truly realizing it: to be able to travel around the country, feeling sand between my toes, tasting freedom on my tongue. There would be nothing holding us back.

"I know," he says smugly. "You don't need to hold the applause."

Turning in his arms, I face his stunning gray eyes that always seem to find me, even when I don't want them to.

"It's ten in the morning. How did you find a caravan?"

His eyes narrow into stilts before his lips spread into a smile. "Is that really the first thing that popped into your head?" He chuckles to himself. "You have such a beautiful mind, baby."

"Don't patronize me."

He silences me with a kiss that makes me forget whatever useless question I asked. "It's called *the internet*." Strong fingers intertwine with mine, and he tugs me along. "Let me show you our new home." Unlocking the door, he pulls it open to let me step inside.

He wears the same look he did when we rode to the horror house all those years ago. A smile stretched from ear to ear and the attitude of a kid who knows he did well and is waiting to drown in the ensuing compliments.

Quaint is the perfect word to describe the caravan's exterior and the most inaccurate word to describe the inside.

The silver taps and handles reflect the morning light as if it hasn't been touched since it was installed. A bed with a mountain of pillows sits at the back, beneath a window with deep green curtains. Perfectly white cabinets, smooth wooden walls, pristine marble countertops, and even the bathroom looks like it has never been used before.

"Did you fix it?" I ask Mickey, slowly exploring the refurbished interior. Someone must have gutted this thing and slapped a new set of everything. I can't imagine when he would have had the time to do it on top of fixing up the horror house.

He shakes his head, slapping my butt as he walks past me to fall onto the bed. "Come here," he calls, holding his hand out for me.

Slipping my fingers into his, I let him pull me to his chest, acting as a barrier between me and the bare mattress. We lie there in silence as he draws patterns onto my back, swirls and love notes. The heat of his intense stare scorches the side of my face.

I was wrong. This whole time I was misguided in my views of Mickey. Roman Riviera isn't a liar who abandoned me. I wasn't nothing to him or a girl he would eventually leave.

I shift to look up at him. "Thank you," I say without really thinking it through.

"For what?" He grins, ready to be showered in praise.

"For the caravan." But that's not what I'm really thankful for.

"Go on," he fishes.

"You gave me everything else I needed when I was too focused on becoming someone else. And then for leaving," I say. Mickey tilts his head to the side questioningly. "You gave me the chance to grieve the child I never was and become the adult I want to be."

I was aimless, in the wrong job, living in the wrong house, surrounded by people who would rather see me fall. I was so bitter and angry from being forced into a version of myself I didn't recognize, but I became friends with myself. And when Mickey came back, he set me free.

"But that's not all I'm thankful for," I add. "Thank you, Mickey, for coming back to me."

"Always." Soft lips press against my forehead before tucking my hair behind my ear. "Don't thank me, Bella. It's the only option I'd ever choose."

"You saved me." Honestly, I wasn't sure how I would have gotten out of there alive without him. Part of me was too scared to, and the other part was desperate to breathe, yet unwilling to gasp for air.

He smiles at me, and I smile right back. "I don't see it that way."

"You're my knight in shining armor, Roman Riviera."

He nods his head against mine. "I am. But you never needed saving. You just needed someone to remind you that you're not alone. And in case I haven't told you, I'm proud of you, baby girl."

My cheeks heat bright red at his beaming smile. "I'm proud of you too, Roman."

Since I was six, he has spent every waking moment looking out for me, finding ways to keep me safe. I couldn't protect him when we were children, but I can now.

Without saying the words, I stare at him, hoping he sees my promise to him.

You'll never go back in a box, Mickey.

The rhythmic hum of the wheels rolling over pavement stops, jarring me awake. My fingers dig into the new bedspread, still crisp and fresh.

Mickey set me loose at the department store to buy whatever I wanted for the caravan. The cupboards are now filled with food, cutlery, and clothes. Fairy lights are strung across the walls over drawings done by both of us. I'm still trying to figure out how much things will move around as we drive before I decide to get anything else.

He even relented and let me buy some bras.

As much as the saying, *"home is where the heart is,"* is true, you still have to make the house—or caravan—feel like a home.

For the first time in my life, I feel content.

The door squeals as he steps inside. He woke up earlier to start driving and let me stay behind to sleep. Well, it's not like I even heard him get up. We started moving, and I connected the dots myself.

A couple of doors and drawers open and close while I feign sleep. The bed dips under his weight as he crawls closer, tucking me into his arms. "Morning, beautiful."

"Morning," I whisper, smiling against his skin.

I could get used to waking up with him around. Though I'd prefer if he's the first thing I see when I wake up. Or, better yet, more nights with broken sleep because Mickey couldn't wait to sink inside me.

"Did you think you could pretend to be asleep?" he muses.

Lifting a shoulder, I peer up at him through my lashes. "I would never."

I yelp when he pinches my butt, bursting into a fit of giggles as his fingers dig into my sides. A bang hits the side of the caravan, making me jolt upright. Suddenly, I can hear sounds. *People.* Laughter and chatter filter through our home, stiffening my joints.

Mickey pulls me back to him, looking the most at ease I've ever seen him. His gray eyes gleam bright silver, and the curl of his lips holds nothing but joy.

I move to pull back the curtain, but he snatches my hand away, rolling on top of me to hold me hostage. "No."

"Mickey!" I laugh, moving side to side. What is he up to this time?

Heat scorches my body when his hard length rolls against the space between my legs. The single move has both of us groaning as he winds his fingers into my hair in a claiming grip. "If you keep moving, we're never getting out of here, and you'll never find out where we are. Nod if you understand."

I narrow my eyes. "I could also just say yes."

"Brat," he mutters, kissing me for one heated second and consciously putting space between our hips. "I pulled out clothes for you. They're on the bench."

My brows hike up my forehead. "You're dressing me again?"

His mischievous grin morphs into a devilish smirk. "You look good in my clothes." He winks. "But you look better without them."

I'm pretty sure I saw the front of my brain with my eyeroll. "That's the cheesiest thing I've ever heard."

He scoffs. "Shut up. You're, like, twelve."

I bite the inside of my lip. "Twelve and three-quarters, actually."

Mickey snorts before helping me to my feet. I use my inhaler, and then we continue with the mindless, nonsensical back-and-forth while he dresses me, helping me step into jeans, pulling on my Mickey Mouse shirt for me, and lacing my sneakers. In the reflection of the mirror, I catch the deeply pinched brows and his murderous eyes as he braids my hair. A bomb could go off outside, and I don't think he'd notice.

He fusses with the ribbons and symmetry for a couple more seconds before nodding to himself. I wouldn't be surprised if he's giving himself a mental pat on the back.

Suited up and ready for my next surprise, Mickey graces me with my unobstructed sight this time, fueling the excited thrum coursing through my veins.

The humidity sticks to my skin as we step into a big parking lot that tickles a distant memory. Families file out of their cars, giggling and donning backpacks, threading between cars, heading in the same direction.

Rounding the caravan, I freeze in my step.

Disneyland.

Mickey is taking me to Disneyland just like Mamá did on my birthday. There's nothing I can do to stop the heat pricking my eyes and trailing down my cheek. I only have a few memories from when I was younger, like watching Mamá cry when she hugged Mickey and Minnie Mouse.

I pull him into a bone-crushing hug before he can move. Everything he's done, he's done for me. How was I ever so blind to see that?

Peppering kisses all over his face, I chant, "Thank you. Thank you. Thank you."

He laughs, beaming down at me. "You can make it up to me later."

Gladly.

A group of teenagers runs past us, darting for the entrance. My muscles itch to do the same, and I decide not to fight it. How much of my childhood was lost hiding away in the bedroom, crying over parents I'll never have, or taking care of the other kids in the house while I was the one needing care? My inner child deserves to live.

I start dragging Mickey along as he chuckles at all my huffing. *He isn't moving fast enough.* "Come on!"

He smiles at me. "It isn't even open yet."

I snarl. "We need to get to the front of the line."

With a relenting sigh and a knowing smirk, we jog the rest of the way until we get to the queue. Once we're inside, he tags along behind me without question, going from ride to ride and feeding me copious amounts of ridiculously over-priced food.

"Those gloves would be perfect for you if you ever fight again." I giggle, loving the grumpy look on his face because of how *ridiculous* he looks with sleeve tattoos, wearing an orange-and-black tie-dyed Mickey Mouse t-shirt—we're matching—black jeans, combat boots, murderous gunmetal eyes, a Daisy Duck backpack, mouse ears, and the big four-fingered Mickey gloves.

He's my own personal homicidal Mickey Mouse. *He's all mine.*

"The material is itchy," he grumbles.

My sloppy, curled fist hits his chest half-heartedly. "Extra padding for when you punch people."

"It's uncomfortable."

Grabbing a creepy Mickey Mouse mask from off the shelf, I put it against his head and tip my head to the side. "Mmm, no. I prefer your other mask." I return it to the shelf just as the alarm on his phone goes off.

He doesn't move a muscle as I strip him of the gloves, light-up lanyard, and the feather scarf I wrapped around his neck. I barely notice his burning stare, too excited for the grand finale. Shifting my weight, I wince from the pain radiating down my legs and up my back. I could really use a massage.

Turning his head to give me his non-face-painted cheek, I give him a big, fat kiss before pulling him out into the night. During the day, the park is stunning and otherworldly. It's nothing short of magical at night, from the twinkling lights and the music streaming through the warm air.

"Come on!" I squeal when Roman slows.

He sighs dramatically, but his lips are drawn in a menacing grin when I snap my attention toward him and his negative attitude. I don't see him moving until I'm pressed against his chest, feet dangling in the air, and arms automatically locked around his neck.

"Put me down!" *Please, don't put me down.* I've been running from ride to ride and standing all damn day. My feet hurt, my muscles ache, and there's a pinch in my lower back. I'm not going to let my pain ruin our night, though.

He shakes his head. "I haven't been able to hold you all day."

Lie. "You hug me every time we wait in line."

"Not enough."

"Fine," I relent, trying to hide my smile in the crook of his neck. Mickey always knows what I need without me needing to say it. "You can carry me, as long as you walk faster."

"This isn't a negotiation, Princess."

"We're going to miss it!"

"Maybe if I throw you over my shoulder, I won't hear you complaining."

My jaw drops. "You wouldn't dare."

"Oops. Did I say that out loud?"

My gaze narrows. "Prick."

"You love me for it."

The only certainty in life is death. But that rule doesn't apply to me. I love Roman Riviera, and that's the only truth I know beyond a shadow of a doubt.

My feet don't hit the ground until banners swing on either side of the bridge and the palace is close enough to touch. A mirage of colors lights up the castle: blue spires and pink walls, and an ethereal hue covering the fortress bricks.

With Mickey's hand clutched in mine, he weaves us through the throngs of families, staring people down (yes, he's glaring at kids with no shame) until we reach the very front, where he folds up a jersey for me to sit on.

A band marches past and dancers and gymnasts twirl and smile as their gowns ripple and sway. I glance up at Roman behind me to find him already looking down at me.

Averting my attention back to the show, a blush heats my cheeks. His eyes belong to me, even in a place with colors and music. I peek another look and giggle silently at his crossed arms and unamused stare as he watches the performance. When he catches me looking, his face softens, lips curling up into a soft smile.

He holds out his hand, and I take it without hesitation, leading us away from the crowd until we reach a secluded spot by the front of the castle. Light colors the contours of his face, glimmering against his hypnotic eyes.

"Dance with me, Princess."

"I can't dance," I breathe, holding on to his hand because I never want to let go of him.

His lips tip up into a grin. "Neither can I. Dance with me anyway."

"I'll step on your toes."

The apples of his cheeks catch the light. "Then I'll say thank you."

"They'll bruise."

"You won't see me complain about having your mark on me."

"Bruises aren't love marks."

He leans forward until his hot breath feathers against my ear. "Do you want to test that theory? Give me thirty seconds, and everyone will take one look at your neck and how irrevocably mine you are."

"I'm not yours." I am his. Wholly and completely.

"*Liar,*" he whispers.

"I'm not a liar either." *Lie.*

"You're right. You're Isabella, my sweet, sweet Bella."

"I'm not."

Leaning his forehead against mine, he says, "You can think that, but just know I'm yours."

"Liar." Biting the inside of my lip, I smile.

"I am. But not to you. Never to you," he promises. "Dance with me, Isabella. Let me hold you."

"I'll trip."

With each excuse, his eyes darken. "When have I ever let you fall? If you did, I'd be right there beside you. We're Romeo and Juliet."

Frowning, I chuckle. "They killed themselves, Mickey."

"Do you doubt what I'd do for you, Isabella? If you're in a grave, I'm in one. I promised you forever. We won't end in death."

"That's so morbid." My smile spreads until I can't take it anymore. There's nothing that could bring me down from this high.

"You make me crazy." Warm hands wrap around my wrists to bring them up around the back of his neck. "Now, Princess, make me the luckiest man in the world and dance with me."

"I—"

"The next word out of your mouth better be yes. I'll repeat myself a third time for you. But there will be repercussions if I have to say it a fourth time."

I pinch the back of his neck as his arms wrap around my waist. "If you had let me finish, you'd know I was about to agree."

The last thing I see is his grin before his lips meet mine, languidly moving as we sway out of time with the music.

At this moment, the world around us ceases to exist. There's no darkness hidden within our pasts or people surrounding our present. There's only us, standing together in the light, ready for whatever we might face.

Wants and needs are usually two separate things, but they're the same thing when I'm with Mickey. Mamá was right; I would be part of a family. I just didn't realize that my childhood tears of yearning for one were for nothing, because my family is right here in front of me, in my arms.

"You'll never feel alone again," Mickey whispers against my lips, bringing a smile across mine.

"I don't need your promises anymore."

"You never did. That doesn't mean you can't want them." Fireworks explode next to us, flashing purples and greens against our skin, but my attention is fixed on the man I've always loved. "I'll make you another promise: From this day on, there will only ever be *us*. Everything we do, we do together," he says. "I love you, Isabella Riviera."

I grin. "It's Garcia."

"Not anymore, it's not."

I kiss him before saying the words that have lived in my heart since I was six years old. Giving him every crack in my fractured heart. *Fate*, that's what this is. Two lost souls finding each other in the darkness and knowing they'll always have a place to call home.

"I love you too, Roman Riviera."

EPILOGUE

ROMAN

Eight Months Later

Alice Benson and Mike Key.

The modern-day Bonnie and Clyde, minus the crime, publicity, and recklessness.

I never thought I would like the silence that comes with safety, but now I find comfort in it. The quiet of the forest or the roaring waves have become second nature. I thought nothing could compare to the exhilaration of standing in a ring, staring at a man who wants to rip my spine clean from my body. But, as always, I find what I need in Bella. Chasing her through the woods, arguing over a board game, and making risky turns on the road because she sucks at giving directions.

I could live like this for the rest of my life and die a happy man.

A slap echoes through the forest when my gloved fists meet the punching bag. It doesn't stave off the desire to beat someone the fuck up, but it makes the burning need more manageable.

I glance over to my girl, sitting under a tree beside the lake, wearing my favorite sundress, brows locked in concentration as she sketches away on her drawing pad.

"Margaret said if I get an A on all my papers, she'll get me a gaming computer." I can barely hear Jeremy's voice from here.

"That sounds like a terrible idea," Bella grumbles, grabbing an eraser off the picnic blanket.

"TJ's aunt bought him one," he protests.

"TJ is also the smartest kid in school and can only play on it over the weekends."

"Ugh. Don't remind me. Margaret still makes me sit at the table with her every day to study. It's basically corporal punishment."

"Trust me, little guy, it isn't."

Their conversations continue back and forth until he gets a call on the other line, then Bella goes back to drawing.

We've created quite the duo with her commissions. Sometimes, we collaborate on a piece to create a contrast of her soft curves and light shading with my sharp lines and dark strokes. Our version of Bonnie and Clyde.

Except she's the star of the show because sometimes I really can't be bothered drawing. I have to be in the right state of mind, and half the time, I'd rather be touching Bella than wasting my attention on some no-name on the internet.

Bella is here, and she's all mine. Except when she neglects me because she's talking to Jeremy on the phone.

She's not the only one working while we travel around the country—twelve states and counting. Thanks to the internet, I can pick up whatever job I want. Including getting my money's worth after I forked out a little too much on a whole ass professional tattoo kit on an impulse.

Am I good at it?

Meh.

Is it up to safety standards?

Eh.

I steal glances at her between punches, my heart pumping double-time when my eyes land on the "M" tattooed on her ring finger in cursive writing. Hidden beneath the boxing gloves, I have a "B" in gothic lettering to match.

Catching my stare, I wink at her, and she rises to her feet, fixing her dress and leaving her drawing pad behind as she skips over to me with a mischievous glint in her eyes. White and dangerously short, swishing around her legs as she moves, her dress is a major distraction. My dick stands at attention at the sight. She doesn't need to do anything, and I'm ready to sink into her mouth or pussy; I'll take whatever she gives me.

I grin as she makes her way over to me, muscles pumped and ready to wrap her smooth legs around me.

As she closes the distance, I reach my hand out for her. Instead of taking it, the little shit grabs my arm, spins around, then throws me over her fucking shoulder. Just like I taught her.

Ain't no way will "*the student becomes the master*" bullshit fly here, but shit, am I impressed she pulled that off on the first try.

I didn't even see it coming.

She plops down, straddling my raging cock with her warm, inviting center. Tilting her head with a shit-eating grin, she says, "Gotcha."

I smirk, chucking my gloves off to feel her warm thighs beneath my hands. "Not just a pretty face, are you, Mrs. Riviera?"

She snorts. "I think I missed the part where we got married."

Shrugging, I say, "You might as well get used to the name."

"You haven't proposed."

She isn't wrong. I sorta sat her down, grabbed her hand, and started tattooing my first initial—well, the initial of her name for me. Much to my surprise, she didn't fight at all; she just complained that I should have waited to do it until *after* we moved on from the beach.

"Didn't need to," I say. She yelps as I spin us over so that she's under me. "You're already mine. No need to put meaningless labels on it."

Roman and Isabella can't get legally married because, apparently, there's a warrant out for our arrests. But Alice and Michael can, and neither of us wants to seal the deal under a name that isn't ours.

She arches a brow. "How many times have you called me your wife?"

I shrug. "You are."

She doesn't get another word in before my head is between her legs for breakfast, and I stop short. Bella isn't wearing any panties. "Fuck, baby girl," I rasp. "You're going to kill me."

Her ensuing giggle makes my cock strain harder against the loose shorts. My tongue descends on her, and *fuck,* if she isn't the sweetest thing I've ever tasted.

I've become an addict with many vices that all revolve around Bella, and I need my daily hit. I don't care when, whether for breakfast, dessert, or a midnight feast, I need to have her coming on my tongue at least once a day. Her taste is too addicting.

Her breathing labors and hiccups as she starts mewling, grinding her hips against my face as I flick my tongue out and lick every inch of her sweet cunt. Bella buckles when I latch onto her sensitive nub.

My hands climb up her body to pull her dress down to her waist. Pinching her nipples, she moans into the sky.

Delicate fingers grip onto my hair, uselessly attempting to pull me away. I'll comply with my terms. I plunge my tongue into her pussy, pummeling in and out until her moans quicken and echo through the forest, crying out my name as she shudders beneath me.

"Ten out of ten, would come back for seconds," I tease, running kisses up and down her thighs.

She's too delirious to respond, panting hard without noticing I've lined up my cock with her entrance. "Any last words?"

Blinking rapidly, she focuses on me, then on the space between us where I run my tip through the wet heat. "Jesus Christ," she moans when I push against her sensitive skin.

"God won't save you from me." I move my hips forward, breaching her tight cunt, and I don't stop.

Bella was made for me, and I was made for her. There isn't a part of her that I don't love. She's the one who brought me out of the darkness and made it feel like life was still worth living, even if I were in a box.

Her moans dance through the air and filter into my bones. I couldn't get enough of her before, and I don't see myself ever thinking I've had my fill.

Moisture drips down my legs from the area where we're joined. "You're always so fucking wet for me." I chuckle, gripping her cheeks between my thumb and pointer finger. "You're my dirty little slut, aren't you, baby?"

She nods frantically as her muscles contract around my length. My hand finds her clit, and I start moving in circles just the way she likes. She always looks so beautiful when she's about to come, fluttering lashes and gasping breaths. The way her nipples pebble into biteable points as her chest rises and falls has my mouth watering for a taste.

Then, for the best part, she throws her head back and screams my name like it's the only word she knows. Her legs tighten around me, and her body convulses with the need for a break.

Without any warning, my release finds me, emptying myself inside her. Her heavy breaths hit the side of my face as I drop down onto her, bracing myself on my elbows on either side of her head so I don't crush her.

Nothing in this life or the next would hold a candle to her, from her glowing brown Bambi eyes to her plump pink lips. Every part of her is perfect.

I can't wait to live the rest of my life with her. To see her the second I wake up in the morning and have her by my side at breakfast. To hear her laugh during lunch and smile during dinner. Then, have her in my arms when the lights go out; all that will matter is me and her.

My sweet Bella.

I must have done something right in my life to end up here.

It wasn't love at first sight. Not in the conventional way.

The moment she spoke, I thought she was only speaking words. I didn't see the net she threw to capture me. But I never fought it. Deep down, I knew this was where I was meant to be.

The easiest thing I've ever done is love her.

If I could do it all again, I would do it the exact same way.

I would pick her. *Every time.*

The End.

Acknowledgements

We, dark romance girlies, love our deranged men. As a dark romance author, the most common question I receive is, "What the hell were you thinking?"

Well, let me set the scene for you.

It all started when I had just spent an unsavory amount of time scrolling through TikTok (when I should have been writing), ingesting copious amounts of masked men content. There was a trend going around about how dark romance readers would react if they were kidnapped (i.e how quickly would we all develop Stockholm syndrome?).

Anyways, fast forward a couple hundred more videos, I was then left alone with my thoughts for two minutes. I thought, "God, how fucked up would it be if they kidnapped us AND killed our family."

Then, the other voice is my head chimed in, saying, "That's so fucked up. I'd read something like that."

Another voice popped in, adding, "Damn, I don't think that exists."

Twenty-four hours later, while I was at work, a light bulb went on in my head. I could literally just write this messed up book by myself, because I forgot that I am, in fact, an author.

However many months and one or twenty mental breakdowns later, Skin of a Sinner will always have a special place in my heart. I love Roman with everything I have, but I want to deck that man. If he were real, I would have a taser on me at all times.

On a more serious note, this book would never have happened without a whole team of people reading through my manuscript and then listening to me freak out about one thing or another.

I want to give an extra special shout out to Eve, V, Sam, Sage and Emily, because you guys had to deal with me blowing up your DMs on a fortnightly basis.

Now, to everyone else that helped me bring SOAS together; Mette, Tee, Charlize, Pia, Cynthia, Jay, Liberty, Dusty, Mika, Summer, Nicole, Kayla and Kirsten.

I hope you all get (consensually) chased through the woods by a masked man.

Stay smutty x
A St. Graves

Be sure to follow me on Instagram, Facebook and TikTok @avina.stg raves, as well as my reader's group "Avina St. Graves' Reapers."

About the Author

From an early age, romance author Avina St. Graves spent her days imagining fantasy worlds and dreamy fictional men, which spurred on from her introverted tendencies. In all her daydreaming, there seemed to be a reoccurring theme of morally grey female characters, love interests that belong in prison, and unnecessary trauma and bloodshed.

Much to everyone's misfortune, she now spends her days in a white-collar job praying to every god known to man that she might be able to write full-time and give the world more red flags to froth over.

Also By

DEATH'S OBSESSION

He's coming for you.
Death is meant to come on a chariot of broken dreams or in the dark
trenches of a storm, not in love letters and gifts.
He did not take my soul when I was meant to die. He did not want it all
the other times that I've offered it to him on a silver platter. Yet, time and
time again, he reminds me that I am his: His night monster, his dark love,
his perfect other.
Death was the only thing keeping me alive. He watches me from his corner,
taunts me with sweet messages, marks my body with his touch as I sleep.
He took the people that I love away from me. Still, no one believed me when
I said that I saw the faceless man on the night of the accident.
No one can escape death.
Me? I'm chasing it.